The Crew

J.M. Hewitt is a crime and psychological thriller author. Her work has also been published in three short story anthologies. Her writing combines the complexity of human behaviour with often enchanting settings. In contrast to the sometimes dark content of her books, she lives a very nice life in a seaside town in Suffolk with her dog, Marley.

Also by J.M. Hewitt

The Life She Wants
The Eight-Year Lie
The Other Son
The Crew

THE
CREW

J.M. HEWITT

CANELO

First published in the United Kingdom in 2023 by

Canelo
Unit 9, 5th Floor
Cargo Works, 1-2 Hatfields
London SE1 9PG
United Kingdom

A CIP catalogue record for this book is available from the British Library.

Print ISBN 978 1 80436 502 1
Ebook ISBN 978 1 80436 503 8

This book is a work of fiction. Names, characters, businesses, organizations, places and events are either the product of the author's imagination or are used fictitiously. Any resemblance to actual persons, living or dead, events or locales is entirely coincidental.

Cover design by Head Design

Cover images © Shutterstock

Look for more great books at www.canelo.co

Printed and bound in Great Britain by Clays Ltd, Elcograf S.p.A.

1

For Piers, Nikki and Ayton

PROLOGUE

She senses that she's not alone. There is no sound, no shadows, no footsteps.

The hairs on the back of her neck prickle regardless.

Someone is there.

She turns around.

Nobody is there.

She breathes out, almost a sigh. She has been paranoid for too long. Always looking over her shoulder. It will take time to get used to this new way of life, that's all.

She scans the horizon. The water that they are anchored in is secluded, rising mountains of white and grey walls at the stern. An empty Aegean Sea at the bow. Inky, waveless waters that soften into black sand: a beautiful, alien landscape.

There is nobody out there. Other than the one she is aboard, there are no other vessels in sight.

She decides to go to bed. She will rise early tomorrow and show willing. If she wakes up half an hour before her shift starts, she might be able to talk Chef into cooking her eggs and bacon. Maybe potatoes and some avocado toast. A huge platter, just for her.

She casts one more look into the dark night and picks up her jumper from where it lies on the anchor trapdoor.

She tells herself she is safe, ready now to return to her cabin, deep down in the belly of the boat. A chill has risen, and she thinks of her bunk, her duvet, of wrapping herself in it, a cocoon until sunrise.

She rubs the side of her neck, feeling the tendons standing to attention, her pulse quickening. Ice travels down her spine. Not so much a warning. Rather, the feeling that is constantly hanging over her recently. So much so, she's forgotten what it feels like to live without that underlying fear.

'*There is nothing here. Nobody is after you.*' Her lips move as she speaks the words silently, trying to talk herself down.

There is a sudden flash, lightning dancing across the Milky Way. The world turns as thunder smashes through her jaw.

The boat has capsized.

The thought is muddled and wrong. There are no waves, no storm; how is this yacht suddenly sinking?

She rests her head against the teak, the aroma of the cleaner the deckhands use filling her senses. Her heart thuds painfully in her chest against the planks. She can hear her own breathing, a wheeze, as if all the air has left her.

I've fallen, she thinks.

Immediately following is the realisation.

I was pushed.

Claret stains the wood. Not unusual. She knows that from witnessing the way these boats are run, watching them day in, day out, drunken charter guests spilling their Merlot, the stewardesses and deckhands fighting over who should clean up the exterior of the boat. But this is wrong.

This is not wine.

Her forehead throbs. The skin there is split.

She plants her hands on the deck.

A foot kicks her wrists.

She slumps back down and curls, foetus-like. Her stomach clenches into a hard ball as she tenses herself, awaiting a further assault.

More hands come into view, more than one person: two, three, a dozen. Is she concussed, or are her persecutors many people?

A kick lands on her forehead, in the same place as the earlier fist that struck her. It comes from a heavy boot, but that, too, is wrong. No shoes allowed on board.

Everything is wrong.

Silence, and for an all-too-short time, blissful oblivion. Then the hands are on her again. Not thumping or pummelling this time; she is being carried.

The world tilts once more, the handrail below her now, her view: over the stern end of the boat. Nausea rises. She swallows time and time again, hearing the click of her throat, loud in the otherwise eerie calm.

The tender is in sight, the small motorboat that they use to ferry guests to snorkelling locations or as a water taxi.

She closes her eyes. She loses minutes, or maybe more, because the shock of the water wakes her. She gasps, panting breaths, in and out, trying to ease the tightness of her chest. Her eyes dart here and there, but everything is jet black. She is out of sight of any lights that are on the land. The water isn't too cold, but it's wrong that she is in it.

Blood and saltwater sting her eyes; rough hands touch her. Many pairs, she thinks, but with the absence of voices and her own sight gone, it is impossible to tell.

Metal on the flesh of her neck. Tight and cold. It holds the aroma of old pennies, rust and things from the ocean floor. Decay.

She opens her eyes a crack and sees an arm, white flesh, straight up in the air, fingers splayed. She watches, horror like a flame licking her insides, as the fingers of the unidentified person fold to hide in a fist.

She knows that is the signal they use to bring up the anchor.

She screams, but it is silent, cut off by the anchor chain.

The sound of rolling steel. The water is gone; she is out now, in the warm Greek air, going up, up, up.

The side of the yacht scrapes at her back. Beneath her, she sees the chain wrapped around her, the anchor itself nestled below her chin.

Her heart, which moments before thudded so painfully, slows horribly. She braces herself for the yell she's heard from the dock several times a day. *Anchor is home!*

3

When it comes to the end of its trajectory, if those words are spoken, they will be the last she hears.

The knowledge, the realisation of what is about to happen galvanises her into action. She struggles, thrashes the lower part of her body, but is no match for the motorised anchor. No match for the person or persons operating it.

The fibre-reinforced plastic morphs into steel at her back. The edges of the anchor pocket.

So, this is what it feels like.

Nearly there.

She closes her eyes once more as the anchor tries to fold itself home.

There is a snap, a gush of blood, staining the port side with its spray.

She doesn't feel it. She doesn't see it.

She is gone.

PART ONE

ELLA

ONE YEAR AFTER THE DEATH OF ASHLEY

Here she is again, standing beneath the plaza at Athens Marina, staring at the 50-metre superyacht, *Ananke*, the sun beating mercilessly down on her bare shoulders.

Despite the heat, a shiver wracks Ella Themis's entire body.

Ananke, named for the Greek goddess of fate and circumstance. Was that what last year's tragedy was – fate?

Ella Themis has been a yachtie for a long time. Her father had been a captain, her siblings deckhands. Her youngest brother, the one who they no longer speak about, strayed from tradition, and went into the forces. They are scattered now. What remains of them, anyway.

Her mother had been the type of woman who holidayed on yachts, and her mother's family were the kind of family who purchased yachts. It is in the blood. At thirty years old, she's worked her way through ten seasons up to chief stewardess. It is the perfect way to run away from real life.

Over the course of her yachting career, she's done the Med, the Baltics and the Rivieras – both Italy and France. The last two years have been spent in Greece.

Last season was a write-off. After the accident, *Ananke* was seized and put into the dry dock while the authorities carried out their investigations.

Accidental death by misadventure had been the verdict.

A young life cut short by an avoidable tragedy. One of those needless, senseless moments in time that makes everyone in the vicinity embrace their lives and let go of the petty stuff. The crew mourned. Some of them cried. Most of them drifted off *Ananke* and finished the season filling in on other superyachts. For Ella, it brought back emotions that she'd already been running from. She spiralled into herself, holding a tight ball of rage in her stomach like a foetus that seemed to kick out, winding her.

Terrifying her.

The world had once been so big with limitless opportunities.

Now, there is nowhere left to hide.

Now, one year later, all of them have come back.

-

The first person she sees on board *Ananke* as she moves down the boardwalk is Captain Carly Lee. Conflicting emotions pull at Ella as she watches her boss on the bow. Like all good captains, Carly is fair but strict. She abhors drunkenness from staff and grudgingly grits her teeth when the guests get intoxicated. She is at the top of her game in terms of professionalism and excellence in all areas. As a female captain on a man's sea, she's worked twice as hard to get where she is, and for that, she rightfully commands respect.

But... seeing her is a reminder of the last fateful journey that *Ananke* took before she was confined to port for a year. The whole point of coming back was to be on the same ship as Carly. However, just for a moment, Ella considers slinking off back down the boardwalk and seeing if there's a position open on another yacht. She'd happily lower her rank, go down to second or third stewardess. Because she's not sure that she can face this.

'Ella!'

Too late.

With leaden feet, Ella makes her way on board. Captain Carly envelops Ella like a mother would. A normal mother, anyway. Ella's mother doesn't give hugs any more.

'I'm so thankful you came back, Ella,' Carly murmurs.

Their embrace is slightly longer and more loaded with emotion than it normally would be for the first meet of a new season. The lingering hug is for the one girl who won't be coming back this year. It is because of her.

Ella pulls back and studies Carly's face. She looks the same as last year. Strong and capable, equal parts ready to smile or to chastise. Her jaw-length blonde hair is pushed behind her ears, shades atop her head. She's dressed in the boat's casuals, polo shirt and shorts, *Ananke* embroidered onto the breast.

'I'm glad to see you,' Ella says, though she's not sure if it's true.

Carly pats Ella's shoulder. 'You're the first one here. Grab your cabin, then we'll get to work.' Her smile downturns. 'The ship's not in a good state. Lots to do.'

It's an unwritten rule on superyachts. At the end of the season, you leave the boat as you wish to find the next yacht you'll be working on. Any decent captain and crew will insist upon this, and Ella has always adhered to it.

But last season, *Ananke* was seized. All of them, crew and guests, had to leave immediately with only their own belongings. Since then, *Ananke* has had police, investigators and insurance officials tramping all over her.

'When is the first charter?' she asks Carly now.

The captain does that strange little grimace again. 'Two days' time.'

Forty-eight hours to get this ship looking like the jewel of the ocean that she's supposed to be. 'I'd better get started then.'

'I'll help, later,' Carly calls over her shoulder as she makes her way back to the bridge. 'I'm going through the mechanics with Sid.'

So, Sid is here too. Ella is glad Carly has turned away before she sees the expression on her face at the mention of his name.

He's the chief engineer, and behind his back, nobody calls him Sid. His name below deck is Slopy, on account of his slopy-shouldered approach to his work. The role of a chief engineer is to ensure the safe running of the mechanical side of the boats.

In this world, on superyachts, there's barely anything in disrepair. Like new cars, it's mostly computerised. Therefore, Slopy spends most of his days and nights sleeping in the engine room.

Normally, on yachts, the engineers muck in with the deck crew, and because *Ananke* only has two deckhands, Sid really should be assisting with the exterior.

He doesn't, however, and it's a bone of contention that ripples through the crew.

Unfortunately, Sid 'Slopy' Lee is Captain Carly's brother. Wherever she works, he's usually to be found too.

Alone on the main deck, Ella can stall no more. It's time to assess the damage, which will inform her of the current workload.

Ananke is a wonderful ship. Before last year, she was the nicest boat Ella had ever worked on. Pieces of her still emit the magic – the mahogany panels, teak flooring, plush carpets in the interior. The gold handrails, smudged with fingerprints of a hundred people, definitely need a clean. Everything does, she notes as she makes her way through the lounge to the stairs that descend to the crew quarters and galley.

She smells the galley kitchen before she reaches it. Pulling up her shirt to cover her nose, she finds herself wishing the world were still back in the time of facemasks as the aroma of rotten food assaults her.

Her makeshift face covering drops as she stands in the doorway and gapes in amazement.

On that fateful last charter, she'd been on the mid shift. She'd gone to bed at around 10 p.m.; her girl on the late shift was responsible for clearing dinner and making sure everything was in order for a breakfast that never happened.

But today, the galley is exactly the way it looked when Ella was escorted off the vessel a year ago.

Ella is livid. Of all the people that have been on *Ananke*, none of them thought to dispose of all the perishables. It smells like a sewer in here, and in two days they'll have guests aboard who will be paying more for their charter than the average person pays for a house.

Throwing open the porthole windows, swearing under her breath, Ella gets to work.

An hour later, she's on the dock, heaving the last bag of rubbish into the already overflowing large bin, and sucking in great gulps of hot Greek air before she goes back aboard.

'Hey, Ella, are you getting on okay?'

Shielding her eyes from the sun, she stares up to see Carly on the aft deck. She's stripped down to a vest, and Ella wonders if the past hour of the captain's work was as horrifying as her own has been. She doubts it, somehow.

She gives Carly a thumbs up and bangs a fist on the side of the bin where she's just discarded almost all the contents of the galley. 'It was pretty bad; food from the last charter was still out.'

Carly shakes her head. 'I hadn't been in there yet; it must have been awful.'

'Seriously, the worst thing I've ever seen,' Ella calls back in reply.

Her words ring around the dock, almost echoing in their stupidity.

Her mind spins as angry tears threaten. The nightmare, the one she has had on repeat every night, flashes before her eyes.

That face, distorted in agony, that neck, the pale flesh torn, the anchor chain embedded in it.

Year-old food, rotten and stinking, is not the worst thing she's ever seen, not by a long shot.

'Ella?'

The calm voice of the captain brings her back to the here and now.

She blinks, forces a smile and jerks her head towards the boat. 'Best get on, still got the cabins to do.'

Carly studies Ella's face for a moment or two longer than necessary. Finally, she nods. 'We'll catch up later; I'll take you for dinner.'

It's not an invitation, but rather a statement.

They don't normally eat together on land. Captain Carly, despite her warm nature, is the boss after all. She's also sober, has been for twenty years, and when Ella and her crew go out, they like to let loose.

Still, there's no crew here yet, maybe not until tomorrow, and Ella can't think of anything she'd like less than to spend the first night of a new yachting season alone in her bunk, thinking about last year.

'I'd like that,' she says in reply. With a final wave, she makes her way back on board.

With Carly ensconced in her own cabin, on the top deck near the bow, Ella wanders the rest of the boat from floor to floor. She starts at the top, on the sun deck, straightening up the loungers as she goes. They are bare, the covers stowed somewhere, and though it is the deck crew's job to maintain the exterior of the boat, she makes a mental note to keep an eye out for the cushions and covers. It was something Ashley was good at: blurring the lines between inside and out, merging the teams, teaching them through her own actions that helpfulness makes for good working relationships.

Next to the sun deck, through the double patio doors, is the bridge deck lounge. An area to relax if rain has hit, or wind, and Ella has never much cared for the opulence in here. *Ananke* is sleek, rich with chrome and teak, but this lounge, with its swirly patterned carpet and gauche bar, has always struck her as rather old-fashioned. With its cigar cabinet for the male guests, she supposes it is a relic of a time gone by. Beyond the lounge are the cabins where the bridge crew sleep. On *Ananke*, this space is reserved for Carly and her brother.

Ella moves past the entrance door to those cabins and trips down the spiral stairs, coming to land at the guest cabins. There are six of them in all: a master, two VIPs and three doubles.

On that last, fated charter, they had only three guests: the Kilfoyles – a husband and wife, and their teenage son. The adults, Piers and Nikki, had the master, and their son was in a VIP.

Ella feels a ray of hope; that leaves four guest cabins made up and untouched, and she wonders if she can get away without stripping the beds and cleaning in those cabins that were not used. She peers into one of the doubles and her heart sinks. Like the rest of the boat, this too has been turned over by the insurance investigators and police.

There is nothing on *Ananke* that has not been tainted by last season's accident.

Pulling the door closed, Ella moves on. She won't start on those this afternoon; she'll wait for her other interior crew to arrive tomorrow. More hands will make lighter work.

She passes through the main deck lounge, glancing left and right, seeing fingerprints and smudges, rings from year-old drinks on the bar, dust, discarded litter.

She keeps walking, out onto the main deck, towards the stern, stopping when she reaches the Jacuzzi.

It has been drained, she notes. One less job for the deckies to do. She looks in the oversized basin, remembering all the nights of fun she has had in here. Bottles of champagne, hard drinking, partying, a pounding bass thumping out, safe in the knowledge that Carly's soundproofed cabin was at the other end of the boat.

Other times, too, with other crews, Ella and the temporary chef who had come to fill in when Luca had a kitchen-related incident and had to go ashore for a couple of days for medical attention. Ella doesn't get involved on board, not any more, not since she became a department head. *Don't screw the crew* – it's the motto they try to live by, but mostly fail disastrously at.

The temp chef was a free pass for Ella. Only there for two days, it suited her, and apparently him, just fine. She hadn't even liked him that much, had admitted to herself afterwards that she'd used him in the hope it might get someone *else* to notice her.

It hadn't.

Aside from those random nights of unbridled passion, this hot tub was the place to unwind after a charter. Secrets were shared here, walls and defences were down, and friendships were made.

She'd sat here, in this very spot, last year with Ashley Mercer, the night before she died.

What had they talked about? They'd had a bottle of Veuve between them, the others drifting away one by one. As the sun had risen on what would be the last day of Ashley's life, they'd sat in companiable, drunken silence.

Ashley had spoken about something... poignant? It was hard to recall. The boozy night, the thoughts of the new season, the worries, inconsequential things were already crowding her brain, leaving no room for anything else to sit and fester in it.

She thinks hard, trying to recall what Ashley had been talking about, when Ella's mind was distracted with her own to-do list and her own bleakness.

I did it; I escaped.

Was that it? Had Ashley said those words?

If she had, Ella hadn't thought much of her phrasing back then; after all, the majority of yachties – herself included – were all running from something. Miserable upbringings, stifling home lives, small towns that suppressed them. Fractured families and, in Ella's case, the darkness of a grief unspoken.

There was something else that night, something... more. Ashley was... was what? Worried? Troubled?

Ella hates that she can't remember.

Because the very next night, Ashley was dead.

2

The Jacuzzi is not a pitstop of good memories. Ella moves on.

She can put it off no more. She will go below deck, start cleaning and organising the crew cabins. The other employees will be here tomorrow; the first thing they will want to do is claim their own space.

She moves back through the lounge and down the spiral steps, past the galley, which looks better than it did a few hours ago. There is a lingering scent, though.

Rot.

Decay.

She leaves the porthole wide open and moves past it into the thin corridor that leads to the six crew cabins.

Ella has her favourite, the one at the very end, furthest away from the galley kitchen, so the sound of Chef having a tantrum is muffled, as is the noise of the guests up on deck if she's on an early shift and they're partying until dawn.

She claims the bottom bunk, and then it hits her with a jolt.

There will be one less crew member this year.

The thought of an Ashley-shaped gap is dizzying, shocking, and she slumps heavily down onto the bed.

They won't be a crew member short, of course they won't; there are other stewardesses to hire. Not many, though, because the virus that escalated to a worldwide pandemic still lingers and some countries where the employees come from are locked down. They will find someone, though. The way they found Ashley last year.

Crews usually change most seasons. It is part of the build-up, the excitement, finding out who you're going to be working and living with for the next few months. Captain Carly, however, likes the crew she's got, and she always requests them first. Because of this, *Ananke*'s deckhands and stewardesses have worked together on and off for around a decade. Ashley was an anomaly, an outsider, but she slotted into their odd little family like she'd always been there.

The knowledge that this year, *Ananke*'s third stew definitely *won't* be Ashley, stabs at Ella.

The grief that never went away sits like a stone in the pit of her stomach. Flames of anger, now an all-too-familiar sensation, lick and spit and coil.

She looks up at the top bunk. She didn't share a cabin with Ashley last season; she was bunking in with her third stew, Brandy. But that last night, Ashley had ended up in Ella's cabin.

Had they talked more, then? Had they shared pieces of their lives until Ashley fell asleep in the top bunk, where Brandy should have been sleeping?

Ella thinks carefully.

Where was Brandy that night? The guests – the Kilfoyle family – were not the raving type. They'd gone to their cabins shortly after dinner, meaning the crew got to grab an unheard-of early night too. And if Brandy hadn't come back to claim her own bed, *why* had Ashley got up and left the cabin in the dead of night?

Ella stands on the wooden slat of the bottom bed and pulls herself up to view the top bunk.

The duvet is in a pile at the bottom of the bed, the pillow at the other end.

It has an indentation in the centre.

Ashley's head, thinks Ella grimly. She traces the outline of it.

The investigators had been in here, the *astynomia* – the Greek police – too. Judging by the state of the galley and the guest rooms, she doesn't think they'd have left the bed that Ashley slept in so neat.

Had they been in here?

She pulls open the wardrobe door. Here they are: all the belongings they had to leave behind when they were escorted

16

off *Ananke* last summer. The items have been rifled through, put back in a haphazard fashion.

Ella skims her eyes over her possessions that she was made to leave behind and picks up a scarf. She won't wear it again, not after it has been sitting on this ship for a year, contaminated with last season's horror.

Ella sighs as she climbs back up on the top bed, her back rounded, head down to avoid hitting it on the ceiling. She hates prepping top bunks *and* sleeping in them, for this very reason. But since she is up here, she may as well strip the bed and check the storage lockers. She works deftly, pulling the cover off the duvet, shedding the pillow, dropping them to the floor to be taken to the laundry.

The cabin door squeaks open. Ella sits up, knocks her head, swears and climbs off the bunk.

Cat stands in the doorway.

Her eyes are red. She's already been crying, Ella realises. Just stepping back on board *Ananke* will do that. How the hell are any of them supposed to work here again? How on earth are they expected to last an entire season?

Cat launches herself at Ella. Ella folds the young deckhand into her arms, much like Captain had done to her.

They part eventually, and Cat sits down heavily on the bottom bunk.

'I didn't want to come back.'

Neither did Ella. But all those people grinding at her, Captain especially.

It'll do you good.

It's best to get back on the horse.

I need my best team with me.

Get yourself some closure.

Face your fears.

It was Captain who wanted them all back, the same crew. Minus one, of course.

'I— I don't know what happened that night,' says Cat. 'I haven't seen or spoken to anyone else.' She turns to look at Ella. 'Have you?'

There is something in her tone, an accusatory quality, as though the rest of the crew have been regularly meeting without Cat.

'I haven't seen anyone. I haven't spoken to anyone in a year.'

And isn't that strange? she thinks now. Isn't it odd that they didn't meet up, after they were all separately questioned, to discuss the grave happenings upon this ship or to hold some sort of memorial for the girl they'd all taken into their hearts? Ella had thought about it, about *him*, most of all, how they'd been wrenched apart. For months after, her fingers hovered over a message she wrote time and time again that, ultimately, remained unsent.

The memories that she's tried so desperately to quash are rising like a tide. In danger of being flooded, Ella closes her eyes and does the breathing techniques her therapist recommended. In through the nose, hold for five, out through the mouth.

But Cat has never been one to shy away from questions. Now, a year on, she's full of them.

'Was it you who found her?' Cat demands. 'Because nobody ever told me anything.'

Ella emits a small gasp, her breathwork interrupted, stunted, shut off completely.

That day comes back. Total, in all its horrifying glory.

3

TWELVE MONTHS AGO

'Why is the breakfast table not set?' Ella is snippy today. She is talking to nobody, because all the crew seem to have vanished.

Ashley is on earlies, and yet, nothing has been done. It is most unlike the girl who is fast becoming Ella's favourite employee.

In the galley, she runs her fingers over the lemons that have not been sliced. The oranges for the fresh juice still sit in the fridge, untouched. In the room tucked behind the pantry, she stares at the two washing machines. Empty. Piles of washing still waiting to be loaded.

These are morning duties that are vital to get done immediately upon waking. The laundry needs to be put on before the early shift stewardess even pours her first coffee.

It is disappointing. Ashley has never let her down before.

She slams her way down the corridor and smashes open Ashley's cabin door. Cat is asleep on the bottom bunk. At the racket, Cat pulls the sheet over her face without even looking to see who is in her cabin and hisses like the creature she's named for. 'Get lost!'

Ignoring her, Ella puts one foot on Cat's bunk and pulls herself up to study the top bed.

Empty.

She feels a slap on her ankle. Looks down to see Cat's flailing hand.

She thinks about apologising. Nobody who was on the late shift wants to be woken before their time.

But Ella's pissed off, so she slams her way back out of the cabin and goes in search of her errant third stewardess.

Belatedly, she remembers Ashley being in the bunk above her own last night. She darts down the hallway to her cabin and peers inside.

Nothing. She runs back to the galley.

'Have you seen Ashley?' She practically snarls the words at Chef Luca as he emerges from the pantry.

'Nope.'

She gives him a look of disgust as he licks his fingers, covered in flour from the fresh bread he's been baking for breakfast. 'The primary guest is up, though, and he looks like he could do with a coffee.' Luca gestures to the CCTV beyond the door of the galley, in the crew mess.

'Shit.' Ella forgets about Ashley for a moment. It's the last day of charter. So far, this guest and his family have had a relatively good time. Apart from the incident the day before.

Ella shudders. She doesn't want to think about that. She hopes the guests have forgotten it. She needs to keep on top of this charter. For the crew to dip in their efforts now would potentially reduce their tip.

As she grabs a pad and pencil and makes her way to the sun deck, she keeps a lookout for Ashley. Come to think of it, where is her second stewardess as well? It is almost eight o'clock. Brandy should be up now.

No stewardesses, a guest who wants morning coffee and no doubt breakfast, and the bloody table isn't even set.

Moving around the upper deck, she sees Captain Carly's blonde head.

Fuck!

If Cap comes down and sees the lack of table décor, they'll all be for it.

Danny, the bosun, saunters past, broom in hand, rag over his shoulder. He is whistling a tune.

Normally, when he appears, Ella is softened by his appearance. Not today.

In a sudden fit of rage, Ella yanks the broom out of his hand. 'Danny, where the hell is my crew?' Her words are clipped and sharp, a hint of panic in them.

He stuffs a wad of Luca's bread in his mouth and talks around it. 'Why would I know?'

She simmers, tries to cool down. Right now, half of *Ananke*'s crew are AWOL, and though Danny isn't her first choice for interior assistance, he's the only one here.

'I need your help. Please, please, go to the top deck and see what Piers wants to drink. Take his breakfast order but only if he requests it. If he doesn't, see if he fancies going on the jet ski before breakfast.'

Danny chews slowly, regarding her with something almost like suspicion.

She swipes at him with the broom head. 'Buy me some time, *please*!'

He snatches the broom back, grumbling, but she knows that he knows teamwork is the key to their tip size.

On borrowed time, she pulls out her radio and presses the call button.

'Brandy, Ashley, this is Ella. Please make your way to the sun deck.'

She won't repeat the call. It will be heard on everyone's radio, and she doesn't want Captain to know she's missing two stews.

While she waits for one or both girls, she starts pulling for breakfast. The last day of charter is usually a nice affair – they go all out, décor-wise – but today there is no time for frills. She sets the most basic of settings, already sweating, a mixture of hot Greek sunshine and stress.

She hears Brandy before she sees her, feet pounding up the stairs, polo shirt buttoned up wrong, stuffing her unbrushed hair under the *Ananke*-branded cap that Brandy would normally never be caught dead in.

'Where have you been?' Ella's words are a hiss, but she's also relieved that she's now at least got one member of staff. 'And where the hell is Ash?'

Brandy seems frantic. 'I overslept. I'm so sorry but, Ella, you know me, I never do this.' The girl's panic is evident as she sweeps her hands out in front of her, toppling the vase of fresh flowers that the provisioner brought yesterday.

Ella catches them before they crash to the tabletop. 'Jesus, calm down. I've got bloody Danny doing stew duties, so relieve him, take the drink orders, then find my fucking third stew.'

She's annoyed because this is an easy three-guest charter. In a job where Ella has catered to a dozen who in turn have brought even more people on board to party the night away, this one is a gift and should be treated as such. The Kilfoyles retired to their suite way before midnight last night, so there's no excuse for any of the crew oversleeping.

But... Ashley hasn't overslept, has she? Her cabin is empty.

Ella smooths down the last napkin on the table and goes in search of Cat, Ashley's bunkmate.

She finds her on the swim platform, hauling the jet skis and sea bobs and various other water toys out of the storage.

'Cat, did you see Ashley this morning?'

Cat glares at her. 'I didn't see anyone. Only you, barging in, waking me up,' she says pointedly.

'Yeah, sorry about that.' Ella's not sorry; it's a yachting way of life to be woken at all hours. 'But I've lost my third stew.' She narrows her eyes at Cat. 'Did you spend all night in your cabin?'

Cat huffs as she hauls a sea bob to the edge of the platform. 'Most of it. Don't know if Ash was there when I went to bed. I don't make a habit of checking her whereabouts before I go to sleep.'

Ella catches sight of Piers and his wife, making their way up the stairs to the deck where breakfast is to be laid out. 'Shit,' she says, 'gotta go. If you see Ashley, send her straight to me.'

It's torturous. The one day she's a stew short, and the guests want *everything*. For the last couple of days, they've been satisfied with fruit, croissants and pastries. Because it is their last day, they want the works. Eggs, bacon, omelettes, mimosa cocktails for the adults.

22

Ella stares at the son of the guests, who so far has spent most of his holiday in the galley with Chef Luca, honing the skills of the profession he wants to follow. Today, when they could do with an extra pair of hands, he's content to sit between his parents, sipping on his mocktail.

When they are finally sated, Ella packs them off to the swim platform so they can squeeze some extra fun into their last few hours. It gives her a chance to search for Ashley.

As she heads to her cabin to retrieve her mobile phone to call Ashley, she realises something has shifted inside her.

Earlier, she was furious. Now, hours after the fact, worry stirs uncomfortably in her stomach.

She calls Ashley's number, standing in her bathroom, staring at her own reflection as she listens to the dead tone of a mobile.

Where is she?

So far, Ashley has proven to be an exceptional crew member. She has never been late for a shift, plus she's helped the exterior as well as carrying out her own duties. She came highly recommended from the *Siren* yacht crew.

But of all the employees, Ashley is the one she knows least about. They've become friends. They've shared small pieces of themselves. They have a connection that's yet to be explored in depth, an almost sibling-like bond.

Yet, she thinks as she makes her way through the ship to the lower deck, Ashley has never fully opened up to her. But the same could be said for Ella, too. Because they all have a story.

They all have a past.

They are all fleeing from something.

She checks every door of the exterior. At the engine room, she sticks her head in, waking Slopy Sid, who is napping at his desk.

'You seen Ashley?' she asks him roughly, taking a slice of pleasure in how he jerks upright at the sound of her voice.

For a moment, he looks like a deer caught in headlights. His mouth works soundlessly, until he manages to squeak out his words. 'Why would I?'

He turns his back on her and pretends to study the screens lit up in front of him.

What a waste of space.

She slams the door closed behind her and resumes her search.

The shout comes twenty minutes later. Seconds pass, then someone lets out a yell that flows seamlessly into a high-pitched scream.

Ella, in the process of heading up to the bridge to inform the captain that Ashley is missing, stops in her tracks.

The radio on her belt crackles to life.

All she can make out over the static is one word, repeated over and over: '*Emergency... emergency... emergency...*'

It is Danny, but she's never heard his voice like that.

'Dan, where are you?' Her own words are steady, but of course, at that moment, she has no idea what's coming.

'P-p-port side,' he stutters.

She swings through the back of the wheelhouse and out of the opposite door. Danny isn't in sight, but Piers is and so is his son.

Ayton, the young lad, has one hand on the railing and is peering over the edge. His neck is red and blotchy, exposed to the sun.

He turns at the clatter of Ella's approaching feet.

'What is it?' Ella asks.

He covers his mouth with one hand, eyes popping, cheeks bulging.

'Ayton?' Ella puts a hand on his arm.

He coughs, more of a choke, before a stream of vomit sprays through his fingers.

Instinctively, Ella steps back.

'Sorry.' The kid's words are a hoarse whisper.

Her training comes back: unflappable in an emergency, that's what she's been taught. And even though she doesn't know yet what this situation is, she grips the boy by his arms and steers him back to sit atop the housing that the anchor mechanism sits in.

She steps back to the railing. Piers still stands there, apparently unaware of his son's distress. Down below, she can hear Danny.

He must be standing in the tender. He is crying, huge, jagged sobs, the like that she's heard before.

Cries that haunt her at night.

Cries she wishes she could forget.

Danny is generally stoic, and suddenly, Ella doesn't even want to see what's happened down there.

But, too late, he's seen her. Hoarsely, he screams her name, and his tone cuts through her.

With one bound she's over the side, using the railings as a ladder, down, down, down until she feels Danny's strong hands around her waist as he lifts her into the tender.

She looks at him first, his face red, his eyes streaming, his cheeks sodden.

'No,' he says, choking on a sob, chest heaving. He pushes her a little. 'Go back up; you don't want to see.'

She's annoyed again, right back to a few hours ago when none of her staff could be found and Danny was nothing but an irritation. Why did he call her down here if he didn't want her to see?

And of course, now she *has* to see.

Had someone described the scene beforehand, she'd have thought she'd have passed out upon viewing it with her own eyes. Or at the very least vomited, like the boy up on deck.

But there's a strange nothing as she looks.

Ashley Mercer, her missing third stewardess, is splayed against the side of *Ananke*. The heavy anchor chain is twisted around the girl's neck, caught so tight that at points, it is embedded deep in the skin below Ashley's chin. Her eyes are open, staring, red where they should be white, all the blood vessels burst.

Above her, she hears a commotion, but the sound is vague and far away, as though she's underwater. Eventually, she drags her eyes away from the monstrosity in front of her and looks up.

She sees the charter guest, Piers. He's staring.

He's not even looking away.

And what is that on his face? Something like… fascination?

Looking just like he did when that other awful thing that happened. Was it really only yesterday? Was it – as some had said – a bad omen, a sign of things to come?

Ella turns away. She swallows hard as her stomach roils.

Above her, another face appears. Ayton, the guest's son, back again. He is a teenager, she thinks. He is an accomplished cook, working in the galley with all the confidence of an adult.

But he is *not* an adult.

'Get the boy away.' Ella finds her voice as she clambers back up to the deck.

More people are there now. They all seem frozen, heads craned over the side of the boat, the kid included.

Ella rushes at him, shouldering him back from the side. 'Away!' she shouts. 'Get him away.'

Piers is still there, and just like the monstrous scenario the day before, he's silent, watching, seemingly unable – or *unwilling* – to drag his eyes away.

Ella pushes Ayton into his father's side. 'Take him away,' she says. 'He does not need to see this.'

Piers looks at his son and blinks slowly, as if only now realising he has been here this whole time.

Ella turns to the wife, Nikki, who has emerged on deck. Like the others, she too is looking over the side. They can't see everything from there, not the way Ella saw it, face on, up close, but they can see enough.

They can see too much.

'Nikki.' Ella says the guest's name quietly.

Nikki looks at her.

'Please,' says Ella, 'please take him away.'

One single glance down at the splayed form on *Ananke*'s port side and Nikki gets it.

She grabs her son with one hand, Piers with the other and, in a huddle, she shoves them all into the door that leads inside the bridge.

Only then is Ella aware of how loud everything is. Danny's shouts, Cat's cries. The heavy metal of the anchor hitting the starboard side as *Ananke* moves in the gentle waves. Static on the radio as Captain arrives, calling for assistance, swearing between gritted teeth.

4

Now, a year later, Cat repeats her previous statement.

'I don't know why I came back here.'

They are in the crew mess, Cat and Ella.

It is unlike any first day of season that Ella has known. Normally, turning the boat over ready for the months she will spend on board passes in a flash. There is work to do, provisions to order, cabins to clean, floors to scrub. It all applies here – indeed, the workload is heavier than she's ever known it – but Cat's right.

Neither of them knows why the hell they agreed to come back here.

'It's supposed to help. Should give us "closure".' Ella shrugs and slumps in her chair.

That's the official line, but Ella knows the real reason.

Ananke's crew are hand-selected by Captain Carly. They have been for years. Carly is afraid that if they don't come back together, now, one year on, they will scatter to other yachts. Captain has spent years putting together her own A-team, and she's at risk of losing them.

It's a compliment, to be number one on Carly's list. As such, they are paid handsomely.

That's why they've all come back, for money and status and the relatively stress-free life of working in a familiar team.

She tells Cat this now, and watches as, momentarily, the younger girl's face lights up with pride.

'You didn't know that, before now?' she asks disbelievingly.

Cat shakes her head. 'It's a nice feeling,' she whispers, somewhat guiltily.

'You earned it, being part of a team that Cap requests every season. Don't feel bad for coming back.'

She glances at Cat, wondering if she should have told her. It's an open secret, really, between the department heads. Captain doesn't want the younger members of her A-team to get big heads.

But right now, that's the least of their problems. Their heads are already messed up.

Ella turns to Cat to ask a question that's been hovering in her mind for the last year. 'Had she done that before?'

'What?' Cat picks at the skin around her nails, already red-raw.

'I know she'd sorted the anchor when it was twisted, the night before… *that night*. I remember Cappy was furious because her deckhands were too drunk to go in the water. But had Ashley done it before that?'

Cat nods unhappily. 'A couple of times that I know of. She was good at it; she was good in the water, diving, swimming underwater and stuff. She was better than me, better than Danny even.' Cat pauses, her eyes far away. 'I bet Captain would have asked her back again. I bet she would have put Ashley in her dream team.' She looks sideways at Ella. 'Not in the interior – she'd have been outside.' She barks a laugh. 'She probably would have taken my role.'

There's a strange bitterness in Cat's tone. Ella chooses not to press her on it. What's done is done; there's no sense in Cat being envious now. After all, Ashley is gone. Cat's spot is safe.

'I didn't see it,' says Cat. 'But they said she untangled the chain, that night, then stood in the tender with the control to shift the anchor to a new spot, like Captain did the night before. But she got… caught up in it.' Cat's voice is thick with tears again.

'Captain is lucky she didn't lose her licence,' observes Ella.

'Captain thought about handing back her licence, quitting altogether.'

The girls jerk their heads up at the newcomer's voice.

'Luca!' A tiny part of Ella wants to hug him, but she's retreated into herself. Loss does that to her, pushes everyone away.

He leans over her, a firm hand on her shoulder as he whispers a greeting in her ear.

Ella remembers Cat, the thing she had with Luca last year, and she pulls back from him.

Cat, however, remains seated, eyes downcast, fingers back at her mouth to worry at the ragged skin that's left around her nails.

The atmosphere is still dense and heavy.

'Shall I make us coffee?' Cat asks.

There is silence from both Ella and Luca.

'I'll, uh, I'll make coffee,' Cat says, and sidesteps out of the mess and through to the galley, hurrying like she can't wait to get away.

'Brandy and Danny are now coming on board,' announces Carly as she comes into the room. She smiles, but it doesn't quite reach her eyes. 'Full house.'

Ella's heart lurches at the mention of Danny's name. Unlike times past, it sinks just as quickly in a sudden flash of sorrow. She hates the words Captain just said. *Full house.* She wonders if the older woman is stupid, mean or just insensitive.

'But it's not a full house,' says Ella. She takes a deep breath and tries unsuccessfully to quash the anger in her own voice. 'We're one person short, and to be honest, Captain, some people are having a hard time being back here.'

Me included.

Carly nods. 'I-I thought it would help. Captain knows best, right?' Her sharp laugh is one of self-deprecation. She puts a hand on Ella's wrist. 'I'm feeling the same as you all, and if this season is to go well, I *need* my team.'

Jesus! Ella's fury, never too far from the surface these days, simmers a warning. It's all about her, about the boat owners, about the season. Forget that a girl died here.

Her emotion must show on her face, for as Cat drifts back past her with the coffee, she lays a hand on Ella's shoulder.

Ella jerks free of her touch.

'I want total transparency.' Captain walks to the door so she is standing between the galley and the crew mess. She turns to

30

include Luca and Cat, sitting silent and stiff, a world of space between them. 'I thought getting back together would help us to heal, and, guys, I'm not always right. But I believe in us, this team. And I'm still certain that being together will help us.'

It's hardly an impassioned speech. When Carly is on the bridge, at the wheel, she commands the sea and the ship. Now, she's clearly floundering.

Like us, thinks Ella. *Like me.*

'We have the Kilfoyles coming aboard tomorrow. We need to turn this boat around. Tonight, I'm taking us all to dinner.' There is a look of resignation on her face as she glances around at her crew. 'After this first charter, I'll release anyone who wants to leave.'

It is something. The knowledge that Ella can walk away without penalty or a blemish on her record is better than the thought of facing the entire season on *Ananke*.

Footsteps approach the galley, low murmured voices. Brandy and Danny are here. Arriving together. Something warm bites at Ella's insides. This time it isn't anger.

Danny comes in first. Ella attempts to meets his eyes, smiles, but looks away at the last minute.

Like Captain said, it's a full house.

Almost, but not quite.

–

She thinks of the previous times she's been in the crew mess with these guys. Hundreds, over past seasons. Some of them she's known for a long time. Danny, for example, has been on the fringes of her career for so long he's like a big brother.

That's what she tells herself, anyway. Tagging him as a family member makes it so much easier to ignore the sensations that stir in her when they work together.

The sense of anticipation for the start of a season is missing. To Ella, and maybe the others, this is the way she normally feels towards the end of the summer. Sluggish, embittered, like she's ready for it to end.

'It might be nice to share some memories of Ashley,' says Captain, when everyone is sitting with their coffee mugs.

Nobody says anything. Doesn't Cap realise that along with memories come flashbacks that are best buried?

Ella looks down at the empty mug in front of her.

Someone needs to say something. *Come on, Cap*, she pleads internally. *If you're so intent on healing us, on keeping us together, how about you start*?

As if she's heard her, Carly does just that. One by one, as if encouraged, as if won over by their leader, other voices pipe up. Small at first, sounding half-choked, before slight smiles break through.

There's talk of Ashley's helpfulness, of her smile, of how happy the girl was. Captain keeps it going, expressive as always, hands darting back and forth. Ella sits back and observes, not joining in, buried half-memories gnawing at her.

'El?' It's Danny, peering at her. He is blurred, just a Danny-shaped vague image.

Ella scrubs at her eyes. 'It's bullshit.' She thought she'd whispered the words, but now there is silence, all eyes on her.

'What do you mean, Ella?' Captain's voice is low, serious, all hand gestures gone, smile vanished.

Ella shakes her head. 'You all say she was so happy. I–I don't know if she was. There was… something… Ashley was worried about something. I don't think she was always smiling.'

Captain leans forwards, elbows on the table, staring intently. 'What do you mean?'

Cat chips in. 'What was she worried about?'

'I don't know!' Ella is louder than she'd meant to be. 'I… I don't remember.'

'Is that why she wasn't sleeping?' asks Brandy.

Brandy's question pulls one of Ella's own to the front of her mind. 'Where were you, that night?' she demands. 'Ashley was in my cabin, in your bed, where *you* should have been. She left, yet you didn't come back, did you?'

Brandy flushes a deep red. 'I've already been questioned, thank you,' she snaps. 'We all have.'

'Yeah, but we don't know what the answers were, do we?' says Cat slowly.

Brandy pushes on, brown eyes flashing at Ella. 'What, you think I had something to do with it?' she snarls.

Captain is up, hands waving, calming, soothing. 'Hey, come on, turning on each other won't help anything.'

'Nothing will help!' Brandy slumps in her chair. 'Nothing's going to bring her back, is it?'

She should comfort her, Ella knows that, but *Ananke* is now a hive of sadness, of anger; the lack of understanding of how and why this happened is smothering them all.

'I want to get on,' Ella says. 'I want to get all the cabins done before dinner.' She doesn't wait for a reply, just leaves the room and all its sadness and heads back towards the crew quarters.

Down the hallway she pauses, glances back. Full house, Captain said, minus Ashley. Only now does she realise that they are two less inside. Sid, Captain's brother, wasn't at the meeting, either.

And it's as if none of them, not even his sister, have noticed.

Back in her own cabin, she empties the clothes from her bag, all these nice things, all these labels that she wears on a crew night out, loving the freedom of being out of uniform. The designer tags that once meant so much but now are meaningless.

She hangs them in the tiny wardrobe, piling last year's clothes into a bag and leaving a space for whoever her new stewardess will be when she joins the boat in a few days. She takes out her toiletries, stacking them neatly in the bathroom. She picks up her bag and is about to sling it into the corridor so it can be stowed in the hold when she pauses. It is heavier than it should be.

She closes her eyes as she remembers.

One year ago, police coming aboard acting like soldiers. There were no niceties in their manner, no empathy for the crew and what they'd seen. They marched through *Ananke*, ordering the crew to leave, with only their passports and essentials. Ella had scooped a change of clothes, for who knew how long she'd be hanging around, and a phone charger and flung them in her bag, hangers and all, before barging into the other girls' cabins to make sure they didn't have anything that would be considered contraband on board. So vivid now, the memory of facing Ashley's bunk, her meagre belongings, the thought of those greasy-fingered police and investigators rifling through her things. She hadn't even thought about it; indeed, now, she barely remembers doing it, but do it she did.

Sweeping an arm across Ashley's little shelf and holding her bag open to catch the few items.

Her passport wasn't there, she remembers that. She also recalls Ashley wanting to keep it with her, as though she was frantic at the thought of losing it. Her mobile phone wasn't there either. Dully, Ella remembered the dead tone when she'd tried to call it that morning. In fact, all that was on that small shelf was a book that Ashley was always scribbling in, a pen, a swimsuit, a T-shirt she slept in and a small handful of money. Her tip envelope wasn't there, and it wasn't in the captain's safe, either. Ella knew that because she stashed hers in the safe, locked away from alcohol-fuelled abandon that might make her spend it all on drunken nights out.

As she'd packed the girl's belongings, one ear listening out for any police marching down the corridor, she remembered another time, another death, other possessions, so many not making it back to those who would have cherished them.

A vague thought: *Ain't gonna let that happen again.*

She'd had a notion of looking at the stuff, reading Ashley's words, holding her items. A little memorial before passing them on to Ashley's family. But then she'd found out the girl had no family. And suddenly, the whole thing was even sadder, and she'd done nothing with any of the items. Hadn't even taken them out of her bag. Had half-blocked the memory of even having them.

Now, one year later, she tips the items onto her bunk. With their presence, she's covered again by blackness.

This was a mistake, coming back here. Captain is wrong. It doesn't matter that she doesn't want to lose her team; none of them will be any good to her, anyway. They won't be healed. They will simply be reminded.

It will be worse when the Kilfoyles come back on board tomorrow. And why are they even coming back to the death boat?

Because it's a freebie. A gift from the boat owners to say sorry for the inconvenience of last time.

Ella is tired now. Tired of thinking of it, of feeling it.

Maybe… maybe just being with Ashley's things might provoke something in her. Anything is better than this bottomless pit of blackness that is occasionally pierced by a white-hot temper.

Ella sits on her bed and picks up the notebook.

The sun sinks lower, enveloping the room in gloom as it moves away from the single porthole. Ella takes a deep breath and reads the first page. Her eyes blur. She holds the book away from her, so the ink isn't smudged from her tears.

Diagrams of yachts, denoting all the points that nobody bothers to learn beforehand, just stuff that's picked up along the way. Ashley was a prepper. Ashley was determined to succeed in her chosen career. Ashley was so precise that in no time at all, she could have been a lead deckhand or a bosun or a chief stew.

It makes the whole thing even more sorrowful.

All this planning. Notes of stew duties, deck jobs, boat parts. Agency contacts, ports and islands they'd visited or were due to. She was a newbie, this was her first real charter, but nobody would know she was inexperienced. She'd even made a neat little paragraph of the Kilfoyles' drink preferences.

After a couple of dozen pages, there are blank ones. Ella flips through, suddenly desperate to read more of funny little Ashley's way of working. It is bittersweet. The anger has softened. Maybe this is what Captain meant about healing.

35

But there is nothing but empty pages, and then, just as she is about to close the notebook, everything changes.

> *I fear I'm being stalked. I know I've hurt someone more than even I ever imagined I could. I know that either I AM being stalked, or I THINK I am, and I'm worried I'm losing my mind.*
>
> *I don't know which one is worse.*
>
> *I don't think I'll survive this trip.*

5

Ella reads the passage over and over.

And suddenly, that conversation with Ashley in the Jacuzzi that night isn't quite so vague any more.

Someone is watching me. Hassling me.

Shit! What else was there? Ella reaches into her memories, one year ago on an alcohol-soaked night.

Someone on the crew? One of the guests? What more of the conversation is there that she can't recall?

But Ella's mind is a blank.

She hauls herself up and reaches for the doorknob, ready to go out and brandish Ashley's words to the crew.

But…

She slips back into the bottom bunk and stares at the notebook. Was one of the crew after Ashley? But why? None of them had known her before the charter.

Had they?

She looks again at the words.

I don't think I'll survive this trip.

Ella puts the notebook in her back pocket and rolls off the bunk.

The crew are in their cabins now, dispersed to get ready for their dinner on the marina. Aftershave and perfume scents are cloying, a fog she walks through. As if this is any other first night of the season. Of course, it's not.

Not to Ella, anyway.

She pauses at Danny's cabin. It's the only one with the door closed.

She pushes it open.

Danny is in the bathroom, towel round his waist, door open, and Brandy is sitting on the bottom bunk.

She stands up when Ella comes in, looks her up and down.

'Are you ready?' Brandy sounds doubtful.

Ella returns her look. 'Are you?' she asks archly.

Brandy leaves the room without replying. Ella frowns. She and Brandy have always had a good working relationship. No, more than that – a friendship. Now, that seems to have changed.

'Dan, how're you doing?' she asks.

'Fine.' His voice is muffled as he pulls a shirt over his head. 'You?'

'Not sure. Danny, how well did you know Ashley?'

He slips his shades over his eyes, even though they're indoors. A move that doesn't go unnoticed by Ella.

'She helped on deck a few times. Didn't know her well, did I? None of us did.'

Ella leans against the doorframe. 'Would you have wanted to know her better?'

He scoops up his phone and puts it in his pocket. 'What do you mean?'

'I mean, did you *like* her? Did you find her... pretty?'

She knows Danny. Knows he's a ladies' man, knows he can occasionally lose his temper. Knows that he was the one who found Ashley that morning.

God, her thoughts are spiralling. To consider that he would do that.

Not him. Anyone but him.

Please.

'Jeez, El, I don't know. I didn't think of her that way.' He strides towards her. His presence makes her step back and he moves past her into the hall. 'Why are you asking stupid questions?'

'Why do you think they're stupid?' she answers back in a flash.

'Pointless, irrelevant, stupid. Whatever.' He walks away, down towards the mess, and Ella is on his heels.

'Where were you that night?'

'In bed.' He stops finally, and his expression is curious now. 'Why?'

'All night?'

'Jesus, Ella, what the hell are you asking me?'

What *is* she asking him? If he lured Ashley out to the tender and wrapped the anchor chain around the girl's neck?

This is Danny. She's known him for years. They've chartered together dozens of times. They've hung out in bars, they've danced, they've been friends. He knows her brothers, he's met her family.

And there has always been something hanging in the air that suggests that there could be more.

I've loved him for years.

The thought flies into her head, unbidden, unwanted.

She banishes it. Another thought comes, just as unwanted. How well does she really know Danny? How well does she know any of the crew who just spend summers together every year? They are thrust together, at the start of every season, but who are they for the other eight or nine months of the year? Ella knows she wears a mask, a kind of armour when she's on charter. She is professional, organised, bossy. Luca is stressed, always yelling, barking orders. She's always suspected he puts it on a little bit, striving for the authenticity of an Italian chef. Cat is scatty; Danny is a wannabe surfer dude. Brandy is aloof; Sid is lazy, creepy, but harmless. Are they all wearing cloaks? Just for appearance?

She doesn't know, not really.

All she knows is what they want to portray.

Herself included.

'I'm just trying to figure out what happened,' she says eventually.

'We know what happened. Ashley tried to untangle the anchor chains, on her own. She failed, big time, and paid for it with her life.' Danny grabs a water bottle from the side. He holds it in his palm for a moment before turning and lobbing it across the crew mess.

Danny is right. Or, at least, he's repeating the outcome of the investigation.

And it fitted, it really did. Even though it was tragic and awful and has scarred them all, the conclusion makes sense.

Because that's what Ashley did. She helped out, all the time, even in other departments, because she was desperate for approval, for that end-of-season crossing to Spain, for validation and success.

Plus, she loved the water. Loved it more than any of the others, even the experienced deckhands like Danny and Cat.

Ella would have let it go. Would have tried to soothe the bruises of her grief. In time, she would have maybe moved on.

But that was before the notebook.

It was before the other stuff that happened, which has wound her so tightly that some days she never smiles at all.

Danny is there now, up in her face, his strong hands on her shoulders, peering at her.

'You're right,' she says. 'But... but I think something happened.'

He takes his hands away and she staggers slightly. 'What do you mean?'

Danny. Friend. Confidant. Colleague.

Danny. Who has always been something more. Something for the future. A potential that Ella's never acted on for fear of destroying what they've got.

But it's destroyed now, anyway. All these relationships, these friendships – if that's what they were – have been sullied.

She has nothing else to lose. But she needs to know that it *wasn't him*.

He slumps down in a chair as she takes the notebook out of her pocket, still open to the strange paragraph, and slides it across the table to Danny.

He reads it. Slowly, and takes so long she knows he's reading the words again. She sits down opposite him, and waits.

'What the...?' Finally, he looks back up at her.

Ella shrugs unhappily.

He flicks it back to her. The book skids across the table and lands in her lap.

'And you think I was following her? You think I was… stalking her?'

'No, I don't!' As soon as she says it, she knows it's true.

Danny is upfront and open. He will confront if needed, tell harsh truths. He has a temper. He's a lot like Chef Luca in that regard. But she's never felt unsafe with Danny and has rarely seen a side of him that would suggest anything other than the man she believes him to be.

Until right now.

He kicks out, his anger startling her, his bare foot landing on a wall panel. The panel buckles.

Ella stares at the indentation. It reminds her of the shape in Ashley's pillow. His rage reminds her of her own.

In response, her own temper flares again.

'Oh, yeah, great way to show me how you couldn't be responsible for Ashley's death,' she snaps sarcastically.

He moves around the table, coming up at her again, his face close to hers. No concern in his features now, just… something she's never seen before, but something she's felt plenty herself in the last year. Before that, even.

'Hey!' Captain saunters in, hands up. 'Hey, hey, what's going on?'

'Ask her,' snarls Danny.

Captain, unflappable, crosses her arms. 'Captain is asking you, my bosun,' she replies.

'Ready! We're ready!' Cat bounces in.

Cat, with her inability to ever read a room.

In the silence, Ella's eyes land on Cat. For someone who came aboard crying, she sure seems to have cheered up. Ella remembers Cat's words from earlier, how Ashley was so good at the role that Captain would have had her back this year, possibly shoving Cat aside to make room for her.

Ella stares at the girl, but Cat seems not to notice.

Captain takes one more look at Danny's face, glances at Ella, and then claps her hands.

'Right. Off this boat. Dinner.' Carly pauses and looks at the others who have trickled into the mess. 'Tomorrow, we pick up charter. This is still our job, our business. We are who we have always been. Professionals, giving seven-star service.'

She claps her hands again. A mother hen, shooing them on their way.

Ella hasn't changed her clothes or so much as brushed her hair. Nights out with the crew are special occasions. Longed-for breaks where, for once, they become the ones who are looked at and looked after. Cat still has that mindset, and Brandy and Luca. Even Sid has emerged from his hole in a freshly ironed shirt.

Like they've all forgotten already what happened on this yacht.

Or like they no longer care.

'Ella?' Captain puts a hand on her arm.

Ella looks down at the clothes she's been wearing all day. 'I'm ready.'

—

She walks the marina quickly, still wearing the clothes she travelled to Greece in, the ones that she scrubbed the filthy galley kitchen in. Unthinkable. But that was before.

Breaking away from Captain, she catches up to the others. She wants to sit next to Danny, doesn't want to leave their friendship like it was back in the crew mess, a mass of hurt and anger.

Not him. Not Danny.

She sees Brandy heading for his end of the table. Thankful for her trainers, instead of the usual heels she'd be sporting on a night out, she overtakes Brandy and slips in beside him.

'Sorry, Danny,' she says, quietly and breathlessly. 'I'd never think anything like that, not of you.' She holds his eye contact, bolder in that one look than she's ever been before with him. '*Especially* not about you.'

He nods. His jaw is set. She knows him well enough to know he's not entirely forgiven her.

'So, what are you saying, then?' He glances around furtively, and lowers his voice. 'You can't seriously think someone hurt Ashley?'

She edges closer to him, matches her voice to his own low tone. 'I remembered something, after I read that bit in her notebook. The night before she… well, you know. In the Jacuzzi, she said someone was hassling her. *Watching* her.' She frowns. 'She said something else, later, the very night before…' Ella trails off, unable to clutch the memory and hold on to it.

'What did she say?' he asks.

She shakes her head unhappily. 'I… I don't remember. We'd been drinking. A lot. It was our unexpected night off.'

His face is a look of amazement. 'You drank so much you can't remember the conversation?'

'Piss off, Danny. You were so drunk you couldn't even be trusted to go in the water and release the trapped anchor.'

He reddens immediately.

She regards him seriously. He was drunk. So much so that Captain wouldn't allow him to do what should be second nature to him. How far gone was he? Drunk enough to…

No.

No.

She shakes her head as if to discard the thought. She'd seen him the following morning, the moment he discovered Ashley's body. He was distraught. Devastated.

Because he was responsible, and everything was different in the cold light of day?

No!

She straightens up and looks him dead in the eye. 'You were drunk; we all were. What happened when you left the crew mess? Did you go straight to your cabin?'

He narrows his eyes. 'Why are you asking?'

'I just wondered if you saw anyone else. If we can establish a timescale, we can narrow it down.'

'Narrow *what* down?' His eyes are huge, disbelieving. 'You really think one of us is responsible?'

They had been docked in the middle of the sea. If Ashley's death wasn't an accident, it comes down to those who were on board *Ananke*.

She looks around the table, at the assembled crew who she's known for years. How many of them can she truly discount? She's seen the best and the worst of all of them, across the seasons. Her earlier thought comes back to her. She spends time with these people for a quarter of a year. Who are they when they are not on charter? What behaviours might they exhibit out of uniform?

Plus, there are three other people that can't be excluded. If she's going to look at her crew, who she has known forever, surely she needs to examine the guests who are, essentially, strangers. But the Kilfoyles are a family. A seemingly nice, decent family.

But there was that other incident... the terrible thing that happened the day before Ashley's death... Piers, the main guest, his fascination at odds with everyone else's distress.

She draws in a jagged breath, not wanting to think of *that* scenario right now.

All that blood, staining the deck.

She shakes her head violently and looks around the table again. Her eyes come to rest on Luca. Volatile, for sure, but from her experience it's a qualification needed to be a chef. Although he'd had some discord with Ashley, hadn't he?

'Slopy,' says Danny suddenly, out of the corner of his mouth.

She looks at Slopy Sid. He's in his chair, on the opposite end of the table. His chin rests on his chest, as though he's about to nod off at any moment. He hasn't, as far as she's seen, interacted with anyone yet; he didn't join in the crew meeting earlier when the others were sharing their memories of Ashley, and nobody has talked to him tonight.

He is an oddball. But the way she – all of them – have always seen him is just that. Strange, but harmless.

How much does she really know about him?

How much does she know any of them?

'I need to open a dialogue,' she says out loud. 'I need to find out where everyone was.'

Danny taps his fork on the table twice, before pointing it at her. 'Where were you, Ella?'

'What?'

He shrugs. 'Just seems fair, if we're going to treat everyone as a suspect – why would you get a free pass?'

'Okay, we'll start with you,' she shoots back. 'Where were *you*?'

That flush again, scarlet, rising up his neck and staining his cheeks.

'Danny?' Suddenly, Ella is cold, despite the heat of the night, goosebumps prickling at her flesh.

He mutters something. So low, so muffled, she doesn't hear it. 'What?'

'I was with Brandy!' This time it's loud enough for the rest of the crew to turn their way. Danny colours even more.

'Oh.' Ella falls back in her chair.

She is deflated. Hurt. Which doesn't make sense because there's never been anything between Danny and her.

Yet.

She sucks in a breath of air and tries to get past it.

The food arrives in the midst of the sudden awkwardness that has hit their end of the table. In silence, she picks at her swordfish. Eventually, when she has forced down half of the meal, she speaks again.

'Maybe we should forget it.' Her voice is cold. She tries to soften her tone. She doesn't want him to know that she's hurt that he spent the night with Brandy. 'It's… I'm being silly.'

She blanches at her own words. Words that are hazily familiar. Words from that Jacuzzi night. Not from her, though – from Ashley.

It's silly. I'm being silly. It really doesn't matter.

Oh, God, more is coming back to her now.

Ella leans her head forwards, praying for silence, hoping Danny doesn't interrupt her as she digs around in her blackened, blocked memories.

It'll be better in Spain.

She had almost forgotten about Spain. Ashley was going to stay on board *Ananke* at the end of the season and sail to Spain.

It'll be better in Spain.

Yes, that's what Ashley said. Which means whoever she was afraid of, if it was someone on the crew, wasn't going to do the end-of-season crossing with her.

But who had originally planned to sail from Greece to Spain?

Captain Carly, Danny and Chef Luca.

That means the three of them are out of the suspect pool.

And Brandy was apparently sleeping with Danny that night. Even the thought leaves a sour taste in Ella's mouth. She feels her lips twisting spitefully as she glances at the girl. Danny liked Ashley, was helping her out, showing her the ropes of the exterior roles. Did that spike something in Brandy? A jealousy, perhaps?

And it still leaves the Kilfoyles, Cat and Sid unaccounted for.

And herself, she supposes, if Danny has his way.

She turns back to Danny. 'You're in the clear,' she says.

He gives her an arch look. 'Thanks for that, Your Honour. Can I ask what made you come to that conclusion?'

'Ashley said everything would be okay once she got to Spain. You were going to do that crossing; so was Luca and Cappy. It couldn't have been you three that she feared.' She pauses, unsure how to phrase her next question. 'Uh, are you sure Brandy was in your cabin? She didn't leave at all?'

He reddens slightly, brushing off her question with a shrug before hurriedly moving on.

'What about that Kilfoyle bloke?' he asks. His tone is suddenly gossipy, as if they are discussing some idle scandal. 'I mean, didn't you find him a bit... weird?'

'The thing... on the deck!' It is vague, the recollection of not only that incident, but everything about the previous season.

Every bad memory of that charter one year ago that up until now, she's managed to semi-block to save her already fragile state of emotions.

What else is hiding within the dark recesses of her mind?

'We need to go through everything.' She grabs Danny's arm. 'And once we clear a crew member, we need to get them on board too.'

He frowns. 'Why?'

'Because they'll have memories of her, things that we might not know. Information that might mean something if it's shared!'

Danny removes her hand from his wrist. 'It's been investigated. It was an accident. It was bloody awful, horrific, but it was an accident. El, do you think you're getting a little... obsessed?'

She rears up again. 'Don't you think it's worth getting obsessed over? Someone *died*, Danny!'

A sudden weight on the bench next to her.

'Okay, guys, what's going on down this end?'

It's Captain, hands gesturing, face troubled.

Ella takes a deep breath but Danny cuts in. 'Nothing, Cap. We're all good, just chatting.' He gives her a winning smile.

Captain looks from her to him, suspicion evident in her features now. 'Okay.' She stands up and claps her hands. 'Guys, your captain is going back to the boat. Please don't forget we have our guests boarding tomorrow. There is still so much to do, so midnight curfew, okay?'

Obedient nods all around.

When Carly has gone, Ella turns back to Danny. 'What was that about?'

He is watching Captain go, her long strides marching back towards where *Ananke* is docked.

He turns to her, troubled. 'I don't want to tell her that you're thinking... this way.'

He thinks Ella's crazy. He's aware what happened, just before Ashley... He's one of the very few that does know, and he thinks she's going to go mad, like she almost did before. Like her mother has.

Her vision blurs with unshed tears.

Another weight lands on the seat, and with a rustle of taffeta, Brandy slides in, glaring at them, eyes blazing.

'What were you talking about?' she hisses.

Ella opens her mouth to speak but clamps it closed.

Let *him* answer.

'Ella is trying to find out where everyone was *that night*.'

'Why?'

'Because she doesn't think Ashley's death was quite what it seemed,' Danny replies.

Brandy stares at Ella. 'It was an accident. The investigation—'

'The investigation didn't have all the information,' interrupts Danny. He looks at Ella. 'Show her.'

She blinks at him. Moments ago, it had seemed like he thought she was losing her mind. She hesitates, for she hasn't truly discounted Brandy, though she's not sure if it is because she is suspicious, or just… angry at her former friend.

'Show it to her.' Danny glares at her and downs a shot from a tray that's being passed around.

Dutifully, cornered by Danny's demand, Ella produces the notebook and passes it to Brandy. 'Keep it to yourself, for now,' she says as Brandy reads Ashley's words.

Brandy closes the notebook. Her eyes are big and round with disbelief. 'Nobody would have wanted to do that to her. Ashley was… lovely. Nobody would have wanted to hurt her.'

Ella stabs her finger onto the notebook. 'Someone *was* trying to hurt her. Or rather, someone was watching her, stalking her.' She takes a deep breath and looks at Brandy closely. 'Ashley told me someone was hassling her.'

Brandy sneaks a look at the others around the dinner table. Ella watches as, one by one, her eyes land on a potential suspect. Is Brandy innocent, or just a really good actress?

'Did you tell the police when they questioned you?' Brandy asks.

Ella feels the heat in her face. 'I didn't remember until today.'

'But we were out at sea that night, anchored; nobody could have got on board…' Brandy's voice is low, almost as though she's thinking out loud.

'Exactly,' Danny says.

'Oh.' Brandy lets off a full-body shudder. 'You think one of us…'

Ella shrugs. 'How well do we really know each other?' She lets her eyes linger on Brandy.

Brandy has been a friend, over the seasons, on the yachts. They've worked together and partied together. They've been each other's confidants. Last season, at the very start, Ella had confided that she feels something for Danny. That once the seasons are over, she still finds herself thinking of him.

They'd been drunk, naturally, because Ella wouldn't normally reveal something so personal to her subordinates. But they were not so drunk that Brandy wouldn't have remembered the conversation when she decided to crawl into Danny's bed.

'Wait, so… you wanted to know where *I* was?' Brandy flushes a deep scarlet and her eyes flash as she looks up at Ella. 'Seriously? *Me!*'

Ella is put out by the fact that Brandy is affronted. 'Why shouldn't we look at you? You were there; you were on board.' Ella fixes Brandy with an ice-cold stare. 'It doesn't matter, does it? Your whereabouts have been accounted for.'

Brandy drops her gaze. All that attitude is gone in an instant, replaced with something that looks like shame.

Shame because Ella knows her friend stayed with the man Ella loves, or shame because of what she did to Ashley?

'Ella…' she begins.

Ella stands up, horrified at what Brandy might say next. She doesn't want Brandy apologising for going with Danny.

Not in front of him!

'Leave it, for now. I… I want to go back to the boat.' She holds up her hand as Brandy stands up too. 'No, I just need a bit of time. I need to check how much work is still to be done.'

She walks smartly off in the direction of *Ananke* without saying goodbye to any of the others. At the edge of the marina, she stops and turns.

The table, minus Captain, are still seated, still pouring, still drinking. Brandy has made her way back to her original seat. Danny sits alone at the other end.

For that, Ella finds she is relieved.

6

Ananke is still in a mess. Not too much on the exterior. Danny and Cat must have got to work this afternoon while she was moping around, devouring Ashley's notebook in her cabin.

But the fact that the outside of the boat is spick and span only serves to highlight that Ella, so far, has accomplished nothing inside.

She glances at the clock on the galley wall. It is just past midnight.

God, the charter guests arrive *today*!

The rest of the boat is silent. Captain has obviously retired for the night. Ella moves through the interior of the boat, and a glow starts within her.

Ananke is a tip. Captain has every right to be on her back, demanding that it is righted before sunrise. But Captain has faith in Ella that by the time she gets up, the yacht will be fit for purpose, a seven-star haven.

No matter what else is going on behind the scenes – missing Ashley, the depression that comes along with her absence, her own memories and the accompanying rage dredged up by Ashley's death, and now the possibility that the outcome of the investigation was all wrong – Ella must prove her worth to Carly.

It is why she is chief stew on Captain's handpicked team. She is productive, organised and works extremely well under pressure.

Or, like Danny said, she is obsessive.

The pressure is on now, and Ella won't let Captain or the crew or guests down.

She doesn't think about it any longer. She flings Ashley's notebook on her bunk and shuts the door, so she won't be distracted.

After *Ananke* is in order, once the guests are on and settled, Ella swears to herself that she will resume looking into what is fast becoming a mystery.

They are back late, the others. So late that it is practically early the next morning, despite Captain's midnight curfew.

The old Ella would be furious, and she would let it be known.

Somehow, now, she can't bring herself to care. Let them try and work in a few hours with a hangover. She won't give her stewardess, Brandy, any grace. She will simply ride her harder.

The sky is just beginning to lighten in the east as they troop back aboard.

None of them seem very hammered, but the aroma of alcohol is coming off them in waves. They are, Ella realises, so damn drunk and have been for so long that they've actually moved past the worst of it and are halfway to sobering up.

Danny and Brandy stagger onto the boat together. Ella moves away from them, unable and unwilling to witness the two of them. What is it with them? Are they still a couple? Were they ever, or was it just a one-night thing?

Brandy.

Her friend, workmate and confidant.

Ella shakes her head softly to herself, picks up the last black sack that is filled with trash and, slinging it over her shoulder, she walks onto the marina and makes her way to the large, industrial bins.

She smells the stench before she reaches the small, concrete fenced-off square that houses the cluster of bins that are used by the dockside restaurants and bars. As she makes her way into the enclosure, she gags.

The bins are overflowing, so much so, the floor is a mass of rubbish. A side effect of the pandemic. The world is slowly beginning to right itself, getting back on track, but there is still so much to catch up on. Refuse collections are obviously not high on the list of priorities.

Ella stares at it. She is absolutely *not* going to wade up to her ankles through what looks like it could be year-old rubbish.

Yet, she can't just dump it here outside, either.

She backs away from the trash station, looks up towards the plaza. It is in darkness now, the Greek spires just about visible in the pre-dawn. She could take the rubbish to the other side of the plaza, where the out-of-action boats are incarcerated. It's a bit of a hike, but maybe the refuse areas down there will be clearer. Besides, she doesn't want to go back to *Ananke* just yet. The walk, before the sun comes up and the heat arrives with it, would be pleasant.

But she's also a little bit familiar with *that side* of the marina. It is completely different to over here. She knows there are people who live there, making temporary homes in the ferries that are currently docked year-round. Those that used to sleep in doorways and on the beach moved in when the pandemic hit. They're not a threat, not that she's ever experienced, anyway, but still…

Ella shakes her head, turns back once more to the refuse enclosure and slings the trash bag in as near to one of the bins as she can get it.

To her left, a pile of rubbish moves. A glimpse of something, long and thin and sleek, that twitches. Ella shudders, turns and sprints back towards *Ananke* before she can see the body that the tail belongs to.

Her cabin is empty when she returns, the top bed undisturbed. So, Cat and Brandy must be bunking in together.

Or have they come to a decision between them? Perhaps Luca is in with Cat, which means Brandy is bunking in with Danny.

If so, if it is still going on between them, it's going to a be a really long season with their new love shoved in her face for the next few months.

Ella strips off, her motions angry, flinging her clothes, soiled with a hard day and night's toil, into the corner.

As she steps into the hot shower, she remembers Captain's words of yesterday.

After this first charter, I'll release anyone who wants to leave.

Never did Ella think she'd ever walk away from a charter season. But faced with watching Danny and Brandy's PDA makes her think that, now, leaving is a distinct possibility. Where would she go, though? Not home, that's for sure.

And then there is Ashley. The mystery of Ashley. The words scribbled in that book that, the more Ella thinks of it, mean something.

Something awful.

Something sinister.

Something that could equate to… murder?

Something that the investigations, both by the police and the insurers, didn't pick up on, because all that time, Ella had the evidence with her.

And she knows now, until that mystery is solved, she won't be going anywhere.

In her towel, she moves back to her bunk. Work is done now. There are five hours until the guests board. Five hours for Ella to delve into her theories.

She stares at her bed.

The notebook has vanished.

–

She stands outside Danny's cabin door. In times gone by, she wouldn't knock and wait for an invitation. She'd barge in. She's always done it, not just with him, but all the crewmates she's known for ages.

Brandy's face comes to mind. Not Brandy now, or tonight, or yesterday, but last year, when Ella was stupid enough to confide in her the feelings she has for Danny.

Ella feels herself hardening as she stands in the corridor.

She twists the handle and shoves the door open.

The light above Danny's bottom bunk is on. He is in bed, awake, half-sitting.

In the top bunk, Ella hears a yell, muttered swearing in what she identifies as Italian.

No Brandy. Just an angry Chef Luca.

She jerks her head, motioning for Danny to join her. He throws back the covers and picks up a pair of jeans from the floor. Ella drags her eyes away from him, dressed only in shorts, abs and pecs and tanned torso rippling.

In the hallway, he closes the door behind him, one eye on her as he drags his jeans on.

'What's up?' he whispers.

'Where's the notebook?' she asks him.

He tilts his head to one side. 'Huh?'

'Ashley's notebook. I put it on my bed when I got back. Now it's gone.'

He scratches his head. To Ella, he is infuriatingly calm.

'It's evidence!' she hisses at him. 'And I'm betting whoever took it is the one responsible for her murder!'

Something overturns in the pantry. Footsteps.

Belatedly, Ella realises the light is on in there. She turns around. *Cat*.

'What the—?' Cat comes towards them, bouncing off the walls, still a little drunk from the night out. 'What the hell? Someone… someone *killed* Ashley?'

Cat is exuberant, loud, and has never learned the meaning of hushed tones or whispering.

Doors open down the hallway, one by one. Chef Luca, still on the top bunk, hair tousled, eyes narrow with sleep. Out of another cabin comes Brandy, eyes wide, hands clutching the doorframe. Suddenly, *Ananke* is thrown into turmoil.

They talk at once, all of them, voices growing in volume, competing to be heard.

Too loud.

Much too loud.

Because Captain cannot hear this. If Carly learns this new information like Ella has, she'll shut down the charter, and the season, and she'll get the Greek authorities *and* the boat owners involved.

55

They will find nothing new. All they will discover is that Ella unwittingly had possession of what could be evidence of a murder *all this time*.

They will not come to a different conclusion, and she could face God knows what consequences for concealing it. Ella knows how they work. Time is money, after all.

How much is one life worth?

'Shut it!' Ella's voice cuts through the conflicting conversations. 'Be quiet.' She prods Danny, shoves at Brandy. 'Get in the crew mess and keep your voices down.'

She talks fast and low, no option now but to spew out what she suspects to the wide-eyed faces around the table. She didn't want to do it this way. She wanted to question them, one by one, probing at them until she could clear them of any involvement. But Cat's big mouth has put paid to that.

Even as Ella explains her suspicions, she can't wholly believe the words that are coming out of her mouth.

The grief, which is just that. Terrible, life-altering, but... normal, all the same. The healing process that Captain Carly believes so utterly in, so she can keep her team together, on gathering the crew and passengers who were all there that fateful night.

Then, the discovery of the notebook, the shame that she's had it all this time and never even looked at it, and the subsequent resummoned memories of Ashley's fear that she was being stalked.

'You think it was one of us?' asks Cat. 'That one of us did... did *that*, to her?'

Ella is suddenly weary. She can't remember the last time she slept properly. It isn't a recent thing. She hasn't had an unbroken night since Ashley's death one year ago. Since before that, actually. Since the *other* tragedy, when her life was shattered once before, and she lost everyone she loved as they folded into themselves and their own grief.

She hunches in her chair and puts her head in her arms. Her motion silences the others.

'El?' A hand on her shoulder.

Light, tentative. Brandy.

Ella shrugs her off.

'Someone took the notebook,' she says. 'I put it on my bed. Now, it's gone.'

'Slopy,' says Cat immediately.

'What about him?' demands Ella.

Cat grips her arm. 'He was listening to you guys, at dinner. Didn't you see him? He actually moved down the table towards you so he could hear better.'

Ella shakes her head. That is the problem with Slopy Sid. He is like a snake, stealthy, silent, sneaky.

All the same, she narrows her eyes at Cat. Is she simply trying to throw Ella's questions at someone else, so they don't land on her?

But Brandy speaks up for Cat. 'Yeah, we went on to Cotton Bar, but he'd already left. He could have come back here.' She darts a glance towards the door that leads to the deck. 'He's probably got it now, reading it…' Her eyes widen. 'Making sure there's nothing that incriminates him!'

'*Porca vacca!*' Luca thumps a fist on the table. 'This is your plan? To accuse, no trial, no questioning? *Vaffanculo!*'

'No! Not… not *accusing*,' Ella protests.

'Just… investigating?' asks Brandy.

'That's right,' agrees Danny.

Luca swings around to face them. 'Wait, everybody agrees with this… this… *farce?*'

'It's not a fucking farce!' cries Ella. 'This is a life! *Was* a life! Ashley's life. If what happened wasn't an accident, then we owe it to her to find out.'

'Nothing happened!' Luca is blustering now, his hands emotive, face incredulous that they could even consider this. 'It was an accident. They said so, the big men, the insurance men. An accident.' He holds out his hands, imploring them.

Ella thinks she knows the reason for his passionate speech. She puts a hand on his arm – a light touch, calming, she hopes. 'It wasn't you. We know it wasn't you.'

She hears a groan from Danny, moments before Luca explodes.

'Who the *hell* are you to investigate me?' He seems to grow before their eyes, a hulk, swelling like a wave before it becomes a tsunami.

Then, there is carnage once more.

–

Ella removes herself from the crew mess. She doesn't care if Captain hears the racket down there. Doesn't give a damn if her crewmates tear each other to pieces.

Outside, the sun is up. There are a few people on the square of the marina. Fishermen are out on the calm sea, shouting to each other from where they sit with their lines, reaching across their bows and sterns, passing metal flasks back and forth. Sharing drinks, food, stories, laughter and personal space.

Covid hasn't vanished entirely, but the world – or this corner of it at least – has relaxed somewhat. She's been around these multi-generational fishermen for years; she bets they never took one iota of notice to the rules of lockdowns and social distancing.

Ella turns away from the fleet of fishing boats and walks the perimeter of the deck. Outside the engine room, she comes to a stop.

Cupping her hands to the glass, she peers through the porthole.

Slopy is not in his usual seat. The room is in darkness, the only light coming from the various switches and monitors that keep everything in tip-top condition.

The cot he uses to nap on is beyond the room, and Ella would bet money that's where he is now.

Like she did with Danny's cabin earlier, she twists the doorknob and nudges the door open.

She doesn't come in here much. It's kind of dank and miserable, and it smells like Sid. It's not massively unpleasant, but it's certainly not the kind of scent that the other guys have.

Danny's is hard work, coconut oil and cologne.

Sid's is a certain level of mustiness. Dust and sweat. Lies and unease.

Ella tries to shake herself out of it.

Ridiculous! All of them have known Sid for years. He's a sad man, no doubt lonely, seemingly friendless. Even his sister doesn't spend much time with him. And Sid has never fitted in with the crew. Never fitted in with anyone. He is either ignored or mocked by everyone, crew and guests alike.

Ella leans against the bank of desks and stares out of the window.

What does that do to a man? What has it done to Sid?

'Ella.' His voice is a raspy growl.

It comes out of the shadowy corner. Ella jumps. 'Slop— Uh, Sid?'

He doesn't move, but as her eyes adjust to the gloom, she can just make out his shape. He's standing in the corner. Just standing. Not fiddling with a computer or anything electronic.

Just… standing.

'What are you doing?' She's not fearful of him. Never has been. He's never been a threat. He's just creepy old Sid, who they leave alone in his basement-like boiler room.

Now, she wonders if that was where Ashley went wrong.

The girl had a good heart. A big heart. Did she see how alone Slopy was? Did she offer him something resembling a friendship? Did Sid take it the wrong way?

She remembers all those times when it was her and Ashley, then the realisation that Sid was there too, just like he is now. Standing. Watching.

'This is my room,' Sid says, his tone gruff. 'Surely I should be the one asking what *you're* doing here?'

To his left, she sees a workstation. It's cluttered, for Sid is untidy, always, wherever he is. Underneath a stack of papers, in among the white and grey, she sees the corner of something colourful.

She storms forwards, snatches it up and holds it to her chest.

Ashley's notebook.

'Why do you have this?' she asks. 'Why did you take it from my cabin? Why were you even in my room?'

He steps forwards, just one pace. Ella stands her ground, refuses to retreat, no matter how close he gets.

An involuntary shudder runs through her. Is that what happened to Ashley? Did she refuse his advances? Did she, too, stand her ground, and pay for it with her life?

'I wanted to know if she'd written anything about me.' He stands in a patch of sunlight. He is unshaven, hunched. Greyer than he seemed when she saw him yesterday, when he was at dinner.

He looks older.

He looks a little bit… broken?

'Why would Ashley write anything about you?' As soon as she says the words, she knows.

Someone is watching me. Hassling me.

Ella draws in a jagged breath.

I know I've hurt someone more than even I ever imagined I could.

She gasps. 'It was you! You were stalking her, hassling her!'

Sid stares mournfully at her.

Sudden silence descends.

7

'Oh my God!' Ella holds the notebook so tight she is in danger of ripping it. 'God, it was... it *was you*!'

'I... I didn't mean to frighten her!' His words burst free of him. He sags against the wall again.

Almost as if it is a relief. Almost as if finally spilling the truth has unburdened him.

'Frighten her!' Ella is seething. She is all rage now, that terrible, heavy feeling. She could hit out in every direction and punch out anybody nearby.

The same emotion she's had for a year now.

'Frighten her!' She says it again, shouting now. 'You *killed* her!'

'What?' Sid squeals.

At the same time, the door bursts open, bringing sunlight in with it, along with Danny. 'What?' Danny says. 'Him?' He turns to Sid. '*You?*'

'Wait... what?' Sid bleats. 'No way. No!'

The truth is within reach and Ella pushes towards it. 'You just said you frightened her. You said that, just now. You made advances on her; she rejected you and you *killed her*!'

'No!' His words are a hoarse scream. He shrivels before them.

The rage drains away. Screaming men are so much worse. She remembers last year, the sound of Danny, finding Ashley, screaming... She remembers a time before that, her father's sobs, her mother's shock that never subsided, that turned her into stone never to be softened again.

Ella is ripped back to the present as Danny spins past her, knocking her roughly aside as he grabs at Sid. Sid cowers, gasping, puts his hands round his head as he retreats into himself.

'I'd never do that!' Sid's cries are stifled as he buries his head in his arm. 'I frightened her, but I'd never hurt her!' He speaks again, but his words are muffled.

'What?' Ella steps forwards, gripping Danny's arms, pulling them down to his sides.

He struggles, just for a moment, before flinging his arms out of her grasp and retreating towards the door.

'What did you say?' she demands of Sid.

He moves an arm, just one, peeps at her like a child.

'I said, I can prove it,' he whispers.

'How?' she snaps.

He looks down.

She edges closer to Sid, goes into a crouch to put herself at his level, as if he is a child. 'Tell me, Sid,' she says.

He puts his arms down and for the first time that she can ever recall, he looks her dead in the eye.

'I recorded it,' he says. 'I've got it all on film.'

–

She doesn't know what they are about to see on the huge screen set up in Sid's engine room. She hopes it's not…

She swallows back bile that has risen in her throat.

Behind her, Danny locks the door and flips the porthole blind down.

The room is in darkness apart from the radar screen and the strange, blinking lights. Ella has no idea what purpose they serve. All she can hear is Sid's breathing.

She swallows again. This time in disgust.

'Hurry up,' she urges him.

He has a USB stick that he slips into a slot and taps on his keyboard. Slowly, he turns to face her. 'You won't… this can't go any further. I don't want anyone else knowing about this.'

There's a stifling heat in the tiny room now.

'It's all right, Sid. Just show us; we just want to know what happened.'

He inhales deeply. His hand that hovers over the keyboard is trembling.

Then, he presses a button, and the screen bursts into life.

The film was shot in this very room. Ella recognises the gloomy interior, the lack of light, the blinking buttons. The camara is focused on the radar screen, the same one that she can see to the left of the computer. A thin blue line runs through it, disrupting the data that should be shown. Then, the camera moves jerkily, to show another person in the room.

It's like a bolt, Ashley, on the screen. Ashley, how she was. Sweet-looking and kindly.

Sid's voice comes from an unseen corner.

'...technical issue, or it might need a new screen. Pain in the ass, these things.' Sid's voice, monotone, as he explains some sort of problem that he's trying to sort.

'Will we have to stay in dock to get it repaired?' Ashley's voice seems to hold a tone of anxiety.

'Nah, don't worry, it'll be a quick fix once I figure out the problem. I'm sending a video to a mate on land, hoping he can advise me,' Sid replies.

On the video screen, there is silence in the room, and then Sid speaks again.

'I... I really like you, Ashley,' he says.

There is a beat before Ashley replies. 'I really like everyone on *Ananke*. You've all been so welcoming.'

To Ella, listening to it unfold on the video, Ashley's voice is robotic, monotone. A lie?

'Can I take you to dinner, next time we dock?' Sid's words come out in a rush, as though he's been building up to it.

Next to Ella, she feels another kind of heat. It is Sid, this time visibly sweating.

Before Ashley can reply, Sid is pushing on. 'I know a great place. You know the plaza, where the ferries are docked on the other side? They have some cute little cafes over there. It's not fancy or anything, but...'

Ashley turns so she is profile on. In the dusky light her face looks ashen.

'No,' she says. 'I... I don't go over that side of the marina. Not any more.'

'Oh,' says Sid. 'It's really not bad. I know—'

'No!' Ashley's voice is sharper than Ella had ever heard it. 'Please don't mention that place again.'

Silence, long and drawn out and awkward. The sound of footsteps, light but hurried. The heavy engine room door opening, a burst of sunlight, then nothing but darkness and the sound of Sid's breathing.

'I scared her.' Sid flips the lid of the laptop closed. 'I wasn't expecting a date or anything, but that's clearly how she heard it.'

'Gross, man, why the hell were you recording that, anyway?' Danny asks, moving up to stand by Sid.

Sid swallows audibly. 'I... I was recording the fault on the radar to send back to the engineer in Athens. She came in... I didn't switch it off.'

'Gross,' repeats Danny.

Ella slips off the stool she's been sitting on. 'Look, you did nothing wrong. I... misunderstood.' Behind Sid, Ella can see Danny's face, confused, still with a look of anger. She speaks quickly. 'You're okay, Sid. Sorry to have bothered you and don't worry, we won't mention this to anyone.' She reaches out, squeezes his repulsive arm, and makes for the door. 'The guests will be on soon; come and join us when we meet them. And maybe have dinner in the crew mess tonight, yes? You shouldn't be stuck in here all the time.'

She passes Danny and grabs his wrist, yanking him out of the door before Sid can even respond.

'What the—?'

She raises her fingers to her lips to shush him. 'Come up to the bow, *now*,' she mutters.

She practically races to the end of the yacht, Danny on her heels.

'What was all that about, El? You *believe* him?'

Does she believe Sid? No, not entirely, even though he put on a pretty good act of being embarrassed and ashamed. Sid is still very much in her frame of suspects, but she doesn't want him to think that. Doesn't want him leaving *Ananke* before she's had the chance to observe him further.

Also, there was something else that struck her as odd in that film she just watched. Something that had nothing to do with Sid.

She draws Danny closer to her and tells him this.

'Sid is sad; he's lonely. He's a mismatch, here, with us. If it wasn't for his sister, he'd never work on superyachts. I never thought before that he's dangerous.'

'Why'd Ashley freak out, then? If it was just a case of him asking her out for dinner, no strings attached, why'd she lose her cool like that?' Danny gestures back towards the other end of the boat. 'You saw the recording. If it was just him asking her out for dinner, then she overreacted.'

'Yep.' Ella winces as she feels her own teeth grinding. 'Ashley was… let's face it, she was gorgeous. Men have probably been fawning over her for her whole life. Why did she react like that to a simple dinner invitation when she must have encountered that all the time?'

Danny slumps down to sit on the anchor housing, a weary look on his face. He pulls a packet of cigarettes out of his pocket. 'I don't know, El. You tell me.'

'There are two possibilities,' she says. 'Either that wasn't the first interaction where Sid had hassled her, or… it was because of where he wanted to take her.'

'To dinner?'

Ella grabs Danny's cigarette and takes a deep drag. She lets out a little groan of appreciation. Right now, she's unsure why she is constantly trying to quit.

'The ferries,' she says, more to herself now than Danny. '*The words she used.* "I don't go over that side of the marina. Not any more." That's what she said, right?'

He looks at her, blue eyes doubtful. 'Did she? It is a bit… crap over that side.' He takes his cigarette back. 'I… I don't know; we should have taken the USB so we could watch it again.'

Her pièce de résistance. Ella unfurls her palm. Upon it lies the stick with the last video of Ashley on it. 'We did,' she says.

Briefly, he looks pleased. In a split second, his face has fallen. 'Regardless, we're still no closer to getting any answers.'

Ella closes her hand and shoves the stick in her pocket. 'We need to watch this again and also find out everything we can about Ashley Mercer. Things we don't know that she might have mentioned to the others.' She turns her head to look out across the marina.

The plaza stands there, tall, proud, concealing behind it that strange part of Athens that everyone tries to ignore.

What is over there that Ashley was so afraid of?

Simultaneously, Ella and Danny's radios burst into life. Captain's voice crackles through.

'Guys, I've got eyes on our guests. Y'all better be in your uniforms and lined up on the dock in two minutes.'

Ella stares at Danny, still in his deck T-shirt and casual shorts. He runs his eyes over her vest, the one she sleeps in, with the rip near the shoulder.

'Shit,' she says, and takes off running for her cabin.

'Copy that, Cap,' she hears Danny say into the walkie. Moments later, he overtakes her, running past the other crew members, all in their blacks, ready to greet the most important guests they'll get this season.

—

She smooths her hair back and glances at Danny who has slipped in to stand beside her. He is still fiddling to get his epaulettes on his shoulder, and he is all fingers and thumbs as he wilts under Captain's glare.

To her left is Brandy, holding the tray of champagne that they always greet their charter guests with.

'What fizz did you pour?' Ella asks.

'Louis Roederer Cristal,' mutters Brandy from the corner of her mouth. 'The 2008 vintage.'

Ella breathes out in relief.

The welcome drinks are her gig, normally. She always studies the preference sheet to make sure the guests get exactly what they want. If nothing specific is noted, she'll trawl their social media. If she can't see anything there (which is rare – the rich love to show their expensive tastes) then she'll order the most pricy from the provisioner.

Brandy, to her credit, has not only remembered Piers and Nikki's preferred brand of champagne, but has even done a half-shot measure for Ayton, topped up with orange juice.

The guests are a hundred yards away now, striding along the marina.

The mother and son are as she remembers them. Nikki, tall and elegant, fresh new highlights glinting in the sunshine, wearing a beige, flowing dress. Ayton, smart casual, yet his togs are undoubtably as expensive as the drink he's going to enjoy.

She studies Piers. Upright and somewhat stocky is how she recalls him. Is it her imagination or has he changed over the last year?

He seems... smaller, somehow. Stooped over.

He has aged.

Ella watches him as he gets closer. Why has he aged? A man of Piers's means has the money and all the tools at his disposal to remain forever young.

Has last year's tragedy put ten years on him?

Has the knowledge of *what he did* done this to him?

Or has he simply been working hard, hunched over his computer, toiling at his business day and night like he did aboard *Ananke* last year?

She narrows her eyes.

She will find out.

'Piers, Nikki, Ayton!' Carly is in pure captain mode, striding forwards to shake their hands. She envelops Ayton in a brief hug. 'We're so glad you came back to us.'

Nikki doesn't emote the same warmth as Captain. 'To be honest, we weren't sure if it was the right thing to do.' She puts a hand on her son's shoulder. 'We're still undecided.'

Ella feels the touch of a hand on her hand. She snaps open her eyes and looks down. Danny's fingers on hers, a caress of... of what? Support? Friendship?

Her heart does a timid little jig. She swallows hard before wrapping her fingers around his.

'We're going to change your mind,' says Captain, gesticulating wildly, as is her way. 'We're going to give you a trip of a lifetime, I promise.'

At Carly's words, Ella disentangles her grip from Danny's. It's as though the Kilfoyles had bad service last time, rubbish meals or disastrous service. Their last holiday was ruined because a murder took place on board.

As if her emotions are written on her face, Piers glances at her. 'We had a fantastic time last year, Captain,' he says.

He locks eyes with Ella. She stares back.

A fantastic time?

Having his young son witness a dead girl's body with an anchor chain embedded in her neck was a *fantastic time*?

Danny's hand is on hers again as though he can feel her fury.

This time, Ella pulls away immediately.

Captain claps her hands. 'So, you've enjoyed *Ananke* previously, but Ella will give you a refresher tour. Then we'll be on our way, heading for our first anchor point.'

At the mention of the word 'anchor', Ayton and Nikki noticeably cringe.

Ella swivels to look at Piers.

The word has had no impact on him whatsoever.

She sets her jaw.

He is the one to look closer at.

And that is exactly what she intends to do.

8

Ella hangs back as Brandy tops off the Kilfoyles' drinks again. She feels a presence at her back. Whirling round, she comes face to face with Danny.

'You've got to chill out,' he murmurs.

She shakes her head and glances back at Piers. 'Why did they come back?' she asks, almost a question to herself.

'Because it's a free charter,' Danny replies. He huffs out a laugh. 'Come on, El, you know as well as I do how much the mega-rich love to get something for free.'

'Even this?' she shoots back. 'Coming back here, to the place where they woke up to any normal person's worst nightmare? Same boat, same captain, same place, same staff – minus one?'

Danny narrows his eyes as he, too, stares at Piers, who is currently draining his second glass.

'Hey.' Danny nudges her and looks away from Piers over the bow. 'You know how murderers can't help returning to the scene of the crime, right? How they inject themselves into the centre of it? Do you think…?'

As one, they turn back and study their charter guest again.

Ella shivers and wraps her arms around herself.

Is that it? Is that why they came back?

Someone clears their throat, loud and over-dramatic. Ella looks up to see Captain on the stairs, glare fixed on Ella and Danny, head gesturing subtly over to their guests.

Danny flits away, but not before he's given Ella one last penetrating gaze.

'Something to think about,' he whispers, and then he's gone.

Ella does the walk-through of *Ananke* for the benefit of the guests, who already know the layout.

As they reach the staircase that leads downstairs, Ayton glances at his father.

Piers gives him a nod. Ayton bounds down the stairs, no doubt in search of Chef Luca, hoping to hang out in his favourite part of the yacht, the galley.

Nikki is the first to bring up what happened last year. 'We followed the investigation,' she says, in hushed tones, once her son has vanished from view. 'An accident, they said.'

It is the perfect opener. Ella takes a deep breath.

'You didn't hear anything that night?' she asks. 'Like, when Ashley realised that she was in trouble?' She stares pointedly at Piers. 'The VIP suite is close to the port side.'

Piers returns her stare, his eyes small and mole-like behind his lenses.

Ella hates that she looks away first.

Nikki snorts and elbows Piers in the ribs. 'This one had one too many Drambuie cocktails.' She turns to Ella. 'He doesn't sleep at home; he's always working. That night, I couldn't sleep for his snoring, but if he got a decent rest I didn't mind.' Her face changes suddenly, and there it is, the past year written on her face too, dragging down her pretty, delicate features. 'I wish I'd paid more attention that night... What I thought I heard...' She trails off, looking rather ill now.

Ella turns sharply to her. 'What did you hear?'

Nikki shakes her head and purses her lips. 'Nothing... I don't think.'

Ella turns to Piers, aware that throughout their exchange he hasn't said a word. 'You slept all night. You didn't go out there at all?'

He holds her gaze again. This time, she doesn't look away.

'First night I've slept like that in decades.' He holds his hands out, palms up, reminding her for a moment of Captain Carly. 'I haven't slept like that since. I doubt I will again.' Something crosses his features, dislodging the carefree jolliness that he wears like a mask.

Like a mask.

That is exactly what it is. His exterior is just that, a front. The armour has slipped, just for a moment, and now she can see just how much last year's charter has impacted him.

He takes his glasses off and cleans them. By the time he has slipped them back onto his face he is back, walls up, professional façade fixed in place.

'Why did you come back?' she asks curiously.

Nikki stares off to sea. When she speaks, her voice is distant, as far away as her gaze. 'When we were invited back, I said no. Then later, I thought, *We can't rewrite it, but maybe, maybe we can replace it.*' She blushes. 'Does that sound stupid?' She utters a harsh laugh. 'It does to me. As if we can ever erase *that.*'

Ella forgets that she is supposed to be showing them the boat. It doesn't matter, anyway, the tour. It's all for show, just like this charter, just like this season. A masquerade that Captain and the boat owners have masterminded to prove that on *Ananke*, everything is okay and is running just like before.

Business as usual.

Ella slumps down in a chair. She's not supposed to sit here, not when guests are on board. In all her years of being a yachtie, her own professional front has never slipped.

Now, she's not sure she can keep it up.

'I saw her the night before it happened, out on deck.' Piers speaks up, startling Ella out of her reverie. 'She wasn't working; she looked…' He shrugs, unable to find the words. 'She had problems, worries?'

Ella eyes him warily, still unsure of his motives, his personality, his very self. 'I don't know. I didn't know her very well.'

And that is the problem. Of all these people, some of which she's known for years, she doesn't know them very well.

She thinks of herself, of the front she puts on to hide her own personal issues, in front of both crew and guests. Ashley Mercer was no different. Ashley Mercer was a bloody riddle. Her life was just as much a mystery as her death is.

Outside the floor-to-ceiling windows, Captain marches past, on her way to the bridge. She raises a hand in greeting to her guests, then stops as she catches sight of Ella slumped in the armchair.

Muscle memory ensues, seasons of professionalism. Ella reaches forwards and pretends to tie the lace on her shoe before standing up.

'What time would you like lunch?' she asks politely, her questions over for now, her stew-face firmly back in place.

'Maybe we can pop our heads in the galley, see what our sous-chef son is rustling up for us?' Piers is equally polite, following her lead.

'Certainly.' Ella smiles and ushers them towards the crew quarters.

–

On her break, she holes up in her cabin and inserts Sid's USB stick into the yacht's laptop. She watches the short film repeatedly, scouring the video for... for what?

She doesn't know.

There is nothing here, only Ashley's change of tone when Sid said he liked her, and her reaction to his suggestion that they go to a down-and-out part of town for dinner.

She can taste disgust in her mouth. Sid, who earns so many tens of thousands a year, who has virtually no outgoings, yet is cheap enough to suggest a crap cafe when he could have taken her to one of the many places the crew go when *Ananke* is docked. And why did he want to go there, to that awful part of the marina? Was it because it is generally avoided by the majority of people in Athens? Was it because it's quiet, secluded, nobody around to witness whatever plans Sid had for Ashley?

Ella's door opens. She whirls around. Danny is there, holding two mugs of coffee, one of which he passes to her.

'Thanks,' she says.

He edges into the room and sits beside her on the bottom bunk. 'Still obsessed?' he asks, gesturing with his mug to the laptop.

For once his tone isn't mocking, nor sarcastic, and she can see the heavy furrow that dents his normally smooth brow.

'I don't know,' she says, eyes on the screen. 'I don't know what to make of it.'

'Brandy said we're getting low on Krug. I said we can make a provision run on the tender.' He catches her gaze and holds it. 'Do you want to join me?'

She knows what he is really saying. The provisioner's van meets them on the dock, but because of the narrow pathways, it waits for them at the steps below the plaza. At the line of the divide between the superyachts and the out-of-commission ferries.

'We're a stewardess down,' she says. 'Captain would never allow it.'

'Cat's going to cover.' He waits for a moment. 'Or we can go after charter once we're docked back there.'

Two more days. Ella will go crazy with all the loose ends and half-formed theories if she can't at least discount something. Or find out something. But what will they find there? Ashley declined Sid's invitation to cross that unseen divide.

Or... did Sid resume pursuing Ashley? Did she weaken under protest? Even if she did, Ashley died here, on the port side of the very yacht Ella is aboard now. There will be no answers in the ferry marina now, one year on.

Will there?

She closes the laptop lid and stands up. 'We'll go now,' she says.

–

'She knows their preferences, Cappy.' Danny is on the bridge, having been accosted by Carly. 'I told her to write a list, but you know what she's like: *If you want a job doing properly...*' He mimics Ella, a passable impression that almost makes her smile.

Carly leans over the rail, peering down at Ella, who has already stationed herself in the tender. 'Don't be long,' she calls. 'And next charter, please anticipate the quantities you're going to need.'

'Copy that!' Ella gives her a fake smile and a thumbs up and waits for Danny to climb down into the smaller boat.

They don't speak as they ride the waves through the ocean. The sun is beginning its descent, an orange globe sparking a pink and red halo.

It is only when they pull up to the port that Danny clears his throat.

'I thought we'd ask around.' He jerks his head towards the plaza. 'Over there.'

A chill descends on Ella. They never go to the ferry side since the pandemic happened and the people moved in. It's got a bad rep, though from the times Ella has had to pass through, she's seen nothing untoward. Just normal people. They don't hassle the crews from the yachts. They're just… there. Looking weary, helpless, hopeless, homeless.

Then again, Ella has never been to the ferries after dark.

Danny tosses her a beanie hat and an unbranded fleece. She puts them on, covering her uniform.

They head up the plaza steps in silence, pausing for a moment at the top.

They set up meals here sometimes. Always ensuring the seating plan is pointing towards the marina where the superyachts dock, and away from the view of the ferry port.

It's a chilly night, and the marina they've just come from is empty of pedestrians. To her left, the ferries sleep. Great, hulking, unwieldy beasts housing the people who got caught here when the pandemic hit.

It wasn't always like this. Pre-Covid, both sides were heaving with people, day and night and practically all year round. The ferries were out all the time.

'I meant to ask, where did you even find Ashley's notebook?' Danny asks as they start up the plaza steps.

Ella ducks her head so he can't see her flush. 'I packed it when the police told us to get off the boat.'

She can feel the intensity of his stare and she brings her head up defiantly.

'When... when it all happened, my family...' She feels a stone lodged hard in her throat and pushes through. 'We never got his things back. We got some, but it was like they'd been picked over.' Ella's mouth twists bitterly. 'I thought about it all the time – them, going through his stuff. Picking it over, like magpies.'

He doesn't say anything, but instead, he drapes his arm awkwardly around her shoulder.

She shrugs it off and moves to the wall that lines the stairs.

'Something's going on down there.' She looks over the side. Almost below them, in the little alcove, there is an eerie red glow. 'Police,' says Ella.

There is unease building in her at the thought of crossing this unseen divide. She turns to Danny. 'Let's just get the Krug and go back to the yacht.'

'No. Let me take a look.' Danny darts towards the stairs, the ones that lead to the place where Ella really doesn't want to go.

'Danny!' She hisses his name, but he has gone. Swearing under her breath, she trips down the steps after him.

He hasn't got far. He is standing at the bottom, motionless, statue-like. She falters halfway, sees the grimace on his face, sees his throat working, looking remarkably like the way he looked last year, when she climbed down into the tender to be faced with—

'Danny?'

He jumps backwards, up one, two, three steps.

Then she sees them.

Rats.

Streaming out of the concrete enclosure where they keep the bins.

She gasps, remembering just the other night when she was considering bringing *Ananke*'s trash over here in the hope these bins might have more room.

She gags, covers her mouth as the rodents race past her, banished from their home by the presence of the authorities who are circling the space, torches lit, speaking rapidly in Greek.

'Oh, Jesus Christ.' Ella backs up too. 'Come on, we're going back to the boat.'

She marches back up the steps, taking them two at a time, not even glancing behind to see if Danny is following her.

She's not sure what is causing her more concern: the rats or the police. She feels bile rising in her throat again and she moves faster, knees pumping, not slowing until she reaches the relative safety and familiarity of the plaza level.

She looks to the right, to the bright lights and the opulence of the marina.

A new sound reaches her ears. Footsteps, many of them, pounding the steps from the direction of the ferries, rising in volume. A stampede.

And there they are, here they come. The people who live down there, in varying degrees of dress – some decent, the newer ones, some with clothes caked in filth who have lived down there a long time. They are fleeing, disturbed by the presence of the police, who rarely come here.

She flattens herself against the wall as they, like the rats, stream past her.

They don't look at her as they hurry across the plaza and down the other side.

The mass slows and gradually trickles to a stop. The last people to pass her are holding hands. She stares at them, transfixed.

The man, a dreadlocked lad, with gleaming skin and fury in his eyes, holds the hand of his companion. She's small and blonde. They are dressed like tourists, clean in body and clothing. The girl is sobbing.

It doesn't look right. The two of them don't look right. He's dragging her along and the whole scenario just screams *wrong*!

The girl tries to pull away from him. It is fruitless.

Someone is hassling me. Someone is watching me.

Ella steps forwards. 'Hey.' Her voice is sharp. She looks at the girl. 'Are you okay?'

The girl stops and drops to her knees. She covers her face with her hands. The man glances at Ella, looks at his companion and takes her arm roughly.

His strength is so that she's dragged along on her knees, her head tipped back, mouth open, harsh, jagged, rattling breaths beating the air.

'*Hey!*' Ella takes the girl's wrist with both of her hands. 'Stop!' she shouts.

Beside her, the girl seems to find her voice. 'I knew her!' she wails. 'She was my friend!'

'El!' Danny is suddenly there, next to them, face red, arms outstretched. 'What's going on?' He jerks her hand free of the girl's. 'What's happening?'

The chain has broken. The man gets behind the girl, shunting her with his tall, strong body towards the stairs that lead to the marina.

'Wait!' shouts Ella, but they have already gone.

She turns and slaps at Danny's chest. 'Stop that man… that girl didn't want to go with him!'

He shakes his head. 'Come on, we're getting out of here.'

Then, just like the couple that have gone before them, he manhandles her down the left-hand steps to where the tender is tied up.

'Jesus, Danny!' Ella wrenches her arms free of his and rubs her wrist. 'What the fu—'

'They found a body.' His voice is sharp as glass and cold as ice.

Ella stops as his words cut through her.

'What…?'

He shakes his head. 'It was… bad.' He clamps his mouth shut and scuffs his feet.

'Oh, God, did you *see* it?' She thinks of last year, of what he found, *who* he found, *how* he found her. 'I'm sorry.' She's contrite and sorry for him, but at the same time, so bloody glad she didn't go all the way down the steps and witness it herself.

She can hear weeping. She checks herself. Not her. It wouldn't be: Ella doesn't cry any more.

Behind Danny, she can see the blonde girl, now crouched on the dock. The man stands over her, still tall, still strong, keeping her in place with one hand on her shoulder, the other at her mouth, barking commands.

Ella takes two steps towards them. Danny grabs her hand. She shakes him off and keeps walking.

'What are you doing to her... oh.' He's feeding her an inhaler, forcing it in her slack mouth, tilting her face back, his hand cradling her head, tender and kind. 'I'm sorry,' she says, 'do you need any help?'

'No.' He glares. 'It's the shock, is all. She'll be fine.'

The girl gulps in air and knocks the inhaler out of the way. 'She was my friend,' she bleats, pitifully and breathlessly. 'We thought she'd gone home, ages ago, like a year ago.' The tears stream down her pale face. 'All that time...'

'Sorry,' says Ella again.

'It might not have been her.' The man's voice is rough. 'That was messed up, man, you couldn't even tell if it was her.'

Ella swallows. Jesus. What sort of state had that body— No. She doesn't even want to know. The memory of all those rats catches at her. Do rats do that – feed on human remains?

She turns to leave. Danny is at the provisioner van now, hefting out a crate and a couple of bags.

What a disaster this little jaunt has turned out to be.

The sooner they get back to *Ananke* the better.

Behind her, the girl's breathing has quietened somewhat. The man murmurs to her, soft words that Ella can't hear.

A scrape of feet as the girl struggles to stand.

Her voice, when it comes, is surprisingly strong.

'It *was* her!' she cries, her voice ringing out in the now deserted marina. 'I know it was her; I'd know that necklace anywhere. It was Ashley!'

She's reached Danny before her steps slow, falter, then stop altogether.

Ashley.

The name is on her mind.

Has been for a year, more than ever these last few days, and will likely be for the rest of her life.

'El, take these bags, will ya?' Danny piles them into her arms.

She will look stupid if she turns back and asks the asthmatic girl what she just said. She will risk more of the man's wrath. Risk Danny intervening and kicking off, getting a black eye or something that the captain will no doubt give him a red card for.

But it's weird…

Is it her mind playing tricks?

I'm worried I'm losing my mind.

Ella puts the bags down and turns around.

'El! For fuck's sake, where are you going?'

She barely hears Danny as she retraces her steps, back to the marina wall.

'Your friend,' she says as she reaches them, 'what did you say her name was?'

The girl looks up at Ella.

The man steps in front of her. 'Why?' he spits. 'You police?'

Ella shakes her head. 'No, I'm… I just wanted… to check.'

The girl shoulders him out of the way. 'Ashley, her name was Ashley.' Her eyes, though still red and wet, hold something akin to hope. 'Did you know her?'

Ella pulls her phone out of her pocket, scrolls the photos until she reaches a selfie of herself and Ashley. She holds it up so the girl can see, feels her face reddening at the girl's confused expression.

Ella shoves the phone back in her pocket. She's being stupid. It's not that uncommon a name and besides, Ella's Ashley is already dead. She knows that. Hell, she *saw* that. She needs to get out of here, out of this horribly undesirable area and back to the place she calls home for a few months of the year.

Ella apologises. 'Sorry, I'm… it doesn't matter.'

'Then why you here?' The man is rough, moving his shoulders, practically squaring up to Ella. 'Why you asking?'

'I thought… I thought it was someone I once knew.' She puts a hand on the girl's skinny, cold arm. 'I'm mistaken; I'm sorry for your loss. I'll be going now.'

She's taken a few steps back towards the van, but the girl is at her heels now, grabbing at her, reminding Ella of a puppy.

'Has she been with you? Is that where she disappeared to?' She grabs Ella's arm, tight claws digging into her. 'He reckons it could be anybody, but he didn't see her necklace.' She yanks on Ella's arm with force. 'It wasn't fancy, just cheap coral, but she always wore it.' The girl glares at Ella, fire in her eyes. 'Someone stole her passport, before she went missing. What was that about, you know?' The girl breaks off and drags the back of her hand underneath her nose. 'I knew something was wrong when it was stolen. We don't do that, right? We stick together, you know?'

Ella shakes her arm free, suddenly needing to get away.

This time, the girl doesn't follow her. She's almost reached Danny when the girl's voice comes out of the darkness, thin and reedy and wavering once more with tears.

'You think you couldn't have known her; you think we're so different from you lot?' The girl's anger comes as a surprise, her inflection, the loaded venom more suited to the man she's with. 'She wasn't a nothing, she was a someone, and she didn't deserve to die buried in trash like that!'

It's the pain that gets Ella. She knows that pain. She knows that the world is still spinning, and the sun is still rising, the moon keeps on coming. But not for Ashley. Not for either of the dead Ashleys.

She turns back to the girl. 'I'm really sorry,' she says, hating the inadequate words. 'You remember her; that's all we can do. We can't beat it or make it right. All we can do is remember them.'

She's talking to herself now. Imparting words of wisdom that are directed internally because it's true. *She'll* never solve this mystery. This girl in front of her, earnest, crying still, will likely never solve hers.

'Sorry.' She looks at the guy, includes him too. 'You guys take care, okay?'

The girl puts her face to the sky. The light from the crescent moon hits the planes of her face. She is washed out, sallow, a strange, sickly yellow and a picture of bad health.

Ella shivers and turns to leave. She doesn't want to come back to this place for a very long time. Next time they dock, she vows she'll stay on board.

The girl's voice follows her steps back towards Danny, *Ananke*, home, safety. 'I won't forget her! Ashley Mercer was her name! And I won't ever forget her.'

The sickle moon is suddenly so very bright, too bright. The world narrows to a tunnel. The sky falls.

PART TWO

1

ANNIE

ONE YEAR EARLIER

Annie Taylor watches as Robyn Seever shrugs off her coat and lets it fall to the ground.

'I did good,' Robyn says.

Annie stoops to pick up the discarded jacket and smiles brightly at Robyn.

'It's great; you did very good,' she replies.

Robyn frowns. Annie turns the wattage up on her smile even more. 'I knew you would,' she says. 'I never doubted you.'

And it is good, this beach, this country, their new home. She breathes in deeply. It tastes of sea air and new beginnings.

She snaps back to the present as Robyn takes her coat out of Annie's arms. Walking over to a nearby industrial bin, Robyn lifts the lid and throws it inside.

'Robyn!' Annie is hot on her heels, up on tiptoe to peer inside.

'What?' Robyn smiles. 'Come on, like we're ever going to need our coats in this place.'

The bins have been not emptied recently. The coat lies near the top, nestled on a bed of old, browning vegetables.

Coat forgotten for the moment, Annie drapes her arm around Robyn.

Athens.

She can't believe they made it. Can't believe their dream has been realised.

England in all its greyscale non-glory has gone. All the muted, depressive hues and days spent shivering are behind them. From now on their days are sunshine, deep blue waters, dense heat, freedom and, most importantly, they are together.

'We should find a place to stay,' Annie says.

'Sweetie, look.' Robyn opens her arms wide, an expansive gesture encompassing all that is now theirs. 'We could literally close our eyes right there on the sand and it would still be better than the bed in the home.' Her voice has a dreamlike quality. 'We can sleep under the stars.'

'The temperature drops at night. And sand isn't as soft as it looks.' Annie's voice is tentative as she points out their future possible discomfort.

'How do you even know that?' Robyn asks, eyes narrowed but still with a smile upon her lips. 'How many times have you been to Greece? How many times have you even seen sand?'

Annie shrugs. She knows the argument is over.

'We can use our coats as pillows, anyway,' Robyn concedes.

Annie's gaze drifts towards the bin, but she says nothing.

Robyn turns away from the sea and faces Annie. She pulls her friend's long, blonde hair, a loving tug. 'We've still got *your* coat, right? A shared pillow, yes?'

Annie smiles. 'Yes, Robyn,' she says.

'Teamwork,' says Robyn.

'Dreamwork,' Annie responds automatically.

And it is dreamwork, their partnership, their friendship. Robyn is the one with the ideas and the plans. Annie is there to smooth them over, iron out any kinks.

It works well, most of the time.

—

It's quiet, even though it is midday. Annie had expected hustle, bustle, waiters and tourists. She'd pictured their arrival so many times over the years, since Robyn had come up with this plan. She'd imagined them slipping into the midst of the city, their vitality and youth and willingness to work spring-boarding them into their new life with offers of everything from accommodation to food to employment.

But in all the years of daydreams, she'd never thought they'd make their escape and subsequent arrival during the tail end of a worldwide pandemic.

Robyn had not even known what a pandemic was.

Half the world is still shut off, locked up, locked down.

Locked in.

They sit outside a taverna, a single waiter on duty. He darts a glance at them as he passes, tidying tables that have had no customers, his face unreadable underneath the facemask he wears.

'Smile at him,' Robyn urges Annie suddenly.

Annie shifts uncomfortably. 'He's not looking at us,' she murmurs.

She glances at him. Her words were partially right. He's not looking at them; he's looking at *her*.

Abruptly, Robyn stands. 'Wait here, I'm going to use the loo.' She jerks her head towards the public restroom on the corner of the marina. 'Get us some lunch, or something, yeah?'

Annie watches her go.

She feels the heat of a gaze on her neck, and turns back to face the taverna. He is watching her still, but he quickly averts his eyes.

Annie sighs and leans back, tilting her face to the sun. Boys are not what this Athens trip are about. It's a fresh start. A chance to work hard and live a life that has so far been denied to them both.

Annie knows what she looks like to other people. Tall, blonde, clear, unblemished skin and bright eyes, the colour of the very ocean that laps upon the shore where they are to make their home. The exterior of Annie has everything, but she doesn't want to rely on that to get on in life.

A shadow falls over her. Annie opens her eyes to see a delivery truck parked in front of her, blocking off the sun.

She sighs and stands up. It's a good thing there's no time to sit around sunbathing. They still need to find a place to stay, a job to provide money for them to eat and pay rent.

As she picks up her bag, she nods at the young waiter hefting bottles of mineral water off the back of the van while the driver stands to one side, smoking a brown, rolled-up cigarette. The young man mutters under his breath, noticing what Annie is sure is his first customer, hanging around the entrance.

Annie hesitates before putting her bag back down on the bench.

'Can I help you?' she asks tentatively.

The waiter looks shocked, then something like gratitude shines on his face.

He thanks her, tells her his name is Tobias. He tells her if she would get the remaining bottles off the van, she can leave them on the ground, and he will repay her with the best gelato she will ever taste.

As he speaks, he hurries towards his potential clients, throwing a glare at the unhelpful driver of the truck.

Annie isn't sure what gelato is, but she knows that she wants some.

As the waiter sets up the couple with a takeaway cappuccino, Annie hefts the large bottles to the steps that lead up into the taverna.

Tobias, after waving off his customers, thanks her profusely.

'No sign of anyone all morning, then everything at once.' He laughs, beckons to her to follow him inside for the promised gelato.

He hands it to her, a milky kind of ice cream, and pauses as she reaches out. 'Your friend... she has gone?'

His eyes are slightly wide as he asks the question. Annie thinks he sounds hopeful.

'Just to use the restroom,' she says firmly. 'She's coming back.' She fixes the young Tobias with a stare and tries to inject Robyn's special breed of confidence into her tone. 'Do you have any jobs going?' she asks.

Tobias looks around the empty restaurant and shrugs.

Annie slumps in her chair.

'Perhaps… in return for a small job, I can give you a good meal…'

Annie smiles winningly, but it falters. 'What sort of job?' she asks cautiously.

'The tables are to be set for lunch; patrons think we might be closed if I don't lay the tables. My chef is off work, so I need to be in the kitchen.' He shakes his head, something like despair crossing his youthful features. 'I can't be in there, out here too.'

Annie breathes out in relief. That sort of job she can easily do. She raises her chin. 'My friend will get a meal, too?' she verifies.

He hesitates, just for a moment, before nodding his assent.

Annie seals the deal with a handshake and gets to work.

This is the sort of employment she would be good at, she thinks as she locates the paper tablecloths, candles and cutlery. Making things nice, inviting. She glances up the cobbled street, noting the restaurants here outweigh the potential customers by quite a margin.

She finishes her gelato as she lays out the knives and forks, casting a critical eye over them and rubbing away any water spots.

Annie is into it, her need for perfection, her enjoyment of work taking over until everything, even her worries about employment and accommodation, is soothed from her mind.

It's not until she hears her name being called repeatedly, rising in crescendo with an accompanied panic, that she's brought back to earth. The forks clatter to the tabletop.

She runs to the railing, sees Robyn standing by the bench where she'd left Annie. Robyn is turning in circles, her body rigid as she searches for Annie.

'Here!' Annie calls. 'Up here!'

'What are you doing?' asks Robyn, running over, clutching a bag that she didn't have before.

'I'm helping out Tobias; this is his taverna but he's short-staffed.' Annie leans over the railing. 'He's promised us a good meal in return. Come on in.'

Robyn takes a step back and surveys the restaurant.

Annie narrows her eyes. 'Where did you get the bag, and the sunglasses?' She walks to the entrance and peers down at Robyn. 'You've got new clothes, too.'

She takes in her friend, recalling the sad amount of euros that they had between them, which they were supposed to be frugal with. It was meant to last until at least one of them had secured a job.

Robyn shrugs off her question with a flap of her hand as she climbs the steps into the taverna. 'Don't worry, it was all cheap enough.'

She walks down the tables, running a finger over the candle holders and paper tablecloths.

Annie hurries to catch up. She raises her hand to touch the security tag on the back of Robyn's new shirt, and in one practised movement she folds it inside the neck, before smoothing the tablecloth that Robyn has managed to rumple.

Maybe this was a bad idea. Maybe it would be best if they split up to search for a job each. After all, customers are scarce; there's no way a restaurant will be able to hire both of them.

She says this to Robyn now, her words carefully chosen as she attempts to explain the economics of them both seeking gainful employment in separate establishments.

Robyn frowns as she listens, then, with a hardened stare, she meets Annie's eye.

'We should stick together,' says Robyn. 'We're in a strange place, we don't know anyone, we only have each other.' She gives off a shudder. 'To think of you with strangers, trying to take advantage...' She trails off and pinches her lips together. 'Besides,' she continues, smiling at last, 'you promised me a good meal.'

Annie nods, resigned for now.

Behind Robyn, in the shadow of the bar, Tobias stands and watches their exchange. Annie smiles brightly and prepares to introduce them.

'Sit, eat.' Tobias gestures with his hands towards the table. He watches only Annie, his small tongue darting in and out of his mouth to lick at nervous lips.

Robyn studies him coldly as she pulls out a chair and sits down in front of the steaming plate he puts down on one of Annie's newly made tables.

Tobias's smile wavers. 'Enjoy,' he says, 'on me.'

'Thank you, Tobias,' says Annie as, with one more uncertain glance at Robyn, he moves back towards the rear of the restaurant.

'This is great,' comments Robyn as she stabs at the spaghetti with her fork, picking it up, putting it down and barely eating anything. 'But what else has he got?'

Annie, almost finished with her meal, tilts her head to the side. 'What do you mean?'

'I mean, lunch is fine, but we need a lot more than a hot meal. Can he offer us a roof over our heads, a bed to sleep in?'

She doesn't mention a job, Annie notices, but she doesn't pull her friend up on this.

It niggles, though. Annie's done something in exchange for this meal. She's hefted all those bottles off the truck, set all these tables. Where has Robyn been? 'I thought we were sleeping under the stars,' Annie says mildly.

'What?' Robyn asks.

Annie backs down. Temper flares from either of them won't help their situation at all. 'Sorry, I… I just meant…' She trails off, curls into herself, shoulders rounded, face averted.

Her gaze lands on Tobias, lurking in the shadows behind the bar. This must be his folks' place, and from the looks of his stance, twitchy and on edge, it's possibly the first time he's been left in charge.

Maybe there is more than a meal here after all. Maybe a temporary job, for as long as Chef is off, and the owners are away. But before she can mention this possibility, Robyn is sitting up, calling the young man over and, mortifyingly to Annie, clicking her fingers.

'Wine,' Robyn says, when he reaches their table. 'Isn't that what you guys drink at every meal?' She tilts her head to one side.

Robyn reaches forwards, touches his wrist lightly. 'This dish is exquisite,' she says. 'Thank you so much, we really appreciate it.'

He's confused, wary, nervous. Annie knows Robyn's self-confidence has that effect on people, and she uses it to the best of her ability.

'Grappa,' she says. '*Vino?*'

He nods. He is uncertain but makes his way back to the bar regardless.

'What are you doing?' asks Annie in a hushed whisper.

Robyn clutches Annie's hand across the table. 'Watch, listen, *learn*.'

Tobias is back, an open bottle in hand and two small glasses.

Nervously he pours, a tiny amount in each.

'Toby.' Robyn shakes her head and gets up from her seat. She stands before him, almost as tall as him, and she sees the flush of his chest in his open-necked shirt. 'Come on, that won't do at all.' She offers him a smile, closed lips, as is her way, because her teeth aren't as straight or white as Annie's, and she takes his arm, leading him gently back towards the bar.

She reaches over, plucks an unwashed glass from beside the sink and, keeping a hold of him, she leads him back to the table and presses a hand to his shoulder, forcing him to sit.

–

Three hours later, Annie is pleased that Tobias has loosened up. He seems more comfortable now, chatting with Robyn as they press him with questions. His mother and father own this joint; they're away for the day and night, helping an uncle over in some place called Chalandri. He is nineteen, and it's the first time he's been left in charge.

The bookings have been dismal, but the season hasn't started officially yet. It's the start of May, and perhaps next week, the restaurant will be busier, the tourists will come, the money lost from the pandemic will be recouped.

He is optimistic, Annie notes. Initially she thought that it was because of his youth, even though he's the same age as them. After listening to him for a while, once his lips have loosened with the wine, she realises his age has nothing to do with it. He has led a charmed life, living here, where he is always warm, his belly is always full, and there is love and attention in abundance.

What must that be like, she wonders, to be raised as such?

'We can help you, tonight.' Annie sees her opening, the chance to earn a little bit of cash that would buy them a room for a night or two.

He opens his arms and gestures round the taverna, which has been empty of other diners since they arrived. 'Maybe there will be nothing to help with.' Tobias laughs.

He is calm now, relaxed in their company, and more than a little drunk.

Robyn squeezes his hand and keeps her fingers entwined with his. 'So we'll keep you company instead.'

At the very least, they might get some more food, thinks Annie as she smiles at the pair of them.

He smiles back at her, all white teeth in a deeply tanned face.

'Can I use your bathroom?' Robyn asks him.

He gives her remote directions. Not to the restaurant toilets but pointing through a beaded curtain, past an empty kitchen, up a flight of whitewashed stairs. When Robyn has disappeared from view, Annie smiles at him again and they finish their drinks in companionable silence.

After a moment, she looks towards the doorway.

They live here, she realises, him and his parents. Their home must be on the floors above the restaurant.

She stands up. 'Can I use the bathroom, too?' she asks.

He rises from his chair too, leading her by the hand in the same direction that Robyn went.

On the first floor, their home is comfortable if not roomy, clean and tidy, and she sees decades of love splashed across the walls in the form of photographs and mementos. Robyn is there, staring up at them, an unfathomable expression on her face.

Tobias gestures to the bathroom, off the hallway.

'I'll be downstairs,' he says. He puts one hand on the wall to steady himself, and Annie sees he is drunker than even he thought he was.

She feels a hand on her arm. Robyn, in front of her, eyes filled with concern.

'How much have *you* drank?' she whispers.

Annie smiles at her friend. 'Not enough.' She laughs, to banish the strange atmosphere that has covered them on the inside of this small, lovely home.

Robyn gives her a quick hug and points to the bathroom. 'You go first,' she says.

As Annie closes the bathroom door behind her, she sees Robyn back in front of the family portraits, studying them intently.

When she comes out, Robyn is nowhere to be seen.

Annie pauses in the hallway. 'Toilet's free,' she calls.

'Okay, thanks.' Robyn's voice comes from an unknown room. Annie waits a moment more, then makes her way back down to the taverna.

—

The little street where the taverna sits is slightly more alive when Annie goes back.

There are a couple more customers scattered throughout the restaurant. Tobias looks harassed again, stumbling between the tables, dropping his pen and pad, fumbling beneath the seats to pick them up.

Annie hurries to him, plucks the pad from his hand. 'I've got this,' she whispers. 'Are you okay to cook?'

He nods, relief lighting his face.

Annie narrows her lips as he makes his way haltingly to the kitchen. She crosses the floor to the customers, writing down their table numbers and orders and making a note of their drinks on a separate piece of paper.

She glances up the stairs, hoping Robyn is nearly finished in the bathroom. She can mix the drinks; Annie will alternate between supervising Tobias in his chef's role and keeping an eye on the front of house.

After all, it's their fault he is drunk, and she feels bad.

But there is no sign of Robyn on her way back, so Annie carries on working, flitting between the kitchen and the restaurant.

Time has passed by the time Robyn reappears. How much time, Annie doesn't know. She's lost herself in her work, finding the rhythm soothing, even taking pleasure in her aching feet.

After another trip to the kitchen to hand Tobias a strong black coffee as he bends over the stove, she sees Robyn lurking in the hallway.

'Where have you been?' Annie stands back and surveys her friend. Her hair is wet but neatly combed; she smells fresh, perfumed even. 'Have you used his shower?'

Robyn grins. 'I had a bath, a lovely long soak. And it's not his shower, it's his parents', and they're not here.' She pokes her head out front and looks around. 'Where's Tobias?'

'In the kitchen, cooking.' From across the room, the only couple left raise their hands in unison and make a scribbling motion in the air. The universal sign to call for the bill. 'Don't disturb him,' instructs Annie as she hurries over to the customers.

Annie wipes her brow. The dinner rush is over. Tobias hangs over the grille. There is a pause now, he tells her, between the diners and the late-night drinkers.

Robyn is at Annie's shoulder. 'Take a walk with me,' Robyn says. 'Back soon, Toby,' she adds as an afterthought.

Annie feels his eyes on her as, arm in arm, they head down the street towards the water.

'You were right,' Robyn says grudgingly. 'It is kind of cold.'

It takes a lot for Robyn to admit she was wrong. Annie puts an arm around her friend and draws her close. 'We have a bed for tonight, I reckon. Tobias will let us stay, don't you think?'

Robyn says nothing. Annie watches her, sideways on.

Her friend's face, normally so pale, already looks like it is starting to burn after just a day in the sun. Her dark hair looks dank, where she has pushed it away from her face repeatedly while working at the taverna.

Eventually, Robyn glances at Annie. 'I bet he'd let you stay longer. Tonight, tomorrow, next week. All summer, I bet.'

Robyn looks away to the water once more, her face in shadow.

–

Annie isn't stupid. She knows how people look at her, how the same people's eyes pass right over Robyn. Unless they're a certain type of person – usually a man – who knows they'll get anything from Robyn, and nothing from Annie. It is the partnership, how they work together. The teamwork that Robyn speaks of so often.

Annie thinks back to their journey, long and arduous as it was. Often, she can hardly believe they hitchhiked here, all the way from London. Robyn had planned their transport in its entirety. Decent people, Robyn proclaimed, would not stop for her, so she'd inserted Annie roadside, only revealing herself when Annie had secured the lift. Slightly shiftier people, the truckers, the bored, lonely men on the road, saw a goddess, and Robyn noted how their eyes dimmed when Robyn climbed in the cab beside her, and then glinted when they saw potential evenings they could have with Robyn, which they'd never reach with a girl like Annie.

It hurts Annie's heart that Robyn has that perspective of herself. Equally, it makes Annie uncomfortable of the role that has been bestowed upon her: a pliability, a purity, a bloody halo, really.

Their future begins tomorrow morning. Annie shivers in anticipation of what Robyn has planned for them.

Annie knows Robyn so well that right now she can tell from her friend's speculative gaze that Robyn has something in mind.

Under the light of the moon, they walk the length of the marina.

It's deathly still and quiet out here. The yachts that are moored are in darkness, the exterior chairs and tables covered, pools of salt and rainwater puddling on them, stained with disuse.

Unused… but open to the elements.

Open to anything.

Or anyone.

Robyn's breath catches in her throat, Annie's signal that genius has hit. She turns to Annie.

'These yachts have been sitting here for two years; their owners are stuck in England, America, Spain, maybe even as far away as Australia. Quarantine rules are still in place for holidaymakers. These owners won't be coming back for their boats any time soon; there's no way they'll isolate before coming out, then spend another couple of weeks locked up in a room just for the chance to get on their yachts for a week or so.'

Annie knows what Robyn is thinking.

These boats are clear and free, a home for the foreseeable future for them both.

–

The restaurant shift draws to a close relatively early at midnight. Tobias waves off the last of his customers and turns to Annie and Robyn.

'Thank you for helping tonight,' he says politely.

'You're welcome. It's okay if we kip down here, yeah?' Robyn says casually.

He is still holding the door open, expecting them to leave also.

'Oh,' Tobias says. 'I… uh…'

Robyn takes his arm and the door closes. 'Just for tonight – we'll be gone before your folks get back.' She winks at him and smiles. 'Annie will even help clean up; there'll be no trace that we were ever here.'

He looks cornered, but Robyn doesn't give him a chance to argue.

'Good man.' She gives his upper arm a squeeze and leads the way through the restaurant and back up the stairs.

The atmosphere has changed from earlier. When they were working, they were a team, Annie and Tobias. Even Robyn chipped in near the end, collecting glasses and depositing them on the bar.

Now, Tobias seems irritated that they are still there. Robyn's face is stony, and even Annie feels a flutter of annoyance. They worked for him, helped him out, saved his ass when he almost got too drunk to cook and serve.

Guilt follows quickly to nestle on Annie's shoulders. It was their fault he got drunk. Maybe they've outstayed their welcome, but one look at the chilly evening and Annie doesn't want to start hunting for a bed now.

She puts one hand on his arm. 'Just for tonight,' she says, and gives him one of her best smiles.

'One night,' he replies as he meets her gaze.

Upstairs, Annie can feel Robyn's annoyance when he won't let her sleep in any of the beds, mumbling about changing the sheets. Instead, he gestures to the sofas, of which there are three at right angles to each other. Resolutely, he takes one of them, as though he plans to keep watch on them all night long.

Annie covers herself with a blanket draped on the back of her sofa and whispers a thank you to Tobias before curling into herself.

Tobias reaches over and turns the lamp off.

'Good night,' he says stiffly.

But as tired as Annie is, sleep won't come. She keeps her breathing steady and even. She senses the shift in Tobias when he finally falls asleep.

As if the strange day has finally drawn to a close, Annie's whole body relaxes. She can feel herself drifting, close to falling asleep herself, when a creaking sound makes her open her eyes again.

It is Robyn, rising slowly from the couch, soundlessly crossing the room and slipping beneath Tobias's blanket, fitting the length of him as he lies on his side, his face to the back of the sofa.

Annie closes her eyes, not wanting to bear witness to the price that Robyn is willing to pay for the night's shelter that has already been given to them.

Later, after, Tobias manoeuvres himself up, climbs over Robyn and retreats to what Annie assumes is his bedroom.

Heart pounding even though she remains still and silent, Annie watches as Robyn, entirely naked, follows him down the hallway. As Robyn raises her hand to push on the door to his room, the door is closed firmly against her palm. Annie hears the click as it is locked from the inside.

Robyn turns back to the lounge. The last thing Annie sees before she closes her eyes again is her friend's face, sneering to cover her sadness.

—

They leave early, Robyn pulling Annie gently from her slumber, a finger to her lips as she guides her through the pre-dawn gloom of the hallways and out through a back door.

Annie had wanted to say goodbye to Tobias.

As they walk down to the marina, Robyn shoots her a look. 'He wasn't very nice to us, Annie.' Her mouth works, and Annie knows she is reliving that moment, where Tobias locked his door to her.

'It doesn't matter.' Annie links arms with Robyn as they make their way towards the marina. 'We don't need to go back there. It was just a stopgap, right? Better things are ahead.'

'You're right,' replies Robyn. 'Onwards and upwards.' She nods, a determined set to her jaw.

'But we want to stay here, in Athens?' clarifies Annie.

Robyn nods.

Annie jabs at Robyn's bulging bag. 'So… perhaps it's not wise to steal from local people.'

Robyn stops and cups Annie's face in her hands. 'I know, you're right. You're always right.' She lets off a laugh and pulls Annie close. 'We'll give it back, once we've made our fortune – we'll return it all. I promise.'

Annie grins. 'Fortune? We're going to make a fortune?'

Robyn releases her. 'You bet. Come on, the future starts *now*.'

–

Today, at sunup, the marina is busy. Night fishermen are heading back into port, yelling through the otherwise still air, hurling nets and boxes filled with their wares. There is no quarantine for them, Annie notes, as they go about their daily business.

The smaller boats are docked within a large square, opposite the motionless yachts that they looked at last night.

Annie is watching the fishermen with awe. Robyn claps her hands in front of Annie's face.

'Look,' she says, pointing to the large, white ships docked to their left. 'Forget those pissy little inflatables; this is where *we're* headed.'

'Those?' In the daylight, they look even bigger and grander than they did last night. Annie shades her eyes with her hand and squints across the marina. 'They're worth millions! Do you really think they're empty?'

'They're empty,' says Robyn to Annie. 'The owners are thousands of miles away; it's too much hassle to get here with all the isolating and everything, so… say hello to our new home!'

Annie takes a hold of Robyn by her shoulders and stares hard at her. 'Look, if we do this, it's on a temporary basis, okay? We take care of the yacht as if it were our own.' She gives Robyn a gentle but firm shake. 'We don't take anything, okay?'

'A home fit for a princess,' Robyn whispers in reply into Annie's hair. She pulls away to look Annie in her face. 'That's you,' she adds.

Annie squeezes her shoulders. 'And you're my queen,' she says. She turns back towards the yachts. 'Okay, let's do this.'

Once the fishermen depart, there's nobody over this side of the dock. They take their time, surreptitiously checking out the front of each yacht, whispering each name out loud. *Aurora*, *Escape*, *Vita*, *Lady*, *Serenity*… Every one of them speaks a promise of a life that both girls have waited to live. They stop at the end of the row and look at the final boat in the marina.

Destiny.

Yes. Yes! This is the one.

As if by unspoken agreement, as one they step off the marina onto the yacht.

The sides are high enough to conceal them from the eyes of anyone across the water, but they bend low anyway, making their way up to the sliding doors, Annie stepping back as Robyn cups her hands to the glass and peers inside.

'All the furniture is covered,' Robyn whispers, her tone high with excitement. 'The owners won't be coming here any time soon.'

Robyn tries the door handle. It is locked, but Annie knows that so far in Robyn's short life, apart from last night with Tobias, a lock has never been an issue.

They leave the door, walking around the side of the deck, and, towards the rear of the boat, a porthole window is hooked open.

Annie reaches for it, but Robyn grips her hand. She moves up close, looking at all angles for some sort of motion sensor alarms. Finding nothing, Robyn puts her hand inside, yanks up the catch and pulls the window open.

'Wait here,' she instructs Annie.

Access is easy for Robyn's straight-up-and-down figure, and she has room to spare as she slithers inside and lands in a neat roll on what transpires to be the floor of a kitchen.

Annie watches as she remains in a crouch, waiting, watching, listening. When nothing but silence resonates around the boat, Robyn stands, gives Annie one more smile, and heads off to explore the interior.

Annie turns to face the open sea. She breathes deeply. She imagines waking to this sight every day, stepping outside on the deck, the ocean and the blue sky and bright sun the first things she will see every day. Her fists clench and unclench. They've wanted this new start for so long, plotted and planned and saved and made several treacherous journeys. Can it really be this simple?

She hears footsteps coming from inside the yacht. She turns; her face falls.

Of course it can't be that simple.

Robyn is approaching, her face sullen, her mouth down-turned. Behind her is a man, walking determinedly.

Annie covers her mouth with her hand. Who is he – the owner?

He sees Annie, raises his eyebrows in her direction.

He taps Robyn on her shoulder, long, tanned fingers lingering on her skin to divert her towards a door. From his pocket he takes a set of keys, opens the door and stands back to let her pass.

Once she stands on the deck next to Annie, he leans against the doorframe and crosses his arms.

'This boat's taken. You'll need to move on.'

His voice is calm, non-threatening and confident. There is a lilt to his tone that Annie recognises. He is British, like her, and with a sinking feeling, she realises that of all the people who have flocked here, they are not the only ones who had the idea of using the unforeseen pandemic to find a roof and a bed.

Annie glances at Robyn, who stands in stony silence. She knows her friend as well as she knows herself, understands that

Robyn is considering putting on her haughty persona, maybe thinking about telling this man who is just like them that her father owns *Destiny*, and he is the one who is trespassing. Annie watches as Robyn looks at her own reflection in the steel wall behind him. They both know that this guy is as street-smart as Robyn. They all know that she doesn't look like the kind of girl who belongs on a yacht called *Destiny*.

'The other yachts, in this marina...' Robyn tails off, holding eye contact with him.

He shrugs. 'All occupied.'

No room at the inn.

Robyn gives it one final attempt. 'And you're sure this one's full to capacity?'

He looks her up and down lazily, and Annie's heart lurches.

He finishes his slow appraisal of Robyn and makes his decision. 'Yeah, they're all full.'

Annie looks down at her feet. She recalls last night, the door closed in Robyn's face, the turn of the lock the final insult.

Annie takes Robyn's hand. She gives a pleasant smile to the man who has claimed *Destiny* for his own. 'Thanks, anyway, see you around.'

They move down the yacht, back towards the point where they can step off back onto the marina. So, *Destiny* is out of the equation, but there are other boats, other spaces. They haven't travelled two thousand miles to turn around and go back to the UK.

He follows them down the slim walkway, perhaps making sure they leave, maybe checking they don't swipe any of *Destiny*'s goods on the way out.

As they make the short hop back onto dry land, he calls across to them.

'Try the ferries,' he says. 'There's more room there. They're generally clean, and the people are all right.' He includes them both in his words, but his eyes linger only on Annie.

Annie follows Robyn, who is giving her best fuck-you walk in case he's still watching her.

Annie glances back. The man has already retreated inside.

3

The ferries.

Try the ferries.

It makes sense, what the guy said. A ferry won't be quite the palace that *Destiny* is, but it's a roof and warmth, comfort and a place to regroup and plan. It's all they need: shelter, and a place to lay their heads.

Annie catches up to Robyn and slips her hand into her friend's.

It's a short walk over, up a flight of steps. Pausing at the top, they stare down at the large, white ships that are in the dock.

Disappointment is coming off Robyn in waves and Annie knows she is still thinking about the opulence of the yachts.

'A ferry will be all right,' says Annie. 'It's just temporary, just until we get jobs and can afford to rent a place.'

Robyn squeezes Annie's hand. 'I know,' she says. She tilts her head back so the sun's rays land on her face.

'We should split up,' says Annie as she looks out over the marina. It's a good view. From here, she can see the potential. The bars and restaurants that surely will be busy later. The hotels scattered beyond the marina, where surely there will be cash-in-hand jobs in housekeeping or kitchens.

She turns back to face Robyn and is aghast to see the angst in her friend's eyes.

'Silly.' She folds Robyn into her arms. 'I meant split up today, just for a few hours, so we can see what's out there, cover more ground.'

Robyn shrugs and scuffs at the ground with her feet. Annie straightens up.

'Meet back here at midday, okay?' She makes sure her voice is firm, the only way to chivvy Robyn along when the other girl sinks into the doldrums.

Finally, Robyn nods her assent.

She stands at the top of the concrete stairs and watches as Robyn trips down them, back the way they've just come. She observes her friend's shoulders, rounded, desolate. Something out there will happen to lift Robyn's spirits. Somewhere out there is a job opening, a potential employer that Robyn can sweet-talk, or a careless shop owner that she will lift something from.

Annie would rather it not be the latter, but Robyn is good; Annie has no fear she will be caught, and if it makes her feel better...

Suddenly weary, Annie sits down where she stands and just like Robyn before her, she lifts her face to the sun.

She's almost dozing when the slap of feet behind her has her sitting upright. A second later, something sharp hits her spine.

She jerks to the side, all Robyn's words of warning making her grab for her shoulder bag, clutching it to her, planting her palm on the hot concrete, ready to face her adversary.

'Sorry, excuse me.' The woman – young girl, really – stops momentarily and puts a hand on Annie's shoulder.

'Sorry,' another girl joins in, almost a twin of the first, both wearing matching polo shirts and sporting bouncy, shiny ponytails. 'Lot of traffic up and down these stairs – you might want to move to the edge.'

They're carrying cooler bags, two each, and their faces are red both from the sun and the weight of whatever it is they're carrying.

'We've got at least two more runs up and down,' pants the first one, 'so... just to give you a heads-up.'

Dutifully, Annie moves to the side of the steps.

They're busy; they said they had more items to haul up the stairs. Should she help them? In return, would they slip her a few euros for her assistance?

But before she can speak, the second woman throws a rushed 'Thanks' behind her as they hurtle up the final flight, blonde hair bobbing with their exertion.

When they make their return, now bag-free but still sprinting, Annie stands up to get a better view of their route.

They run together along the marina, moving out of sight momentarily behind the large, concrete pillars before emerging on the walkway of a boat. It's not a boat like *Destiny*, this one – it's even bigger, three times the size, but not quite a ferry either. At the rear of the deck is a hot tub, half a dozen people in it, drinks in hand, watching lazily while the blonde women pick up two more cooler bags each and stagger back off the vessel, heading once more towards the stairs.

These girls are employees, she deduces, and by the looks of it they are used to physical, hard work and would most likely politely decline her offer to help. They dodge into the small, plaza-like building and are out in mere moments. Dashing past Annie again, they pay her no heed this time as she's no longer in their way.

Waiting until the sound of their hurried steps has diminished, she hauls herself up and pads softly into the building at the top of the stairs.

She walks through several archways supported by columns in typical Greek design, narrow passageways, more steps up to what seems to be simply the frame of a building, open on all sides to the elements. She stops there, gazing around in wonder.

But it's not the astounding view across the port and beyond it to the open sea that has her breathless. It's the table in the middle, set for six, conch shells and starfish adorning it, wine coolers and gold-trimmed plates, three different-sized drinking glasses per setting nestled beside long, wooden platters that are currently empty.

The people in the hot tub must be coming here. She reflects on this: those people already drinking, leaning back in warm, gushing, bubbling water, watching casually as two young women make endless trips up and down the marina steps to make something beautiful like this.

Oh, how money talks.

Annie moves over to the table and inspects it. The napkins are designed in an intricate flower shape. It's art, really, and a small smile plays on Annie's lips as she thinks of the kitchen roll they use back at the home on a rare takeaway treat night.

Turning away from the table, she inspects the rest of the room. The easterly part of it is in full shadow, multiple alcoves as part of the room's labyrinthine design. Another corridor lies obscured there.

She can stay there, or in an alcove, in relative shade and comfort, Annie realises, until the meal is over. There will be leftovers, she'd be willing to bet on it, and if they can save their meagre money stash rather than buy a dinner tonight—

Voices, more of them this time, coming up the stairs. She recognises one of the women's tones now, and this time there's a man with them.

Annie slides into the gloomy corner of the room and narrows her eyes to slits as she watches them move around the table.

A chef has joined them, carrying more cooler bags, and he darts around, setting plates of peppery-scented pastas in the long, wooden troughs on the table.

'I'm not doing anything else up here,' he pants as he puts the serving spoons down with a clatter. 'It's fucking ridiculous, okay, Ella?' He turns to his colleague, the first woman who accidentally kneed Robyn in her spine back on the steps. 'No more dining up here. We're short-staffed as it is; just send them into town for fancy meals in the future.'

The one called Ella rolls her eyes. 'If they request it, we have to do it. Come on, Cheffy, you know this.'

'Then you can bring the shit. I'll cook it, back in the galley; you lot can bring it up here.' He jabs a finger over his shoulder. 'I'm not doing that trek again, okay?'

The other girl puts a hand on Chef's arm. 'Think of the tip we'll get,' she says. 'Just keep the end game in sight.'

'Your inspirational bullshit...' Chef jerks his arm away from her touch, but there's a smile in both his face and his voice now.

Chef salutes them, throws them a farewell, and retreats the way he came. 'I'm not coming to collect it when they're done,' he calls. 'You can get a deckhand to be the dogsbody.'

'Whatever!' yells Ella. She turns to her friend. 'He's such a twat.'

The second one pulls a face. 'Just think of the—'

'—tip, I know.' Ella smiles. 'What do you reckon it'll be?'

Blondie shrugs. 'At least twenty-five.'

Annie drifts off in her concealed state. A tip of twenty-five euros. That's a decent, if smallish, meal. Possibly drinks too. Though she's willing to bet these girls live on their yacht all season round. They have no need to save their money for food. The angry chef probably cooks for them once the guests have left.

'Thirty grand, maybe.' Ella grins, her teeth very white. 'And that's nearly four grand each.'

Annie feels a spike in her chest. Just in time she claps a hand over her mouth to stifle her gasp. Not twenty-five or thirty notes. Grand. *Four thousand each.* A fortune, split between the crewmates.

And what do they do, these crewmates? They work hard, but they live in a place like this, in ports like these, on boats even bigger than *Destiny*.

They do for a wage what Annie happily does for either a pittance or for free.

Annie watches as they check the table over once more, then, murmuring about how it is time to collect the guests, they depart back the way they came.

Annie comes out of her hiding place once they have left and puts a hand on her chest to still her thundering heart.

She could do this. She could make a table beautiful, elegant, interesting. She can fetch and carry and clean. She can pour drinks and tend to any rich person's needs. The chef himself was complaining that they are short-staffed.

Thoughts of Tobias, his small taverna and the yacht that wasn't to be their destiny vanish. A fire is lit. She needs to track down

Robyn and tell her that for once, Annie has come up with the plan.

--

At the foot of the stairs, sitting on a concrete wall, Annie pauses for thought. Yes, she has got a plan and yes, she needs to bring Robyn in on it. But she swallows down her excitement.

She can't just stroll onto one of these yachts and into a role like the one that girl Ella has got. She knows there will be applications, they will want to know her experience and, the biggest hindrance of all, they will want proof of her identification. It's not that she hasn't got ID; she has her provisional driving licence. But these big boats are made to travel; what if they go through international waters to another country? They would expect to see her passport, and that's one thing she hasn't got.

Disappointment bites at Annie. Not for the first time, she rues the day that Robyn convinced her to escape from their dreary home in England without saving up a bit of money and getting their passports. If they'd waited, they wouldn't have entered Greece illegally. Now, they're stuck here, without means for gainful employment.

But, as is her way, Annie forces a smile on her face. There are no obstacles that have stalled them or stopped them so far.

There will be a way.

There *must* be a way.

She stands up, brushes herself off and makes her way determinedly into the hub of activity in the marina.

--

Two hours later, armed with all the information required to make this dream a reality, Annie decides it's time to get back to Robyn.

Those biting teeth of pessimism have gone now, sunshine in their place, and a bounce in her step.

Robyn is already there, standing at the top of the stairs in front of the plaza. Annie sprints up the concrete steps, blonde hair streaming behind her.

'Hey!' Annie throws her arms around Robyn, pulling the girl close to her before drawing away.

Robyn smells like smoke and spirits. Annie wrinkles up her nose and hopes wherever they end up tonight has a shower.

'How did you get on?' Robyn pulls Annie's bag off her shoulder and peers inside, rifling through the information leaflets that Annie has put in there.

'Good.' Annie draws Robyn to sit beside her. 'Really good, actually.' She beams.

Robyn's eyes are wide and round at Annie's excited tone. 'What?' she demands.

Annie pauses for effect. 'I think I've found the perfect job.'

Robyn's face falls for just a moment. 'Oh,' she says.

Annie catches her friend's tone and frowns. 'You sound disappointed! Come on, Rob, this is huge. It's what we need if we want to stay here.'

Robyn shakes her head and attempts a smile. 'Go on, then, tell me everything; I can tell you're bursting. Spill it.'

Annie lays it all out. She starts with the scene inside the plaza, gesturing behind her to the grand building as she speaks. She tells Robyn about the food, the table, the drink. She keeps her eyes on Robyn's face and watches the magical moment when she mentions the tip that the yacht girls were anticipating.

Two red spots appear high on Robyn's cheeks. She grips Annie's wrist. Her mouth works, but speech won't come.

'I know.' Annie giggles. 'Imagine it, Robyn.'

Both descend into a quiet stillness as they envision it.

Where they came from, it wasn't poverty. They were fed, watered, given a bed and a roof over their heads. But money was always tight in the home. They had essentials, but for so many years they have yearned for more.

This is the place for more. This industry, with its opulence, luxury and fortune in abundance.

This is the place.

Robyn finally finds her voice. 'Did you get us a job?' she asks, her voice breathy.

Annie's smile slips a little and she sighs. 'No. I got all the info, on the low, like, but this is where we run into problems.' She raises her eyes to meet Robyn's. 'We need a passport.'

Robyn pinches her lips together. Annie can practically see the cogs working inside her mind. 'Oh-kaaay,' she says slowly. 'So, we need to forget it, then. Go with our original plan for cash-in-hand jobs.'

'Maybe there's a way we can apply for one...' Annie trails off, knowing how stuck they are. 'There must be a way. I don't want to stay like this, living day to day, spending every morning looking for a bed for the night. Never having our own place, never having... security.'

Security.

It's the optimum word. It's what they've been deprived of their entire lives. Relying on the home to continue to have them there. Relying on the foster parents who came and went, dangling possibilities of forever-homes that never materialised.

'Let me think about it,' Robyn says. She stands up, staring into the distance. 'Come on, we'll find tonight's bed, and once we're sorted, we'll figure out tomorrow's problems.'

For the first time, Annie notices Robyn's own bags. Two of them, cheap plastic carriers. She looks up at Robyn and back at the bags. 'How much money do we have left?'

Robyn winks. 'I haven't spent anything yet.'

Annie closes her eyes briefly, knowing better than to ask.

'Come on.' Robyn gestures over to where the hulking ferries lie in port.

Together, they walk the length of the marina in companionable silence until they come to a stop beside one of the large ships.

Silver lettering on the side says *Ocean Song*.

Robyn gives Annie a critical once-over. 'Try and look like you belong here.'

They hop from the marina wall to the deck, no gangplanks left out for them around this side. In front of an open door, a man stands sentry. Annie peruses him, takes in his gleaming, ebony skin, dreadlocked hair. He's tidy, clean, wearing cut-off shorts and a whiter than white vest. He lives here, and the clean and fresh look of him makes her more hopeful for living conditions.

'We're looking to crash, just for a night or two,' says Robyn. She tilts her chin up to him, inserts a strength into her voice that tells him she takes no crap, that she knows the drill (even though she doesn't), and that she's as entitled as he is to shelter and a place to lay her head. Annie watches her with admiration.

'You stayed here before?' His eyes are lazy, but his voice is rougher than she'd expected.

'Here, there, you know how it is.'

His gaze flicks between them, as if weighing them up against each other. His eyes linger on Annie.

'Payment?' It's the request Annie dreads yet at the same time expects.

It doesn't mean money; they all know that. Robyn has paid for things with many different currencies, none of them coins or notes. Annie, so far, has avoided this.

'Here.' Annie takes one of Robyn's plastic bags and gives it to him.

He opens it, studies it and his eyes linger on the second bag Robyn holds.

'Feminine stuff,' Robyn says. She grins at him. 'Nothing in there for you.'

He looks at them both for a while longer before taking the first bag and stepping aside. 'Cabins are all full. You might find a space in the dining room. One night only.'

One night only! Annie feels the fury coming off Robyn that this man who also doesn't belong here is laying out the rules.

But one night only suits Annie just fine. The sooner they have to leave, the sooner they can start making an actual, feasible plan. She hates this, all the bed-hopping, last-minute chances that they have to grab. Annie wants an actual bed. One that she pays rent for, and one that there's no chance of getting kicked out of.

A glance at Robyn tells her she is biting back a sharp retort. Grabbing Robyn's hand, she ducks past him and into the gloomy interior.

The boat is huge, and seemingly empty. Annie knows that it won't be later. All the residents here are outside in the sunshine, soaking it up, clinging on to the warmth before the sun dips and the cold comes calling. They'll be outside hustling, for coins, for drugs, for a single chance to make it in a world that has nothing for them. This is the start of tourist season, but the pandemic is not a thing of the past, and pickings will be slim.

Ignoring the sentry's instruction, Robyn thunders up the stairs, Annie trying to keep up, towards the decks where the cabins are located.

She opens every door, only stumbling across people inside every few tries.

'Jeez, sorry,' Robyn says, making a big thing of stepping back and looking at the cabin number embossed on the door. 'Wrong cabin – all these hallways look the same!' She throws the startled occupants a cheery smile, slamming the door behind her, going on her way.

She works like a dervish in the unoccupied cabins while Annie stands by the door, pulling out drawers, rifling through mostly empty wardrobes, finding a coin here, a pack of cigarettes, condoms, even. She pockets everything she sees. In the final rooms at the end of the second floor they've pillaged, she rips a duvet and pillow off both bunks.

'Come on,' she orders Annie. 'Let's find this dining room.'

The dining room is sad. There are no lights, clearly no electricity, and the room, about as big as an assembly hall, has a pungent aroma that makes Annie's gag reflex kick in. Around the edges a few people are huddled, undistinguishable shapes under sheets, hollow eyes, souls lost and adrift.

'Oh, God,' Annie murmurs.

She's never seen anything like this. Annie spent all her life in the home. It was a crap way of life, she wanted more, always, but in that place, at least she had a bed, food, warmth. The landscape was grey, but here, it's black as night.

There are times when Robyn wasn't in the home. Annie knows her friend ended up in places like this. For Robyn, this is semi-normal and not all that shocking.

But Annie knows there's more out there, so much more to be had.

'All right,' Robyn says with one glance at Annie. 'Chill out, we're not stopping here.'

Annie sags against her with relief as they back out of the room. She keeps a tight hold on Robyn's hand, hating that it's so dark in here.

She's been on a ferry before, a couple of times, actually. Once on a jolly over to the Isle of Wight, when the children's home was flush with a donation. Then again to Cork. Of course, they took a ferry some of the way on their long journey here, too. The dining room on that trip to Calais, once they'd sneaked out of the back of the container lorry, was nothing like it is here.

Beside them, in the corridor, is a fire door. *No Entry* says a helpful sign next to it.

Robyn pulls it open.

The engine room is another matter entirely. Emergency lighting is on, and even though it's gloomier down here, the air seems fresher, less stale.

Robyn puts the pile of duvets and pillows on the floor near to the door, making a place, rifling through her one remaining bag to examine her wares. Not feminine products, as she'd told the sentry, but long-life pies, bottles of water, shampoo and soap and biscuits. Prized items that he would have willingly taken from them.

Robyn slides the bag under the duvet. Annie, still standing, looks around.

The engine room is silent apart from the random creaking of the pipes that run around the cavernous hull. Annie imagines eyes watching her from concealed shadows, ears listening. Everyone on this boat will be waiting for opportunities. They will if they're smart.

She thinks of all the hidden dangers lying in wait. 'I'll take a walk round; you wait here with our stuff,' she tells Robyn.

The engine room is roughly the same size as the dining room, several decks above them, and it takes Annie ten minutes to do a lap of the room. She peers in every corner, cranes to check behind each pipe. The room is empty of people, but there are tell-tale signs of occupancy. Folded sheets, plastic bags much like the ones Robyn had. Bottles of half-drunk water, hats and shoes and small piles of clothes.

She's glad she scoped out the room instead of Robyn. Robyn would be searching for anything they can make use of, but, despite the sentry's words and Annie's own ambition, this shelter could be home for a while. Annie knows better than to shit where she eats. Robyn isn't so cautious.

Completing her lap of the room, Annie settles down next to Robyn.

Robyn has curled herself around one of the pies she stole, eating as if it's the first meal she's had all day.

It is, Annie reminds herself, thinking guiltily of the fresh fruit and croissant breakfast she'd treated herself to down on the marina when she was researching the job she so desperately wants.

'These boats, the ones you want to work on. They're classy, right, nothing like this?' Robyn gestures around the bowels of the ferry. 'They're for rich people, like the mega-rich?'

'Superyachts,' interrupts Annie. 'They're called superyachts.'

Robyn blinks at her. 'Yeah…' she says. 'Superyachts, right. And you want to be a waitress on one of them?'

'Stewardess,' Annie breaks in again. 'They're called steward-esses, not waitresses.' She swallows as she thinks of that beautiful yacht, the gorgeous table, the confidence of the girl called Ella, of the money she makes, of how she commandeered her crew, even the grumpy chef. 'Yeah, I want that,' she whispers.

'It sounds like hard work.' Robyn leans back against the wall.

'It is, but the money is worth working hard for.' Annie sighs. 'But you can't just stroll onto a yacht. You need references, a CV, a *passport*.' Annie emphasises the last word.

Robyn flicks her a glance. 'We'll work it out,' she says.

Annie's heart beats a little faster. 'Really?' she whispers. 'You think there's some way?'

Robyn smiles and puts her arm around Annie. 'Have I ever let you down before?'

Annie leans into her. 'Never,' she says.

4

In the early evening people begin to trickle into the engine room. In groups of two and three, finding a place, building a nest, just like Annie and Robyn have done. Robyn sits with her back to the wall. Annie studies each newcomer.

Before long, the room is lined with people. There is minimal chatter here, even though some of them must have slept alongside each other for days, weeks, months, even. The clusters stick together, she notes, just like she and Robyn do.

She'd thought they would come in, kip down and settle for the night, but the sun has long gone down, and yet a few people are still wandering. Round and round, up and down, as if they're doing nothing more than stretching their legs, the way one might do on a long-haul plane journey.

Not that Annie has ever been on a plane, but she's seen plenty of them on the television. She shifts, restless, wishing she could go to sleep but there's too much whirling through her mind. She stands up and turns to Robyn.

'I'm going to have a walk around,' she says. 'Back in a minute.'

She stops when a hand closes around her wrist. In the gloom, Robyn's eyes are shining up at her.

'Be careful,' Robyn murmurs.

Annie nods, touched by her friend's concern. She walks the perimeter, much like she did earlier. Now every space is filled, though she notices each little group or couple leave a respectable space between themselves and their neighbour. Others are still walking, slowly, in no hurry, whispering past her, averting their eyes, like spectres on a ghost ship.

When she returns to her spot, she sees another girl there. She's not encroaching on her and Robyn's space, but, unusually, as far as Annie has seen, she is on her own. Discreetly, Annie glances at her.

No, she isn't normally alone. She is usually with a couple, the man who acts as sentry on this ship, and another woman. A quick look around tells Annie that they are nowhere to be seen this evening.

She shrugs to herself. Maybe they had a disagreement. Not uncommon, especially living, breathing, sleeping alongside each other every day.

Annie sits down next to Robyn and pulls her duvet around her. 'New neighbour,' she remarks in a low voice.

At the comment, the girl glances at them. She offers a brief smile, so small that Annie wonders if it were even real.

'Hi,' says Annie, shyly but kindly.

Robyn jabs an elbow in her side.

Annie leans back and closes her eyes.

The lights, that strange, greenish glow, dim even further, as if someone has flicked a switch.

Annie can feel the change as, beside her, Robyn relaxes, for the first time since they arrived.

Back in the home, for all their childhood and youth, they had a routine. At lights out, once the day workers had gone home and all the kids were in bed, a member of the nightshift staff would pull the heavy, velvet curtain across the front door. It would close with a snap and a rattle, the noise distinct, and for as long as Annie can remember, Robyn had always taken that sound as one of safety. There was security in the cover of darkness. Robyn could relax; the day was over. No more scrapping, no more thieving, no more looking over her shoulder until the following day. According to Robyn, no threats came at night-time.

Annie felt the opposite. She longed for the daylight, for the shadowy corners to vanish.

The gradual reduction of the greenish glow of the engine room is the equivalent of that faithful old curtain snapping closed.

Safety for Robyn, fear for Annie.

She hears a sound and her eyes snap open.

To her right, the other new girl, the one who has slept alone, has shifted in her slumber. Her pitiful bag – a blue and white striped plastic carrier – has toppled off her knee.

Annie feels a deep sympathy for the girl who seems to be on her own. She lets off an involuntary shiver, glad that she's always got Robyn by her side.

The rest of the long night passes for Annie in uneasy, fitful starts.

–

They move on early, Annie eager to get outside into the bright new day, away from this terrible, greenish glow.

Robyn stretches, makes conversation with Annie, even throws a casual 'Good morning' to the people who trickled in last night, and who are now making their way out to spend their days above board, seeking money, seeking sunshine, seeking food and water and a better place to be.

The girl beside them wakes up as the engine room comes to life. She spots her bag on the floor, upended, and with a flushed face she shoves her things back inside it and joins the steadily growing queue of people departing the boat.

Robyn wraps her cold hand around Annie's. 'Come on, let's get out of here.'

Up they go, the metal stairs clanging beneath them as they climb higher, finally pushing through a fire door and emerging onto the deck. The sun is hot, even though it's early, but there is no time to pause and enjoy it.

Robyn links arms with Annie and they come out onto the dock, the shabbier side, making for the concrete stairs that will take them past the magical plaza and on to the place where Annie wants to be.

In the shade of the stairs, Robyn stops and dodges into the shade of the plaza.

She has a smile on her face, so infectious that Annie can't help but return it.

'What?' Annie says.

Robyn reaches into the front of her shorts and withdraws the source of her glee.

Annie blinks at it. 'A passport?' she says. Her mind tries to stack up all her questions in order before settling on the most important one. 'Where… what… who does *that* belong to?'

Robyn thrusts it towards Annie. In its wake travels a smell, unwashed, stale, ripe, which Annie tries to ignore.

Annie traces the dark blue cover of the passport. 'It's new,' she says. 'They were a different colour before.' She hands the passport back without opening it. 'You need to return it. It's not ours. It doesn't belong to us.' She doesn't even want to know who it *does* belong to. She only knows this isn't the way she wants to start their new beginning.

'Jesus, Annie, you've really got to stop being so… so nice. This is a dog-eat-dog world, survival of the fittest. Every man for themselves.' Robyn's voice is low but ferocious.

The silence stretches on, bogged down in the sudden fatigue between them. Robyn moves first, pulling Annie's bag over to her and inspecting the contents. She pulls out a bar of soap and holds it up.

'Shall we have a swim? Cleanse ourselves, get clean, chill out for a little while. Discuss it more later.'

Annie knows it's Robyn's way to a peace offering. She meets her friend's eyes, takes the hand that's reaching out to her.

–

On the sand in a small cove, they survey the landscape. It's early, the fishermen either well out to sea or already returned from their night fishing. No tourists yet, and so they strip down to their underwear and sink into the water. It still holds a chill from the winter, but Annie embraces the cold. She feels her skin tightening, the saltwater a welcoming sting. She uses the soap to scrub every part of her, leans her head back and dips her hair into the ocean. When she's done, she bobs over to Robyn and passes her the soap.

Under the cover of a mild wave, Robyn slips off her pants and lets them drift away on the tide.

She stands up, totally naked, and throws the soap back in Annie's direction but purposefully just out of reach. It plops into the waves, and Robyn lets out a laugh at Annie's startled face.

The sound brings an answering giggle from Annie. She looks at Robyn full on, open, alive, joyous.

'You think I won't find it?' she calls.

Robyn crosses her arms, a challenge.

'Right.' Annie raises her hands up above her head and executes a perfect dive into the crest of a wave.

Annie dives again and again, emerging like a mermaid to holler and wave at Robyn, who has retreated to the shore.

Annie strikes out, lean arms cutting through the water as she races back and forth. Annie can swim well, could have been a champion had she the means and opportunities. But girls like her and Robyn don't get a shot at things like that.

When she's panting from the exertion of the swim, she makes her way back to join Robyn on the beach. She pulls on her top and shorts and flops down beside her, enjoying the feel of the sun drying her off.

Time has passed, the sun has moved in the sky when she feels the eyes on her, a half-knowledge in the back of her mind, and she checks the ocean first, noting that it's empty all the way to the horizon, before twisting her head to look behind her.

It's Tobias from the taverna, standing where the cove meets the sandy strip of beach. He's a way away, in the glare of the sun, but Annie recognises his gangly frame, his slightly awkward stance.

Annie's heart does a little judder in her chest as Robyn sees him too.

Boldly, smiling slyly, Robyn stands, grabs her shorts and shirt but doesn't put them on. Annie feels the heat in her face, not just from the sun, as Robyn sashays up the sand towards him, swinging her non-existent hips.

As the sun dips behind a small, fuzzy cloud, the horror hits as Annie realises it's not Tobias any more. She can still see him, off to one side, looking up and down, off towards the ocean, looking anywhere but at Robyn in her full naked non-glory.

There is a man where Tobias originally stood, older, greyer, deeply tanned. His eyes are the same shade of blue as Tobias's, but this man's eyes are glinting with coldness.

Annie can feel the tension taut between the man, Tobias and Robyn. She breaks into a run up the beach towards them. She reaches them as the older man speaks.

'Thief!' the man snarls at Robyn, spittle flying from his furious mouth.

Robyn glances at Annie as she skids to a halt beside her. There is no fear in Robyn's eyes, only a dark and dangerous glint.

Slowly, Robyn pulls on her vest, steps into her shorts, and tugs them up her legs. Clothed, she faces the man down.

'I am not! I did nothing,' Robyn snaps at him. She flings a hand to where Tobias stands, a picture of shame and embarrassment. 'Ask him what he did.' Robyn stretches herself up to her full height, and sneers at the man who is clearly Tobias's father. She drags her hand down the front of her shirt, the thin cotton clinging, transparent, to her boyish figure. 'Ask him what he did to me, *with* me, in your fancy fucking home.'

Annie's hands flutter nervously as she dares to look at the man.

Robyn's counterattack has clearly shocked him, as have her words. He didn't expect that, she sees with unease. His silence is further compounded by the dimming of the fury in his face. He is unsure, hesitant.

'Thief,' he says again, but it is quieter this time, not as much weight behind his words.

Robyn smiles coldly and continues to stare at him defiantly.

He retreats, marches over to Tobias and puts an arm around the boy's thin shoulders.

'You don't come back; you stay away.' He looks Robyn up and down and ignores Annie. Now he is further away from Robyn, he seems to get a bit more momentum going. 'Filthy creature,' he spits. 'Girls like you… disgusting!'

He drops his arm from his son's shoulders and marches back up the road towards the town.

Robyn glares at Tobias. To Annie, it seems Robyn is ready to unleash upon him for his father's wrath. But when she glances at Tobias, it's not Robyn he is looking at. He is looking at Annie, his eyes no longer dreamy with longing, but hard and glinting with a barely concealed disgust.

He has lumped Annie in with Robyn now, she sees. Despite her own differing personality, he doesn't see them as separate people any more. To him, no doubt to his father, they are one and the same.

Thieves.

Disgusting.

Robyn sees the look he throws Annie. She rears up, twisting her face into an ugly smile.

She turns back to Tobias. 'I'll cut you,' she says. Her voice is so low, so normal-sounding, that for a moment Tobias looks confused.

'W-what?' he asks.

She takes a step closer to him. 'You look at her like that again and I'll cut you.' She lifts a hand towards his face. He jerks backwards, stumbling on the uneven road.

Annie slips her hand into Robyn's and draws her away, back to the beach.

5

'That girl won't need the passport,' says Robyn.

She's pulled it out of her pocket, slapping it against her palm and waving it in Annie's face.

They're both dry now, both covered in a new sheen of sweat. Half from the heat, half from the altercation with Tobias's father.

Annie ignores the passport and grabs a tight hold of Robyn's hand. She hates how the older man spoke to her friend, hates the words he spat at her.

Thief. Disgusting creature. Filthy.

The cutting words hurt as much as if they had been directed at Annie herself, and she holds on to Robyn, hoping Robyn can feel her love transferred, skin to skin.

They're sitting on the wall again, watching the superyachts and their occupants up close.

'You need to look at the passport for what it is, a gift,' says Robyn.

'She might need it,' says Annie. 'She might want to go home.'

Annie wonders where home is for the girl on her own who lives in the engine room of the ferry. She hasn't checked, still refuses to so much as open the passport and look at the person that Robyn has decided Annie should be.

'She can't go home. Not yet, not with the flights how they are, the quarantine period, the isolating each side. And you think she's got the money for a plane ticket? Do you think she'd be living in a ferry if she had any money?' Robyn persists.

Annie says nothing as she watches a child skip past them, one hand clutching an ice cream, the other tugging at the sleeve of an older woman.

Much like the child is doing, Robyn tugs on Annie's arm. 'We can use it, just for the season, or even just for a week. Just to see how you get on.'

Annie is watching the yachts now. On the one closest to them, guests are on board, half a dozen well-groomed men and women clustered around a semi-circular bar on the top deck. A stewardess holds a bottle of something and pours it into four of the glasses. She puts the bottle down, picks up a metal cannister, shaking it left and right, over her shoulder, like Annie has seen in the movies. On the deck below, four young men in matching polo shirts are hard at work. One of them is swishing a broom around, two more are attaching cables to a much smaller boat, while the fourth calls out distances and instructions to raise the tiny boat up from the water.

'You can do all that,' breathes Robyn, watching too.

Annie makes a *pfft* sound.

'You can!' Robyn's excitement is growing now. 'This isn't a pipe dream. It could be reality. Our reality, the one we've always wanted.'

'I don't know how to make cocktails,' protests Annie.

'So you haven't got bar experience; I'm sure it's not a game-changer. Annie, look at what you can do!' She points out the champagne pourer, the guy one floor below, pushing the brush around. Even the two that are climbing all over the sides of the yacht, clipping the cables, tightening ropes where their boss tells them to. 'Look, they're not in charge, the ones doing the work. They're doing what they're told, what the gaffer tells them to do. Jesus, Annie, that's you all over.'

Annie's mouth turns down a little, affronted at Robyn's notion that she's a dogsbody.

'What about you?' Annie asks. 'We can't *share* one passport, can we? Where will you sleep while I'm on board if I get a job?'

Robyn evades Annie's sudden torrent of questions.

'Let me worry about me,' she says sternly. 'I'll be fine. To be honest, I'll probably get a good job and a place to lay my head much easier without you hanging off my arse.'

Annie sighs and looks back at the yacht. What would it be like? she wonders. To have a job to go to every day, to have a bed to sleep in each night. To have a wage given to her, to no longer live hand to mouth, day to day. To bring back money for Robyn, so her friend, for once in her life, can live well. Robyn wouldn't have to live in the engine room of a ferry or use her body as a kind of currency for meals.

She attempts to ignore the knowledge that doing it this way is *wrong*.

Annie turns to Robyn. 'I need to figure it out; I can't go in looking like a novice,' she says. 'There's qualifications needed, certificates and stuff like that.'

Robyn nods, her face calm, but her fingers that grip at Annie's give away her excitement.

Annie continues. 'I need to get everything in order. I'll need a CV, I reckon, things to put on it. I imagine I need to register at one of the agencies...'

'Yes,' says Robyn. 'We can do all that. I can help you.'

Annie stares at her. 'Just for a couple of weeks. Just to see how I do. If it works out, we return the passport, we do this properly.'

Robyn nods eagerly.

Annie stands up and brushes herself down. 'Where do we start, then?'

Robyn stares past Annie, over her shoulder. The question is loaded, Annie knows, and really quite unanswerable. Robyn can't do anything. If Annie is going ahead, this one is all on Annie.

The change is a little unsettling, but also rather freeing.

Annie digs around in her bag and comes up with a few crumpled euro notes. She puts the majority in Robyn's hands, closing the girl's fingers around the money, and stuffs the remaining few back in her bag.

'Will you eat?' Annie pleads. 'And just chill out for the afternoon.' Annie leans forwards and kisses Robyn's cheek. 'You never relax; it's always you doing all the work. Promise me that for once, you'll take it easy today and let me do everything.'

It's not strictly true that Robyn does all the work. It is correct that her friend is normally the one with the ideas, but execution is left to Annie.

'You got the skills,' says Robyn all the time. 'You're organised, innit?'

Left to clean up the mess, a lot of the time, is often Annie's thought.

But this one is different. This plan is one that Annie is actually on board with.

Apart from the identity theft, of course.

As Annie hurries back down to the yachting hub, she can feel the hard edges of the passport through the thin material of her bag. She slips her hand inside and holds it for a few seconds before letting it go.

She still has not looked at it. Hasn't yet perused the person she is about to become.

Because once she does, there's no going back.

As Annie drifts around the shipping offices and the yacht staff agency, plucking more leaflets and information from the stands outside, she thinks about her words from earlier.

If it works out, after a couple of weeks, we return the passport, we do this properly.

Words spoken in haste, because if she was intending to return the stolen passport, she would never be able to work in this harbour again, because she would have already become known by that name. She would have to move on.

And Annie is sick and tired of moving on.

If Robyn were beside her now, her friend would tell her to think about that particular problem later.

It is with a sense of unease that Annie follows the path that she knows Robyn would have taken and pushes the thoughts of practicality aside for now.

She doesn't want to speak to anyone, not yet, not until she knows the basics. Or, at the very least, hold a conversation about this industry without looking like a complete amateur.

The contents of her bag are growing. From the brochure, she found a website for those wishing to start a career within this industry. Using the computer shop in the town, just past the taverna, Annie carefully formulated her own certificates that she'd need to be employed on a yacht. She is now the proud owner of a falsified Basic Safety Training certificate, and an ENG 1 medical pass.

She sweats as she waits for them to be printed out, sure that the woman behind the till knows exactly what Annie is doing.

She clenches her fists, wills herself to stay calm as she waits for the shouts of '*Imposter!*'

Instead, the woman simply says, 'Ten euro.' Her voice is muffled by her facemask, and she keeps her eyes on an iPad next to her, which is showing some foreign sitcom.

Annie takes her papers and her change, whispers a 'Thank you' and makes her way back down to the marina.

Unobtrusively, she mingles in with the yachties, watching the way they talk, how they always seem to be in a rush – too much of a rush to pay attention to a stranger in their midst.

Eventually, the town beyond the port falls quiet. Siesta time.

Annie tucks her new certificates inside her notebook. Perched upon a wall for a five-minute break, she strokes the cover.

Palm trees, a sunset sky, the ocean glittering.

Robyn bought her this notebook, ducking into a shop as they walked from the cove earlier. She knows Annie well, knows that she will want to make notes on everything she learns before jumping into the unknown.

And Robyn did actually *buy* her this notebook. She left the receipt inside, proof of purchase, wanting Annie to know that she believes in her enough to spend what little cash she has, when she could have easily stolen it.

It pleases Annie, as Robyn no doubt knew it would.

The crews of the yachts have dispersed somewhat, melting back to work upon their big boats, ready for whatever their afternoons hold for them.

Annie slips the notebook in her bag and leans back to lift her face to the sun. She sniffs as the aroma of a nearby barbeque wafts over to her, before wrinkling her nose as burning plastic and chemical scents encroach on her senses.

Annie sits up and glances at the town behind her.

Flames!

She doesn't hesitate. Slipping the shoulder strap of her bag across her body, she leaps from the wall. She's off in a sprint, up the cobbled street. No pause for thought, just the knowledge that there's danger, and people may get hurt.

On the deck of the nearest yacht, she spots a huddle of crew, staring up the hill.

'Fire!' Annie yells.

She's walked this street many times in the last couple of days. Knows how narrow it is, knows that the surrounding restaurants would impede the route of a fire truck with their tables and chairs scattered in the path.

Halfway up the cobbles, she stops and looks back. On one of the larger yachts, the crew are out, hosing down the deck. A deckhand stands, hose in hand, water gushing out while he stares open-mouthed up the hill.

Annie sprints back to the bow of the yacht.

'Hey!' she calls, waving frantically. 'Hey, will that hose reach up there?'

As though galvanised by her words, he gives her a quick nod, flicks a switch on the hose so the water slows to a trickle, and lowers it down to her.

Others are there now; the girls on the yacht beside her are calling out, gesturing to her, yelling for their deckies to hand them their own yacht's hoses.

Back up the hill, Annie drags the hose behind her. She pulls up short, an anguished cry falling from her lips as she sees the source of the fire.

Tobias's family's taverna.

Despite the way he looked at her earlier, the scene in front of her still brings tears to her eyes. The tables on the veranda, with their cheap, paper cloths, are ablaze. The flames have caught in the dry, wind-free heat, and are licking a path towards the wooden beams of the taverna's structure.

Other crews arrive, standing with their own hoses, which are frustratingly too short to reach the building. Neighbouring restaurateurs emerge from their siestas, shirtless, to stare at the taverna's blaze.

An old man snaps his braces into place and looks at Annie and her hose. He turns, calls something in Greek that she doesn't understand. Moments later a woman trots out of her joint with two large, white, plastic buckets. He gestures to them, swirling his hand in the air.

Annie understands. She points the hose into the bucket, craning down the hill to the white yacht where the deckhand is on board, shading his eyes.

'Switch it on!' Annie yells.

A horrible ten-second wait before the hose bulges and water spurts out.

Annie fills each bucket, watching the old man's painfully slow progress as he hobbles the few feet to the taverna, his shaky hands losing much of his water along the way. On his second trip back, Annie passes him the hose and takes the bucket from him.

She's faster, much more stable than the old guy, and soon there is a rhythm going.

Splash, fill, splash, fill.

The rhythm jumps and starts, like a scratched record. Annie glances around to see other crews alongside her, following her lead. In the distance, she hears bells and horns honking.

They keep going, working in a chain now, buckets passing hand to hand, dampening down the flames that smoulder upon the marbled floor of the veranda. The taverna itself is another matter. The beams have caught alight, flames rising upwards.

Annie wants to make sure Tobias and his family are out, but each time she opens her mouth to speak the smoke clogs her airways, making her eyes stream and her body wrack with coughs.

'Here, put this on.' She feels a hand gripping her arm, forcing her to put her bucket down.

Annie looks up into the face of the girl she knows is called Ella. Ella holds out a length of material. It's a tube scarf, one like motorcyclists wear, like the ones she's seen the deckhands sport when they're on deck and the sand has whipped up into a frenzy.

Annie takes it and slips it over her head, pulling it up to cover her mouth and nose.

'Thanks,' she gasps, her voice muffled.

Ella's hand is back on her arm, more pressure now, preventing Annie from picking up her bucket. Ella looks off to the left, further up the hill.

'The fire crews are here,' she says. 'We need to shift those tables.'

They are off again, stalling in their attempts to battle the flames with their homemade devices. Forging ahead to the tables that hamper the fire trucks, an obstruction preventing them from reaching their destination.

They shove the tables and chairs aside, assisted by a couple of other locals and deckhands.

Then, the fire truck is through, the men leaping from the side, unreeling their hoses, getting far closer to the flames than Annie and the other helpers could.

They have stopped the fire spreading, Annie can see from the other restaurant and bar owners who cling to each other, fright mingling with relief in their eyes.

As another coughing fit takes her, Annie removes her bag from her body, puts it on the path and sinks to sit on the kerb. Ella is down the hill, collecting bottles of water from grateful locals. She heads back to Annie, passes her a bottle and sits beside her.

'That was something, huh?' Ella wipes her face with the bottom of her shirt, leaving a black smear of soot across her cheek. 'I'm Ella, by the way. Ella Themis.'

She's tall, very tanned, but so fresh-looking that Annie thinks maybe her skin tone is from her ethnicity, rather than life on deck.

As Annie shakes her hand, she asks about Ella's unusual surname. To her ears it sounds foreign, though Ella clearly sounds American.

'Greek,' says Ella. 'On my father's side. It means "justice".' Ella gazes towards the chaos over at the taverna.

Annie follows her gaze and lets off a full-body shudder at the thick, black smoke that pours from the building. 'It's awful,' she whispers.

'It would have been a lot worse if it hadn't been for your quick thinking.' Ella knocks her bottle against Annie's in a mock toast. 'Nice work. Which boat are you on?'

Annie stares dumbly at her. 'Pardon?'

'Sorry, I assumed... are you not a yachtie?'

Despite the panic and the fear of what's just taken place, Annie feels a warm glow.

She starts to shake her head, and then she looks back to Ella. 'I'm trying to get into the industry,' she says, injecting as much confidence into her voice as she can muster.

Ella shrugs. 'Well, you're organised, clearly, and you think on your feet. You shouldn't have a problem.' She scrutinises Annie, eyes travelling up and down her body. 'Have you got experience?'

'Not on yachts, but I've done some restaurant work, house-keeping.' She pauses and makes believe she is Robyn, filled with all her friend's sense of entitlement and bravado. 'I can do it; I know that much.'

Ella's eyes are still on her. Red-rimmed and veiny, much like Annie imagines her own eyes appear. 'Are you with the agency?'

'Not yet. I was actually on my way there.' Annie utters a laugh and pulls at her own shirt. She'd dressed with care this morning, as carefully as was possible seeing as she had next to nothing. Now, her clothes, a pink, pastel skirt and white top, have smudges of dirt on them, and she knows she reeks of smoke from the fire. 'I'm not going to make the best impression now, am I?'

Inexplicably, her eyes fill with tears. She doesn't know why. There's tomorrow, after all; it's not the end of the world if she doesn't get a job today.

Behind Ella, she sees through the rapidly diminishing crowd three figures, cocooned in blankets. She recognises the silhouette of Tobias, hunched over, and that of his father, who stands in the water-sodden street, his hands on his head, staring at the ruins of his life's work.

Annie turns her face away so she doesn't have to see their despair.

Or so they don't see you.

She shudders, not knowing why she thought that, realising belatedly that Ella is still staring at her.

She attempts a weak smile at the other girl.

'I'll vouch for you,' says Ella suddenly.

Annie blinks, unsure of what she's talking about. 'Sorry?' she says blankly.

'I know Joan down at the agency. You were a hero today; I'll put in a good word. I'm a chief stew on a yacht. Joan and I go way back.' There is a hint of pride in Ella's voice.

Annie is taken aback. She puts out her hands to steady herself, knocking her bag over in the process.

Ella laughs, puts out a hand and hauls Annie to standing.

'But... but you don't even know me,' protests Annie.

Inside her mind she can hear Robyn's voice, yelling at her for looking a gift horse in the mouth.

'I know what I saw. I know you rushed headfirst into a potentially dangerous situation with no regard for yourself. That's the sort of person who we look to employ in this business.' Ella points to Annie's bag, the contents strewn on the path. 'Grab your stuff; let's go.'

Annie crouches down to scoop her paltry items back into her bag. She picks up the passport last, flicks it open and looks down at the face that is supposed to be her own.

After a moment of hesitation, she closes the passport and slips it in her pocket.

'I'm Ashley,' she replies. 'Ashley Mercer.'

The choice was taken from her, Annie realises as she sits across from Joan in the agency.

Or perhaps it was fate that brought Ella into her life at that moment, forcing Annie to make a snap decision on whether she was going to go along with Robyn's plan to use another girl's name.

When Ella has departed with a cheery wave and a 'Come find me later,' and Joan is moving around the office to gather paperwork and forms to be completed, Annie studies the passport.

This girl, this Ashley Mercer, is a passable imitation of Annie. Both blonde, both slight of build, both British. They are not twins by any stretch of the imagination, but a smile can make all the difference to a person's face. In the passport photo, Ashley looks almost stern.

Carefully, Annie smudges a finger along the photo in the passport, leaving a streak of black that slightly obscures the photograph in the little blue book.

Much better, Annie thinks guiltily.

'I like to start my girls out as day workers.' Joan is back, carrying a pile of folders that she puts down on the desk that sits between them.

'Day workers?'

Joan nods. 'You go aboard when a yacht comes into dock and the guests depart. You clean up, inside and out, just housekeeping. Once I've got an idea of how you work, I'll consider you for charters.' Joan wears half-moon glasses and she peers over them at Annie. 'Ella has recommended you, and that's quite an accolade in my book.'

There is no smile on Joan's face, and a flash of fear shivers through Annie. She needs to prove herself to this woman, needs to convince the gatekeeper of the yachting industry that to take Annie on would be a good thing.

'I'll do whatever it takes,' says Annie. 'I can do anything, cooking, cleaning, bartending, and if I don't know how to do it,

I'll learn. I learn quickly, and I make notes, and once I'm taught something I don't have to be shown again.'

Joan nods, flicking through her files now.

'*Siren* needs a day worker; it's coming into port shortly.' She stares at Annie again, looking doubtfully at her. 'You'll need to change; you can't go on board like this. Even if you did put out a fire, there are standards that need to be kept at all times.'

Annie nods eagerly and rifles through her bag. She pulls out her purse, frayed and tattered, and from inside she withdraws the last of her cash. Holding up the few notes, she shows them to Joan. 'I'll go now, get a nice shirt, some working shorts – would that do?'

There is a long moment of silence as Joan peruses her. Then, little by little, Joan's somewhat rigid face begins to soften. The flinty, grey eyes are suddenly more mellow, and Joan's lips curve up into an almost-smile.

'I've got some clothes, leftovers from old seasons. They should fit you.' Joan clears her throat and stands up. 'Come on, love.'

There is a kindness in Joan's words that until now Annie had no idea existed. What was it, she wonders, that set that switch in the older woman's mind?

As she's led into a backroom with a shelving area of polo shirts and shorts, Annie realises.

Joan could see she needs a chance. Joan, from sight only, and Ella's words, thinks she's deserving of a chance.

Freshly clothed, Annie ties her long blonde hair back, picks up her bag, and emerges back into the dusty, old-fashioned office where Joan awaits.

Joan appraises her, nodding with apparent approval. She hands over a piece of paper. '*Siren* is coming into slip seven,' she says. 'It will be helpful if you can work for as long as they need you, and they'll probably want you again tomorrow morning.'

Annie takes the paper, folds it neatly and puts it in her pocket. 'Thank you,' she says seriously. 'I won't let you down.'

Joan raises her eyebrows, a cynical *we'll see* written upon a face that's seen all the girls who have no doubt come and gone over the years.

Outside, after the gloom of the office, the sunshine is almost a surprise. Annie hesitates in the marina. She is supposed to report directly to the yacht called *Siren* to commence work. Once aboard, she is expected to work until they tell her she can leave. When will that be? Five o'clock, office knocking-off hours? Seven, eight, nine o'clock, or even later?

Annie doesn't care how long she has to stay, but she is worried that Robyn will be concerned if Annie doesn't meet up with her soon.

They have no phones, no means of communication. But this is her one chance, *their* chance. Annie can't throw it away.

With a quick look at the berth map on the wall outside the agency, Annie locates slip seven and hurries on her way to her future.

She takes a deep breath as she walks onto *Siren*. She puts her facemask in place, ever mindful of the possibility of *Siren*'s captain scrutinising the borrowed passport too closely. She isn't that worried about Joan; the older woman had squinted for a moment over the passport and hadn't even mentioned the smoke marks that Annie had attempted to obscure the picture with.

Will the people in charge on *Siren* look closer? Do they do some sort of technical database check? The fear lurches inside. *What if I'm found out?*

On the deck of the boat, out come two of her new colleagues.

'Hey, you must be Ashley?' asks the taller of the two.

A sharp pebble lodges in Annie's throat. A split second where she's about to automatically correct the girl. Then she remembers. That's her name now. She pushes past the blockage and forces a smile that they can't see under her mask.

'Hi, yes, I'm Ashley. Ashley Mercer, it's great to meet you.'

'Pippa, Roxy.' The girl points to herself and her colleague. 'I'm chief, she's second. Day worker, right?'

It's as though she's so busy she can only afford the time to say a few words of a full sentence.

Annie hesitates, long enough for her to see Pippa's dramatic eyeroll.

'Yep,' Annie says hurriedly, swallowing down her natural, drawn-out conversation to match the girl's speed of words.

'This way.' The woman who is apparently her boss turns sharply on her heel, signalling for Annie to follow her.

They pass several more people on the route, all who smile or raise a hand in greeting.

'Are you okay doing laundry?' Pippa asks. 'Mundane, I know, but we need help turning this boat over.'

Mindful that Joan from the agency will probably ask Pippa how she did, Annie nods eagerly. 'Anywhere you want me,' she says. 'That's what I'm here for.'

She's sure she sees a flicker of relief in the girl's eyes, and once she's deposited in the laundry room, after the world's quickest induction, she vows to work her hardest to clear the piles of clothes, towels and bedding as fast but as thoroughly as possible. Speed is of the essence here, she reckons, but attention to detail is needed too.

She works speedily, just like she used to when she was on washing duty back in the home. Sorting the things that can go on a high-temperature wash, delicate items put to one side, shoving the quick-wash things in first, so as soon as that cycle is complete, she can fold and iron when the next loads are on.

She works methodically, as is her way, taking pleasure in a job well done as the piles decrease in size.

Two hours have passed when Annie hears the clatter of feet on the stairs that lead down to the laundry room, and Pippa sticks her head around the door.

'Wow,' she says, casting a critical eye over the room. 'Nice work.'

Annie smiles, pleased. 'Thanks,' she says shyly.

'Listen, the engineers need to take the boat out of harbour while they test the sails. Just… hold on to whatever you can, and be careful with the iron while we're on the water.' The eyeroll comes again. 'It's a bloody nuisance, to be honest, so just… be warned.'

It's a thrilling piece of news. Annie hadn't expected to leave the harbour.

She gives a thumbs up to Pippa, who, once the information has been imparted, dodges out as quickly as she came in.

She's grateful for the warning once they get underway. Pippa wasn't kidding about telling her to hold on. The boat lurches left, then right, righting itself only momentarily before beginning the whole rocking motion again.

'Hey, Ashley, right?'

Annie clings on to the worktop above the washing machines and turns to face a new visitor.

'I'm Kofi, lead deckhand. Pippa told me to tell you to take a break.'

'Oh, awesome, thanks,' she says, daring to let go of the side and staggering towards Kofi.

He laughs and she joins in. 'This is actually pretty great.' She smiles as she balances with one hand on the doorframe.

'You can come on deck if you want a real experience,' he says, and at her eager nod, he beckons at her to follow him.

She bursts out onto the port side, gasping at the spray of seawater that comes over the side, lunging for the rail as the boat does another gyration.

Up ahead, on the bow, she can hear whoops and cheers. Clinging on to the side, legs far apart for balance, she makes her way to where the action is.

'Are we having fun yet?' Roxy sticks her head out of a port window, shouting over the noise of the ocean.

'It's brilliant!' Annie calls back, grinning so wide she can taste saltwater on her teeth.

The deck opens into the bow, and Annie hears a crashing sound above. She looks up to the sky, gasping again at the billowing sails, all three of them out to capacity, the wind beating into them and pushing them onward.

All the crew are on board, shrieking and clinging on to each other with every tilt of the boat, unexpected excitement in their working day.

Annie reaches Kofi, who got to the wheel a lot faster than she did. He stands with the captain, Piotr. Both are grinning from ear to ear.

This is their world, she thinks as she watches them radiating joy. *This sail is what they live for.*

Kofi spots her and beckons her to the helm. '*Siren* is a hybrid, a combination of motor and sail. Any excuse to get the sails up and we take it!'

'Are you enjoying it, Ashley?' asks Captain.

She grabs the handrail again and laughs, a sound of pure pleasure. 'It's amazing!'

It seems like only seconds have passed before the winds suddenly drop. A collective groan goes up, and Annie realises she can stand without falling.

'That's it?' she asks, disappointed.

Kofi shrugs. 'Until next time.'

Annie takes her cue from the others, all drifting back to the interior. Running now that she doesn't have to cling on to anything for balance, she hurries back to the laundry room, the joy of the sail lifting her up as she finishes up the last of her tasks.

—

The digital clock on the crew mess wall tells her it is ten o'clock. A rumble of panic sits like a stone in Annie's stomach as she imagines Robyn's distress at her being gone all day.

'You're okay to come back tomorrow?' asks Pippa as she sees her off the boat.

Annie nods. 'Eight a.m., right?'

Once she's off the passerelle, she breaks into a sprint towards where the great, hulking ferries sleep.

She hears Robyn before she sees her. Legs pumping, she runs the length of the dock, rounding the corner to see Robyn next to the gatekeeper, the same one as last night. When she reaches them, doubling over to catch her breath, Robyn grabs her arm and pulls her into the gloom of the ferry.

'What were you quarrelling with him for?' pants Annie.

Robyn pulls her along the corridor and yanks open the door that leads down into the engine room. 'He wanted to close the doors! Jeez, Annie, I've been so worried about you; where were you?' She shoves open the engine room door, pushing Annie in ahead of her.

Their place by the door is gone, a couple huddling in the spot where Annie and Robyn slept the night before. Robyn mutters under her breath and pulls Annie past the rows of sleeping bodies.

'Here.' Robyn inserts Annie into a gap big enough for the two of them.

Annie, suddenly exhausted, sinks to sit upon the hard floor. 'I've been working,' she says. 'I got a job.' Even just saying the words is thrilling enough to chase away her fatigue.

Robyn's eyes glint in the darkness. 'Tell me everything,' she says.

As Annie relays her day of adventure on *Siren*, she recalls what started her off on the path to becoming a yachtie, and her eyes darken.

'The taverna caught on fire,' she whispers. 'Robyn, it was awful; Tobias and his family barely made it out. The taverna is just a shell.' Annie covers her mouth.

The stench of smoke, the orange flames, the pure adrenaline rush settling over her once again, making her skin fizz and her eyes water.

Robyn leans in close. 'You stink of smoke.' She draws back, regards Annie warily. 'Were you there, at the taverna?'

Annie remembers Ella's words. *You were a hero today.*

But for reasons she can't fathom, she doesn't want to repeat them to Robyn.

'Yes,' she whispers, the full memory of the burning building where they spent a night fresh in her mind.

Robyn's face is whiter than usual. 'You shouldn't have been there,' she says, her voice cracking.

Annie shrugs. 'I helped, a little bit.' She remembers Ella's words. 'It could have been worse.'

From her pocket, Robyn withdraws a phone and hands it to Annie. From behind her she produces another one. Two iPhones. Older versions than the ones she saw on the crew on *Siren* today, but phones all the same.

Annie covers them with her bag and glances furtively around.

'Relax,' says Robyn. 'They were cheap because they're old, but I got SIM cards, so we can stay in touch when you're working.' The look she gives Annie is deep and meaningful. 'And I won't worry about you like I did today.'

Thoughts of the fire and the lingering fear melt away as Annie draws Robyn in for a hug.

'I don't know what I'd do without you,' Annie murmurs.

They remain close, arms entwined, for the rest of the night.

–

The following morning, Annie walks down to the marina for her second shift on *Siren*, with Robyn trailing her.

At the midway point of the plaza steps, Annie pauses and pulls Robyn to sit on the steps beside her.

'What are you going to do today?' she asks anxiously.

Robyn shrugs.

'Will you eat?' Annie asks, rifling in her bag for her ever-dwindling stash of cash.

Robyn nods, but Annie can see her attention is elsewhere as she stares through the moulded balustrade towards the town.

Annie follows her gaze. Midway up the hill lies the still-smouldering remains of the taverna. Annie shivers.

'Poor Tobias,' she murmurs, unable to forget the intensity of yesterday's furnace.

Robyn says nothing.

Annie pushes herself up. When Robyn begins to stand, Annie puts a hand on her shoulder.

'Stay here,' she says. 'I'll be back when I've finished my shift. Buy yourself a breakfast, and be good, okay?' She pulls Robyn in for a brief hug, letting her go as her friend's sour scent assaults her nostrils. Annie forces a smile. 'Go swimming again,' she says lightly.

Before Robyn can reply, Annie is gone, tripping down the stairs, entering the throng of people. Head down, Annie zones in on the person in her sights, and hurries along.

'Ella!' She reaches the girl, panting.

Ella turns, a flicker of recognition in her face, a ready smile on her lips. 'Ashley, good to see you. Heading back for day two?'

Annie nods. 'How did you know?'

'Pippa's a good friend of mine,' replies Ella. 'I trained her. We chat.'

That figures. Both have the same mannerisms, the same way of talking, like there's so much to do and so little time. 'Thank you so much for what you did yesterday. You didn't need to vouch for me, but I'm really glad you did. I... I owe you one, really.'

Ella tilts her head to one side. 'You can buy me a drink with your first pay packet.' She grins to let Annie know that she's joking. 'Where're you staying, by the way, in case I hear of any more jobs that come up?'

Annie feels the freeze in the base of her spine. She can't tell this glamorous, put-together woman that right now she's bunking down with the homeless in the ferries.

As the silence stretches on into an awful awkwardness, the ice spreads throughout Annie's body. Her mouth works, but no sound emerges.

Ella frowns, just a minute motion, and suddenly, all the potential that was heading Annie's way is in danger of being lost. Still, she can't bring herself to speak.

'If you're moving around, what about a phone number – do you have a mobile?'

With great physical effort, Annie pushes through the mental block. 'Yes,' she manages. 'Wait...' From her bag she pulls her new phone, the one Robyn got for her cheaply, and navigates to her number. She reels it off for Ella, who types it in her phone, then presses the call button. Annie's phone buzzes, just once, before cutting off.

'Save that number as mine,' Ella instructs. 'Gotta go now, but we'll catch up later, yes?'

'Yes,' breathes Annie, but Ella has already gone, in the wind, darting off just as quickly as she appeared.

–

This time, on *Siren*, she's on housekeeping. Replacing all the pillowcases, sheets and duvets that she washed yesterday. It's a more arduous task, more physical, but Annie's got a taste for this work now, and she wants to stick with it. Not just day working, either, but the full-on charter experience. From the connection she's made with Ella, and the efficient work she's doing on *Siren*, Annie reckons she stands a good chance of getting her name put forward for proper, long-term employment.

There are still logistics to figure out. The name on Annie's bank account doesn't match that on her passport, and the name that she's using going forwards. She'd fed Joan at the agency a sob story of her bank account being cloned, and how she's having to use her married sister's account.

Joan had hesitated before setting it up. 'You'll need your own account,' she'd warned. 'So set up a new one as soon as you can or let me know once yours is up and running again.'

Crisis averted, but only temporarily.

Annie has other worries too. What if she runs into the real Ashley Mercer? Has she noticed yet that her passport is missing? Will she search her memory for the two new girls that slept beside her in the engine room of the ferry just two nights ago? How long will it take for her to put two and two together?

And then there's the worst thing of all, playing on Annie's mind.

This morning, as she reached the peak of the plaza steps, Robyn beside her, Annie caught a glimpse of Ella down in the square, blonde ponytail swinging, that confident gait that, in Annie's eyes, told her that Ella knows her worth.

She envisaged it, just for a brief moment, introducing the two of them, her oldest friend, or, rather, her *only* friend, and the woman who, unless Annie has got it totally wrong, is beginning to *feel* like a friend. Somehow, she couldn't imagine the three of them together.

Annie practically ran from Robyn to Ella, but she doesn't want to delve too deeply into the why of this.

She gets back to work, shaking out the final duvet in the master suite of *Siren* before she goes in search of her next task. After all, today is for completing all her work, and giving the very best impression that she can.

But thoughts of Robyn sit heavy inside her as she works. She remembers the first time they met. They were young, tiny little things, undersized for their eight-year-old frames.

They had both been in and out of various homes forever. Nobody knew where Robyn came from, only that she'd been found naked, squawking, flesh tinged blue, on a pavement in Osbourne Road, in the east end of London. Whoever had left her there had literally placed her on the edge of the path, next to the road. No clothes, no blanket, not even a plastic bag. The umbilical cord that had bound her and her unknown mother had been crudely hacked off. It wasn't even tied.

The social worker had called her Robyn after the woman who had found her and had taken her to the hospital. Annie remembers when they were in their early teens, Robyn having dreams about the mysterious saviour Robyn. She'd wanted to know the woman whose name she wore, the person who'd cared enough to pick her up, messy cord and all, and deliver her to a place of warmth and safety.

But the older Robyn had long since died, and that was that dream shattered.

From then on, Robyn always told Annie not to have dreams that relied on other people.

Annie's was a similar story. She was also found, new-born, in London. That was where the similarities ended. Annie was discovered in the West End, on the steps of a fire station, wrapped in not one but two blankets, her cord tied in two places with string, and an unsigned note of apology.

Robyn fantasised that they were actually blood sisters, that their silly, silly mother had made another pregnancy mistake and, feeling awful at how she'd dumped poor Robyn, cold and naked to the world, had at least taken care with Annie.

Once, she'd shared this new dream with Annie. Annie, even back then clever and practical, had pointed out the odds of this wouldn't be likely, nice as it was. Annie was only a few months younger than Robyn.

Robyn had felt foolish and embarrassed in front of Annie.

It was the first time Annie had realised she had hurt Robyn, and so started her trend of making it better.

'We're as good as sisters, anyway,' Annie had soothed.

That was how they rolled from thereon. Annie: the nice one who could always find a kind word. Robyn was the leader of the show, the planner, the doer, the mastermind.

And though Annie loves Robyn with every fibre of her being, she allows the thought that has been drifting around the edges of her mind to finally materialise.

She's enjoying this short separation, the independence that it's given her, and the chance to forge ahead on her own and find out who she really is.

But it is just temporary, she reminds herself. Just a little break. Soon, she'll be back at Robyn's side, the dream team together again, where Annie belongs.

PART THREE

1

ANNIE

The end of her short stint on *Siren* comes too soon.

All afternoon, as she nears the finish line, Annie keeps an eye on her phone, which remains frustratingly, resolutely silent.

When it finally beeps, nearing sundown, Annie snatches it out of her pocket. It's a text message from Robyn, a photo of her friend, on the middle ground of the plaza, a wide smile on her face, the grand structure behind her.

Annie puts the phone back in her pocket and does a final walk-through of the pristine yacht. There's a sense of deep satisfaction in her work, but seedlings of disappointment nestle alongside because she's leaving.

On the boardwalk, she bids goodbye to Pippa.

'You'll call me if you need me again?' she asks anxiously.

'Yep, no problem, good job, and thanks again!' Pippa is already back on board, ponytail flying behind her.

Annie heads back towards the square, inhaling deeply, at a loss for what to do now.

She's not Ashley any more, and she's not sure if she'll ever get the chance to be her again. It's a shame, because though it doesn't sit right how she got to be the other girl, when it came down to it, she liked being Ashley Mercer, helpful and hard-working and seemingly well liked.

Then she hears a shout.

'Ashley! Ash!'

It's the shortening of the name that makes her pause. The familiarity of a nickname, bestowed upon her, she sees as she turns around, by a department head.

Annie turns around. 'Ella, hi!' Annie sends up a silent prayer that Ella has some good news for her and isn't just asking her how the final shift on *Siren* went.

'We're short-staffed. I need another body. The role is for a stewardess, but they're expected to assist on the exterior when needed.' She looks Annie up and down, pauses for just a moment before saying, 'Are you up for it? It will be a trial run, see how you handle an actual charter.'

Annie swallows. 'Seriously?' she asks. 'For real?'

'Pippa said you did good. I already knew that, but I wanted you to clear your second shift, make sure you're not a one-trick pony.' Ella winks.

Annie takes a deep breath as she prepares to sell herself. 'I'm new but I'm keen, and I'm more than willing to work. I really enjoyed working on *Siren*. I worked in the laundry, mostly, but I'm sure I'd be just as productive—'

Ella lifts a hand, effectively cutting her short. 'I know, Pip told me. Can you come on tonight?'

Annie blinks. 'Come on board? Tonight?'

Ella does a perfect imitation of Pippa's eyeroll. Annie sees where it all manifested now. She wonders if she, too, one day will be like these women, talking in clipped sentences, rolling her eyes at stupid questions.

'Yes, tonight. Do you have your passport?'

'Yes,' says Annie quickly.

And with that one word, everything changes again.

Ananke is a showstopper. It's a fifty-metre superyacht, only a little bigger than *Siren*, but somehow it seems like double the size. It has four outer decks and three below. It's not a hybrid, like *Siren* was. There's no sailing here, just pure, unadulterated motorised luxury.

'Sailboats like *Siren* are meant for adventurers,' explains Ella on their approach to the big boat. '*Ananke* is where the money is.

But for the guests to pay the price, we've got to make it worth it for them. *Anything* they want, they get. Got that?' she asks as the passerelle lowers to allow them to board.

There's that feeling again: that there might be a double standard here, payment in kind, the one she's learned from living alongside Robyn all her life.

She catches Ella's wrist. 'Are we expected to...' She swallows, can't even bring herself to say the words.

'Anything,' says Ella firmly, marching onto the walkway.

When Annie doesn't follow her, Ella turns. 'What?' she says.

'I don't know if I could,' Annie manages to say. 'I mean, I'm not a prude, but...'

The now-silent night is broken by Ella's peals of laughter. 'Jesus, Ashley,' she says, coming back towards where Annie stands on the dockside. 'I didn't mean *that*! Shit, if any of the guests so much as lay a finger on you they'll be off the boat. Got that?'

So, Ella is also a protector, like Robyn.

No, she realises. Ella is simply her boss.

It is interesting, she thinks now, as she takes her final steps aboard *Ananke*, the personalities Annie takes from those she meets. Protector, protected, leader, follower, sayer, doer.

Hunter.

Hunted.

Annie shivers, wondering where that thought came from.

She tunes back in to Ella, who is still talking, reeling off duties and instructions. A couple of people flit past, pausing for a handshake or greeting. All crew, Annie supposes, though it's hard to tell in their street clothes. She flails for a moment, wondering how she's going to keep track of everyone, learn all these names.

She thinks it is anxiety she is feeling, then revisits the emotion. No, she realises, it's excitement, anticipation.

'Where did you come from?' asks Ella as they make their way to the crew quarters.

'London,' says Annie. And then, to divert further questions, she asks, 'What about you?'

'Here, there, everywhere.' Ella shrugs.

Annie follows her along the corridor of cabins in silence. It's not much of an answer. As if sensing Annie's thought, Ella turns to face her.

'Everyone in yachting is either running from something or chasing something.' Ella pushes open a door. 'I don't even know why I still ask that question. Where we come from is neither here nor there. Who we are now is all that matters.'

Annie stares at her; the words coming from her chief stew are a lightning bolt of everything Annie's been feeling but has been unable or unwilling to say. Hope is building, ferocious now, upon hearing that past lives don't count, history is over and done with. Some things belong in the past.

'Yes,' Annie whispers. 'That's exactly it.'

She follows her crewmate through an opulent lounge, through a swinging door and three flights of stairs that wind down into the bowels of the boat. It's not like the ferry here, where you go down those fire stairs with an impending sense of fear as you descend into the gloom.

The light is constant in this stairwell, from cleverly placed portholes and circular lights set into the woodwork of the steps.

'Crew mess,' says Ella as they walk through a small dining area. 'And the galley kitchen, pantry, through there, our sleeping quarters.'

'Cool,' says Annie. 'It's more spacious than I imagined.'

Ella nods. 'This is not one of the biggest yachts I've worked on, but they're all designed so cleverly. Hidden storage, literally, like, everywhere.' As if to demonstrate her point, Ella pushes a panel in the wall of the hallway. It slides up and in, and lo and behold, what Annie imagines are the crew's luggage and suitcases are neatly stowed inside.

'You're sharing a cabin with Cat,' Ella informs her as they carry on at a fast pace down the corridor. 'Hope you're all right with the top bunk.'

She pushes open a door and Annie steps inside.

Hope you're all right with the top bunk. Annie feels her eyes filling at the sight of her very own bed. Not a makeshift one, not a thin duvet on a hard floor, but a real, purpose-built bed. Surreptitiously, she wipes her face on her shirt sleeve and looks away from Ella's curious glance. 'It's still so warm out,' she says by way of explanation for her stupid tears.

Ella checks her watch. 'You'll be okay to be up at six? We'll go through everything properly in the morning. I'll introduce you to everyone tomorrow, as most of them are back in the marina. If you're hungry, there's some grub in the crew mess. Help yourself.'

Annie nods. 'I'll be up at six,' she says. 'And… thank you.'

Ella calls out a good night, closing the door behind her as she leaves.

Annie turns back to the bunk again and surveys her bed.

Hope you're all right with the top bunk. What would Ella say if she knew that this bed is like manna from heaven? That since she started her trip to Greece, she's only slept in the passenger seat or the containers of lorries, a beach, on a couch, on the floor of a disused ferry's engine room.

She shakes her head to dispel memories she'd rather not revisit, hoists her bag up to the top bunk and nimbly climbs up herself. She settles her things around her, making a place like she's used to.

From her pocket she takes out her phone and stares at the empty screen.

She thinks of the soft mattress underneath her, and the ferry where Robyn will lay her thin, stolen duvet down to rest tonight. The image hurts, and her eyes blur with further unshed tears as she taps out a text message.

> I got another job. On a different yacht this time. Had to come on board to start early tomorrow. Will you be okay? xxx

Annie watches the phone. But just like earlier, it stays frustratingly and resolutely silent.

She will stay awake, she decides, so she can introduce herself to her new roommate when she comes in. But her eyes grow heavy, until she decides just to rest them for a short while.

It's her last thought as sleep catches at her, and for the first night in as long as she can remember, there are no dreams at all.

2

There's a body in the bed beneath her when she wakes. A huddled shape under the duvet, snoring heartily, noisily, then murmuring and, finally, giggling.

Annie sits up in the bed, her face aflame.

There are *two* people in the bunk below her! And oh God, what if they don't know she's there, and they start something up down there? The embarrassment would be huge, too much to bear on her first day aboard!

As quietly as she can manage, she slips down from the bunk, landing with a soft thud on the floor.

'JAY-SUS!'

The voice startles her, the volume making her cringe.

Annie holds out her hands, a position of surrender, as the bedside light is switched on, and two tousled heads emerge from the small bottom bunk.

'Hi, morning, sorry, I'm Annie,' she says in a rush. 'I just came on board last night.'

'Fuck,' says one of them, the man, as he groans, clutches at his head and dives back underneath the pillow.

'I'm sorry,' whispers Annie.

The girl emerges, stretching, all tanned limbs, muscled arms and legs that go on forever.

'Ignore Luca,' she says. 'He's always grumpy in the morning.' She grins at Annie. 'I'm Cat; are you my new roomie?'

Annie nods. 'I'm really sorry,' she apologises again. 'I didn't realise…'

'It's okay.' Cat drags her fingers through her short, ebony hair and stretches once again. 'What time is it?'

'Ten to six,' says Annie.

'Fuck.' Cat jabs an elbow into Luca, who responds with a roar.

'I can just…' Annie gestures towards the door. 'I'd better go upstairs.'

She slept in her clothes of the night before, and she hadn't even used the bathroom, brushed her teeth, her face, but she'd rather turn up on time looking like a bag lady than be late for her first morning.

She smooths her hair as she traverses the hallways, trying and failing to remember the route that Ella took last night. Worries are piling up on her now: she's given Ella her passport; will they keep it, scrutinise it, carry out checks on her? What about the bank stuff – does that go through Joan at the agency or is she now employed by this boat? Is the agency even involved, seeing as this gig came on the back of a recommendation? Will her new boss do even more thorough checks on her, on this bigger, plusher, richer yacht? Or will it be the opposite, considering she came straight here from *Siren*? Will they be so accommodating as to pay her money into an account that – as far as they are concerned – isn't in her name? Can she open one in Ashley's name, to cover her tracks? And finally, is she destined to be Ashley Mercer for as long as her career lasts?

No, she decides. Ashley is a person in her own right. At some point, Ashley will want to go home, or even to move onwards. Ashley can't want to live in the engine room of a disused ferry for the rest of her life. Perhaps the girl had just hit upon hard times, like lots of the community. Now the world is starting to open a bit more post-pandemic, surely she'll want to be on her way. Without her identification, she might be stuck in there forever.

Annie stops, halfway up the winding staircase. She hadn't thought of that before. She hadn't thought of any of this before.

But there's no time to ponder upon it now. She can hear footsteps behind her, and she steps back against the wall as Luca, the man from the bottom bunk, flies past her up the stairs.

He gives her a small nod, and she recognises him as the angry chef who was in the plaza where she first saw Ella.

After a second she follows in his wake, heading towards the voices of what she imagines are her new crewmates.

–

After a very brief introduction to the captain – a woman, to Annie's astonishment – called Carly Lee, Ella takes her to the laundry and selects her uniform for her.

'Change in your cabin, polo shirt for now – later we'll change into the smarter ones for the guest arrival. Back to the mess when you're ready.'

Back in her cabin, Annie slips on the smart, black shirt to ensure it fits. She has a stripe on her sleeves, she sees, as she studies her reflection in the mirror. One stripe, or epaulette, as the technical term is. It's the lowest ranking, but to Annie, it's everything.

That one single stripe is, to her, an image of the rung of a ladder. Just one step, but she's on it all the same.

Impulsively, she takes a photo of her reflection and puts it in a message to Robyn. She didn't hear from her friend last night, after she sent her the new message, and the lack of reply has been playing on her mind since she woke up.

She thinks of Robyn in that ferry room, *alone*. They travel in packs, people like herself and Robyn, or at the very least in pairs.

She shakes her head and screws her eyes closed. She's spinning. Of all the people in that engine room, Robyn is the one who can take care of herself.

–

'I've got your passport,' Ella says when she heads upstairs in her polo shirt. 'We keep it in the safe on the bridge, and you can get it to go back ashore after each charter if you need it.'

Yesterday, Annie spent ages before leaving *Siren* smudging her fingers with newspaper print and rubbing it over the photo page so it merged in with the sooty mess she'd created previously. Now, she's not sure if it was a good idea or if it simply highlights the falsification, making the viewer look closer at it where before they might have just given it a cursory glance. It's the first that it has been mentioned since she handed it over, and it doesn't sit well, that it's in a safe on the bridge. Anyone could look at it up there. She'd rather have it with her, in her pocket, safe from prying eyes.

Annie thinks about her fake persona as she gets to work in the master cabin, following Ella's orders of stripping, remaking a new bed, and cleaning '*literally from top to bottom*', as per Ella's words.

She wants her own name back, she decides. But, even more importantly, she wants to do this life properly. She can keep all the experience she gets here, in Greece. She can transfer it all to a new CV. She can get documentation in her real name. It will mean going back to England, somehow, illegally, of course. Unless she can try to claim some sort of asylum here, visit an embassy, and get a new passport from here?

No, that won't work. They'll know she gained access to Greece in an improper manner.

Can she… Annie hardly dares to consider it, but could she… *confide* in someone?

Not yet. Wait, there's no need to act right now. Wait until you know these people, wait until you are sure there is somebody you can trust.

The word of warning is the voice of Robyn.

Robyn taught her a lot, and most of it makes sense.

She takes a last look around the master suite, pleased with her work, and on her radio, she calls Ella to let her know she's finished.

'Copy that,' comes the static-ridden reply. 'Change into your blacks, then come up to the boarding deck.'

Annie does as she's told, hurrying to her cabin and slipping into the black shirt. The thrill of that single white stripe still fills her with excitement all over again, and she wonders if that feeling will ever fade.

She wonders if, one day, she might have a sleeve that boasts two or even three stripes.

As she leaves the room to head up to the deck, she sees the second stewardess who gave her a rushed hello earlier, Brandy, sprinting down the corridor towards her, divesting herself of her work clothes as she runs. Annie flattens herself against the wall again, a replay of that very morning when Chef, also late, came thundering up the stairs.

'I'm so late,' Brandy yells as she skids into her own cabin. 'Cover for me, Ashley, and get the champagne ready.'

Once more, Annie does what she's told, stopping in the galley to check on the preference sheets how many guests are about to board, before heading back up to the deck where the passerelle is, grabbing a bottle of champagne and the correct number of glasses.

'Where's Brandy?' asks Ella, eagle-eyed as she spots Annie doing the job meant for the second stew.

'She's right behind me; I just thought I'd get these ready.' Annie tells a semi-lie, hoping she's not caught out.

'I've got it.' Brandy sidles up to her, tips her a wink and a quiet 'Thank you,' and takes the tray from her.

Under Captain Carly's scrutinising eye, they line up along the deck. Ella walks the line, issuing instructions. 'Shirt tucked in, please, Danny,' and 'Tie your hair back, Luca.' She says nothing to her own department, just gives a slight nod to both Brandy and Annie.

Then, the guests are there, a curious mix, thinks Annie. A newly-wed, slightly older than middle-aged couple and their various offspring. The woman, Cynthia, has insisted that all the crew refer to her as Mrs Olsen, and her husband, Phillip, is to be called Doctor.

There had been a Pippa-esque eyeroll from Ella as they checked over the guests on their preference sheets earlier. Cursing from Luca, the chef. Apparently, so said Cat, along with wealth comes certain expectations, and a heightened sense of entitlement.

'We do what they want, and we bite our tongue, and think of the tips,' were Ella's parting words of wisdom.

Annie isn't worried. She knows people like this. Not with this extremity of riches, of course, but people who are to be handled with care.

Demanding people who can turn at any moment.

Annie is gracious as the charter gets underway, a small smile, polite words, lowered eyes. Silently expressing to Doctor and Mrs Olsen that yes, she's aware of their status, that they're the boss, that what they want they get. That she's here to serve them.

Robyn would *hate* it. Scraping, bowing, kissing ass. Just another reason why it was always going to be Annie on board, rather than her friend.

The offspring, stepbrothers and sisters of varying ages, are slightly harder to perceive. Their respective parents have made their wealth, the mother through investments and the doctor through a dedicated medical career. Annie can appreciate that, but the kids, it's all been handed to them and yet their own sense of entitlement seems to be even bigger than that of their parents. As a result, the children are rude, demanding and completely missing any semblance of manners at all.

Annie lets it wash over her. Every time she feels a little spike at their attitudes, she pauses, looks out over the railing, or out of a porthole. The view from the place that she now calls home bursts the bubble of annoyance instantly.

They anchor in what she thinks is the same cove that *Siren* passed on her impromptu sail, just a couple of days ago. The yacht tender – the small vessel used for ferrying crew and guests to land – is lowered into the ocean, and the guests are taken ashore for lunch and sightseeing.

It's breathing space, and as Ella and two of the deckhands have gone with the guests, the atmosphere aboard relaxes.

'Four hours of calm,' says Brandy to Annie. 'Four hours to chill, girl.'

Brandy isn't slacking; breakfast has been cleared away, the endless glasses they've been supplying to the guests are cleaned and dried, and there's no table to set for lunch.

However, doing nothing doesn't sit quite right with Annie. She's sure there's always something to be done on a yacht this size, so she leaves Brandy in the crew mess and wanders through *Ananke*, running a critical eye in each room. Guests' cabins haven't been used long enough for the beds to need to be changed, the bars are fully stocked and the floors are freshly vacuumed.

On the top deck, she finds Cat, arguing with a man she's yet to meet.

'Hey, Cat,' she says, and nods to the stranger, awaiting an introduction.

When none is forthcoming, Annie sticks her hand out. 'I'm Annie, the new third stewardess.'

'Sid, chief engineer,' he says. His eyes, dark with irritation, light up as he's introduced to Annie.

Beside him, Cat mutters something under her breath that Annie doesn't hear. In response, Sid glares at Cat before stalking away, dipping his head as he slips back inside the interior of the boat.

'I just came to see if you need any help with anything,' says Annie. 'Interior is all good.'

Cat is still scowling, but at Annie's words she lunges forwards and grips her hand.

'I think the anchor is twisted,' she says, her voice full of angst. 'I left it, I didn't watch it and I think we spun around while we've been docked. Danny's off at the beach, and Sid won't help me. I really don't want to tell Captain that I fucked up.'

'Why won't Sid help you?' asks Annie. 'I thought he was the chief engineer?'

'He is, that's the problem. It's not a mechanical issue, therefore not his domain.' Cat turns and spits her frustration over the side. 'That's why we call him Slopy Sid because he's lazy as hell!'

'I thought everyone pitched in on board,' says Annie. 'If he's so lazy, why doesn't he get the boot?'

Cat smirks. 'Because he's Captain's brother. Family ties, and all that crap.'

Annie nods, understanding now. She peers over the side. 'Surely it's just a case of doing a dive, untangling the rope?'

Cat rubs at her jaw. 'That's what I need to do.'

Annie frowns. 'You don't like diving?'

'I love it! But I'm on antibiotics for an ear infection; I'm under strict orders to stay out of the water.' Cat joins Annie in peering over the railing. 'But nobody is here; nobody will see me, right?'

Annie shakes her head. 'Give me ten minutes to get changed. I'll go down there.'

Cat stares in astonishment. 'You'd do that? I mean, for me?' Her glee turns doubtful. 'Can you even dive?'

Annie laughs. 'Like a mermaid, I've been told. I just need to get a costume on.'

Cat grabs her arm. 'You'll need a suit; you can use mine.'

In the wetsuit, Annie sits on the platform and prepares to topple off the side. She's discarded the air tank for now, sure that in such a short space of time she won't need it. Excitement surges in her, like the waves she's about to fall into. This is it; this is the adventure she's been craving. Not only diving, which she loves and is naturally good at, but this sense of camaraderie, teamwork, helping a colleague in need.

A *friend* in need…?

And she's not doing anything wrong. She's been told she can take a dip when the guests are off the yacht. If Captain comes down to the deck, that is simply what she's doing.

Annie takes a deep breath and lets herself fall backwards.

It's a different world down here, underneath the ocean. There is no noise, no sound at all except the water rushing in her ears. It's crystal clear, tiny shoals of razorfish, sea breams and red mullets rushing past her.

But she's not here for the aquatic life, she reminds herself, as she turns in the water and heads towards the anchor ropes.

The port-side chain has twisted, she sees, opening her eyes wide underwater and peering through the bubbles. Not badly snarled up, just a snag, she sees thankfully. She grabs it with one hand, yanks at it roughly, and lets out a hiss of joy that emerges as bubbles as it frees itself.

She points her feet and rises slowly to the surface, emerging from the water at the bow.

Cat is already cheering, spinning round and whooping.

Annie laughs and shushes her.

Cat runs to the platform and hauls Annie out of the water, enveloping her in a hug.

'You're a freaking legend, Ashley,' she says. 'I owe you one.'

Annie peels the suit off, laying it out to dry in the sun on the deck. 'I enjoyed it,' she says truthfully.

Cat claps her on the back. 'Ella wants to be careful; we'll poach you and use you on the deck team.'

Annie preens under the compliment. 'Thanks, Cat, but it was no problem. You'd better keep watch; they'll be coming back in a while and I'm going to get dried off.'

With one last grateful hug, Cat has bounded away.

Annie watches her go.

This is what teamwork is, she thinks. Helping another human. Doing it for nothing in return, just because you can, just because it feels good to assist another.

Sid wanders past, all smiles but no speech. Annie gives him a little wave. He averts his eyes, blushes as he dips his head and scuttles back inside his engine room.

He's shy, she thinks. And he kind of reminds her of Tobias, uncertain of himself, almost bashful.

She's told Cat she was going to her cabin, but she sits down on the deck and looks out over the sea, wanting to appreciate the moment. So far, today has been a good day.

She turns around, checking out the sandy cove that they're anchored near to. Palm trees, white sand, blue water. The beach is deserted.

Annie shivers. There's nobody in sight, so why does it feel like someone's watching her?

Cautiously, Annie leans her head around the side and stares down the deck and over at the beach.

There is nobody there.

Paranoia.

Annie laughs at herself, but the sound is uneasy to her own ears.

–

When the guests are ferried back on the tender, carnage ensues once more.

To Annie, it's simply a busy dinner service. 'Carnage' is the word used by Chef Luca, his curses the song of the galley, Ella's eyerolls keeping a beat in time to his tune.

Annie loves it.

When she takes a ten-minute break between courses in the crew mess, Captain Carly passes by.

'How're you doing, Ashley?' she asks.

Annie swallows past the name thrust upon her and beams. 'Good, thanks.'

Captain speaks with her hands a lot, Annie has noticed. She's had little to do with her so far but from what she's gleaned, Carly is straight-talking, no-nonsense and likes to speak in the third person about herself.

'Captain saw you helping Cat, earlier, with the anchor,' she says.

Annie feels herself redden. Captain wasn't supposed to know – nobody was!

She says nothing.

Carly wags a finger at her. 'Captain knows everything. Captain watches everything. But don't worry, I like it, the teamwork. And I saw you; you were good in the water.'

Annie smiles shyly. 'I really love it out there; I feel… at home in the ocean.'

Captain raises her eyebrows. 'You must have been training for a long while to dive like that?'

Annie smiles politely. It's not the case at all. Once, she was placed in a foster home where activities were the plan of each day. Ambition and goals were encouraged, and the family had the money to test the potential and enjoyment of all the kids they took in.

That was where Annie discovered she loved the water.

Annie loses herself in a daydream, remembering that short time she'd spent there. For a while, it seemed like the Havershams might become more than a temporary family.

Annie began to do the one thing that Robyn had always told her was the most dangerous of all.

Annie began to hope.

It all fell flat, though, after Robyn had been allowed to come and visit her one weekend. Soon after, Annie was back in the group home full time. The Havershams' contact had become a lot less after that, until it tailed off altogether.

After that, swimming became just an occasional treat at the local baths.

'I didn't get much chance to get in the water, but I'm hoping that might change here,' Annie says.

Captain reaches out her expressive hands and pats the table in front of Annie. 'It will,' she says with a wink. 'Just keep it up, what you're doing.' Another wink, another pat. 'Captain's happy.'

Carly's words are a lift. A boost, that whatever Annie's doing, so far, is a good job.

She just needs to stick at it. Keep to her high standards, and then, this could be a gig for the whole season. From what she's seen so far, this industry's employees mostly rely on connections and word-of-mouth recommendations. It's a chain reaction. After all, she did a good job on *Siren*, and Pippa's endorsement has brought her here.

As she reflects on the conversation, she remembers Captain's words. *Captain watches everything.* The relief is like a flood, covering her body.

That feeling of being watched earlier, the paranoia that hit. It wasn't a danger signal; it was just the captain, keeping an eye on her, and, no doubt, all her crew.

A darkness descends quickly, smothering the joy that the captain's conversation brought. Annie still hasn't heard from Robyn.

While she's on her break, she heads down to the cabin she shares with Cat and reaches for her phone.

It's still switched on silent, has been all morning as she's not sure of the protocol of having a mobile on her while she's working.

There is a single message waiting for her, from Robyn.

> You look like you're having a great time.

Filled with relief that Robyn is okay, Annie falls back on her bed and holds her phone to her chest.

Moments later, she's freshened up in the tiny bathroom and is running back up the stairs to find out what Ella wants from her next.

'Walk-through,' says Ella. 'Check all the exterior; if you pass the guests, ask if they need anything.'

Annie does as she's told, smiling politely when she comes across the family, who are scattered throughout the yacht. They stare at her with blank eyes, like she's a ghost, or a minor irritation. With their hands already full with cocktails and champagne, they wave her away.

They've left a trail of debris in the wake of the route they've taken. Towels lying on the damp deck, jackets and bags flung down haphazardly, phones and laptops on a sun lounger. Annie folds, tidies, places the electronics out of the sun, wondering when the last time was – if ever – any member of this family ever had to pick up after themselves.

She doesn't mind, though. She thinks of the wage that will be incoming, repeat bookings, a whole season spent earning. A pot of money that will go towards a deposit for a little place to rent for the two of them. A bed each. That's all Annie wants, the chance to give Robyn a proper bed like the one Annie is currently enjoying.

As Annie approaches the port side that overlooks the beach, the back of her neck prickles once more. She straightens up, stares around her, sees nothing and nobody. But there's a very real feeling of eyes that are not just casually observing her but *searing* into her.

She spins around in a full circle, scanning the decks and the horizon.

She thinks of those back in the ferries, Ashley Mercer, the *real* one, on the hunt for what was stolen from her. Those who were with Ashley, people who protect their own. Tobias, who simmered with distaste the last time he saw her, his fury and that of his family probably heightened now they've lost their taverna, even though it was nothing to do with Annie.

Tobias knows her name. Her *real* name. He has ties with the yachties; would any of them have mentioned her, told him that Ashley Mercer, aka the hero of the hour, had been the one who had the idea of dragging the boats' hoses up to his place? Would they have pointed her out in the crowd, when all the helpers had sat among the aftermath of the fire, gulping down the water that grateful restaurateurs had handed out?

She imagines him, confused at the fact they're calling her Ashley.

The anger of his father, turning his scathing glare on his own son, who had been taken in with his trusting nature by a girl that, as far as he was concerned, had given him a false name.

Despite the hot Greek sun, a violent shudder wracks Annie's body.

The feeling of being watched lies hot and heavy on her skin.

Breathing quick like she's run a mile, Annie ducks into the interior of *Ananke*.

In the narrow hallway, she leans her head against the cool wall and puts a hand on her chest to still her thundering heart.

3

They are not in the marina any more. Who could have followed *Ananke*'s route out here to the open sea? It is a ridiculous notion, yet, still, Annie knows there were eyes on her when she was on deck.

Would anyone on board know where *Ananke* was heading and preparing to anchor? Could it be as simple as someone back in the marina going into the offices and agencies on the dock and asking for the yacht's route? Has Ashley's passport usage been logged back on land, lying in a logbook somewhere for all and sundry to view? Is Ashley, or her pals, after her now?

But it wouldn't make sense. Why not just report the passport as stolen and point the authorities in Annie's direction?

But she knows the answer. People like Ashley, the same as Annie and Robyn and all the people residing in the ferries, don't go to the police.

Or is whoever is watching Annie getting their intel from somebody on *Ananke*? Is anyone even watching her?

But that knowledge of being watched was exactly that. A knowledge.

How can she ask someone without sounding weird? She can rephrase it, maybe. Ask Ella or even the captain if the routes that *Ananke* takes each charter are planned out beforehand and if they're listed anywhere.

Yes, she thinks. That doesn't sound too odd. It's just a simple query about the procedures and protocols of this industry. Annie is a beginner; she's full of questions – it's normal.

Isn't it?

Annie wishes she had someone else to confide in. Her gaze lands on Cat's messy bunk. Her roommate seems great, but she doesn't know her well enough yet to know if she is a trustworthy keeper of secrets.

The same goes for all the crew.

All the people she's encountered.

There has never been anyone else before.

Just Robyn…

She thinks of messaging Robyn, but she knows her friend. Robyn would become inflamed with fury. Annie can see her now, stalking through the engine room, flinging accusations, causing enough of a stir that the gatekeeper might kick her off.

No. Her friend has a spot to sleep, one that's in high demand, even though it's nothing like Annie's comfortable bunk.

Annie won't jeopardise that.

This thing, if it even is a thing, she will have to work out on her own.

—

'Do the guests know where they're going before they come on board?'

They are nearing the end of the dinner service, the rush and panic is winding down, and for the first time all evening the crew can slow down and catch their breath.

Brandy, on the early shift, has already been sent down for the night, as has Cat. In the galley, it's just Ella and Annie, and Luca, wielding his cloth as he begins the big clear-up.

'How do you mean?' Ella is distracted, peering at the current guests' preference sheets, checking the following day's weather, calling out at intervals to Luca what stock they'll need from the provisioner in the morning.

'I mean, are the activities planned out beforehand? Like, when did we decide to anchor in this particular cove?' Annie bites her lip, wondering if her question sounds totally foolish.

'No. Captain decides pretty much last minute, depending on the weather. That gnarly weather from a few days ago is still in the area. Cap knows this inlet is sheltered; it's her go-to.' Ella barks out a laugh. 'Her port in a storm.'

Annie smiles politely. 'So she doesn't stick to the same route, the same places to drop the anchor? What if people wanted to know where *Ananke* was? Like, if they had to make contact in an emergency?'

Ella looks at her strangely. 'Officials would see the radar. They can always radio the yacht.'

'And nothing is laid out in plans before the charter?'

'No. Why would they be? There are thousands of islands in Greece; only a couple of hundred are inhabited. Captain picks and chooses, depending on tides, weather.' She looks at Annie curiously. 'Why do you ask?'

Annie fixes a bright smile. 'I'm just wondering.'

'She wants to learn!' shouts Luca from the walk-in fridge. 'She's not bored and jaded with this life.'

Ella dips her head. 'Give it a couple of seasons.'

It's a good opener to her next tentative question. 'So… do I get to stay, on *Ananke*, for the rest of the season?' She holds her breath.

But Ella is distracted now, swearing quietly over something missing from their provisions. The window of opportunity has come and gone, oh-so-brief.

'Carry on the way you have, you'll be fine,' Ella says, pulling the list off the wall and marching to corner Luca, still in the fridge. 'This charter is your trial run,' she yells over her shoulder, as the fridge door closes behind them.

Trial run.

One more full day to go.

Then she'll be in.

Or she'll be out.

—

There is something special about crawling up to her top bunk at the end of a long day. The cabin is dark, peaceful; the bottom bunk is thankfully Luca-free. Cat is sleeping, dead to the world. Though she's exhausted after a hard day's graft, Annie is far from sleepy.

She wishes she'd brought a book on board, something to make her eyes as tired as her body. But after tomorrow they'll be back in port: she can go to town; she can buy a book or even two or three with the tips she's made so far.

She tells herself she is safe here. There is nobody looking through her porthole. There is likely nobody observing her from outside either, from the land that they've docked close to. Ashley Mercer is not stalking her. Tobias and his father are not either.

It's just that old paranoia, she tells herself. Muscle memory from the arduous journey here, hiding from officials, melting into crowds and queues that neither of them had any right to be in.

Annie screws her eyes closed, praying for sleep to come.

—

The final day of the charter dawns grey, with hard pellets of rain, and swollen, low-hanging clouds. The storm that Ella mentioned, coming back for a second go.

Annie did sleep, but apprehension has taken root and remains upon waking, a sense of unease that she's sure is more than the weather outside.

Today, she will learn if her trial charter was successful, and if she's got a job on *Ananke* for the next few months.

She attempts to dare to be a little confident. Ella and the captain and the rest of the crew haven't had any problems with either her work ethic or her attitude. The only problem that could arise is one of formality.

And does she really want to spend her first charter season – if she's successful in getting the job – under a cloud of anxiety at getting caught in a big, fat lie? More than just a fib. *Identity theft.*

No.

Annie wants to be Annie.

She wants to look forwards, not back over her shoulder. Wondering who is onto her, watching, plotting their vengeance.

It might mean the end of her role on *Ananke*, but at least now she knows she can do this job, she knows she loves it and she knows she's found her tribe in folk such as those on this yacht and *Siren*.

She's going to do this properly. She will return to Athens Marina, go back over that awful side that is so grey and dreary. She will track down Ashley Mercer and give her back her passport. She will explain to Robyn that she wants to do this properly, *legally*. Then she will catch up with Ella, explain the whole situation to her. She'll leave nothing out; she'll be honest and truthful. And maybe, just maybe, Ella will find a way for her to stay on board as her true self.

—

At noon, Doctor, Mrs Olsen and their various scowling offspring bid them adieu. Mrs Olsen hands a fat envelope over to Captain and thanks them for their attentiveness in a cool, mechanical voice. Her eyes are concealed behind oversized, black shades. She gives them all a pinched smile in turn, tucks her hand into the doctor's arm, and sashays off the boat.

At the after-charter round-up, Annie stands in the background and accepts her tip envelope with quiet gratitude. At the end of the meeting, as seems to be the norm after the guests' departure, Ella cracks open the champagne and passes a glass round to everyone, apart from Captain Carly, who toasts them with orange juice.

'I want to thank Ashley for joining our little family, and for fitting in and stepping up. It feels like you've been with us a lifetime, Ash,' says Cat, raising her glass. 'Here's to my roomie!'

Annie hopes they think the blush staining her face is one of embarrassment for being the centre of attention, rather than the mortification she feels at the lie that is her name and her life.

Will Cat still be so jubilant, so friendly, once Annie confesses that she's been living a lie?

Ever the optimist, she hopes so.

'Clean up, top to bottom, aim to be finished at three.' Ella, having drained her bubbly, claps her hands at her interior team. 'We've got the night off, and we'll start work tomorrow at ten. New charter starts the day after.'

Annie drifts away, down to the now-empty guest cabins, grateful she's going to be working alone for the next few hours. Now that she's decided on what to do, she wants it to be over and done with.

She cleans in record time, stripping the beds, shoving it all in the laundry, wiping down all the maple with the polish, scrubbing away the fingerprints and smears from the light switches and wardrobe doors.

It's nearing 3 o'clock when Ella comes down to the master suite to find her.

'Finish up,' she says. 'We're done for the day; anything else can wait until tomorrow. We're heading to the beach bar now, then dinner, drinks. You're coming, right?'

Annie takes a deep breath. How easy it would be to say yes, to follow the girls to the beach, to have dinner, to return to *Ananke* without tracking down Ashley, without giving her carefully prepared speech to Robyn, without confessing to Ella.

But there are other worries that lie down there, in the marina. Ashley, whose passport Annie is currently using, running into her before Annie has had a chance to return the girl's identification. Robyn, who wouldn't fit in with Ella and her gang *at all*. Tobias and his angry dad, casting scathing, furious looks at the girl who let her friend rip off their home and then fled.

'I've got some things to do; I'll try and meet you after dinner,' she lies.

'Sure,' Ella says. 'I'll text and let you know where we end up. I'll see you later.'

Once Ella has left, Annie pulls out her own phone. No further texts from Robyn. The blank screen is mocking, and it fills her with worry for her friend.

–

The rain has turned torrential when she makes her way off *Ananke*. She's looking at the raincoats hung neatly on the pegs in the crew mess, wondering if she can borrow one. She is sure they were there for the whole crew to use but doesn't want to assume. She takes one anyway, knowing that she won't leave her job and new life without handing it back to Ella. Knowing that by having the item, she will have to face her boss and whatever consequences follow.

It is only when she heads along the deck, coat over her arm, that she hears the captain's low tone coming from the engine room.

The door is ajar and she knocks tentatively, wondering who else is in there. Pushing it open, she peers inside.

Sid, or Slopy, as Cat refers to him. She remembers Cat's words, that he's lazy, that Captain is obliged to keep him on because they're siblings. Annie can identify with that sense of duty.

'Sorry to bother you.' Annie holds up the mac. 'Is it okay to borrow this?'

'Of course.' Captain spreads her hands expansively. 'Are you heading out in this?'

'Just for a while, then I'm meeting the others.' Annie wonders whether to test the boundaries on Captain for a confirmation on her employment status. It's not like her to be pushy, but she really wants to know where she stands. She holds herself up straight, injects a little of Robyn into her stance. 'I'm hoping Ella will have some good news for me later, that I can stay for the rest of the season.'

Captain gives her a thumbs up. 'Good luck,' she says, before sweeping past Annie and heading towards the bridge.

Annie pauses in the doorway, unsure if she should be disappointed or not. She'd thought the decision to keep her on would be up to Captain, but seemingly the ball lies in Ella's court.

Oh well.

It doesn't change anything, anyway. She still wants to be herself, *Annie*. Whether it is on *Ananke* or not.

'Hey.' Sid's voice comes out of the gloom. Annie turns away from the door to face him.

'All right, Sid?' she greets him.

He moves forwards, mobile phone in hand, pointed at one of his computer screens.

'I've got a technical issue, or it might need a new screen.' He shrugs. 'Pain in the ass, these things.'

'Will we have to stay in dock to get it repaired?' Annie asks politely.

'Nah, don't worry, it'll be a quick fix once I figure out the problem,' Sid replies. 'I'm sending a video to a mate on land, hoping he can advise me.' He jiggles the phone in his hand. She sees now he is recording the screen.

Or he was, but now it is pointing at her. She gives an awkward smile that she's sure comes off as a grimace.

There is a strange moment of silence before he speaks again. This time, his words are tentative. 'I… I really like you, Ashley,' he says.

She feels a jolt at his words. Attempted come-ons are always awkward for her, and this is definitely unwanted. However, Sid seems like a spare part on this yacht. He doesn't seem to mix with anyone. And he is the captain's brother. Could he make things difficult for her? For her onward journey? Is this going to be one of those awful scenarios where she is supposed to offer herself to him to keep her place on this boat? A casting couch situation.

She feels her face burning as she searches for the right words. 'I really like everyone on *Ananke*. You've all been so welcoming,' she says lightly.

'Can I take you to dinner, next time we dock?' He blurts the words out, almost before she's finished talking.

Before she can think of a gentle let-down, Sid pushes on. 'I know a great place. You know the plaza, where the ferries are docked on the other side? They have some cute little cafes over there. It's not fancy or anything, but...'

It is all she needs to hear for her to no longer care about hurting his feelings. 'No,' she says. 'I... I don't go over that side of the marina. Not any more.'

Not after tonight, she adds silently.

'Oh,' he says. 'It's really not bad. I know—'

'No!' Ashley's voice is sharper than she's ever heard herself. She doesn't want to be a bitch to him, it's not in her nature to be that way towards anyone, but just the thought of it, of going over to that awful side of the marina, next to the ferry that was her temporary home... Where Ashley is. Where Ashley's friends are. Possibly running into Tobias and his awful father. Annie shudders. Any of them could call her by her real name. To have that happen, in front of Sid...

She blinks slowly. Unless Sid already knows that could happen. Unless that is what Sid is banking on...

Has it been him, knowing her truth all along? Watching her? She takes a deep breath. 'Please don't mention that place again.'

He makes no reply. Annie wants to say more but can think of nothing. She turns back to the door, yanks it open and hurries out into the rain.

The marina is almost deserted, nobody lurking, she concludes, as she furtively looks around for anyone who looks like they might be watching her.

Waiting for her...

She turns back to *Ananke*, fully expecting to see Sid on the stern, observing her, but there's nobody there either.

She pulls up the hood on her borrowed mac, puts her head down and makes her way towards the plaza.

Under the cover of the place that borders the rich and the homeless, Annie feels like she's entered a different world. How quickly one gets used to the opulent life, she muses, as she heads through the shelter to the top of the stairs that look down at the desolate ferries.

She can see *Ocean Song*, still in the harbour, still nestled among all the other ones that are not in service. It lifts her spirits slightly, and she knows in her bones she's doing the right thing. Ashley Mercer will still be there, still bedding down in the engine room. She might not even have realised her passport is missing, and Annie can just say she found it on the floor.

She starts the long trek down the concrete steps.

The time has come to start making things right.

—

The engine room is freezing, and Annie wonders if it was this cold when she was sleeping in there. The green lights are not on yet, it's still too early, and there are only a handful of people scattered around the floor.

Robyn isn't here. There's no evidence that she is even still sleeping down here, but it doesn't mean she's not. Robyn would pack her meagre belongings up each morning and either stash them somewhere safe or carry them with her.

Annie does a loop of the room, peering behind the pipes, whispering an apology when she comes across a sleeping person.

Back to the entrance door, and there's no sign of Ashley Mercer.

Annie does another lap, this time asking each person if they know Ashley, if they've seen her.

Dull, heavy-lidded eyes stare back at her. Annie suppresses a shudder. Did she ever look like that? So... lost?

'Haven't seen her for five days.' The only answer she gets is from the dreadlocked man who seems to act as some sort of gatekeeper for *Ocean Song*.

She's about to move on, when he stands up, towering above her. 'Have *you* seen her?'

Annie can't decide if his tone is menacing or not, and she shakes her head.

'How do you know her?' he demands as she turns to resume her journey round the room.

Annie feels caught. She doesn't want to confess her sin to this guy. He seems to know Ashley, seems to... care?

Next to him, a pile of blankets moves, a pale, white hand emerges, a face tucked into the material to stifle a cough. Another young woman, Annie sees. One she doesn't recall from the last time she was on this boat.

Despair catches at her. Is there no end to the number of young, seemingly lost residents of this engine room?

The girl folds into herself. Her breathing is shallow and ragged, trailing off into a wheeze.

Annie looks at the man, who is still awaiting an answer from her.

'Is she okay?' she asks him, gesturing to the girl on the floor.

As if only just realising his companion's plight, he leans down and rifles through his filthy bag.

'She's asthmatic,' he says, glaring as though it's Annie's fault. 'And this is getting low.' He holds up a blue inhaler, shakes it in Annie's face as though to prove it's practically running on empty.

Annie backs up a step, the vision of that inhaler triggering a long-buried memory that she's fought so far to the back of her mind it's almost entirely blacked out.

'Sit her upright,' she instructs the man. 'Try and get her a hot drink with caffeine.' She looks around the engine room, only now noticing the dust motes floating in the gloom, and the damp air down here. 'She'll be better off upstairs, in the air.'

His expression softens ever so slightly.

'Thanks... uh...?'

'Annie.' As soon as she introduces herself, she wishes she could take it back. Right now, it's best to stay as anonymous as possible. But it's as though he barely heard her. This guy has other things on his mind.

As Annie goes on her way she glances back, sees him hauling his friend up, her thin arms around his neck, his grunts of effort as he helps her towards the door.

She sees the inhaler poking out of his back pocket. Annie closes her eyes, her own breathing difficult now, and lets herself remember.

–

Stefan was his name. Stefan Archer. He lived in a huge house, and his mother was on the board of directors for the children's home. He came along sometimes, when they held fetes and occasionally on day trips when the funds were in a good place.

He was an awful child. In fact, she imagines that the offspring of the Olsens – the guests who just left *Ananke* – were much like him growing up. A sense of entitlement, a knowledge of security from his family, and his parents' intact marriage, and their money and their warmth and never-ending flow of food available, that gave him not compassion, the way his mother seemed to have, but something almost like empowerment.

He liked to taunt the kids at the home, a classic bully, snide remarks, open-palmed slaps and a bitterly twisted, red mouth.

Like Tobias, like Sid, like so many before and since, Stefan made a beeline for Annie.

Annie, being who she was, tried to understand his behaviour. 'I think he craves his mother's attention,' she explained to Robyn. 'His mum is always here, with us. I think he wants her to himself but doesn't know how to tell her.'

Robyn's fists clenched until her knuckles were ice white. 'He's just an arsehole,' spat Robyn.

Annie stared at her friend. Mostly people were not just arseholes. There were reasons for their shadowy sides, usually deep-rooted in their past.

Annie shrugged and said that it didn't matter. They were fifteen years old. Their dream of escape was already birthed, Robyn leading the plotting and planning. Time would pass. One day, she wouldn't have to see Stefan ever again.

Carnival time, the summer they turned sixteen. Stefan was still around, worse than ever. Somehow, he'd failed to grow, to fill out and shoot up like the rest of the kids that he'd known for years. It belittled him even more, and while his stature remained minuscule, his rage seemed to expand.

They had hay bales at the carnival, a yearly event that stretched through the garden of the children's home, across the road, which was closed off for the event, and along the neighbouring shop fronts. It was for the little kiddies, really, but Annie enjoyed the almost holiday feeling that it conjured in both residents and staff alike.

Stefan was there, recruiting his little gang of hangers-on, kids that would rather join him than be beaten by him. Annie stayed out of range, not for her own safety, but more so that Robyn didn't flip her lid and be subsequently punished by being sent inside.

The inevitable happened, though; of course it did. Lately, Annie had thought that he only went for her because of Robyn's reaction.

He sidled up to Annie, sitting upon a hay bale with some of the youngsters. Watching his approach, she sent the kiddies away to the food stalls, and braced herself.

He said nothing. His hands did the talking, pale, bony fingers lingering on her bare legs, face leaning close to hers, eyes never meeting her own.

Annie pulled away, her senses heightened. This was different. Even though Stefan looked like a boy, he wasn't. He was feeling adult things, and wanting to try them out, regardless of whether someone was willing or not.

Then Robyn was there, grabbing him by his neck, her fury lending her a strength far greater than Stefan's. She shoved his face into the hay bale and held him there.

For too long.

Far too long.

When does did defence become attack?

Annie used both her arms to pull Robyn away. Finally, Robyn let go and Stefan emerged, sneezing, wheezing, batting both girls blindly away.

Stefan staggered away. Annie groped for Robyn's hand. Now, even at sixteen, they took comfort in the physical from each other, but Robyn shook Annie off, put her closed fists in her pockets and sauntered away.

She heard him before she saw the crowd gathered around him. A rattle, snake-like, his face, white and sweating, his lips blue. His mother stood over him, roughly patting down her son, pulling his pockets inside out before her own hands went into her hair, pulling at the roots before she turned to those concerned people standing around her.

'Help him!' she shrieked, so far removed from her normal calm, warm exterior that Annie barely recognised her.

'They can't find his inhaler,' said a boy, one of Stefan's recruited friends.

Annie stared at his face, his horror written there for all to see. Paramedics fought their way through the stalls and took him away, oxygen mask over his face. Chest barely moving now, skin as grey as a winter sky.

The party was over. The kids drifted around in two packs. One team secretly pleased but aware enough not to show it. The other, traumatised, and quiet, the horrific scene bringing back memories of who they'd lost, and how they ended up here.

An update later, from grave and serious staff. *Alive, but very poorly*, the outcome softened for their wide-eyed and scared audience.

Later, still stinging from the turn of events, Annie had crawled into Robyn's bed.

'I know he was awful, but nobody deserves that,' she whispered into the darkness.

Robyn, her face ghost white, agreed. 'I know,' she said. She sounded shaken, her voice trembling, her fingers twisting in the sheets.

Mrs Archer didn't come around so much after that.

The memory always ended there, in the bed they often shared. Now, in the wake of the same rattle but from a different source, Annie lets herself remember it fully.

The next morning, Robyn was up as soon as the curtain that was pulled across their front door was opened, the clatter of the rings that held the heavy drape in place Robyn's own alarm.

Annie lay in the bed, throwing the covers off, the day already warm. She reached behind her to flip the pillow to the cool side, flinching as something went flying past her face to land on the floor beside the bed.

She peered over the side, staring for what felt like an eternity at the blue inhaler that lay on the carpet.

She buried it deep in the bin outside the front door and resolved never to think of her discovery again.

4

She passes the engine room girl later, sitting on the dock, head tipped back, the drizzling rain still ongoing, but the air fresher because of it. She looks better, thinks Annie, her cheeks pinker and her chest rising and falling in a more natural motion.

Annie smiles at her as she walks past.

'Hey, you were asking about Ashley.' The girl's voice is a hoarse whisper, and Annie moves closer to her.

'Yes,' she says, 'do you know her?'

'She's gone.' The girl clears her throat then coughs, leans over to catch her breath. 'She moved on without us, without even saying goodbye.'

Annie crosses her arms across her chest, visions of this girl, or her male friend, visiting *Ananke*, asking questions about their missing one, Ashley Mercer, and the confusion on Ella and Cat and Captain's face as they look at the girl that they believe to be Ashley Mercer.

Annie backs away from the girl. That wouldn't happen. The homeless move on all the time. It's a knowledge, for any of them, all of them, to not be surprised when someone ups and leaves, surely?

'I've got to go,' Annie says. 'I'm glad you're feeling better.'

Without waiting for a reply, she turns on her heel and hurries off the boat, away from *Ocean Song*, leaving her past behind her.

She finds Robyn, eventually.

They meet at the bottom of the plaza, on the bad side of the concrete steps.

The rain has slowed to a drizzle. Temporary, probably, and Annie stands in her own shirt, the jacket that bears the name of *Ananke* folded up as small as possible and stowed away in her bag.

'Have you seen Ashley?' Annie asks.

'Who?' Robyn flicks her wet hair out of her face. It makes a slapping sound as it hits the back of her coat.

'Never mind. Look, I got you some money.' Annie digs in her bag, pulls out the envelope that contains the two-thousand-euro tip that she got on *Ananke* and passes it to Robyn.

Robyn takes it, whispers a thank you, and puts it in her pocket without opening it.

Annie peruses her friend. Robyn looks grubby, sad and worn down. Annie's heart cracks a little. 'We're going to check you into a hotel,' she says decisively. 'I don't want you staying in that engine room for one more night.'

Robyn utters a laugh. 'Hark at you, a couple of nights on a floating palace and a simple roof and a space to sleep isn't good enough for you any more!'

Annie smiles, her tensions melt away a little and she draws Robyn close to her. 'I want to take care of you, for a change. Come on, let's find a place for you.'

Robyn draws away. 'I got stuff to do, but don't worry, I promise I'll find a nice place to kip for tonight.'

'Not just tonight,' Annie says in a rush, thinking on her feet now. 'Hopefully I've got a job for the season. With the money, we can get you a decent room, and in the daytime, you can go apartment hunting for us, okay?'

Robyn shrugs. 'If you like.'

Annie frowns. There's a scratch on Robyn's cheek. Two inches long, red, angry. Annie looks away, but the image remains. What happened? A scrap over territory? Over food? Over a spot on the floor where the number of bodies outweigh the space?

'You'll get a hotel, yes.' It's not a question. She takes Robyn's arm, making a mental note of the bed and breakfasts she's seen on her travels around the marina.

'Wait.' Robyn pulls her arm away. 'You're not staying with me?'

Annie shakes her head. 'I have to stay on board, if I've passed the trial successfully.' She glances over her shoulder at the bright lights of the square below. 'I have to go and meet my boss now, find out if it's good news.' It's not strictly true. She wants to continue her search for Ashley, for she's sure the girl couldn't have moved on far if Annie still has her passport. Then, once she's located her, she will make her confession to Ella. But somehow, after the trouble Robyn went through to get Annie the passport to a better life, she doesn't want to admit her intention to her friend.

'Whatever.' Robyn pulls her phone out of her bag and holds it up. 'I suppose if I'm in some fancy-nancy hotel, at least I can charge this up!'

Annie rolls her eyes, then, realising what she's done, she smothers her laughter at the thought that she's joined that club of Pippa and Ella.

'What are you giggling at?' asks Robyn as they head once more towards the stairs.

Annie shakes her head. 'Nothing. But yes, please keep your phone charged. Get a hotel, not just for a night. There's enough in that envelope to keep you going until I finish the next charter, then I'll bring more.' And, just in case Robyn doesn't get it, she takes her friend's hand. 'There's plenty of money in there, Robyn. You can *buy* things that you need. You don't need to steal anything any more, okay?'

'Whatever,' Robyn says again. She holds up the envelope. 'Cheers, Annie.'

'No worries.' Annie glances around, eager to be gone, almost desperate to be back on the safe side of the marina.

They part at the crest of the stairs. Robyn turns left, back to the ferry side, Annie pulling her hood up again as she heads back the way she came, relieved to be heading down the right-hand side, hating the fact that Robyn has to take the other path, hoping her friend heads inland to find a decent bed for the night.

Down the concrete steps, across the marina, her speed is gaining momentum, when she hears someone call her name. Not her real name. *Ashley*.

She jerks to a stop and looks over her shoulder. It's Roxy, from *Siren*.

She's up in the plaza and Annie starts to sweat. What is Roxy doing up there? She is probably just using it as a cut-through, but how long has she been there? Did she see the tip envelope that Annie handed over; is she wondering why she is giving her money away? Did she hear their conversation? Does it matter?

Roxy is ascending the steps now, coming back into the marina. Panic grips Annie's insides and twists them roughly.

She thinks back over her talk with Robyn. Words and sentences jump at her, spiking her with fear. Her asking Robyn, *Have you seen Ashley?* Telling Robyn, *You don't need to steal any more*.

And, worst of all, Robyn using her real name: *Annie*.

If Roxy heard anything, Annie doesn't want to face her questions.

Annie throws Roxy a wave, mimes tapping a watch. *I'm late*, she hopes the action conveys, and then she turns, and sprints across the still-damp marina, into the portion of this port that she is starting to think of as where she belongs.

She checks her phone, sees a new text message from Ella, informing her she's in Cotton, a bar and grill restaurant on the port.

Annie doesn't go there immediately. She makes her way around the marina, eyes darting this way and that, searching for any trace of the girl whose name Annie has borrowed.

Finally, she sits on a semi-circular seat beneath a palm tree. Behind her, the ruins of the taverna are her backdrop, the smell of long-lingering smoke still in the air. She shrinks into herself, ever mindful of the eyes of Tobias or his family on her.

She ignores the stench of the burned taverna and considers her options.

Options.

She wrinkles up her nose. 'Failings' would be more accurate.

Today she'd tasked herself with returning the passport to its rightful owner, and tracking down Ella and telling her the truth about herself, her name, and hoping against hope that *Ananke* would still welcome her.

Futile.

She takes Ashley's passport out of her bag and looks at the picture, purposefully smudged to conceal that the girl is not herself.

Annie's gut wrenches.

Today, she was going to give Ashley back her passport, but Ashley is no longer here. Ashley's friends haven't seen her.

Ashley is gone. She could be anywhere.

Tears are threatening again. This time, Annie lets them fall freely as she looks bitterly at the passport.

She can't give it back now because the owner is no longer around to accept it.

Where does that leave Annie? She can give up on a season on *Ananke* that could lead to another life that she's only envisaged in her wildest dreams. Or she could go back down the hill, find Ella in the bar, accept the position of the permanent job she's hopefully going to offer her.

She can resume her role of Ashley Mercer. If Roxy wasn't standing in the shadows eavesdropping, and was simply passing through, and if Annie can manage to evade this marina and its occupants' prying eyes as much as possible for the rest of the season, then there is a chance still to make this new life work.

A flicker of light dulls the ache.

She could *actually become* Ashley. After all, Annie Taylor's life so far has been pretty rubbish. Being Ashley would be a new start, the beginning of a whole different life. A break from all that has been before.

Annie shivers and closes the passport.

She'll live a life for the girl who this once belonged to. She will shed Annie Taylor like she's nothing more than an old skin. Every time she introduces herself as Ashley, it will be a quiet commemoration for the young woman who never got a chance like the one Annie has been given.

She is romanticising the situation. She knows that. It's what she does.

It makes things bearable.

Annie puts the passport back in her bag, slings it over her shoulder and, still with her head down and her hood up, she winds her way to Cotton. Annie scopes out the bar. It is packed and she knows from Ella that it is popular with the yachties. There is no sign of Roxy, though. Nobody in there from the ferries, no sign of Tobias or his parents.

Ella is on the terrace, along with Cat, who is sitting on Luca's lap. Brandy is dancing with Danny, the bosun, and in the corner, Sid the engineer is sitting, his chin on his chest, clearly dozing. She recalls their encounter from earlier and eyes him warily.

Annie sidles in next to Ella. 'Is he all right?' she asks, nodding towards Sid.

Ella raises her eyes. 'That's his usual stance; you'll get used to seeing him like that.'

Annie laughs. It feels good to laugh, to be joyous, to feel the way she does now she's here with her crew, rather than the lost and desolate wave of dread that she feels when she's over the other side, the ferry side.

'You will, right?' Ella asks suddenly.

'Huh?' Annie is confused.

'You will get used to him sleeping every-bloody-where, because you are staying, aren't you?'

Annie smiles shyly. 'If you'll have me,' she replies.

'Good!' Ella reaches across Annie for the large jug of sangria and pours it into two glasses. 'We'll toast, then, to *Ananke*'s newest crew member!'

Annie clinks her drink to Ella's. There are things she wants to ask, stuff that needs clearing up. Like, is it okay for her wages to go into a bank account that doesn't hold the name of Ashley Mercer? Like, are whatever checks they run on board over and done with now; is she in the clear? Although that last question is one she can never ask.

She doesn't ask anything, though. She wants to enjoy this moment, this celebration, like any normal person would.

Any person who is not a fugitive. Who doesn't have terrible secrets. Who doesn't fear the consequences of their true life being exposed.

'Here's to the rest of the season.' Annie lifts her glass again, as if hoping by doing another toast it will dispel the uncomfortable thoughts.

'Longer, if you want,' says Ella.

Annie looks at her inquisitively.

Ella takes a long sip of her cocktail. 'After the season's done, *Ananke* is sailing to Spain; they're doing a crossing over the Med. They keep a skeleton crew on board – I think Danny's going, maybe Luca. There's a place for a stewardess if you want.'

Annie gapes at her. To finish the season and then cruise off to Spain would mean there would be no chance of coming back to Athens Marina.

It will also mean leaving Robyn behind.

Impossible.

She's never done that. Never even contemplated it. Something needles at her conscience. She can't imagine ever doing that.

Can she?

'But… what happens once we get to Spain?' she demands.

'You pick up work there, another crossing back, or set yourself up for the next season and do it in the Med.' Ella shrugs. 'Nobody ever does a crossing and ends up without a job lined up.'

'Bloody hell.' Annie is amazed. 'But don't you want to do it, or Brandy?'

Ella shakes her head. 'I've got other plans. Brandy is going home. It's yours if you want it.'

'I do!' Annie gasps and claps her hand to her mouth. She hasn't thought about it, about what it would mean. Annie considers everything, always, and yet she's just made a split-second decision that will keep herself and Robyn apart.

Unless… unless there's a way to get Robyn to Spain, too…

'Good, that's settled then,' Ella says calmly.

Like it's no big deal, like she hasn't just changed the course of Annie's entire life.

In the lull of conversation, Annie thinks about it. Greece was never her goal. To be fair, it wasn't Robyn's either. Both were happy to just get out. Annie had always thought it a pipe dream, a madcap plan to get out that was just words, something that would never come to fruition. Greece had turned out to be the easiest route for two girls with neither passports nor money. Now she has the documentation that will allow her to cross borders on a yacht. She will end up in Spain; she will get work there. If they can get a passport for Robyn, or some way for her to follow, maybe even get her on a yacht like Annie, they could be set.

Forever.

She will really become Ashley Mercer. Annie Taylor will no longer exist.

'Thank you, Ella,' Annie says. 'But what about you? Brandy is going home, you said; are you, too?'

A dark cloud crosses Ella's face, as sudden and sharp as a rain shower. It takes her an age to reply. 'I don't know,' she says finally.

There is a chill in the air. Annie isn't sure if it is from the earlier storm, or something else. She lets out an involuntary shiver. She likes Ella, a lot, but doesn't feel she knows her well enough yet to enquire about her home life.

'Well, I'm really grateful for the chance to do the crossing,' Annie replies. 'I'm grateful for everything.'

Ella smiles, though it doesn't quite reach her eyes. 'Enough work talk, let's dance.'

Dance they do, on the terrace of Cotton, where the storm seems to have finally been chased away. Ella seems to loosen up.

Annie drinks more sangria than she really should, but for the first time she feels she can let go. She hasn't got to hold back, hasn't got to remain sober. She refuses to let her paranoia in, and she dances like she's not in the danger zone of the marina, as if nobody is watching her, as if she's got nothing to hide.

After what seems like hours of dancing and drinking, Annie spots Sid. He's awake, standing on the veranda, his eyes narrowed as his gaze follows her around the dance floor. Their eyes meet for a second, until Annie makes her excuses and slides out of his eyeline to the ladies' room.

When she emerges, Sid has vanished.

It is nearly 3 a.m. when they cluster together and make their way back to *Ananke*. As they walk across the marina, she realises it's just her, Cat, Luca and Ella who are left.

Cat falls back to walk alongside Annie.

'Ella told me you're officially one of us now.' Cat grabs her in a hug, breathing vodka fumes in her face. 'I'm so happy; you're just lovely.'

Annie squeezes her back. 'I'm really glad I'm here too.'

And she is.

She stands back and lets them all down the passerelle ahead of her. When the door closes behind her colleagues, she turns back to the railing, leans on it and looks over the port.

The huge square is emptying out now. In a few hours, it will be light, the time of day that, for Annie, brings safety along with sunrise.

And a few hours after that, they will be off the dock altogether, moving out into the Aegean Sea, away from Athens for a few days, far from the port and the ferry. Robyn is safe, ensconced in a hotel to enjoy a taste of a life that she's never had before.

The group has splintered once she goes inside. Ella has vanished, presumably gone off to bed. Only Luca and Cat remain in the crew mess. Their manner is altogether different than that of earlier. They are glaring at each other, Luca's face stony, Cat's livid. Too much alcohol, too many tensions. A lovers' quarrel.

Annie cuts through the atmosphere on her way to her cabin, murmuring a good night in her wake.

-

She rises early, filled with excitement at her first full day as an official stewardess. The next lot of charter guests are not arriving until 10 a.m., but there's clean-up to do. Technically, Annie hasn't got to report for work until 8 a.m., but she can't lie still in her bunk, the excitement nipping away at her feverishly.

At just gone 6 a.m., she showers and makes her way up to the deck with a black coffee.

The sunshine makes all the difference, she thinks, as she strolls the perimeter. Deck clean-up isn't her domain, but she checks all the cushions of the sun loungers as she passes them, pulling off the stained ones and folding them over her arm to take down to laundry.

As she approaches the stern, she hears voices, one sharp as a whip, unhappy, louder than Annie's ever heard it. The other voice sounds somewhat sleepy, sullen.

It is Captain Carly and her brother, Sid.

Annie stops in her tracks. She's almost upon them, but Captain isn't her normal cheery self and Annie doesn't want to stumble upon a private conversation.

She turns to backtrack the way she's come, but too late: the captain spots her.

'Hey, Ashley. What time did you guys get back last night?'

Annie pauses. Is 3 a.m. too late, according to the captain? She decides to answer truthfully; after all, she's new — if there is a curfew, nobody has told her about it.

'Three o'clock,' she says. 'Is that… is everything okay?'

Carly shakes her head, her mouth fixed in a thin, straight line. She gestures to Annie to follow her. Placing the cushion covers on the side, Annie duly treks down the passerelle after Captain.

'As you can see' — Captain gestures with both hands to the port side — 'everything is not okay.'

There is graffiti on the side of the beautiful *Ananke*! But it's not the vandalism that shocks Annie, it's the words in red spray paint.

ANNIE IS A LIAR

5

'Oh my God!' Annie covers her mouth with her hands. 'I... I'm so sorry.'

Carly glowers at her. 'It's not your fault, is it?' She narrows her eyes. 'Unless you're responsible for this.'

Ashley. My name is Ashley.

These people, the boss, her colleagues, her *friends*, they don't know that *she* is Annie.

Do they?

She thinks of Sid, last night, watching her. His seemingly out-of-the-blue invitation yesterday, to take her to the ferry side for dinner. She thinks of Tobias, his angry father, of the dreadlocked gatekeeper, of his asthmatic friend, of the girl whose identity Annie is flaunting like the prize that it is. Did they watch her last night; did they track her back to *Ananke*, watching with barely concealed envy at her escaping to the light side to resume a life that she's really not entitled to be living?

She recovers as quickly as she can, dropping her hands and turning to face the captain.

'Of course I'm not responsible, but I'll get right on to cleaning it up.' She leans forwards over the rail, touches the still-damp paint. 'The stuff the deck crew use on the teak after red wine has been spilled on it, that should do the trick.'

Carly seems to sag before her eyes. 'I really appreciate it. Look, I don't mean to snap. I'll wake the others, get them on deck. We've got guests coming in four hours; this *cannot be here.*'

Annie nods. 'I'll get right on it, Captain.'

She dodges past the captain, flying down the deck to the exterior supply cupboard. She grabs a bucket, rags, the acetone, soap and a scrubbing brush, and runs it all back to the stern.

Danny is there now, the bosun, bleary-eyed and scratching his head as he stares at the graffiti. Captain stands ramrod straight beside him.

'It wasn't here when we got back last night,' he tells the captain.

She shakes her head and storms back aboard. 'I can't look at it. This is our absolute priority. You think the Kilfoyles are going to be happy to pay thousands of euros to step onto a vandalised superyacht?'

'No, I promise you, Cap, it'll be like new in no time.' He holds out his hands and Annie passes him the bucket of supplies.

'It had better be.' Captain fixes them with a glare, looking from Danny to Annie.

Sid, Annie notices, has already sloped off somewhere.

Because he's ashamed of what he's done, perhaps?

Or because he had nothing to do with it?

'I'll help,' Annie tells Danny quietly. 'We'll get it fixed.'

Despite her proclamation of not being able to look at the paint that stains the side of the million-pound yacht, Captain comes out every fifteen minutes or so to inspect their progress.

Annie takes the hard brush and scrubs and scrapes until her arms are numb. She thought that despair might lend a hand to her work, but instead, a deep fear has descended upon her.

Annie twists her arm in circles to ease the growing ache and glances furtively around.

Is whoever's responsible for this watching her now?

Thankfully, *Ananke* and her crew will be out of this marina in a few hours, and they won't come back here for another few days at least.

Another thought occurs to her. She drops the brush and turns to Danny.

'The CCTV cameras, in the crew mess – can we see who did this?' She wants to take the words back as soon as they're out.

What if the vandal is caught on camera? What if Captain searches for whoever it was, sets the Greek police on them, and they lead the authorities back to Annie and her lies?

'No, it's live-stream only, not recorded.' Danny slams his rag into a bucket. There is anger in his motion. 'Beats me why on a piece of property worth as much as this they wouldn't have security.'

Annie agrees with him, but inside, she is relieved.

'It's looking better,' says a voice behind her.

Annie starts and turns to come face to face with the captain.

Carly's face is softer now, more like the captain that Annie is getting to know.

Annie stands back beside Danny and together they appraise their work.

'I'll buff it up,' decides Danny, slinging his rag in the bucket and heading off to the supply room. He turns halfway down the dock. 'Thanks for helping, Ashley. Exterior isn't your place, so I appreciate you stepping in.'

She nods at him. Normally, she'd glow under such praise, but the knowledge that the message and the attack was aimed at her has sent her mood spiralling.

'Yes, good job, Ashley.' Captain spreads her hands and gives her a half-smile. 'I was edgy before. Someone was supposed to be on night watch. Someone let me down.' She aims her words towards the closed door of the engine room, Sid behind it. 'Your captain is a fair captain. But she wonders if she's *too* fair. I'm wondering if I need to put a tracking app on my crew's phones to make sure they are where they need to be.' She speaks in her jovial tone, but Annie isn't sure if she's entirely joking.

'I can do a night watch; I'm happy to step in if you need it,' says Annie, desperate to make up for the mess she's inadvertently caused.

Carly lays a hand on her arm. 'You're all right.' Her eyes slide back to the room where her brother has stowed himself away. 'It's... difficult.' She shrugs. 'It's family, you know what I mean?'

Yes. Annie does. Even though Robyn isn't her blood, she's the only family Annie's ever had. The sense of responsibility, of covering for them, protecting them, of sometimes turning a blind eye.

Captain claps her hands. With that single motion she's back. Boss lady, leader, in charge.

Annie takes the hint. 'I'll do a final check-through; the guests will be here soon.'

Captain nods. 'Thank you,' she says.

With one lingering look at the closed engine room door, Carly walks back to the bridge, the opposite end of the boat to where her useless brother resides.

–

The Kilfoyles are a family of three.

Annie watches them as they make their way down the dock towards *Ananke*. She thinks of the previous charter with the Olsens – the aloof wife, the demanding siblings – and she crosses her fingers behind her back, hoping after the drama that's already taken place this morning that this family will be less work.

They've got their son with them, a smart-looking teenager, and Annie feels herself relaxing somewhat as he makes his way along the line of crew who are there to wait on him hand and foot for the next four days. He shakes each hand, pausing to listen to each name given to him. Beside Annie, Brandy introduces herself so quietly the lad asks her to repeat her name. Annie is impressed; some people, adults yet, would already be drifting on to the next person in line.

The father, Piers, is equally as polite, as is his wife, Nikki. They chat to Captain about *Ananke* and all her features, the various coves and islands they'd like to sail to, and the snorkelling opportunities.

Annie smiles to herself. This is a proper family. They're not going to drink the bar dry; they're going to go to bed at a respectable hour; they're here to see the wonders that these Greek islands have to offer.

While Ella shows them around the yacht, Annie goes to the bridge and looks at the map on the wall. She's memorised the places they want to go to; Hydra, Sifnos, Agistri are all islands 100 kilometres or more from the marina. They will anchor there; they probably won't come back to port for the whole charter.

It is as though a weight has been lifted off Annie's shoulders. She will be far away from any potential run-in with anyone on land long enough for them to—

To what? To move on, forget about Annie?

Regardless, it is four days of respite, so long as strange Sid keeps his distance, and Annie resolves not to think about it for this trip. It might mean staying on board whenever they do return to Athens, but after this next couple of months there will be Spain. That's what she needs to focus on. She needs to start thinking of a plan to get Robyn across the sea into another new country.

Glancing at the huge digital clock above the controls for the boat, she sees it is time to start setting for lunch.

In the galley, she finds the son of the charter guests, Ayton. He's at the workstation, grappling with a bunch of mint.

Annie doesn't know Chef Luca too well, but from what she's seen of him so far, he's snippy, moody and almost always on edge.

'Oh, hi,' she says to the boy. 'Are you okay, can I get you anything?' she asks, anxious to remove him from the galley before Chef discovers him in his domain.

'Leave him, he's my sous-chef today.' Luca emerges from the large walk-in fridge, kicking the door closed behind him. 'You set your table, young third stew, and leave us men to our work.'

'Oh!' Annie smiles, surprised by Chef's tone. He is jokey, for once, his stern words a pretence, she sees as he winks at Ayton. She addresses the young charter guest. 'What are you serving for lunch?'

'Lamb, we're making the mint sauce from scratch,' says the young boy. 'We'll be serving it with escabeche of vegetables, all locally sourced and sweet potatoes roasted in coconut oil.'

'Wow.' Annie is impressed. She leans close to him and in a mock whisper, asks, 'Can you make some extra so the crew can have it later?'

He looks back at her, equally as serious. 'Sneak me a beer at lunch and it's a deal.'

Annie laughs as Luca flicks his tea towel at her and she dashes, squealing, from the galley.

As she moves up to the top deck, she muses on the newest, youngest charter guest. Here is a young boy — an almost young man, really — who obviously has very rich parents. He doesn't have to work, probably will never have to, if his folks can afford a trip like this, but he seemingly has a passion for cooking. He has the knowledge, clearly. And he wants to construct this dish, rather than direct others.

What a difference from the previous charter guests' offspring.

What a difference from Stefan, whose mother was in a similar position of wealth, but who wanted to only prod and scare, mock and bully.

She hears laughter from the galley. It is bittersweet. Opportunities that come around, like the one she's been handed, are a whole world of riches in themselves.

The father, Piers, sits himself at the table as she builds the decoration around him. On the deck below, she can see his wife, lying on a lounger, a book held loosely in her hand.

Piers is working, laptop out, and for a moment she gets the feeling he's irritated.

At her?

She swallows back this newly discovered, ever-present paranoia. 'Can I get you a drink?' she asks as she puts the last of the cutlery in place.

He pushes his glasses to the top of his head. Without them, he doesn't seem to hold quite so much power. His eyes are small and tired-looking.

'I'll have a gin, straight up, no ice,' he says. 'Thanks.' He nods to his laptop. 'It doesn't stop, not even on holiday.'

She busies herself behind the bar on the top deck. 'I'm sure it will still be there tomorrow,' she says lightly, as she brings his drink to him.

He stares at her for a moment, then glances down to the next deck where his wife has just accepted a cocktail from Brandy.

He gives a small smile and shuts the lid of his laptop. 'You're right.' He picks up his glass and descends to the deck.

His wife gives an exclamation of unexpected delight, and Annie thinks she knows what this family is about. Him, slaving away of an evening, his wife, waiting… waiting… waiting for him to put down his work.

The charter guests are off the boat after lunch, bellies full of Ayton and Luca's lamb with all the trimmings.

It is the time to breathe again, to regroup, clear, tidy, prep for the next meal, the next cocktail hour, the next excursion.

The afternoon has been busy but perfect.

Then, just as the sun is starting to set, it all goes wrong again.

6

It starts with a bird on the top deck.

Danny was the first to see it, a black lump, feathers moving in the breeze, black beak tucked under a wing.

Annie heard the call over the radio, summoning everyone who was free to the upper deck to look at something.

'Dolphins?' Brandy, folding napkins in the crew mess, looks up hopefully.

'Really?' Annie is thrilled at the thought of seeing something one would only normally get to witness on a paid-for excursion.

'Come on!' Brandy throws the napkins down, grabs Annie's arm as they make their way hastily up to the top deck.

Ella and Cat burst through the door after them, excited at something new happening among the process of a usual working day.

'Oh,' Cat says. She's pushed past them all, the first to see it, and unsuccessfully she tries to turn and go back the way she came.

It's a crow, Annie sees. It's not moving. It's not injured as far as she can see, but its eyes stare balefully, straight at her.

'Shoo!' Captain Carly comes up behind them, and the crew part to allow her through.

It doesn't move.

'Has it broken a wing?' asks Cat in a hushed tone.

'Who knows? We need to get it off, though,' says Danny through gritted teeth.

'Can't we… help it? Look after it until we're back on shore?' asks Brandy.

Captain's mouth is a thin line. 'Not a chance. It's bad luck,' she says. 'Birds on board carry the souls of the dead.'

Annie shivers.

'But that's just an albatross, isn't it?' pipes up Brandy. 'And only if you kill it?'

They stare at her, and she reddens under her colleagues' gaze. 'I paid attention at school,' she says defensively, by way of explanation.

'Any bird is bad luck on a boat.' Annie turns to see Sid, who has come up from the darkness of his quarters to see what the commotion is.

Is it Annie's imagination, or is he looking at her when he speaks?

The crow lifts itself onto its legs and spreads its wings.

The assembled crew holds a collective breath.

'He's going to fly away; he was just taking a break.' Brandy's voice is gleeful.

'Doesn't matter, the thing has still been on here,' Sid replies, his voice heavy and despondent.

Ella stares at him. 'You don't believe that superstition, do you?'

Before anyone can reply, and before the bird can take flight, a scream echoes around the top deck.

Annie flinches at the sudden racket, turns and ducks to escape the huge cloud of white and grey descending.

'What the—?'

Seagulls, two then three, finally half a dozen culminating in a whirlpool above their heads.

The crew hit the teak, shielding their heads in unison. Feathers rain down, the cries from the new birds rising in a frenzied crescendo.

Annie hears someone retching. She dares to glance up, sees the kid of the charter guest, Ayton, standing by the rail on the port side, small hand over his mouth, his cheeks bulging.

Black feathers have joined the snowy ones now, and Annie swipes frantically at her face as one plants itself on her cheek.

The crow can no longer be seen among the flock of gulls that are tearing it apart.

Annie crawls around her crewmates towards the lad, reaching up and turning him around so he doesn't see anything more.

'Let's go down here,' she gasps, herding him, pushing at his small body, but it's as though the kid is frozen in place.

At the bottom of the stairs, she sees his father, looking up, clearly wondering what all the fuss is on the upper deck.

'Take him,' she says, 'please.'

Piers comes up the stairs, but instead of retrieving his son, he brushes past him.

Annie puts a hand on his arm. 'You don't need to see,' she says.

He flicks her hand easily off him, doesn't even look at her as he makes his way to the site of the brutal scene.

Then, as one, the grey birds take flight, gone as quickly as they arrived.

A single gull remains, walking around the deck, pecking at the few pieces of the crow that stain the teak. The gull's entire left flank is red.

'Danny!' Captain's voice breaks the shocked silence.

Danny springs into action, whipping a cloth out of his pocket and laying it over the largest of the claret puddles.

'Cat,' he snaps. 'Cleaning stuff, *now*.'

Cat turns in the direction of the cupboard as she flees past them all. Annie sees the tears that course freely down her face.

'Drinks for the guests,' says Ella as she marches after Cat. She fixes Annie with a hard glare. '*Strong* ones.'

–

Later, once the deck is clean and all evidence of the massacre has been scrubbed and polished away, they discuss it in the crew mess.

'I've seen plenty of nature's horror, but nothing like that. Not here, not on a yacht in the middle of the ocean.' Luca is the first to bring it up.

He's tough, Annie thinks. He's all hard edges and grit, so if it troubled him, it truly was terrible. She'd thought it might be her own sensitivity, but now, looking round the table at ashen faces, she knows it was as bad as she'd thought it was.

'I tried to get the boy away; I asked his dad to come and get him, but he didn't,' says Annie. She hears the wobble in her own voice and swallows hard.

'I know, right? What the fuck was that?' Danny rears up, furious suddenly.

They fall silent again.

The atmosphere in the mess is heavy, hanging low just like those clouds that covered Greece in yesterday's summer storm. Annie had thought it had passed. But since last night when she boarded *Ananke* as an official team member, everything seems wrong.

It started with the graffiti, she realises. Then this... this murderous shit-show that everyone witnessed.

'A bad omen.'

Annie snaps her head up and turns to Danny.

'What?' she asks.

He shrugs. 'It was a bad omen. A sign. This season is going to be shit.' He throws his hands up. 'The vandalism too, it's all a sign.'

Annie shivers. It is as though he can read her mind.

'The yacht's name, look at what she's called!' protests Danny.

They stare at him, and Ella provides the answer for the blank faces. '*Ananke* is goddess of fate and circumstance,' she informs them.

'So... we're protected, by our vessel?' Cat sounds hopeful.

Danny's face is serious, granite hard. 'Nope,' he says. 'The opposite, in my opinion.'

Annie gets up and leaves the table. She retreats to her cabin, the talk in the crew mess still fresh in her mind.

—

Fate and circumstance. Bad omens.

Annie knows it is ridiculous. She's always believed there is not really such a thing as luck.

To lead a good life isn't luck. More often than not it's hard work and determination.

She thinks about those guests in the master and VIP suites above her head. They are not lucky to be where they are. Somewhere, along the way, they made decisions that turned out to be fruitful, allowing them to earn the cash to do with as they wished.

But luck is an entirely different notion to omens, fate and circumstance.

What is written will be done.

Annie looks out of the porthole window. It is ink-black out there, who knows what other omens setting their sights on *Ananke*.

Robyn always relaxes when nightfall comes. Annie has never understood how she takes comfort in darkness. In Annie's world, along with the night come the monsters. Once the sun goes down, her vulnerability is heightened. If half the world is sleeping, they are not there to protect or keep watch.

Annie lets out a groan and covers her eyes with the palms of her hands.

At night-time and lights out, vulnerability comes to visit. Apart from Sid – who should be awake keeping watch but is probably sleeping, or maybe keeping watch in an entirely different way to how he should be – everyone aboard *Ananke* is dead to the world. *Ananke* is open to attack.

It is stupid, silly, and Annie isn't usually given to flashes of paranoia. That's more Robyn's style, not hers. Annie sees the best in everyone, but the events of the day have taken her beliefs and twisted them. They lie hot and heavy in her gut, along with her deception and secrets.

'Nobody is coming to attack this yacht. Everyone on board is a friend.' She says the words out loud, but they do nothing to settle her.

She is alone here, in this cabin. Cat hasn't come to bed, even though *Ananke* has been sleeping for a while now. She's probably bunking in with Luca.

But what if she's not? What if it's Cat, sociable, confident Cat, who has heard word from the marina that Ashley Mercer aboard *Ananke* isn't who she says she is? What if she's the one who Annie should be wary of, and not Sid? What if Cat is working on the say-so of someone back on land, and is right now scribbling more awful graffiti on *Ananke*'s smooth and shiny surface?

The thought has her sitting up in her bunk.

Her heart is a painful beat in her chest.

Annie throws back the cover, and in her night attire of shorts and vest, she slips her feet into her trainers and leaves the cabin.

A check, a night-watch patrol, just the perimeter of the boat, every deck, just to make sure.

The night is warm, the sky cloudless. The moon is full, and it dips into the water on the horizon, a pale, huge lamp that casts a beam all the way down the Aegean Sea to *Ananke*'s hull.

Over the port side, she sees a tiny pinprick of light. The night fishermen? But it's only one lamp. Like the shoals of fish, rarely do they head out alone.

Annie flees up to the wheelhouse. She bursts in, ready to shake Sid awake, ready to ask him if he's working with someone back on land to frighten her.

But the wheelhouse is empty. Sid isn't there at all.

She glances at the closed door that leads to the captain's quarters.

She can't wake her up.

Can she?

No. It is a ridiculous thought. If she turns into that fearful girl, that overreactive, paranoid employee, her life on *Ananke* will be short. There will be no crossing to Spain.

There will be no new life.

And that crossing is her end game, she realises, as she slips back onto the deck and pulls the door to the bridge closed behind her.

It is her goal, and all she needs to do is stifle this paranoia and get through the season here in Greek waters.

She returns to the deck and peers through the night at the lamplight on the water. She can't tell how far away it is. She can't even figure out if it is moving or not.

It is just… there.

Annie looks down at the lights that *Ananke* emits underwater. Blue streams that cast such a beam through the water she can see the shoals of fish that interweave them. Do the lights cast such a beam on her, announcing her presence on deck for all to see?

In her white top and shorts, she's hardly concealed.

Slowly, Annie retreats inside.

Hardly daring to believe she's doing this, she pads down the hallway to Luca's cabin, which he shares with Danny. She turns the handle slowly, opens the door just a crack and peers inside.

She sees a man's foot sticking out over the edge of the bottom bunk. In the top, she counts three arms, one large, hairy, the other two, slender but muscled, and tanned.

Cat, Danny and Luca, all accounted for. It doesn't mean that they're innocent, but they are asleep, and not skulking round the yacht to spray more accusatory graffiti.

At the end of the hall, she nudges open another cabin door. One hunched shape in each bunk.

She breathes out and quietly closes the door behind her.

In the crew mess, she sits on the bench behind the table where they all eat their meals. It faces the bank of CCTV, half a dozen screens showing various sides of *Ananke*. The film is live-stream only, she remembers from questioning Danny earlier. She's never seen anyone really look at the screens, apart from Luca, who stands here when they serve his meals to guests, and he tries to discern whether the food is to their pleasure or not. It has no sound on it, no recording facility set up here, because the only thing that counts on a superyacht is whether the guests are happy or not. Security is not needed. Policing is a ridiculous thought.

Annie watches the screens, flicking from one to the other, fearful of what will happen if a boat the size of their own small tender sails right up to *Ananke*, wondering what she will do if she catches sight of a figure slipping over the railings.

Annie hopes she'll never have to find out. But hope isn't a strong enough weapon.

She stares at the screens, watches the pixelated sky as it slowly changes.

—

She wakes to the sound of pots clanging. Bolting upright on the bench, she draws in a hiss of startled breath.

'Serious?' Luca is there, smashing down his morning bread roll trays on the table. 'You are sleeping in here?'

She pushes her hair back out of her face and glances at the screen. 'I must have fallen asleep,' she mutters.

'Yeah, too much stalking people all night,' he says with a glare.

Annie's heart flutters, a worried butterfly beating on her ribcage. 'W–what do you mean?'

'I mean, what are you doing spying on people in their beds in the middle of the night?'

Oh God. He *saw* her when she peeked into their cabin last night?

'I was looking for Cat; I was worried when I woke up and she hadn't come to bed.' It sounds lame to her own ears, but how can she tell this brittle, prickly man her real fears?

'Cat's a big girl; she can sleep where she wants. If you're trying to collect some sort of intel to take to Captain, don't even bother. Carly's not interested in gossip. The work getting done is all she cares about.'

'No!' Annie is aghast. 'I would never… it's… it's nothing like that.'

His fury turns into a leer. 'Oh, yeah, hoping to catch a bit of the action, were you?'

Her horror switches to an anger that matches his from a moment earlier. When she speaks next, it is pure Robyn.

'As if – you think you're something worth watching?' she mocks him.

He casts her a black look and moves away.

Annie sits back in her seat. It always amazes her when her 'inner Robyn' comes out. She doesn't call upon it often, but she's grateful for the spark when it is needed, for what her friend has taught her over the years.

She wants to put her head in her hands. She wants to go to her bunk and replace the eight hours' sleep she lost last night, but neither is an option. In an hour she must be showered and ready to report for duty, so she drags herself back to her room for a quick change.

–

After breakfast, she's tasked with going to land in the tender with Danny, to pick up a diving professional that will take the guests deep-sea diving.

'Are we going back to Athens?' she asks nervously, as Danny flings the lines to Cat and powers up the tender.

'No, just across the way.' He points to a not-too-distant island.

Annie sits in the back and tries to relax and enjoy the ride.

The instructor is waiting on the dock, tanks at the ready, and Annie helps Danny load up the gear in the tender.

'Hey, I'm Sebastian.' The instructor greets her with an outstretched hand and a wide smile.

She shakes his hand. 'Nice to meet you, I'm Annie.' She introduces herself, immediately at ease with his seemingly friendly nature.

'Good to meet you, Annie.'

At the same time, she feels Danny's eyes burning into her back. 'What?' Danny asks, confused.

The sudden silence stretches on.

7

A slow burn starts inside her, creeping up her body to stain her neck and face red with embarrassment.

Recover it. Fix it. Do it now.

'Ashley.' She corrects the instructor loudly, injecting intent into her tone, but keeping her face down lest either of them see the blush staining her cheeks.

'Ah, sorry, Ashley,' says Sebastian.

He moves on to Danny, talking ten to the dozen, recommending waters that would suit their purpose today while Annie busies herself releasing the line.

The next time she dares look at Danny, he is deep in conversation. Has he forgotten about it already? Has he, like Sebastian, thought he misheard? Or, Lord above, is he thinking of the vandalism on the side of *Ananke* this morning?

Annie is a liar.

She sits in the back of the tender, another thought starting to bloom.

Does Danny already know her real name?

She gazes out to sea as the superyacht gets ever closer, no longer enjoying the ride, her thoughts lost in the depths of her own deception.

–

They need someone to accompany them on the dive, and Danny asks Annie if she wants to go along with them. Annie puts her woes aside momentarily, pleased to be entrusted to go as the sole member of the interior team, even more so when she finds out once she's served drinks and nibbles, she will be allowed to go in the water.

They're not big drinkers, Piers and Nikki. Like true adventurers, they're more interested in the ocean, and soon enough they've dropped the small anchor of the tender in a sheltered cove off the island of Sifnos.

Once more, underneath the waves, Annie finds her peace. Nobody can see her down here. The only eyes upon her are those of the marine life, moving past her, not caring about her presence. Not caring about her sins, past or present. Not out for vengeance.

She executes a swan dive, going down, down, into the depths where barely any sunlight reaches. She weaves in and out of the rocks, plucking a handful of shells off the seabed and bringing them back to the surface. Back in the tender, she pores over them, her treasures, that nobody else has touched for many, many years.

The mainland of Sifnos looks inviting from the deck once they are all back on board *Ananke*. Captain has told the guests about the monastery and the quaint, traditional chapels that are worth a view. The guests know of the island, have business acquaintances or friends who own a place there, and they want to visit for an overnight stay with their pals.

Captain assures Piers *Ananke* can anchor here overnight, the guests can go on land and the tender will pick them up whenever they wish to return the following morning. It's an unexpected night off for the crew, as the guests are going to eat on Sifnos too.

'You handled the lines well when we were out earlier. And your diving is very good,' says Danny.

Annie gives him a grateful look, pleased that he's not mentioning the weirdness of her introducing herself by the wrong name. 'Thanks,' she says. 'I love anything to do with the water.'

He cocks his head on one side and studies her for so long she starts to get nervous.

Here it comes, the question about the cock-up of her name earlier, or the confession that he knows exactly who she is.

She braces herself.

'Do you want to have a go at driving the tender when we've dropped the guests off at the island?'

It's so far from what she expected him to say that she's astonished.

He looks down at the sandwich he's demolishing. 'You don't have to, just… if you're interested in getting deck experience.' He shrugs. 'It was just a thought.'

She pulls herself together. 'Yes!' she exclaims. 'Please, I'd… I'd love the opportunity.'

It's so close to being ruined, she thinks, later, once they've all moved on to their evening chores. Chances and good omens are being thrown her way and she's nearly blowing them with her ever-increasing paranoia.

She waits on the tender, looking out to the island where they're headed. It's a short ride, swimmable, really, she thinks.

The shuffle of the family at the side brings her back to the present. She gives them her hand, helping them one by one onto the small boat. Danny hops on board, as sure-footed as a goat on a mountainside, and herds Annie to the bow.

She watches him as he takes the wheel, the easy back-and-forth controls, nothing as taxing as Carly captaining the superyacht. Once Danny has them pointed in the right direction, he shifts along the seat, handing her control. She squeals as they bounce over the swell, zigzagging towards the sandy beach.

She slows it right down as they enter the shallows, pushing against the waves that are breaking shyly upon the shore, holding it steady as Piers, Nikki and Ayton are helped off the tender by Danny.

'I'll be right back,' calls Danny as he ushers them up the beach. 'Try and pull up alongside that dock, take it nice and slow, no rush.'

Annie's heart races in her chest as she looks at the small wooden platform that stretches out past the waves. It's a good thundering of her heart, she thinks. Good nervous – excited that she's being trusted with this. For the first time in days, she's not frightened.

She spins the tender, going slow like Danny told her, letting the throttle out gently, moving at a diagonal towards the platform. Dusk is falling, that grey time of day, post-sunset, pre-darkness.

The dock is chest height, and she's concentrating so hard on not bumping the tender against the struts that it takes a moment for her to see the cluster of people gathering.

Half a dozen of them, she realises now.

It's not that interesting to watch, she tells herself. *I'm hardly bringing a gigantic ship in to port.*

Nevertheless, she feels a pinprick of relief when she realises that they are not watching her at all. Most of them are kids just sitting on the dock, legs in the water, and a few couples have walked to the end to look out at the last of the sun as it settles beyond the horizon. Behind them, Annie sees Danny walking back towards her, having deposited the Kilfoyles at a beachfront restaurant.

She gives him a smile and a thumbs up, pleased that even with the cluster of onlookers, she's kept the tender steady in the water.

She loses sight of him for a second, and she reaches up and grabs on to the side of the dock, standing on the side of the tender to give herself height.

That's when it happens.

The sense of how out in the open she is, of the crowds watching her, the sheer number of people, who could contain anyone from back in Athens. Her flesh rising, her senses prickling.

That very real sense that she's being watched.

Annie's foot slips and she bangs her chin painfully on the edge of the wooden platform. She lets out a yelp and claws at the side to haul herself upright. The tender has skidded away from her, pushed by her feet as she slipped. Annie holds on to the dock, mortified at what she must look like, ever conscious of *Ananke*'s name on her uniform and the embarrassment she's bringing both the boat and its owners by looking like such a novice.

Clinging on, she peers through the legs of those gathered, desperately hoping that Danny has almost reached her. Arms reach out to her, exclamations of concern mingled with laughter as she's hauled up onto the dock.

She stands up, apologising profusely, head down in shame at her overreaction to something that didn't even happen.

A feeling was all it had been.

A dread of who might be in this gathered group.

She can see Danny clearly now, as he breaks into a run towards her. Annie moves forwards, hoping he didn't witness her humiliation.

'Ashley!' Danny is skidding down the dock now, pushing people out of his way.

Annie blanches as he grabs at her upper arms. 'Ash, what are you *doing*?' His tone is harsher than she's ever heard it, his eyes flashing. So far removed from his usual self. She struggles from his grip, staggering back with a gasp as he lets her go as quickly as he pounced on her.

'Shit,' he grunts, pushing her to one side, sprinting down the remainder of the dock and executing a running leap off the edge.

The tender has moved, floating away on the turning tide. Annie puts her hand to her mouth.

'I'm sorry!' she cries, but Danny is in the water, striking out towards the boat now.

She hears more titters from the pedestrians on the platform, sees Danny's face, red, his clothes soaked. Without a word or a single look at her, he clambers into the tender and steers it back to the dock.

'I'm sorry,' she says as she gets in.

He doesn't reply. Annie takes a seat at the stern; no more driving the tender for her.

She should be angry. At herself, for being so affected, and at whoever has implanted this in her, for stalking and scaring her. At *Robyn*, for stealing the damn passport and for thieving from Tobias in the first place. But for the short ride back to *Ananke*, it is simply failure that sits atop her shoulders. Failure accompanied by a stabbing fear.

Cat is on the deck. Danny throws her the lines; Cat ties them with quick efficiency.

'Have fun, guys?' she asks cheerily.

Danny climbs off the tender and makes his way inside without uttering a word.

Cat holds out a hand to assist Annie. 'What's his problem?' she asks.

Annie shakes her head. She doesn't trust herself to speak. If she even looks at Cat, the tears that have been softly threatening will spill over.

She chooses the long route back towards her cabin. She doesn't want to run into Danny in the crew mess. She pretends she doesn't hear Cat as the deckhand calls her fake name behind her.

In her notebook, she flips through the pages of notes she's made on what she's learned so far. It seems like somebody else's life. Or a life that was hers, had the potential to belong to her, but is now sliding away.

She picks up her pen. Not the pretty pink one that Robyn bought her, but a standard-issue biro she found in the crew mess.

> *I fear I'm being stalked. I know I've hurt someone more than even I ever imagined I could. I know that either I AM being stalked, or I THINK I am, and I'm worried I'm losing my mind.*
>> *I don't know which one is worse.*
>> *I don't think I'll survive this trip.*

She looks at the words she's written towards the back of the notebook. They seem dramatic, reading them back, but they encapsulate exactly the way she's feeling.

Like she's losing her mind. Was someone out there? It certainly felt like someone was watching her. But who?

She knows the why, or at least the various possibilities.

Annie snaps the notebook shut and puts it under her pillow. She leaves her cabin, working her way through the boat towards the crew mess. Luca is the first person she sees.

'Did you tell anyone in Athens we were going to Sifnos?' she asks roughly.

That Robyn tone is coming out again. She can hear it, even feel it in her own stance, but she's too troubled to care.

'Well?' she demands. 'Did you?'

'Who,' he says, 'the fuck is Sifnos?'

'It's an island!' she says impatiently. 'We just went there; the guests are having dinner there.'

He returns her glare, but it's as though he's wary of her; it's not as piercing as it usually is from the sometime-stroppy chef.

'I didn't even know where we were.' He frowns, his face tight and almost ugly. 'What's your problem, new girl?'

'Hey.' Ella pushes through to the pantry, looking from Luca to Annie. 'What's going on?'

'Did you tell anyone on land that we're in Sifnos?' Annie demands.

'No. Why would I?'

Annie moves on her way, determined to catch each crew member and ask them the same question.

One of them is feeding information back to Athens. One of them *must* be.

As she walks past the engine room, she sees the shadow of Sid, moving around in his slow way. She knocks on the door and puts her head in.

'Help you?' He looks up at her through sleepy, slack-lidded eyes, which widen when he sees who his visitor is.

Common sense brings her sharply back to herself.

She is Annie. She is the force of positivity. She is happy and hard-working, and she radiates joy.

She is not this unknown, unwanted personality that has threatened to overspill recently. She is not suspicious, brittle, edgy. She doesn't simmer with a slow-building fury. That's not her.

At all.

'No, sorry to disturb you.' Annie retreats and closes the door behind her.

Behind her, she hears the squeak of the door as it opens again. Her name is called, Sid's voice husky, rising in volume.

She doesn't turn around. She puts her head down and scuttles back along the deck.

What is she doing? What must her crewmates think of her, acting like this?

She needs to put things right. She needs to find Danny, apologise for the mistake she made with the tender, and tell him she's appreciative of the chance he gave her, and should he trust her again, she won't let him down.

She nods to herself.

That's what is important. Securing her future career, not chasing a phantom cohort around the yacht.

'Hey, have you seen Danny?' Spotting Brandy on the upper deck, Annie calls up to her.

'On break,' Brandy says. 'Crew mess.'

'Thanks.'

Annie goes back the way she came, retracing her steps past the engine room, through the door and down the winding stairs towards the crew quarters.

She shivers as she steps out of the warm night air into the chilly, air-conditioned interior. Is it her imagination or was Brandy cooler to her than normal?

The near hysteria is back, full force, bigger than before, despite her promises to herself to remain the girl who she was when she first came aboard *Ananke*.

Has Brandy heard of the mess she caused with the tender off the shore of Sifnos? Or the aftereffect, her snapping, first at Luca, then at her own boss, Ella? Or is Brandy off with her because someone back in Athens has been feeding her stories? Or, even worse than tales – the truth!

She can hear them as she descends the stairs that lead into the crew mess.

'She just went... like... she wasn't even there any more. Wasn't present. She just dropped the lines, the tender went sailing off, and she didn't even notice!' Danny's voice, high-pitched with indignation, floats up the stairs.

Annie flattens her back against the wall.

'She's a fucking weirdo.' This from Luca.

Annie closes her eyes.

'Shh, Luca,' Ella scolds him. 'She just asked a simple question of you, is all.'

'Bullshit!' Luca explodes. 'And anyways, you don't know the half of it. All the weird and crazy shit. Sneaking around, spying…'

Annie stuffs her knuckles against her lips, stifling a cry that threatens to erupt.

No.

No! It's all falling apart. She's only just started, but it's all falling apart!

8

'What do you mean, spying?' Ella asks, intrigued now.

She needs to fix this right now, before Luca tells Ella that Annie opened the door to his cabin in the middle of the night. She'd told him she was looking for Cat, but Luca is going to put a different spin on it, she knows that much about him. What if he knows she also looked at Ella and Brandy while *they* were sleeping?

She forces her feet to move, clattering down the rest of the stairs, purposefully announcing her arrival.

'Hi,' she says. 'Danny, can I have a word?'

'Sure.' He leans back and folds his arms.

Annie swallows a grimace. She'd been hoping to take him out of the crew mess, doesn't want to spill her apology in front of both the gruesome Luca and her own boss, Ella.

She pushes on regardless. 'I wanted to apologise to you, the mistake I made with the tender, earlier, by not tying up the lines. I'm so sorry, you trusted me, and I–I screwed up.'

He sets his mouth in a grim line and nods. Annie can feel Luca and Ella's eyes on them.

'Come on, D–man.' Brandy sweeps into the mess, fixing him with a stare. 'You're not telling me you never made a single mistake when you were learning as a green deckhand?'

Annie's breath catches in her throat. Brandy has stood up for her. Brandy isn't mad, or cold, or off. Or… is she playing at another game entirely by pretending to be on Annie's side?

Danny throws his hands up. 'It's fine, it's a mistake. Of course she's going to get things wrong. It's… it isn't…' He catches Annie's eye. She holds her breath, wondering where he's going with this. 'It's fine,' he finishes. 'I'm sorry, it's no big deal.'

'And anyway, she's *my* girl,' says Ella. 'She's not on the deck team, she's with me, so please don't get yourself worked up over a non-member of your staff.'

Luca barks out a laugh.

'What?' Ella whirls around to face the chef.

'That's rich; you get your nose in every department, my kitchen, the deck team.' He shunts out another guffaw. 'That's real rich, that is.'

Ella lets rip at him, Danny inserting himself between them, but unheard in among their quarrelling, raised voices.

Annie backs away. 'I'm really sorry,' she says. But, deep into their own quarrels that she caused, nobody hears her.

—

She's not expecting to be invited on the return trip on the tender to collect the guests, and when Danny calls her to the deck, she imagines that's what he's going to tell her.

'Hey, Ashley,' he says as she approaches.

He is standing in a slice of moonlight, his face pale and ghostly.

'Hi,' she says. 'Danny, I am so sorry about not tying up the lines on the tender. It was a stupid mistake.'

He shrugs. 'It's a rookie mistake, and that's what you are, a rookie. I'm guilty of forgetting that because you seem like you've been a yachtie for years. Also, Ella was right, you're not even a deckhand. So, I'm the one who should be apologising.'

She clutches at his words, first the apology, but quickly moving on to the praise he just gave her. *You seem like you've been a yachtie for years.*

She glows under his compliment. 'Thanks,' she says shyly.

Then she pulls on her Robyn reserves, tries for confidence.

If you don't ask, you don't get, Robyn always says.

'Does that mean I can steer the tender again when you pick them up from the island?' she asks boldly.

'You can, but Captain's just informed me they're definitely not coming back tonight. They're having dinner with their friends inland and they're staying until morning.'

'Oh.' Annie is conflicted. She'd wanted to show Danny she was worthy of a second chance, but she can't deny she's relieved they won't need to go to Sifnos in the dark. She pictures it, the landing platform abandoned, the beach desolate, the feeling of eyes on her from the shadows of the palm trees.

She diverts her attention to Danny, who is still talking.

'Sorry?' she asks, realising he is waiting for a reply to a question she didn't even hear.

'Captain has given us some free time. We have to stay on board but we're getting food delivered via the water ferry so Chef can have a night off, and we're allowed to have a few drinks, too.' He stares at her intently, as if confused at her lack of excitement. 'Cheer up, it's good news, isn't it?'

'Oh, yes, brilliant.' She gives him a high five, falsely jovial once more, hating the carefree act she's wearing like a cloak, wishing she could trust someone here enough to confide in them.

'So, we'll order in for about eight o'clock. Captain's eating with us, then we can let loose for the night.'

She nods. 'See you later, then.'

She resumes her duties, feeling the light atmosphere from her crewmates at an unexpected night off. Even Chef is happy, grinning at her as she passes through the galley, apparently his beef with her 'spying' forgotten and forgiven. Annie tries to match her glee to theirs, succumbing a bit once Cat joins her, stripping off her uniform as she hurtles down the hallway to the cabin.

'Night off!' she shrieks. 'Night off, bitch!'

Annie laughs at her antics. This time, it isn't forced.

I can do this, she thinks. *I, too, can believe I am as free as they are.*

—

'Did you come here with anyone, to Greece, I mean?' asks Ella as she tips the bottle of Veuve and pours the dregs into Annie's flute.

They're in the Jacuzzi, waiting for the water ferry to deliver their dinner. Beyond the stern, the sun is sinking into the sea. Violet sparks the horizon, beaming red as it touches the water.

Annie narrows her eyes, considering the question, wondering why Ella is suddenly asking it now. When she answers, she chooses her words carefully. 'I came here for something new.' She tips the glass back and drains it. 'I… I didn't have the best childhood.'

If Ella notices that her initial question was avoided, she doesn't pick her up on it.

She sneaks a look at the other girl, noticing that her boss is more than a little drunk.

'You know what, Ash.' Ella points a finger at Annie. 'We come into this industry to find a family of our own. That's what we are, all of us. Just seeking to replace what we left behind, or what we never had.' Ella grimaces, before adding, 'Or what's not there any more.'

Annie listens carefully. There is an undertone to Ella's voice. To Annie, it sounds like bitterness. She remembers Ella's expression when they were on the marina, the way her face changed when Annie asked her if she was going home at the end of the season.

It is almost like Ella understands.

'That's exactly it,' Annie says. 'That's what I needed, a new start. And I did it. I escaped!' The words hold an epic meaning for her, but she still feels a thin sheen of anxiety. She hasn't escaped entirely, not quite yet.

'We're all running from something,' replies Ella. She slurs her words. 'I hope you find what you're looking for here.'

Annie wants to ask Ella what she's running from, but something on Ella's face stops her. Her boss, though friendly, seems private. Closed off. It's ironic, thinks Annie. She would probably understand Ella better than anyone.

Annie squints as the sun dips once more, then sinks entirely. The half-light they'd been bathing in has vanished. 'This is a new life for me. This is a dream come true. This is a fairy tale. I... I just need to make it to Spain. I think it will be better there. I'll find what I'm looking for there.' She nods her head, as if affirming it to herself.

'You don't like Greece?' Ella's voice jolts Annie back to the present.

Annie shakes her head vehemently. 'I love it. But...'

'But what?'

Is now the time to tell all? Annie takes a deep breath. 'Someone is... hassling me.' She shakes her head; the wording she chose is wrong. 'Someone is watching me.'

The water sloshes over the side of the Jacuzzi as Ella sits upright. 'Who?' she demands.

Tell her. Tell her. Tell her everything.

Annie loses her nerve. 'It doesn't matter.' She shrugs once more, misery heavy on her shoulders. 'It'll be better in Spain.'

Ella is silent for a long time. Eventually, she asks, 'Do you mean someone on board? Someone we work with?'

What are you doing? Internally, Annie screams and scrambles to backtrack.

She shakes her head. 'It's silly. I'm being silly. It really doesn't matter.' She gives Ella her brightest smile, tries to bat away the other girl's concern.

'I won't pry, but I'm always here to chat. My role is to look after my team, right?'

Annie gazes at the girl who she feels is more friend than boss. A woman whose exterior screams out that she's in control. But there's also a sadness there, or a hardness. It is difficult to distinguish between the two.

Something that, to Annie, is as noticeable as her own fearful mood must be.

'I... I'm here too, to listen, you know?' Annie blushes. 'We haven't known each other very long, but I like you.' Annie ducks her head shyly. 'And I've got a good listening ear.'

Ella purses his lips and stares off towards the horizon.

'I know,' she sighs. 'Thanks.'

She has an armour, realises Annie. The same style and brand as the one Annie sports herself.

Secrets… secrets… always hiding, ducking and diving. She'd thought her own life was tough. It seems no matter how shiny things appear, if you look closely enough, everything has some tarnish on it.

The sun has long since gone down, and the fresh night air pinches at her.

'Cold?' Ella reaches over the side and passes Annie a towel. 'We should get out. Dinner will be here soon.'

Annie climbs over the edge of the Jacuzzi and wraps herself in the towel.

'Thanks for listening,' Annie says. 'I'd appreciate if you didn't mention anything.' Annie's head is spinning, the Veuve hitting her now, wondering if she's said too much.

Across the dark sea, a beam of light heads towards *Ananke*. Annie feels the sudden tension in her shoulders as she stares at the oncoming vessel.

'The water taxi, bringing the food,' Ella says, stumbling a little as she peers into the dark water.

On the deck above she can hear Danny, calling to the approaching taxi to come around to the platform.

'Oh, great.' Annie breathes out, smiles with relief. 'Thanks again, Ella. Hey, you get dressed, I'll help bring dinner down.'

Dropping her towel, she pulls her shorts and shirt on over her bikini and heads up the stairs to the landing deck.

'Hey, take these.' Danny is there, holding the Styrofoam containers, stacking them up and holding them steady with his chin.

She takes them from him, handling them carefully. She smiles at the delivery man.

The water taxi is a small boat, around the same size as *Ananke*'s tender. The rear of it is covered by a canvas roof. He must have other deliveries, as she can see other boxes stacked up on the rear seats.

When all their food is on board, he gives a salute to Danny and retreats to the wheel.

'Next time!' calls Danny. 'Cheers, mate.'

The water taxi spins in a loop, sending up a spray of water from the rear engine. As it moves away, Annie pauses.

Is there another person in the taxi, in the rear seat, hood up? Or is it just the shadows, a trick of the dark night?

'Hey,' she says to Danny as he strides past her. 'Who... who is that?'

'That's Les,' Danny says. 'He's the provisioner, and he also runs the taxi service.'

'No,' says Annie. 'Did he have a passenger? Was there someone in the back of the boat?'

'Didn't see anyone.' Danny has turned away, his mind on the meal, moving speedily down the stairs to deliver the goodies to the masses.

She's sure the food is good, but Annie tastes nothing. Finally, she abandons the meal that's laid out buffet-style in the crew mess and reaches for one of the bottles of wine that's open on the table.

Vaguely, she's aware of her crewmates' chatter, of the captain's voice, the small talk that these guys so easily fall into.

But all Annie can think about is that water taxi, and the person she's almost sure was sitting in the rear of it.

'Does that water taxi ferry people, as well as food and provisions?' Her question comes out louder than she anticipated.

Seven pairs of eyes stare at her.

Annie shrinks a little, realising she has interrupted the captain, who, it seems, was in the middle of one of her seafarer tales.

'Sorry.' She utters a nervous laugh.

The Veuve mixed with the wine is hitting her now, and she sits back in her chair, feeling the heat in her body. She needs to get out of this room before she says something really stupid.

She stands up, wobbles and grabs the edge of the table.

'I just need to...' She gestures towards her cabin.

As she flees through the door, she hears Captain. 'Is she okay?'

Annie doesn't wait to see what the answering replies are.

She grabs her mobile from her cabin and takes the long route to the deck, avoiding the crew mess. She can still hear the others in there, talking, laughing, arguing.

On the top deck, she stares out into the inky sea. There is no moon tonight. The clouds pass over it in a never-ending reel. The sea is tipped with white froth as it whips up around *Ananke*'s hull.

She glances to the wheelhouse. It is empty. Captain is downstairs, sharing an impromptu meal with the crew in the mess. She wonders where Sid is, for he wasn't with the others inside. Is he sleeping, as usual, in his small room? Or is he up here somewhere, in the shadows, tiptoeing in her wake?

Annie slips into the bridge and, with a glance around, pads over to the safe.

It is ajar, she can see. Why wouldn't it be? Everyone is like a family on *Ananke*; they have no secrets. They have no fears or anxieties.

Only Annie has those.

She opens the little metal door to see the stack of passports. Some burgundy, some blue, some black.

Annie rifles through the blue ones, checking the pages until she gets to her own.

Not her own, she thinks guiltily, *Ashley's*.

She darts out of the bridge, back to lean on the railing, holding the passport close to her chest.

She will keep it with her now, close to her. She imagines if it were to remain in the safe, someone on the crew would be poking around in there, poring over her personal information, seeking some sort of proof of whatever it is they already know.

From now on, she's going to keep everything close to hand, including her secrets, and she's going to keep her eyes wide open.

9

'Ashley!' She startles at the sound of her new name, and looks up to see Captain heading her way, Cat weaving in a none-too-straight line behind her.

'I was just…' Annie trails off, stuffing her passport in her pocket and folding her arms across her chest. 'What's wrong?'

Captain's face is fraught with tension. 'We're spinning, didn't you notice? The damn anchor is caught again.' Carly gestures towards the interior. 'Danny's had too much to drink to go in the water.' She turns her head to glare at Cat. 'So has this one. I need to find Sid to help me.'

Sid.

Annie supresses a shudder. 'There's no need, I'll do it.' Annie walks past Captain, heading towards the platform.

Captain catches her arm. 'How much have you had to drink?'

'Just a couple of glasses, I'm fine.' As she says the words, she realises even though it's a lie, the words themselves are true. The alcohol fug has gone. Her mind is clearer than it's been in days, months, years, even.

'I can, too!' shouts Cat.

Captain gives her a withering look and puts her face very close to Cat's. 'Don't make me regret giving you guys the night off. Get inside; me and Ashley have got this. Find my errant brother and send him to me.'

Annie trails after the captain, nerves fluttering inside her now. Does her boss really want her to go into the water? It's one thing during the day, when she knows that she'll emerge from the waves into bright sunshine, warmth on her shoulders.

But her fears grow when Captain pulls a tank out of the storeroom along with her own branded wetsuit.

'No, I… I can do it. You don't need to go in the water,' says Annie.

Captain gives her a look, one eyebrow arched. 'Captain is double your age plus a few, Ashley. I can manage some manual labour.'

'But I can do it, without all that gear.' Annie takes the tank and rests it on the floor. 'Honestly, I'm quick, and I've done it before. I know exactly where to go. You stay on deck.'

She waits for Captain to leave the room before removing her passport from her pocket and sliding it into the folds of a towel that she shoves underneath the bench.

It's going to take slightly longer than last time, Annie realises as she executes a dive into the depths of the Aegean Sea. The lights with their eerie blue glow show her the way to the anchor chain, but it's dim down here, no sunlight breaking through. Finally, she finds her way to the chain.

Ananke has moved in a slow circle. All that time they were in the Jacuzzi and enjoying their dinner, all the time that Annie was sneaking around the bridge and the safe, the lines have been twisting around each other in a slow dance, barely noticeable from the deck. She pummels her way to the surface, breaking through, one hand on the porthole of the starboard side as she calls up to Captain to raise the port anchor slowly.

'I'll move it out of the line,' Annie calls.

Captain falters. It's against protocol, Annie knows. But so far, the boat has only moved in one full turn. If she continues to spin all night, the lines and chains will be a rat's nest tangle. She can see by Captain's face that she's fuming that her deck team are incapacitated or absent.

'I've got this, Captain,' Annie reassures her.

'I'll get in the tender and watch her.' Chef Luca is there, appearing like a shadow. 'We've got this, Cap, don't worry.'

Annie nods and prepares to go back under. 'Raise it slowly, and don't worry, I can get out of the way if I need to.' She gives the captain what she hopes in an encouraging smile.

She waits until Luca has clambered down into the tender, and Captain has the remote for the port anchor control.

She hears the buzz as it whirrs into life, the sound Annie wakes to, that she hears all day whenever they prepare to pull or drop anchor. It is different here, louder, fiercer, being so close to her. One false move and that anchor would slice through a limb or knock her unconscious.

But Annie is confident in this manoeuvre. She's more at home in the water than on dry land. And she knows she's got the skills to see this through.

It will go some way to setting right the near-miss of the tender escaping the dock. If she pulls this off, her name, albeit not her real one, will taste glorious in the mouths of her superiors again.

Using the hull of the boat, she pushes herself down, peering through the water as the anchor raises, inch by inch, oh-so-slowly. When it is slightly above the line that it's caught on, Annie bursts back to the surface.

'Hold it there!' she says, and without waiting for a reply, she flips over, points her fingers down, and cuts through the water to the anchor. The anchor is cold, wet and gritty in her hands.

As she pushes on the metal, she grabs the line, drawing it towards her, effectively freeing the anchor from its knotted prison.

She lets herself rise to the surface, tipping her head back as she breaks through the waves.

'Done,' she says, swimming in a crawl to the platform, where Luca hauls her out.

Captain Carly stamps down the stairs. 'I'm so grateful, Ashley, and you too, Luca. But I am mighty pissed. Where are my deck crew? Where is my engineer?' Her hands, always expressive, cut through the air in angry slices.

Luca helps Annie to stand and gives his boss a small salute. 'We'll call it a night, guv,' he says. 'See you in the morning.'

'I'd get in your cabin,' Luca says grimly, as they head towards the interior. 'And if Cat is in there, tell her to stay there.' He nods towards Captain, who is already marching in the direction of the crew mess. 'You and I are on her good side right now; best to keep it that way.'

Annie likes the fact that she's currently onside. Not only with Captain, but Luca too. She's sorry for the others, Danny, drunken Cat, but they chose to get smashed. Annie still needs to keep her head down, make a good reputation for herself. The crossing to Spain must not be put in jeopardy, and her actions are just another tick against her name. Hopefully, tonight's narrowly diverted crisis has only helped her mission.

'Thanks for your help, Luca,' she says. 'Good night.'

Much like she did with the captain, before the dive, Annie waits for Luca to disappear inside the yacht. When the door has closed behind him, she darts back into the dive gear locker and retrieves the passport from its hiding place from earlier.

Back in her cabin, sleep won't come.

Cat is dead to the world, snoring in the bunk below her. Annie's glow over saving the day from the twisted anchor dims. Finally, in the early hours, it is extinguished altogether.

All she can think about is whether Sid is still AWOL, or was he not missing at all? Was he – sneakily, stealthily – observing her from afar? Is he even now planning some further desecration of her character?

She throws back the covers and climbs soundlessly down to the floor.

She allows the darkness to envelop her before she slips out of the cabin. The hallway is deserted. From behind Danny's door, she can hear a juddering snore: either him or Luca. The pantry, galley and crew mess are in darkness, just the emergency lighting at ground level casting a beam bright enough for Annie to walk.

Up to the lower deck, out into that burst of strangely warm night air. She walks to the starboard railing, peering over the side.

All she can do now is remain alert against the unknown. It's not like this when Robyn is by her side. Her friend is like a forcefield, or a shield, protecting her from… well, from everything.

From people like Stefan.

Annie shudders at the memory, both of what happened to the boy and what Annie discovered.

Robyn would protect her now, against her unknown, unseen adversary. Robyn would sniff them out, hunt them down, warn them off. But that would be jeopardising Robyn, no matter how tough her friend thinks she is, and Annie's not prepared to do that.

The only thing she can do now is to remain on guard and clear-headed. She will be on constant watch of her surroundings, like she is right now. She will sleep when she gets to Spain, when there's two thousand miles separating her from this island and whichever inhabitant has got it in for her.

For now, for tonight, and probably tomorrow and the nights following, Annie prowls and prowls. Tiredness does not touch her yet; adrenaline pushes her gently. It is like being back in the home, in bed, eyes wide, waiting for whatever waits for *her* in the dark.

Should it come, she will be as ready as she can be.

As the sky lightens to grey, and the first fingers of the sun rise from the horizon, she sits down on one of the loungers and leans her head back.

With daylight comes safety.

Another night has passed.

She made it through.

–

Someone leans over Annie in her bed, their teeth grey, evidence of decay in a sneering smile. Brutal fingers grasp the tender, the pale flesh of the inside of Annie's arm. They twist her skin cruelly, pulling and turning it until Annie can hold the pain inside no longer.

She screams and wrenches her arm free.

Her persecutor opens their mouth and joins her in a scream, louder, longer than Annie's, piercing the night sky.

Annie scoots back, flailing out, unable to believe she fell asleep and let the monster on board. The attacker keeps coming, pushing one hand over Annie's mouth, the other on her shoulder, pushing her back down before bringing her back up, shaking her violently as if Annie is nothing more than a doll.

'Shut up!' the voice hisses in her ear.

Annie goes slack. She tastes the palm of the hand covering her mouth, a mixture of soap, cleaning products and seawater.

Annie wrestles herself free and pushes the other girl backwards.

The girl staggers, throws out a hand to steady herself against the railing.

'Get off me!' Annie gasps, struggling upright. 'What are you *doing*?'

Her attacker comes up in her face, one finger pointed, reminding Annie suddenly of a younger Captain Carly. 'Saving your arse!' she shrieks none-too-quietly. 'Sleeping up here, for everyone to see!'

Brandy. It's Brandy. And it was just a dream.

Annie rubs her face with her hands. 'What time is it?' she asks.

'Just gone six. We've got to set up for breakfast. Danny and Cat are taking the tender to collect the guests from the island.'

Danny and Cat are going. Annie's spirits sink a little lower. She'd thought she might get the opportunity to drive the tender again.

'Punishment, Captain said.' Brandy is still talking. Annie tries to focus on the girl.

'What?'

'Captain said she was really pissed with them, for getting so drunk last night they couldn't sort out the anchor.' Brandy looks at her quizzically. 'Didn't you hear her yelling?'

Annie looks down at the sun lounger. 'I heard some of it.'

'Hey, were you here all night?'

This is not good, thinks Annie. The previous night when her cabin felt claustrophobic and she was hauntingly hemmed in, worrying about someone climbing aboard, Luca had found her sleeping in the crew mess. If this carries on, if the crew start to exchange stories, they'll realise how messed up she really is.

Her chance for freedom will be snatched away. She can kiss goodbye to Spain.

She grabs Brandy's hand. 'Don't mention this, will you?' she pleads.

Brandy snorts. 'Of course not, we stews have got to stick together. Come on, you can lay the table; I'll make sure everything from last night has been cleared away before Captain goes downstairs.'

The day is bright, sunny, already extremely hot, so Annie sets the breakfast plates up outside on the upper deck. As she lays the table, she spots Danny and Cat heading off in the tender towards Sifnos. Cat's long, black hair streams out behind her.

We're all running from something, isn't that what Ella said, in the Jacuzzi?

What is Cat escaping from? she wonders. Or Ella, who sounded like she was talking from personal experience. Or Danny, Brandy or even grumpy-yet-helpful-at-times Luca.

Troublesome families, quarrelling, warring parents, argumentative siblings?

Or something bigger? Something – or someone – as dark as what is happening to Annie.

–

Later, they find themselves on a partial break. The guests are back, fed and watered. Piers has gone back to his laptop, Nikki is sunning herself on the same lounger that Annie slept on, and their son, Ayton, is with Luca, in the pantry. Together, they are discussing lunch plans.

Annie is in the crew mess, folding the napkins she's just ironed, and piling them neatly to one side.

'I heard about you, last night,' says Ella as she places a steaming coffee on the table.

Annie reddens. So Brandy told her after all, that she'd spent the night on the deck.

'I… I'm sorry,' says Annie. 'It won't happen again.'

'What?' Ella pauses, coffee cup halfway to her lips. 'Don't be silly; Captain is thrilled with you. I'll tell you, Ash, you carry on like this, once you get to Spain, you'll be able to have your pick of jobs, deck or stew. You're heading in the right direction.'

Annie is so fraught at the near slip-up, it must show on her face. Ella puts the mug down and leans in. 'What did you think I meant?' she asks. Her voice, previously light, is laden with suspicion.

Annie swallows and thinks fast. 'I thought you were mad because I'd been doing deck work again.' Her tone is calm. Annie doesn't know whether to be thrilled with her deceptive quality or saddened. She never used to be able to lie so well.

Ella sits back in her chair. 'Are you sure everything is okay, Ashley?' she asks quietly, her gaze flicking to the pantry next door, where Luca and Ayton can be heard chatting about ingredients, their voices intense.

Annie straightens her shoulders and gives Ella her biggest smile. 'Everything's great,' she says.

It will be.

It will be.

It will be.

10

It's like a mantra for the rest of the day. She carries it with her, whispering the words to herself as she carries out her stewardess duties.

The day itself is uneventful. The guests are happy to stay on the boat. Nikki and Ayton use the various water toys, and even Piers is persuaded away from his workload to join in the fun. Annie studies him surreptitiously, reddening as she continuously catches his eye. Is *he* watching *her*?

Ridiculous. Piers knows nothing of her deception. She's certain that someone like him would never have come into contact with the ferry people.

Although it's perfectly possible he has been in Tobias's presence, or that of his furious father.

Annie puts her head down, averts her gaze and gets on with her work.

The activity means the deck crew are, for once, busier than the interior. Brandy and Ella take the weight off their feet. Annie is invited to join them in an extended break, but she declines, preferring to stay busy.

She takes the opportunity to walk the decks, all three of them, round and round. Annie sees Captain on the platform, laughing with the guests, and she slips into the wheelhouse and picks up Captain's binoculars, standing over the controls and sweeping the landscape and the horizon with her gaze.

There are plenty of vessels out there, and with the stronger lens, Annie can identify the people visible on board. Another superyacht, a hybrid, like *Siren* was. *Bliss* says the name scrawled in metallic green paint along the port side.

She sees crew members like herself, ferrying trays of drinks to the guests on board, their own slide out, jet skis swirling in circles around the perimeter.

There are fishing boats too, larger ones, with nets mechanically attached. Men with withered skin, brown as berries, doing the job that has been in their families for generations.

The water taxi cuts into her view. She stares at it until her head begins to hurt. She's not sure if it is the same one that delivered their meal the night before.

She puts the binoculars down where she found them and thinks about the possibility that there was a passenger on that vessel.

The shadowy figure she thought she saw.

She thinks of the words she scribbled in her notebook, that she might be losing her mind.

Right now, she doesn't know which is preferable: that someone is following her, watching her, or she's going crazy.

The number of boats out on the water doesn't soothe her. Where she thought she might find safety in among the volume of water traffic, it actually works against her.

There is more to watch. More people to keep track of.

She sees Captain's blonde head approaching the stairwell that leads to the bridge, and she ducks out of the opposite door and resumes her guard of *Ananke*.

She is going to be exhausted.

She has weeks more of this. The work during the day is physical. The other crew members sleep for their full eight hours as soon as their heads hit the pillow.

Annie is young and fit, but she knows realistically she won't last the season living this way.

And once again, after the sun has dipped, and the moon has risen, and it is time for bed, she lies in her narrow bunk, eyes wide and staring as the clock ticks on, eating into her sleep allowance until she throws off the covers as she knew she would.

The crew mess is in darkness, but it's not empty.

A small figure is hunched over the table. Annie draws a sharp breath and cringes backwards to the corridor.

A stranger on board!

The person at the table turns. It takes a long moment before Annie feels herself sagging with relief.

It's just Ella.

'You startled me,' Annie says. 'Are you okay?'

Ella's eyes are dark and glinting in the gloom. Annie lets off an involuntary shiver. The girl who Annie is beginning to think of as a friend suddenly looks an awful lot like Robyn. Sad and small but masking it with a thin shield of bravery.

'I'm fine. Can't sleep.' Ella shoves something underneath the table, but not so quickly that Annie doesn't see what it is. A bottle of gin.

Annie doesn't know where to look. They are on charter. Absolutely no drinking when guests are aboard is Captain's number one rule.

Annie busies herself getting a glass for a drink of water. Who is she to judge? Ella has simply broken a rule. Annie has broken the law.

Ella flings a towel on top of the bottle, stands up and heads past Annie. At the door, she stops and turns round. 'Ashley...'

Annie tilts her head.

'Why don't you make us a tea, join me in my cabin for a while?'

It's like a light inside her, or a warm glow. Ella, for whatever reason, also doesn't want to be alone tonight. Annie holds her breath, wondering if tonight will be the night that both of them break past this block and confide in each other.

Hope blooms in her chest. A problem shared…

Annie smiles. 'I'd love that,' she says as she gathers up two cups and heads to the hot water urn. 'Thanks.'

'Do you have brothers or sisters, Ash?' Ella is in her own bed, Annie atop Brandy's bunk.

Annie lets the question wash over her. 'A sister,' she replies eventually.

Technically, it's yet another lie. In her heart, her soul, her mind, however, Robyn is as good as blood.

'What about you, El?' Annie asks, attempting to steer the conversation away from herself.

'Brothers.' Ella's voice is very small. 'Four of them.' Her voice cracks noticeably.

In the bunk above, Annie doesn't hesitate to flip herself off the bed to land on her feet next to Ella.

In the dimmed light, Annie is aghast to see tears rolling down Ella's cheeks.

'What's wrong?' Annie whispers.

Ella dashes her tears angrily away. 'You've got a sister. Ash, do you sometimes think it would be easier if you were an only child?'

Annie sits on Ella's bed, near her feet. She doesn't know where the question has stemmed from, but she considers it.

All the messes that Robyn has got her into. Like the one she's in right now. If Robyn hadn't insisted on entering Greece illegally, hadn't stolen Ashley's passport... Why hadn't they waited? Why didn't Robyn get a little job, like Annie had, back home, and save up for the identification and air fare and do it properly? Why did Annie let herself be persuaded by Robyn's madcap plans all the time?

'I wouldn't be in the mess I am now,' says Annie in answer to Ella's question.

Ella sits up, tilts her head to one side. 'What do you mean?'

Annie reddens, unable to believe how comfortable she feels with this girl to let slip something like that.

Annie shrugs. 'My sister is... complicated. She took something that wasn't hers to take.' She sneaks a peek at Ella, wondering if she's really going to go so far as to spill the truth. 'She implicated me in something.' Now, she looks at Ella full on. 'And I can't get out of it now. Not without losing everything.'

Ella stares at her, her own woes seemingly forgotten. 'Wow,' she says, 'like, what did she do?'

Annie doesn't answer right away. She looks around the cabin, at the bed she's sitting on. She thinks of what tomorrow will bring. Food, a wage, shelter. She thinks of losing all that if she were to tell Ella the truth.

Her nerve gone, Annie pinches her lips together. She feels traitorous, blackened inside to have had such thoughts about Robyn. She considers Ella's question again.

Life without Robyn. A childhood navigating growing pains on her own. Trying to deal with the Stefans of the world by herself. No love laid upon her. No protection.

'It doesn't matter,' Annie says. She needs to steer the spotlight away and she rattles her now empty teacup. 'Do you want another tea?'

But Ella hasn't finished. 'You don't think it's stupid to be so close?' Ella urges, her voice high, emotional. 'If anything were to happen to her, who else have you got?'

Annie sits back down on Ella's bunk and folds her legs underneath herself. 'I… I don't have anybody.'

Ella's fingers dance across the sheet to clench Annie's wrist. 'Take it from me, it's worth thinking about. The alternative, when you're left alone *after* being so close…' She gulps back a sob and Annie realises belatedly just how drunk Ella is. 'You're young; distance yourself before it's too late. Don't let people get so close that when they're gone, once it's over, you've got nothing and nobody.'

It's the most passionate speech Annie has ever heard Ella give. She doesn't understand it; Ella's words, combined with the look on her face – absolute, utter devastation – frighten her.

'Ella?'

Ella jolts and pulls her hand away from Annie's.

'Don't rely on her; don't count on a man. Don't depend on anyone but yourself,' Ella says roughly. 'That way, you'll never be let down.'

Annie doesn't know how to respond. It's her own hand that reaches out now and covers Ella's.

'You've been hurt,' Annie says. 'I'm sorry. I'm here, to listen.' She squeezes Ella's fingers.

Ella doesn't answer. Instead, she reaches below her bunk and produces a bottle of vodka. Without asking, she pours them each a double shot and they drink in silence. It should have been uncomfortable, but somehow, in that moment, Annie feels a connection with her superior. Neither of them wants to be alone, but after Ella's outburst, it seems that no further conversation is required. There will be no secrets shared tonight, Annie sees that now as she clambers back up into the top bunk. Regardless, for the first time, here in this tiny cabin, with someone else with her, she feels slightly safer.

Vaguely, Annie wonders where Brandy is. She is, after all, lying in the girl's bed.

At some point, Annie is aware that Ella's breathing has changed. Slow and steady now – her boss is obviously asleep.

The walls, their closeness so recently a comfort, seem smaller somehow.

Annie hangs her head to her chest, all hope and positivity gone.

Just like earlier, and the nights that came before, precious sleep eludes her.

–

The night is still hot.

The horizon is an unseen thing. Annie knows it is there, but darkness covers everything. On the starboard side there is no breeze at all, and she slides to sit on the teak beside the anchoring mechanism.

Her breathing is quick and fast. Is this a panic attack? One that is ongoing, not to be lessened or eased until she is out of Greek waters, in a different country?

Worry isn't a stranger to Annie. It is always there, always has been. Since she was small and learned of her origins, she wondered if it were a symbol of her beginnings. Wondered if that tiny, helpless baby somehow knew that the absence of the arms that had once held her was a kind of foreshadowing.

Her constant up to now has been Robyn, and there was not only safety there, but love, too, in being Robyn's chosen one. Overprotective and weighty but love all the same.

Now, there are other people in her life. Her crewmates seem to like her, but to confide in them, both of her own sin and the worries she's facing, would cause damage. They would be complicit in the fraud she has committed.

What would they do, though, those that profess to like her? Captain, Ella, even Cat, would they surround her like guards against this persecutor who, technically, has not done anything to Annie? Or would they push her away, close ranks with Annie left outside, kick her off the boat and report her to the authorities?

Annie puts her head in her hands.

Tomorrow is the guests' last day of charter; *Ananke* will be returning to port. Annie dares to admit to herself that, for the first time, she's not desperate to get back to land, back to the familiarity of…

Robyn.

Annie covers her mouth with a trembling hand.

To think it is a sacrilege! Like swearing in church, but much worse. Annie lets a small cry out, releasing it through her fingers into the howling wind. She doesn't want to think of why.

Correction: she won't even let herself consider the reasons behind this awful, wicked thought.

The tell-tale creak of the heavy anchor below, shifting on the seabed, brings Annie out of her horrors.

She looks up, over the side, at the far-off lights of Athens town. Annie blinks and turns in a slow circle.

The lights were not there earlier. When she came on deck and looked over the railing, she could see nothing, not even the horizon. The boat has spun; the anchor is caught, *again*.

She needs to wake Danny, or the captain, but her night-time activities are already under scrutiny. They will want to know why she was here, on deck, and not sleeping as she is supposed to be. Luca has already caught her up all night in the crew mess, and Brandy woke her from the sun lounger just this morning. She's been making stupid mistakes, and soon the department heads will start to talk, if they are not already. Exchanging information, discovering that Annie isn't getting her eight hours' break. They'll deem her unfit for work. Then where will she be?

Stuck in Athens, with her harasser somewhere close by.

Shit!

On tiptoe, she peers over the side into the inky black water.

She's done this before, more than once, and has been successful each time. The previous time it was also dead of night, and she managed it then by using the downlights of *Ananke* that glow blue through the water.

The small tender is right below her; she can use it as a launching platform.

Annie picks up the foot-long remote that controls the anchor's rise and fall, and clambers down the side into the boat with it clutched to her chest.

She knows someone is there before she sees them. It's a smell, a scent. The moment isn't human. It's animal.

It's feral.

Annie, like the hunted so often do, freezes.

A small, pale hand, with scratches on the back, comes up to sweep the hood of a green mac from her face.

She looks like she's floating on the surface of the ocean. The boat she is perched in is tiny, smaller than the fishermen's vessels.

Nothing more than a rowboat with a minuscule motor attached to the back.

Robyn smiles. 'Hello, Annie,' she says.

Goosebumps cover Annie, from her head down to her feet.

Annie blinks at her friend. The remote for the anchor slips from Annie's grasp. It bounces down to land in the tender with a clatter.

Robyn has a chipped front tooth. Annie wonders what happened this time. It is a vague thought, one that is not important. It is fleeting, and then the freeze has gone, and Annie knows she is face to face with the stranger who has been haunting her.

Not a stranger, some part of her mind shrieks, *it's just Robyn!*

'Rob—!' Annie's voice is louder than she intended, starting with relief, ending in fear. Only one syllable of her friend's name emerges before she swallows back her cry. 'What are you doing here?' she whispers.

The sweet smile has gone; it was just a cover anyway. The snarl that Annie has so often seen, but has never before had directed at her, is fixed in place.

That word comes to mind again. *Feral.*

'What are you doing here?' Annie repeats. 'W-what's wrong?'

Robyn meets Annie's eye. 'You left me,' she says simply.

Annie's mouth falls open. 'You... you knew I was here!' Indignation soars. 'I gave you my tip money!'

The fear is gone, so suddenly that the fury that arrives in its place rocks Annie.

Robyn's eyes glint in the darkness. Small, black, shiny pebbles in a pale face. 'You think that's all it takes? You think you can throw some cash at me and I'll stay quiet? You think you can *run off to Spain*, without me!'

Annie stares down at her, her mouth a circle of shock. How does Robyn even know about the crossing to Spain?

'You've changed, Annie. You think you are hot stuff now, getting this job, using me to get out here and then ditching me.

You used me, like everyone else.' Robyn turns her head, spits over the side. 'After all I did for you. Tobias, that girl from the ferry. Everything I did, and you planned to leave me here.'

The heat of the night drains away. Annie feels cold. 'W-what do you mean, all you did?'

'You're such an idiot!' Robyn's voice quivers in a hiss. 'The fire, the girl, I did that for you, Annie.'

'You set fire to the taverna?' Annie's hands clench into fists. 'Why? Why would you do that?'

But she knows why. It's not about Annie, not really. She remembers that night. Tobias, using Robyn's body as a vessel, retreating afterwards to his room, turning the lock so she couldn't follow him. His father's anger in the following days. The names he called Robyn.

Annie leans forwards and grips the side of the tender. 'What do you mean, that girl? Which girl? W-what did you do?'

Robyn smiles triumphantly. 'She was looking for her passport. I did you a favour, Annie. I was looking out for you.'

Annie breathes out and wraps her fingers tighter round the side of the boat. 'No,' she says, 'please tell me you didn't hurt her.'

Robyn moves then; in a single leap she's clambered from the tiny boat she arrived in, into *Ananke*'s tender.

Annie turns her back, glancing upwards at the ladder-like railings of *Ananke*'s side. She hauls herself up, the anger dissipated, dismay back in its place. She uses her fear. It lends her strength as she grips the top railing of the lower deck. Hope bursts up and out, bright like the Greek sunshine that Annie deeply loves.

But Robyn is behind her. Annie freezes for a vital second. She will scream when she's drawn breath. She will run the length of *Ananke* and she will reach the captain's quarters, yelling her head off to wake both Sid and Carly. The lie doesn't matter any more. She knows now – has always known, really – what Robyn is capable of. The tables have turned, and now it's her turn to face Robyn's wrath.

The fire alarm.

It is a sudden thought, bristling up and jostling for place in her mind. There are several, all of them pointed out to Annie when she had her induction.

Where is the nearest one?

The boat has remained in a slow turn; the lights of distant Athens are dimmed by tears she didn't even realise she was shedding. She doesn't know where she is; did she climb down the starboard side, or the port?

It doesn't matter. She will retreat in her plan. Forget the fire alarm; she will scream, and scream, and scream until someone comes to her—

Why isn't she screaming already?

Annie opens her mouth but she's on an out-breath, and all that emerges is a small huff of nothingness.

She gets a foot on the second to top railing, lifts her other leg to swing it over the side.

Free!

Freedom!

Almost to safety!

Something smashes into her right ankle. Pain holds back for a second, then it blooms, worse than any hurt she's ever felt.

She looks down, knows it is a mistake to do so.

Her foot is at a strange angle. Below, on the tender, Robyn is looking up at her, the anchor control in her hand, that terrible, awful, broken-toothed smile on her face.

Robyn's hand snaps up, her fingers curling around Annie's injured ankle. She squeezes, adjusts her grip and yanks on her foot.

Annie sees her own fingers as they slide down, first knocking against the railings, then the cold, smooth side of *Ananke*.

In the hull of the tender, she folds in two, stunned by the sudden descent.

It is instinctive to curl into herself, foetal, quiet and still, just like she was found all those years ago.

Robyn's hands are on her, moving up and down her limbs, her fingers pinching, her fists thumping. With one hand across

Annie's chest, Robyn's fingers twist their way into her pocket. She withdraws her hand, sneering as she holds up Ashley Mercer's passport and the mobile phone she gave Annie. Annie follows the trajectory of the phone as it is hurled into the sea.

Annie unfurls herself and goes into a crouch on the side of the tender. She dares to look at her adversary.

A single swipe. It feels as though Robyn has a meaty, man-sized paw, instead of those tiny, pale hands.

The water is a shock. So much cooler than the waters she's played in, swum in, done deck duties in. For the very first time, the ocean is not her friend.

Something ice-like touches her neck, even colder than the Aegean Sea.

Even though it will antagonise her, Annie speaks anyway. It suddenly is vital that for once, Annie speaks the truth to Robyn. It is time. It has been years that she's held it inside. She hasn't let herself say it before. She hasn't even let herself *think* it.

'I *was* leaving you,' Annie says. 'I *was* going to Spain at the end of the season. Alone.' It is the truth, she realises now. And, just to make sure Robyn really understands her intentions, she adds, 'Without you.'

Robyn is working fast, whipping up the spare chain that coils around the anchor pocket. She doesn't stop spinning it, even when she looks into Annie's eyes.

There is sorrow there, Annie sees, in that face she knows even better than her own.

Robyn is sorry, but she still can't stop.

Still *won't* stop.

And Annie won't retract her words.

Annie clings on to the side of the tender. Beside her, those blue, guiding lights glow. An invitation to do what comes naturally. To flip, dive, swoop. She could easily cover the width of *Ananke* underneath her hull. She could find an air pocket and stay there until sunup.

But though the intention is there, her brain is foggy; her vision is cloudy from the blow to her head. Instead, she remains where she is, concentrating on her former friend.

'I know you were leaving me,' says Robyn. 'I always knew you would, one day.'

Which is funny, because even Annie didn't know until now.

Face to face, the same pose they've been in so many times. Like when they kneeled on Annie's bed, sharing plans, whispering, plotting their future.

Always together, then, now, forever.

'You hurt me.' Robyn is sobbing now.

Real tears. Not the fake ones she sometimes brings out. Her cries wrack her skinny body.

Even though Annie knows where this is going, where it will end, she is still sorry to have caused tears like this.

But she won't say it. She's said those words to this girl so many times. She won't say it now. Never again.

The irony doesn't escape her, of the façade she places on her like a shield. She tilts her chin up, sets her jaw.

Tough girl.

Pure Robyn.

'Are you even sorry?' Robyn's question is a juddering sob. She pauses, chain loops in her hands, held aloft, as though she's about to place a crown on her friend's head.

It isn't a way out. This isn't a situation where, if she says the correct appeasing, mollifying words there will be an exit, a happy ending.

There are no happy endings.

Annie takes a breath. 'I had the best time. I had the time of my life here, without you.' She feels tears, or it might just be seawater, flowing down her face.

It feels cleansing.

She smiles, and tastes blood on her tongue.

'I'll never be sorry,' Annie says.

The crown falls to rest around her neck. Annie can't or won't fight it.

Robyn presses the button on the control, and the anchor rises up, tucking itself neatly into the pocket on the side of *Ananke*, until it meets its obstruction.

Eventually, it grinds to a crunching halt.

PART FOUR

1

ELLA
PRESENT DAY

All Ella can think about on the short tender ride back to *Ananke* is how confused she feels.

The words of the girl back in the marina replay over and over in Ella's mind.

Ashley Mercer was her name! And I won't ever forget her!

'I don't understand any of this,' Ella mutters out loud.

A body, just discovered tonight, of a girl who bears exactly the same name as Ella's dead stewardess.

Danny doesn't hear her over the roar of the radio. In some distant corner of her mind, Ella can hear Captain's voice coming through, demanding to know their whereabouts.

Danny hunches over the radio. She doesn't hear what he is saying to placate Carly. She doesn't care.

That is a revelation in itself. All these years, dozens of seasons under her belt, her only goal to make the captain and the guests happy. Right now, she couldn't give two shits if Carly fires her.

'…medical issue.'

Ella snaps her head up at Danny's words. He feels the burn of her glare and glances at her over his shoulder.

Ella stands up and walks to him. 'What was that?'

'I told her you fainted.' He shrugs. 'She wanted to know what's taking so long.'

Carly is waiting on the platform, her eyes filled with concern. She holds her hand out to help Ella up.

'I'm fine.' Ella brushes her away.

There must be something in her tone because Carly drops her hand. 'You're sure?'

'Yes.'

'The guests are winding down. Why don't you get an early night?'

There is nothing more Ella would like than to crawl into her bunk and pull the cover over her head. But if she does that, she might very well not get back up.

'I'm fine.' To her left, she sees Brandy heading her way. 'Brandy,' she calls, 'knock off for the night; I'll take it from here.'

Ella cleans and cleans. These guests, the Kilfoyles, are not ravers or party animals; they were not back on their original charter, and they're not now. There is no need to scour the decks of wine stains, or high-heel marks left in the plush carpets. She could easily go to bed with the knowledge that if Captain were to do a random walkabout, there would be nothing out of place.

But to scrub takes physical toil. She is immersed in the action. She hopes with this motion will come a lightbulb moment that explains everything she's learned tonight.

So she cleans.

But still, nothing makes sense.

At some point in the night, she finds herself next to the anchor housing. She sits down heavily upon it and pulls out her phone.

She taps out a message to her old friend Pippa.

> Pip, you know the stew we had, Ashley – do you
> know much about her?

Almost immediately, Ella's phone rings. Pippa.

'Hey, how are you? How's the new season?' Pippa, as always, is brusque and straight to the point.

'Weird.' It's true. Season starts are normally joyous. Everyone is refreshed, rejuvenated. The tiredness comes later, then the sniping starts and the bitching and suddenly, it's all over. Everyone still bounces back the next year, though, ready to go again.

'I heard you're back on *Ananke*, same crew, same guests.' Pippa's tone is laden with caution.

'Yes, it's... not good.'

'It was always bound to be that way, one person missing and all that.' Pippa sighs. 'It was so sad. I barely knew her, but she was... pretty awesome.'

It is the opening that Ella needs. 'Do you know her backstory?'

'Nope. Never got the chance to ask,' comes Pippa's reply.

'Did anything strike you as odd about her?' Ella asks.

'Like what?' But before Ella can answer, Pippa moves on. 'Actually, there was something... Roxy saw her, the night she left *Siren* and joined *Ananke*. She was in the plaza, handed her tip money over to another girl.' Pippa sighs suddenly. 'Look, to be honest, I wasn't really listening to Rox. Busy, you know? I only remember that part because there's no way in hell I'd be parted from my tips, right?'

'Right.' Ella frowns at the screen.

'Look, it was weird, okay, that's all I know.' Pippa's tone changes; suddenly she's ultra-serious, the Pippa that Ella trained. 'Why are you asking?'

'It doesn't matter.' Ella is weary now; all the toil, the fainting episode, the mental strain, the once-grief-turned-betrayal has caught up to her. She glances at her watch. After midnight. She has to be up and on deck in less than six hours. 'I'll let you go, Pip. Good chat.'

'El, when are you next back in the marina?'

'Tomorrow, I think. Last day of charter.'

'Let's catch up. I'll bring Roxy, see if she can remember anything else.'

Let it go. Just... forget it and get on with your life.

Instead, Ella finds herself nodding into the phone. 'Okay, see you then.'

Ella dozes fitfully. There are no nightmares; she's not asleep long enough for any to form, and for that, she's grateful.

Before dawn, she throws off her thin sheet, pulls on her uniform and heads towards the crew mess.

Danny is there, his eyes thin from lack of sleep, his hands cupped around a coffee that looks like it is long cold. She slides in next to him on the bench and peers at his mug. A film has gathered on the top of it.

'Need a refill?' she asks him.

'Yeah.' He glances at the clock on the mess wall. 'Couldn't sleep?'

She scoops his mug up and grabs a fresh one from next to the coffee machine. 'Nope. You too?'

'Thinking about… everything. That girl, last night, the consequences for us…'

She turns to face him. 'What do you mean?'

'Maybe not for us, but whoever first employed… whoever she was.' He accepts the fresh coffee from her and frowns. 'Where did you get her from?'

'A recommendation from Pippa. Pip got her from the agency.' At the mention of her friend's name, she recalls their conversation last night. 'I spoke to her, Pip. She said Roxy thinks there was something weird going on with Ashley.'

'With not-Ashley, you mean.' Danny's frown is still in place as he stares into his mug.

Ella flaps her hand. 'Whoever.' She takes a long sip of her own coffee, strong and black and very much needed. 'Pip is going to meet me when we dock later; she's bringing Roxy along.'

Danny flops his head back and rolls his eyes. 'I think you're concentrating on the wrong thing here.'

She sits back down, opposite him this time, a questioning look on her face.

'It's like this,' he says, 'someone is going to be in the brown stuff when it gets out that our Ashley wasn't really Ashley. If it comes down to the wire, it's going to be seen as fraud. We probably won't get out of the dock again all season, another investigation will open, all those questions.' He raises his mug and points it at Ella. 'You want to go through that again?'

She can't suppress a shudder. But she also can't stand the thought of the lack of truth. She thinks back to last night, the walls around those people who lived alongside the real Ashley Mercer. They are not supposed to be here, any of them. Are they going to even speak up and officially identify the girl from the dumpster?

Ella closes her eyes. 'It's such a mess,' she whispers.

A hand on hers. She opens her eyes and meets Danny's. There is a tenderness there that is something new. Previously, his looks have ranged from casually appreciative to borderline flirtatious to an almost brotherly friendship.

Footsteps clatter down the spiral staircase.

Ella snatches her hand away from his as Brandy comes into the crew mess. 'Dudes,' she says as she ties her hair back. 'Is the coffee on?' Brandy moves to the machine.

Ella sits back. Brandy and Danny. She had almost forgotten.

She shakes her head, flipping thoughts of him and his hand-holding away.

She mustn't forget. Danny is a player. Her feelings are not reciprocated.

She stands up and heads towards the stairs. No word of a goodbye to either of them.

As she makes her way up to the deck, Brandy's voice drifts up the stairwell.

'What's with her?'

Ella doesn't stick around to hear Danny's reply.

—

The Kilfoyles eat their last breakfast on the upper deck. There is a strange atmosphere surrounding the table. The air is heavy, not like an impending storm, but sorrowful, grey.

It is the last time they will see each other. Ella realises that's what the emotion is. They are not dear friends, these guests and the crew, but they shared something that has wrapped them up in a strange bond, a shared tragedy. Yet, after today, they will likely not see each other ever again.

The meal is a quiet affair, a brief moment of respite when Ayton comes up alongside Chef to present a tray of freshly baked, homemade croissants. The crew cheer him.

It's a lovely scene, but Ella feels her heart hardening. Apparently, it shows on her face.

Danny takes her arm and moves her a few feet away from the table.

'What's wrong?' he says, adding, 'Apart from the obvious.'

She can feel the ice growing in her bones, starting at her head, spreading downwards like the old, dying roots of a plant. 'I'm fine,' she replies coolly.

'No, you're not. You're… you're like you were before, a couple of years ago.' Danny narrows his eyes as he scrutinises her. He grips her upper arm tightly. 'Don't do this; don't go back like that, El.'

She thought he'd never noticed. She thought she'd kept herself in check, all this time.

'We're off tonight. We'll have drinks, just you and me,' Danny says.

It isn't a question, and it's what she's wanted for so long. But that ice is in her now, in her core, and she pulls her arm from his.

'I'm meeting someone,' she says.

'Pippa and Roxy?' he asks. 'Fine, we'll meet them, then we'll have drinks.'

She is tired, again. All she really wants when the Kilfoyles leave is to crawl into her bunk and sleep for the rest of the season. Or pack her bags and go…

Go where? Not home. Home is not a sanctuary like it was in her youth. Home is a house in California where family members dutifully visit and spend time in a grey, cracked fog.

She is better off staying on *Ananke*. At least here there is noise and clamour. At least here she will be kept busy. Too busy to let thoughts of Ashley—

Captain's voice calls her over the radio, interrupting her thoughts. An instruction for her, Danny and Chef to meet to discuss the next charter.

Ella scoffs. So much for Captain releasing them from the season if they want to go.

With a sigh, Ella heads towards the crew mess.

The preference sheets for the next guests are on the table. Danny and Chef are already reading them. Cat is there, pouncing on them, not reading the captain's glare that this meeting is for department heads only.

'Cat, scram,' Ella says. She slides in next to Chef and eyeballs Danny. 'Do you want to keep your staff in line, Bosun?'

Chef titters. Catching Carly's eye, Ella sees a twitch of her lips. She knows what that means. Captain thinks she's back, on board, remaining here for the summer.

Captain has got what she wanted.

Ella ignores her. She can walk any time. And she may well do that. Captain shouldn't get so comfortable.

'Who have we got, then?' Ella asks, leafing through the papers. She is all business.

For now.

—

They line up on the dock, dressed smartly in their uniforms. Ella looks down the line, sees the slight gap where the third stewardess would normally stand between Brandy and Cat. An unconscious space.

One that Ella will need to fill, she realises reluctantly.

If she stays, that is.

It won't be easy. In fact, it will be just like last year. Only last year, she got lucky with the girl Pippa was able to recommend.

Or unlucky, as it turned out.

Maybe Pippa has another girl for her. She will ask her tonight. Ella doesn't need to know anything about the girl who called herself Ashley. That's over, done, in the past. She just needs a third stew.

She needs to move on before this darkness eats her up even more than it already has.

She feels a sharp elbow in her side. She gasps, turns to glare at Danny. He frowns deeply, nodding his head pointedly.

Shit. Nikki is there, right in front of her, waiting to say goodbye.

'Sorry,' Ella murmurs, holding out her hand for a shake.

Nikki pulls her into a swift embrace. 'You did a wonderful job,' the older woman says. 'We're so pleased we came back, and we're so sorry for... your loss.'

Ella's eyes immediately fill with tears. She blinks them away before pulling back from Nikki and fixing her expression into one of professionalism.

'Thank you,' she says politely. 'Have a safe trip home.'

Nikki keeps her hand on Ella's wrist and draws her slightly away from the line. 'Was there another deckhand on board last year?' she asks. 'One that didn't come back. Ron... or Rob?'

Ella shakes her head. 'No, it was just us last year. And... uh, you know.'

Nikki nods. 'I keep thinking about that night. I almost mentioned it when we got here, a couple of days ago, but... but I'm not sure.'

Ella puts her head on one side as she regards Nikki. 'What are you not sure of?'

Nikki takes a deep breath. 'I thought I heard an argument, last year. Someone on the deck. It was late, like, really late. It sounded like they were having a set-to.'

Ella feels a tremor run through her. Yet another snippet of information that she's never heard before. 'Who was it?' she urges Nikki.

'It was weird. It wasn't like a screaming match. More like a hushed argument or maybe not even that. Scuffling, perhaps.

Maybe the crew just joshing each other. I didn't think it was anything until I heard her say his name.'

'Rob?' Ella asks. 'You're sure that's what Ashley said?'

Nikki's face falls. 'No, that's the thing. I'm *not* sure. It was the middle of the night; I was half asleep; whoever was out on deck wasn't being loud. It might not have been Ashley. It might not have been a man.' Nikki takes her hand off Ella's arm and runs it through her own hair. 'I'm sorry, I just… it's hard to know that she was down there… *dying*… and nobody had any idea that she was in difficulty. And of course, nobody else was there, because they would have helped her. Right?' Nikki sniffs and wipes at her face with her sleeve. 'I keep thinking about it. About *that night*. Going over and over it.' Nikki glances at her, her eyes alert now. 'You know there's this thing, that if you weren't paying attention, or you try too hard to remember something, your mind fills in the holes. I wonder if that's what I'm doing, filling in holes with things that didn't even happen.' She runs her hands through her hair and looks downcast again. 'It can drive one crazy. Sometimes, I think it's driven *me* crazy. That's why I never said anything, when I was interviewed after the accident.'

Ella can feel the captain's eyes on them now. Like a laser beam, the heat of that stare. She can practically read Carly's thoughts.

The clients should leave happy, not crying, Ella!

Ella squeezes Nikki's shoulders. 'I'm so glad you guys had a good time; that means the world to me.' Her words are loud; there's a fixed smile on Ella's face that is as fake as Ashley's name. But the last thing she needs is Captain grilling her, accusing her of sending the client off the boat in tears.

She can feel Carly's exhalation of relief, and with a quick hug for Piers, and a slightly more lingering one with Ayton, Ella steps back into line and waves them off.

–

Brandy is on her case as soon as they get back on deck.

'We're going to get another stewardess, right?' She trots after Ella, hot on her heels as they make their way below deck. 'Because with Slopy-bloody-Sid refusing to help out, there's only two on deck; Cat can't help us, and I don't wanna spend all season understaffed.'

'I'm on it, B,' Ella says as she dodges around her, heading for her cabin.

'For real, yeah?' Brandy swivels to stand in front of Ella, blocking her way. 'It's only the second charter and I'm knackered already.'

Ella's temper flares, quick and hot. 'Maybe if you get your eight hours each night and quit having visitors in your bedroom, you'll have a bit more energy!'

'Whoa!' Brandy slams her hand on the doorframe of Ella's room. 'What does *that* mean?'

The annoyance dips and fades fast into a heavy weariness. 'Forget it. I'm getting another stew, so just… chill. Okay?'

Brandy's arm remains in place. Ella moves forwards, leaving Brandy no option but to drop her hand to her side. Ella slips into her cabin and closes the door.

Shoulders sagging, Ella sinks onto the bottom bunk.

This is the thing she always forgets and is rudely reminded of at the start of a season.

Nowhere to run, nowhere to hide.

Nowhere just to sit and be.

Nowhere just to sit and… think.

She can hear her out there still, Brandy's voice cutting through the door. She's cornered someone else, probably Cat, and her moaning is very audible.

Ella pulls off her uniform and slips into her shorts and an old shirt. She snatches up her bag and phone, wrenches open the door and barges out, shouldering a still-whining Brandy on her way past.

'Where are you going?' Brandy bleats at her.

'Off the boat,' Ella snaps.

They are gathered in the mess; she can hear their voices. *Ananke* is claustrophobic now and Ella needs some space. She needs to walk, to not have Danny's voice chipping away in her ear, or Brandy's, or Cat's. Ella does a sharp turn up the stairs and cuts through the guest quarters to avoid them.

She stops speed-walking once she's at the marina. The sudden loss of motion has her pausing for thought. She looks left, towards Cotton, and the other bars and restaurants. She could walk in there right now and have a shot with someone she's met before. Old crew, old adversaries, old friends.

Ella turns away from the bars and looks beyond the plaza.

The ferries are there. The dumpsters with all the rats. The place where nobody goes unless they are desperate.

The place where – according to Sid's little recording – Ashley *really* didn't want to go.

Not Ashley, she reminds herself. But the girl who took her name. The real Ashley isn't there any more either.

Ella shivers and turns left, past the bars, past the lines of superyachts, past the fishermen's cove. She walks on and on, not stopping until her trainers sink into the soft, white sand of the next inlet along.

Only then does she slump down to sit on the beach.

–

She dozes, on and off, feeling her body unwind as she sips at her bottle of water and watches the sea.

It is peaceful here. Empty. Normally, at the start of the holiday season, this beach would be heaving, bodies packed on every spare inch of sand. The virus is still causing havoc on travel, though, and only those who can afford to isolate a week either side of their vacation are here.

Even then they're not *here*, on a beach holiday. No, those people, the ones like the Kilfoyles, are on the superyachts, not slumming it in waterside hotels.

Ella's phone beeps, disrupting both her reverie and her peace, and with a sigh she plucks it out of her bag.

It's Pippa, telling her she's already in Cotton, Roxy is with her, and is Ella coming to join them?

Ella puts the phone away and struggles to her feet.

Maybe a drink with her old friend is needed. Too much time alone leads to wallowing, which leads to overthinking. To dwelling on things that she has no power to change.

Determinedly, Ella makes her way back towards the marina.

2

They see each other at the same time. An awkward pause where Ella isn't sure whether to greet her or not. In the seconds that pass, the other girl makes the decision for her.

'Hi.' Ashley's – the real Ashley's – friend's voice is throaty, but she looks better than she did the last time Ella saw her.

'Hey.' Ella throws her a little wave as she approaches. 'How are you?' She looks around, remembering the dreadlocked bodyguard-type guy. 'Where's your mate?'

She jerks her head towards the ferries. 'Packing up our stuff.' The girl sticks out her hand. 'I'm Shaneece, by the way.'

'Ella.' The girl's grip is surprisingly strong for someone so weak-looking. 'You're moving on?'

'Yep. Mason doesn't want to hang around, not with… you know.' The girl swipes at her eyes. 'He doesn't want to be here when they start asking questions about Ashley.'

It doesn't escape Ella, the irony of this. Nobody will ever be held to account for any of this. Shaneece and her man, Mason, and the rest of the homeless community won't talk because they are not supposed to be here. Ella herself, and Danny, are reluctant to get too far involved. Questions will be raised if they go to the police about this girl who was using someone else's passport. Ella might face some sort of punishment for the accidentally concealed evidence. Captain's licence will be revoked if the correct checks were not carried out.

And they weren't. Ella had trusted Pippa.

Pippa had trusted the agency.

Heck, Ella had trusted her own judgment, witnessing how Ashley had raised the alarm over the fire at the taverna, and her subsequent quick thinking with the hoses.

The questions that will never be answered are endless, suffocating, stifling.

'The photo you showed me, that wasn't Ashley, but I'd seen her before.' Shaneece speaks up, interrupting Ella's thoughts.

Ella's heart leaps. 'You had?'

'Yeah. She was new, came to the ferries with a girl friend.' Shaneece wraps her arms around herself. 'She didn't have much to do with anyone, but she was kind to me, once. Didn't like her friend, though. There was something off about her. Something real shady. A lot of people thought the same way.'

So, fake-Ashley had a friend. She wasn't totally alone, like she'd said.

Ella recalls the conversation, that hot tub night again.

Did you come here with anyone?

Ashley had claimed to have come here alone.

Hadn't she?

I came here for something new.

Ella feels a jolt in her chest. Fake-Ashley hadn't answered Ella's question at all.

Someone is hassling me.

It'll be better in Spain.

Then another memory, a fresh one that until now Ella had forgotten.

She implicated me in something. And I can't get out of it now. Not without losing everything.

Ella gasps out loud. The girl that Ella knew as Ashley wasn't in cahoots with a partner in crime.

She was *running* from her. From someone she professed to be her *sister*, but who Shaneece says was her friend.

'Who was her friend?' Ella demands.

Shaneece jumps at the sudden edge in Ella's tone.

'Robyn was her name.' Shaneece shrugs. 'She kept to herself. But she took Ash's passport, or at least, Ash was convinced she

264

had. Ash went to find it, find her, but we never saw Ashley again. Not until the other night… when they found her…' Shaneece's words end on a sob.

The passport. The one that Ashley, *fake*-Ashley, wanted to keep with her as much as possible.

The passport that nobody ever found after she'd gone.

There it was, the missing gap all this time, and what she had meant when she said she'd been implicated in something terrible.

'The photo I showed you, of my friend.' Ella is cautious now, aware that she's getting in deeper than she should. 'Did you know her name?'

'Annie,' says Shaneece. 'She said her name was Annie.'

—

Ella staggers across the marina. She doesn't know where she's headed. There's a vague notion that she's supposed to meet up with Pippa, but right now, she can't even think straight.

Now she has two more names, and neither of them mean a thing to her.

Annie.

Robyn.

The graffiti on the side of *Ananke*, this time last year.

Annie is a liar.

Nikki's words from this morning.

I thought I heard an argument. Who is Rob?

Her name rings out across the square. Ella jerks her head up and sees Pippa, waving at her from the terrace of Cotton.

Danny is there, feet up on the railings. Beside him is Roxy.

Ella changes direction and hurries over to the bar.

Pippa trots down the stairs and gives Ella a quick hug.

'…so good to see you, girl. We're both on this island, but I never see you!'

Ella tries to focus on what her friend is talking about, but all she can think about is the bombshell she just learned about.

Pippa drags Ella up to the terrace. 'Keep in mind that we didn't really know Ashley, before she moved to *Ananke*,' says Pippa. 'She was just a day worker, but… everyone liked her. I think she could have had a long career if…' She tails off awkwardly.

'It was real sad,' says Roxy sombrely. 'She was cool; everyone loved her.'

There it is again, that love and adoration for a girl that nobody really knew.

She throws Danny a look as she sinks onto the cushioned chair next to him.

'What's up?' His face is one of concern, even though she hasn't said anything to him.

'Later,' she tells him, out of the corner of her mouth. She turns to face Pippa, who is pouring a glass for Ella from a jug of sangria. Ella takes a long pull and a deep breath. 'Pip, you got Ashley from the agency, right?'

'Yep. Joan said she was totally inexperienced, though she'd done some service work back home and proclaimed to be a natural around water. Joan undersold her; Ashley was a gem.'

'Why was Ashley in Greece? I mean, who'd she come here with?'

'Nobody,' Roxy chips in. 'Said she was alone.'

'But Pippa said she gave her tip money away?'

Roxy nods eagerly. 'Yeah, it was dead weird. I saw the exchange; they were obviously friends. And the strangest thing…'

'What?'

'Ashley asked this girl if she'd *seen Ashley*.'

'Huh?' Danny, previously lounging in his chair, sits up. 'Say that again?'

'I know, weird, right?' Roxy downs her remaining sangria in one and pours another. 'She said that this other girl, her friend, didn't need to *steal any more*!'

Ella sits forwards in her chair. 'Have you seen this other girl again?'

Roxy shakes her head. 'Nope. But you know what it's like, people come, people go. That's just our industry, then there's the ferry people.'

'You think this other girl came from the ferries?' Pippa demands. 'Wait, do you think *Ashley* came from the ferries?'

Her name wasn't Ashley! Ella wants to scream it, but, although Pippa and, by extension, Roxy, are her friends, something tells her to keep this new knowledge quiet for now.

'And another thing,' Roxy says, pausing dramatically, 'I don't think her name was even Ashley.'

'What?' Pippa pounces. 'You never told me that!'

'I didn't think much of it at the time. Didn't think anything until she'd died.'

Just like Nikki, Ella thinks. All these little pieces of information on their own are worth very little. But after the fact, added up, it's a revelation.

'Well, what was her name?' Pippa demands.

'Annie. That other girl, she called her Annie.'

Pippa wrinkles up her nose. 'I don't know, Rox, I mean, are you *sure*?'

At her superior's question, Roxy's face falls. 'I... I think so. I don't know. I called her, she saw me, she looked... weird when she saw me there. She didn't stop and chat.'

'Anyway, Annie could be a nickname, or... I don't know.' The mood around the table, far from jovial to begin with, dips and silence falls.

'Annie.' Danny speaks up and Ella turns to look at him.

His brow is furrowed, like he's deep in thought, and Ella knows that at any moment he's going to join the dots on where he has seen that name before.

Plastered over the side of *Ananke*, the graffiti he had to clean off a year ago.

Ella stands up. 'Hey, we've got to get back,' she says hurriedly to the girls. 'Thanks for the drink but we've got to turn the ship around for the next charter.'

Pippa, understanding the fleeting lives that the yachties live, doesn't try to dissuade her. She envelops Ella and Danny in a quick hug.

Ella prods Danny's arm. 'Come on,' she says, 'I've got lots to catch you up on.'

'That name,' he says, when they're out of earshot of the bar, 'Annie! Do you—'

'Yes,' she interrupts him. 'It was the graffiti written on *Ananke*. "Annie is a liar". I remember it,' she says grimly.

'Oh,' he says. 'Yeah, that too. I'd forgotten about that.'

'Woah, wait, back up. What do you mean, "that too"?'

They are on the fringes of the marina now, and Danny draws her to sit on a bench. 'Do you remember when I took Ashley across to the island, let her drive the tender?'

Ella nods, remembers it all too well. 'She lost the boat, right?'

'She didn't tie it up, let it drift away. She was off that day, inside her head.' He glances around and lowers his voice. 'We picked up the diving instructor; she introduced herself to him as Annie!'

'What!' A jolt passes through Ella. 'Why didn't you tell me?'

Danny appears to be deep in thought. 'It wasn't a big thing. The guy said, "Nice to meet you, Annie", or something like that, and then she corrected him. Said her name was Ashley, made out like he'd misheard her. But he didn't; I heard her say it too.'

'The girl she was with is called Robyn.' Ella says it out loud, and there is immediate relief that she's no longer the only one in the know.

'How do you know that?'

'I saw a girl from the ferries. She also said our Ashley was actually called Annie. And she came here with this Robyn, but…' Ella trails off, heaviness now outweighing the relief of moments earlier.

'But what?' Danny asks.

'I think this Robyn was blackmailing Ashley, or *Annie*, rather. I think our girl was trying to escape. The crossing to Spain was her end game; it was her chance of a future. And I think Robyn ended that dream.'

Danny's intake of breath is sharp. 'You think this Robyn killed Annie?' He barks out a laugh of disbelief. 'We were anchored, El, she didn't come aboard and kill her.' A moment's silence and Danny's eyes narrow in suspicion. 'El, you don't think that's what happened, surely?'

It wasn't. Ella hadn't known what to think. The whole thing was a bloody mystery.

Until now.

Ella nods. 'That's exactly what I think.'

This time his laughter is loud and long. 'It's not like we were docked here, in the marina. You think this girl sailed out to *Ananke*, climbed aboard and killed our third stew?'

'Nikki Kilfoyle heard an argument on deck that night.' Ella locks eyes with Danny so she can see his expression when she tells him. 'Nikki said whoever it was used the name Rob.'

Danny narrows his eyes.

Ella pushes on. 'I think this Robyn was out of control. She was a bully. She was a controlling psycho. Annie was trying to get away and she so nearly did.'

It is all Ella can say before the tears come. Finally, it is the release she's been holding inside, not just since the death on *Ananke*, but before that…

She can barely breathe through the sobs. Danny envelops her and she takes comfort in the fact that he knows that this breakdown isn't just for Annie.

'You're thinking of him, too,' murmurs Danny.

Him.

They never discuss him or what happened. Ella tries not to even think of him. Danny knows how he died but doesn't know why. He even met him, once, when they all ended up in Florida at the end of one season. Ella does her best not to let him inside her head. They all do, all her family. It's why they're so fractured.

But this parallel with Annie, it's brought it all back to the surface.

She nods into Danny's chest.

'You never talk about him.' Danny's voice is quiet now, tender.

Ella gasps out another sob. 'I can't,' she manages to say.

'It's brought it all back. The accidents were similar, both tragic.' Danny's voice is mild. 'I understand.'

She pushes him away, suffocating suddenly. 'You don't,' she manages. 'You don't understand at all.'

He doesn't press her. For that, she's thankful.

Silence falls. Ella looks out to sea. She can see *Ananke* from here, the gold lettering backlit against the rapidly falling night sky. The sea is inky black, so different from the tempting azure blue during the day. There is no music on the marina tonight, barely any people. The only sound is the gentle breeze rustling through the palm fronds.

'Hades didn't die like they said he did.' The words, once she's said them, are out now. She can't take it back. Alongside this feeling is that name. The name she never speaks any more.

Her brother's name.

Hades.

She feels Danny's eyes on her. She knows if she turns to face him, he'll be looking at her curiously.

'What do you mean?' Danny asks gently. 'He... he had an accident with a rifle.'

She takes a deep breath, remembering the story that her folks put out there.

'Not true.' She swallows hard past the lump in her throat. 'Hades killed himself.'

It is like an echo around the marina, the words she's wanted to say for so long but hasn't dared for fear of them reaching her parents. Words that would make them spiral even further down.

'No!' It is almost a shout from Danny, so loud she cringes into herself.

She feels something on her arm. It is his hand, finding its way into her own.

For once, she doesn't push him away.

Danny speaks again. 'He... he had an accident, on the army base, with the... the gun...'

Ella shakes her head. 'He didn't. He killed himself.' Her voice is blunt and dull, just like her emotions.

'Why?' Danny's tone is full of confusion.

She understands that question. Hades wasn't the sort to do that. Hades, like the rest of Ella's siblings, lived a charmed life and had done since birth.

Until the day came when his life was no longer charmed, nor good, and Hades could see only one way out. Ella searched her memories of her brother for clues she might have missed, red flags and warning signs of something underlying that had slipped under her radar. She could recall nothing.

'He was being bullied,' she whispers now.

'At work? In the forces?' Danny's hand grips hers even tighter.

Ella nods. 'He didn't tell anyone. We didn't find out until later.' A tear drips down her face and lands on their joined hands. 'Until after it was too late. From people who won't say anything officially.'

'They didn't do an investigation?'

'No.' Ella pulls her hand out of his. 'You know how it is.'

Cover-ups. *Ananke*'s owners were no better. Go through the motions, wipe the boat clean and carry on as though nothing happened. Never mind that loss of life occurred.

'And it wasn't a rifle,' she says, 'it was a handgun.'

She looks at Danny for the first time. He is pale. It might just be the moonlight, but she doesn't think so.

'And you're sure of this?' he asks cautiously.

'Self-inflicted, they said.' And here is what she's been thinking about. She locks her eyes on his. 'Just like they said Ashley's – *Annie's* – death was an accident.' Ella tilts her head back. The sky is a blanket of stars, some brighter than others. 'It's not in their best interests to dig too deeply, is it?'

Danny makes no reply. He remains next to her, and she's aware that he is shaking ever so slightly.

'I found nothing about Hades' persecutors. In the end, I had to leave.' She pauses, and says, 'I can't go home again. Everyone is so broken.'

Once. Just one time she'd gone back to the house they'd grown up in. It was no longer a home. The stench of death was as real as if Hades' body had been laid out in the kitchen. One by one, her brothers had made their excuses and had fled. Back to sea, back to yachts, back to a life that kept moving fast enough to keep the past at bay.

'I told her that we're all running from something or looking for something. She was too, but it caught up to her.'

Danny murmurs his agreement.

She turns to him now. 'I need to find this person. I need to track down this Robyn. Because, Danny, *she killed her.*'

Danny nods. 'But she's not here any more. If what they said was true, that she's responsible for the real Ashley Mercer's death, she wouldn't have stayed here.'

He is right. Ella knows that, and maybe, she admits to herself, that's the problem. She will never find the girl who took Annie's life. Just like she'll never find those responsible for ending Hades'.

'God of the underworld,' she whispers.

'Huh?'

She tries for a laugh, but it comes out as a sob. 'My parents named my brothers for Greek mythology. Hades is – *was* – the god of death. You know the story, how in death he was trapped. Just like in life.'

His arm comes around her. 'I didn't know that. So, what about you, El, who were you named for?'

This time it's a real laugh. 'They ran out of ideas when they got to me. I just go by my surname.'

'Themis? And that is…?'

She sits up a little straighter. 'Goddess of law.' She pauses, looks straight at Danny. 'And of justice.'

–

'I'm so sorry about Hades,' Danny says as they make their way back towards *Ananke*. 'I always liked him.'

'I know you did.' It's true. They got on like a house on fire when they met.

'You mustn't let this beat you. Hades and Ashley wouldn't want that.'

It's funny, she muses, as they walk alongside each other. She wasn't Ashley. Her name was Annie, but she doubts they'll ever get used to calling her that.

Not that they'll need to call her anything. She's gone. She's not coming back. Just like Hades.

Yet their persecutors will go on, go forwards. They won't change.

She considers Danny's words. *You mustn't let this beat you.* But it is too late. Ella is beaten.

And yet, time moves, the world spins, the sun goes down and the moon comes up. Ella has no choice but to go on.

She knows she might heal, somewhat at least, in time. But the very fact that justice will never be served weighs heavy on her.

She tells this to Danny now, as they approach *Ananke*.

'Not police justice,' she clarifies. 'Personal justice. For me.' She thumps a hand on her chest, enjoying the sting of her fist. 'For me,' she says, quieter now.

Had she imagined confiding this in him, she would have expected him to laugh. He doesn't. Rather, he nods his agreement.

She shrugs to herself. It's a moot point. Retribution, legal or otherwise, is lost to them. Robyn is in the wind. Hades' tormentors are unknown.

On the passerelle now, Danny's hand is on the small of her back as he guides her onto the vessel. She can see the others through the glass. Lounging, chatting, drinking.

Nothing is different to any other season, except that everything has changed.

Danny's hand is still on her spine. She feels the tickle of his breath as he moves up close behind her. 'Stay with me, tonight,' he murmurs.

Ella shivers. How many years she's been waiting to hear those words.

She opens the door and slips inside. Away from him, the others. Away from everything.

3

She doesn't see him the next morning. Doesn't see any of the crew. She's up at dawn, hurrying off *Ananke*, down the boardwalk to the marina.

This time, she's not looking for Pippa, or Roxy, or Shaneece or the man, Mason. She must leave it all behind her if she's to have any sort of future at all.

Dan is right. If she's not careful, this thing will not only beat her, it will eat her.

She thinks of her mother as she crosses beneath the plaza. Her beautiful mom, once an absolutely stunning woman, now she is wizened, stooped, sleeping her days away in a haze of pills. And her father, previously tall and proud, now smaller, somehow, and grey in both hair and skin. Her brothers, once tightly bound, now scattered, like she is, running as fast as they can from their broken matriarch and patriarch.

They have been eaten. From the inside out.

Ella feels her face harden.

She fears the rage will be there forever.

In the yachting staff agency, Joan is there, on her own, speaking on the telephone. She raises a hand in greeting when Ella comes through the door, holds up five fingers.

Ella is glad she's busy; she has no wish to stop and make idle chat. Instead, she slides the piece of paper with her requirements over the counter.

'Call me if you have anyone,' Ella says on her way out.

She's halfway across the marina when she hears her name being called and the clatter of feet behind her.

Ella turns. Joan, poor old near-to-retirement Joan, is running towards her. The older woman stops, leans over to catch her breath.

'I got a new girl on the books, totally green, but right now, the way things are, it's all I can offer you.' She holds out a piece of paper. A CV, Ella sees, and she takes it from Joan.

Ella thinks about asking Joan if she's done all the proper checks, used the newish database where all the details have been held. But truthfully, Ella knows better of Joan. The woman is old-school, preferring paper files and fax machines, a relic of her time.

She won't be trained now, she's so near retirement. There is no point in trying to pull Joan into the twenty-first century now.

There is little point in anything, any more.

'Thanks,' Ella says. 'I'll give her a call.'

She turns to leave again, but Joan stops her. 'I'm sorry, about the other one. It was... a shock.'

'Yes, it was.' Ella stares past Joan, out to sea. She doesn't want to hear anything more about the girl they lost.

'Such a lovely girl,' Joan says, but Ella is already walking away.

It could almost be a normal day, a normal season, when she walks back onto *Ananke*. She can hear Chef's voice above everyone else's, barking in anger to a deserted galley. Brandy, smoking on the deck above, rolls her eyes as Ella comes aboard.

'No smoking on the sundeck,' Ella says, tilting her head to observe the girl above her.

Brandy holds her glare for a second before flicking her cigarette overboard.

Ella moves past Chef, ignoring his rants, which are usually over something or nothing, and slips inside her cabin.

She closes the door, but there is resistance, and a yelp. Brandy is there, pushing her way inside the cabin.

'I know what you're thinking.' Brandy's tone is hushed and quiet. 'I get it, now, why you've been so off with me. You think that last year, me and Danny... when I was in his room—'

'Stop!' Ella holds her hand up, doesn't want to hear.

276

Brandy grasps her wrist and lowers it. 'He was talking about you. All night, it was about you.' Brandy lays a hand on Ella's cheek, tender and gentle. 'I would *never*… It's always been you, for him.'

Shockwaves shiver through Ella. For the first time, she can think of nothing to say. Brandy enfolds her in her arms, a brief embrace, before backing out of the cabin.

Ella wraps her arms around herself and looks around the tiny room.

Ashley's – *Annie's*, she corrects herself – notebook is still on her bed.

She stares at it, wondering if she will ever feel a sadness for the grief that has touched Ella, or whether this simmering, red-hot anger will be the overwhelming emotion for the rest of her life.

–

She doesn't join the others for dinner in the crew mess. Takeout, apparently, because Chef Luca has thrown a tantrum and is refusing to cook for them. From her room, Ella can hear Carly's soothing tones, placating him, then changing to annoyance as she reminds him that it's literally his job to cook for crew and guests.

They are all falling apart, she realises.

Rows are not uncommon, but normally, they blow over as quickly as they started. Now, it seems that they are all sharing Ella's rage.

She has passed it to them, similar to the virus that still swirls around. They are all infecting each other. There is no other outlet for it. Just like Ella's family, they are eating each other alive.

Ella taps out a text to the girl that Joan offered her, asking to meet tomorrow for an interview. A reply is forthcoming immediately. The text is eager and hopeful, and for a moment Ella imagines this girl, optimistic and outgoing, ready to start her yachting life.

Just like Annie.

4

The girl is rooming in a shared house with three other girls. They are not there, her roommates, because they're already employed on other boats.

The house, set far back from the marina, is horrible. Small windows, barely any light, with threadbare rugs on the stone floor and sagging, old sofas. Cheap accommodation, simply a place to lay one's head while the occupant waits to get a job that will take her out to sea. With no light comes no warmth, and the living room that Ella sits in is freezing. There has recently been a fire in the hearth, but there is nothing but ashes in it now. The room is a strange combination of mustiness and old, fried food.

Her interviewee sits stiffly in the chair opposite her. A deeply tanned face and small, dark eyes peer at Ella, partially concealed behind a curtain of black hair. A dye job, Ella sees, and a bad one at that.

Ella's heart isn't in the interview. The girl isn't right for the job.

She was aware she was a newbie, Joan had told her as much, but she's not even getting anything that would make up for her lack of experience. There's no spark in this one; that something special that Ashley – *Annie* – had, is missing.

Annie was green, but also open and eager to work, to learn. Ella thinks of her notebook, all those neatly written research points. She feels a sharp pain her chest.

Minutes have passed, Ella realises with a jolt. Sitting in silence, and her interviewee is too polite to have so much as cleared her throat.

Ella looks down at the notes she has prepared. The words blur in front of her eyes. She stares instead into the cold, bare fireplace.

'Would you like a drink of water?'

Ella drags her eyes from the fireplace.

'Yes,' she says. 'Thank you.'

Ella hears the kitchen tap grinding in another room. While the girl is gone, Ella moves to the window. It's too high up and too dirty to see out of. She doesn't need the view anyway. Beyond the thin glass is the marina, the plaza, the no-go area of the ferries that sit in port, rusting and salted and slowly falling apart. Behind them is the sea that Ella knows so well, a haven in daytime, unforgiving at night. Upon it, *Ananke* sits proud, holding all her occupants' secrets.

Ella turns from the window and paces to the other side of the room. The ashes smoulder in the fireplace; the grate has not been cleaned in a long while.

Nothing in here has been. That someone would live this way yet apply for a job of which more than half is housekeeping doesn't bode well.

She nudges at the grey ashes with a poker leaning against the cracked tiles. In the kitchen, the tap creaks once more. A floorboard, loose from its spring, knocks a squeak from elsewhere in the house.

Ella crouches by the fireplace and swirls her finger into the ashes.

She can feel her heart, surely as loud as the loose floorboards in this rickety place. A prickle at the back of her neck sends a jolt through her. Ella stands up and shoves her hands in her pockets.

'Here's your water.'

It has the faintest shadow of a lipstick mark on it. Ella ignores it.

'Can you start work tonight?' she asks.

A flash of surprise crosses the girl's face. It is gone in an instant.

'Yes,' she says. 'That would be great.'

PART FIVE

1

ROBYN

She doesn't feel like the same person who stepped onto Athens Marina a year ago.

There was a magic inside her then, and a hope. She'd never felt optimism before. It had tasted strange, that unknown emotion.

Back then, she'd looked at Annie, who shone so brightly she was almost haloed, and wondered if this was how her friend felt every day.

It didn't last, of course, that feeling. It went downhill with Tobias; it gained speed when Annie went off on the boat and Robyn was left to deal with Ashley Mercer herself. It accumulated in an explosion when she realised the extent of Annie's betrayal and acted out her revenge.

She remembers that day of the taverna blaze. Annie was off on the marina, researching everything she'd need to know to get a job on one of those fancy boats. Robyn watched Annie for a while that day. High up on the plaza wall, through binoculars that she had relieved a careless tourist of, she studied her friend down at the marina below. Her bag was beside her. Robyn gave it a pat. She'd gone shopping earlier.

She hadn't paid for any of her wares, though.

Annie was as close to the docked superyachts as she could get. Watching, listening, perhaps, to the conversations on board, picking up hints and tips. Every so often Annie's shoulders would hunch, her blonde hair falling across her face as she scribbled intently in the notebook Robyn got her.

After a while, she saw Annie chatting to a couple from a boat called *Harold*, who traipsed down the walkway onto the dock.

It was a man and a woman, not much older than herself and Annie. This boat's employees sported turquoise shirts, the name of the boat stitched onto the breast.

Annie talked mostly to the girl. Robyn watched the young man, wondering what he was thinking as he stood so close to such perfection. Using the binoculars, she zoomed in on his face. He had a pretty neutral expression, but his fingers twitched at his side.

'What are you thinking?' she whispered out loud. 'Are you thinking of touching her?'

Her knuckles burned with pressure as she clenched her fist, and she lowered the binoculars.

Not him. Nothing could happen to him. He was in the industry that they were trying to get into. It wouldn't be wise to jeopardise their future, not when they'd come so far.

Not him, not this area down here that held so much potential.

But behind her, beyond the plaza in the twisty, cobbled streets, there was someone deserving of Robyn's wrath.

Robyn took a slow walk back into the town, black shades covering half her face, oversized and anonymous, just how she liked it. She didn't look like herself any more, not with the dungarees that swamped her thin frame, not with the red cap she had on, all her hair stuffed inside apart from a few strands hanging loose around her face. Blonde, thanks to the hairpiece she'd relieved the pharmacy of earlier. She turned her bag the other way around, so the motif didn't show, and lastly, she slid on the facemask that she kept in her bag.

Robyn wasn't worried about catching Covid. Maybe she should have been, she thought, but right now, this facemask, the same kind that everyone was sporting, was far better as a disguise than a potential life-saving device.

It was quiet here now, shutters down on a lot of the restaurants. The breakfasts and early lunches were done. Now, the town slept during the hottest part of the day.

The metal shutters were halfway down on Tobias's taverna. It was so easy for Robyn to slip underneath, to stand on the patio area where she'd dined only the day before. It was so easy to squeeze out a few drops of lighter fluid underneath each table, so, *so* easy to strike the match and watch the cheap paper coverings and cotton tablecloths smoke, ignite, spread.

It was so easy to duck out again and walk through the empty streets back towards the dock, divesting herself of the cap, the hairpieces, the dungarees and the facemask.

It was such an easy choice to deal with the real Ashley Mercer.

The sun was going down. Black skies were incoming. The dock emptied of people.

Robyn wandered down the dock, pausing at the three-sided concrete structure that housed the large, orange skip-bins. They had not been emptied recently. Four large bins, and every one of them was overflowing. She wondered if the trash on the other, nicer side had been emptied recently. She imagined it was different here, where the homeless community lived and slept, with no trade and industry going on.

A mountain of rubbish, foul-smelling and – to Robyn's concern – moving.

Rats.

Robyn's mouth twisted with displeasure. She took the dungarees out of her shoulder bag and pushed them down between the stacked refuse bags, shuddering as the pile of trash undulated.

'Hey.'

The voice was so soft that Robyn thought she might have imagined it. She shook her head, trying to clear the seawater that was still in her ears, and pushed the material further in.

'Hey, you!'

This time the voice was stronger, clearer. Robyn whirled around to come face to face with a stranger.

She was young, Robyn's age, maybe. A girl who looked a bit like Annie, small and slender with blonde hair.

'Yes?' Robyn asked.

The girl's eyes darted around as the rubbish bags continued to rustle. Robyn crossed her arms. 'Well?' she asked.

The girl pulled herself up to her full height and stared bravely at Robyn. 'You took my stuff. I need it back.'

Robyn studied her. She'd taken a lot of stuff in the last day or so, none of it rightfully hers. Who was this woman – a shopkeeper from one of the touristy places Robyn had helped herself to items from? A pharmacist? A restaurateur?

Robyn's eyes dropped to the blue and white plastic bag that the girl clutched. It all came back to her.

The girl from the engine room who shared her and Annie's sleeping space. The girl on her own. The passport girl.

'I haven't got anything of yours,' Robyn snapped. 'Go away.'

But the girl didn't move. A wannabe tough little thing, Robyn thought, but despite her continued stare, the fear in the girl's face gave her away.

'I saw what you did, earlier, in the town,' she said. 'So why don't you give me back my passport and I won't say anything about it.'

Robyn felt a tell-tale heat inside her. 'What did you see?' she asked. 'What do you *think* you saw?'

'The fire.' The girl lifted her chin again, a little more defiant now. 'You were bad. Those people are good; they give us food, sometimes, when they can spare it. Water and… and they're nice.'

Not a wannabe tough thing. A wannabe good girl. Like *Annie*.

Robyn rolled her eyes. *They're not nice.* Robyn had seen first-hand the way the father treated girls like her.

Robyn tilted her head as she looked at the scrap in front of her. Did this girl get a different treatment? Did people – outsiders, those on the right side of the fence – look at her the way people looked at Annie? Or was it simply Tobias showing kindness to this girl, without his father's knowledge, just like he'd done for Annie?

Robyn concealed a sigh, stalling for time as she figured how to play this one out.

'I can't give it back,' she said. 'I need it. But I'll trade something for the passport. Something far better than your passport, which you can't even use.'

The girl blinked at her, thrown by the softness of Robyn's tone.

For a long time, they watched each other. Robyn open and friendly, the girl wary at first, before it slipped away piece by piece.

Finally, the girl came to a decision. 'All right,' she said. 'What have you got to trade?'

Robyn smiled and gestured the girl closer.

It wasn't so easy after all. The girl – the real Ashley Mercer – was a fighter. Robyn was surprised, then angered as she felt a sharp kick to her leg, a nail clawing at her cheek.

The anger assisted Robyn. She finished the job quickly.

—

She hung around, close but out of sight, keeping an eye on the bins, waiting for the body to be discovered. But nobody ever came to empty them. Nobody seemed to give a damn about the mounting piles of rubbish that contained the remains of a girl who'd never really belonged anywhere.

Despite what she'd done, the knowledge that Ashley Mercer wasn't missed made Robyn sad.

I did it for you, Annie, she told herself. *I did it for us.*

The next time she saw Annie, she'd expected the wage that her friend handed over. She hadn't expected her to be concerned about the whereabouts of the girl whose name Annie had taken. She hadn't expected Annie to be having such a grand time away from Robyn. She hadn't expected Annie to leave her that night to rush back to her posh old boat.

She hadn't expected to overhear what she did a few days later.

On the marina, the good part, Robyn sloped around, trying to stay under the radar, simply on the lookout for one of these yachties to get so drunk on their night off that they got careless with their designer bags and the purses they contained.

Robyn sat beneath a bar, drawing out a single cocktail that she'd bought with Annie's money.

'Ella said that new girl, Ashley Mercer, is doing the crossing to Spain.'

They were the words that had Robyn paying attention. The name had her ears pricking up.

'The day worker?' The girl's companion's tone was impressed. 'Nice going – the newbie must be good to get that gig.'

A single exchange overheard.

Annie was planning to leave her.

It changed everything.

She began to follow Annie with earnest, paranoia taking root now that this crossing could happen at any moment, any day. She used the tracking app that she'd installed on Annie's phone, stealing bikes, small boats, hopping in taxis and spending the money she was supposed to use for a hotel room. Standing in coves and inlets, watching the big boat and the occupants aboard, only letting out a breath of relief when she caught a glimpse of Annie.

Robyn waited for the text message or phone call from Annie to fill her in on the news that they were going to Spain.

It never came.

The Greek sun seeped into Robyn's skin, filling her with a burning that she knew one day soon was going to explode.

One night, when *Ananke* was docked, the heat within her spilled over.

Robyn navigated the tiny boat out to sea to meet her friend.

It was hard to withstand, that knowledge that Robyn had known what Annie was subconsciously planning. Annie herself had no idea until Robyn made her see.

That's how well Robyn knew her. That was how tightly bound they were.

When it was over, it was like a little bit of Robyn had died too.

Robyn had tried hard, before Tobias and Ashley and the devastating last night with Annie. Did her best to remain calm and nice and clean and normal.

Afterwards, post-Annie, she returned to who she was, regressed to who she'd always been.

Robyn. *The bad one.*

The fury replaced the magic and the hope.

Without Annie, she thought she might die herself. After *that night*, after the tiny, stolen fishing boat eventually put her on a beach with sand as black as her soul, she knew vaguely that she wasn't near the marina any more.

It didn't matter. Nothing did. And as she staggered out of the vessel with the strange, black sand dirtying her bare feet, she wondered if she were alive at all, or if this were some sort of underworld. A purgatory, maybe.

She doesn't know how she survived, because for a long time she did nothing. She didn't eat. All her plans were lost to her. She was totally alone.

At times, as the sun beat down on her and she lay in a doorway of a urinal at the edge of the unknown cove she'd found herself in, blistered and dehydrated, she didn't even know where she was, or how she came to be here. Sometimes, she didn't even know who she was.

Sometimes she woke to a bottle of water at her feet. On occasion, there would be croissants or slightly stale bread rolls. She took them all, never wondering where they came from, or who had left them. She let her skin flake and peel and looked with a kind of half-hearted interest at the red, raw flesh that was left. She wondered why it didn't hurt.

Towards the end of the summer that never was, she left the doorway of the urinal.

Now she felt the pain that had been missing for so long. On the soles of her feet that, upon closer inspection, she found were covered in yellow and black bubbles. Infection running wild.

She waded into the sea until it was chest high. To the left, she saw the white tops of the ferries that she had once called home. She started in that direction. The tide was low and at some point, she found herself in that same cove where she had once bathed with Annie.

Who knew, all this time, she was only next door to Athens Marina.

Back in that place, months after the event that had nearly ended her, the marina under her hot, swollen feet, Robyn started to come back to life.

She wondered if Annie were smiling down on her when, in December, she relieved a group of drunk tourists on a stag weekend of enough euros to keep her going through until spring-time.

She didn't utter up a prayer of thanks, though; it didn't seem right to.

She could stay here, she realised. There was no danger, because nobody ever remembered Robyn, and nobody had really known she existed anyway.

She got herself a room in a house and went to work.

–

Transformation is easy with money. Often, Robyn thinks about the struggles – both internal and real – with Annie's passport and the issue with her bank account. They should have waited, she acknowledges, like Annie always wanted to. Should have got enough money to *buy* themselves a new identity, the way Robyn has done. She has everything she needs now. Official papers, the basic first aid certificate requirements, a driving licence, a passport *and* a bank account.

She thinks of Annie sometimes, but not as much as she imagined she would.

She could have let her go. Could have cut her loose to sail off into the literal sunset, bound for Spain beyond the horizon.

She's glad she didn't.

Now it is *her turn*. She's learned enough, from sitting unobserved on the docks and beaches and marinas and coves. She's picked up phrasings and words that were once so foreign to her. It is the only good part of being the one that nobody ever looks at, the one that nobody ever realises is even there.

She's soaked it up. Not like a sponge, not like Annie would have. But enough resonated for her to give it a go.

She doesn't think much of the woman who interviewed her. She was cold, uninterested and clearly bored.

Robyn doesn't care. She is not working on a yacht to make friends. Friends suck. Annie was proof of that. It's all about the money.

When she has replenished her stash, she will have the funds and the freedom to decide what comes next.

—

Robyn is all smiles as she boards the yacht. She is channelling Annie, her smile, her openness, her willingness. She is putting on her very best jolly-hockey-sticks persona as she follows her new boss inside.

'It's a beautiful boat,' Robyn exclaims, her cheeks hurting from the stretched grin she has fixed in place.

Ella glances back at her over her shoulder and offers a tight smile in return.

Down a set of winding stairs they go. The air is frosty, goosebumps spiking on Robyn's arms. She follows Ella through an open door, where she is thrust upon a gathered group.

Her new colleagues, she presumes. She switches the smile back on, raising her brows to ensure it reaches her eyes, and pauses for introductions to be made. For the last week she's been repeating her new name to herself.

Roberta Steel.

Nice and simple. A bit of her old name in there. A new surname, one that she has chosen.

One that suits her.

That's what she is: made of steel.

But Ella keeps moving, beckoning for Robyn to follow.

'Your bunk is this way,' she says without breaking her stride.

Robyn stumbles, taken unawares, caught in an awkward moment. She'd mentally prepared to show herself at her shiniest, happiest best to meet this gang, but maybe introductions will come later.

Her smile drops, and she nods at the assembled group before picking up her pace and trotting after Ella, who is almost out of sight down yet another corridor.

Robyn can feel eyes on her as she follows Ella. Consciously, she straightens her spine as she walks.

Her yachtie colleagues are not as bouncy and joyous as they appear when she has watched them from afar. When they are on charter, they are always smiling. It doesn't mean anything, she tells herself. Their apathy, their blank stares. They are tired, maybe, with all the prep work to get a new season underway. Their strange moodiness and the frosty air has nothing to do with Robyn. Why would it? They don't know her, after all.

She finally catches up to Ella, who is standing beside an open door, arm outstretched to gesture inside.

Robyn stands uncomfortably close to Ella and peers inside.

She has a room of her own, two beds to choose from.

'Get settled in,' says Ella in a monotone. 'Get some sleep; we'll start training tomorrow.'

Robyn frowns at the door as it closes behind her. That's it? She has to sit in here all night? No dinner, no involvement, no questions?

She rubs her arms, shivers a little bit as she stands in the corner of the small cabin.

It doesn't mean anything, she tells herself again. It isn't fear that has caused these icy fingers to lay claim to her skin. It's cooler down here, is all. As it should be with the air conditioning that a superyacht like this has.

Maybe she could go back out there, make a cup of tea, offer everybody else a warm drink.

She closes her hand over the doorknob and as she touches it, adrenaline flows through her.

What if Ella locked it?

With an audible gasp, she wrenches at the handle.

The door flies open so fast it almost hits her in the face.

She barks out a laugh, loud in the silence of the boat, and leans her face against the doorframe.

'Gotta get it together,' she says to the empty hallway.

She straightens, makes a conscious effort to amble casually back towards the crew mess.

But when she reaches it, the room is deserted, empty, all the lights switched off.

Back in her room, she closes the door and leans against it. Is it her imagination, or does it somehow seem smaller in here now? Like the walls have shifted ever so slightly, closing in on her.

She looks at the bed; it is inviting, as small as it is, so she climbs up to the top bunk and wraps the duvet around herself. She thinks of the scratchy blanket she had in the shared house, and the old cover on the ferry.

'I did it,' she whispers out loud. 'I made it.'

But her words, like her smile of earlier, are forced.

—

Some hours later, she is staring at the ceiling of her cabin. She hears the others as they turn in for the night. They are not quiet. Nor are they mindful that it is late, and others might be sleeping. She wonders where they have been, why the crew area was in darkness, why she hasn't been invited to wherever they had been hanging out.

One by one she hears their doors close. She tries to take comfort from the sound, just like that old curtain being pulled across the front door of the home. She whispers to herself that all is safe, it is okay to rest now. She closes her eyes so she doesn't have to look at the walls that now seem even closer than before.

As much as she tries, sleep won't fall upon her. It doesn't, these days, as though that period of being half-unconscious has given her body all the rest it needed.

Sliding down from the top bunk, she pulls on the clothes she came in, for she hasn't been given a uniform yet, and she pulls open her door.

Tiny opaque lights line the hallway. She follows them as they lead to the stairs, winding upwards where the room opens into some sort of lounge. The emergency lighting up here is not needed, because a full moon shines a silvery way through the floor-to-ceiling windows.

She pauses a moment before pulling the door open, mindful of an alarm that would signal an intruder. But that's not what she is, she realises with a start.

She belongs here.

So why, if she does belong here, hasn't she been given her uniform yet?

The sudden thought makes her uncomfortable, and she decides not to pursue the question.

On the deck, she moves to the railing, pulling her jumper off as she goes to feel the hot night on her skin. The very fine hairs on the back of her neck prickle as she senses that she's not alone. There is no sound, no shadows, no footsteps, rather just a sense that she is being watched.

She turns around.

There is nobody. The deck is empty.

She turns back to the water. The moon is casting a path that stretches from the horizon to land. The sea is calm, the smallest of waves lapping at a black-sanded beach.

Robyn has seen that black sand before, but it is a like a half-memory of a time that didn't fully belong to her. A beautiful, alien landscape that scorched her feet.

There is nobody out there. Other than the one she is aboard, there are no other vessels in sight.

She will go to bed. If she gets up early tomorrow, she might be able to talk Chef into cooking her eggs and bacon. Maybe potatoes and some avocado toast. A huge platter, just for her. It strikes her that she doesn't know which one of the people she walked past earlier is the chef. That feeling again – how odd it was that she wasn't introduced to anybody.

Like it isn't worth anybody getting to know her.

Like… she's not going to be around for long enough.

Just like before, in her cabin, the yacht seems suddenly smaller than it did previously.

Stop it. She talks herself down, tries to find that optimistic cheer from earlier.

It seems distant now, like a far-off memory. Her confidence has vanished in a slow trickle since the moment she was led down those stairs and past all her crewmates without introduction.

She looks at that black sand again. It doesn't look as close as it did just moments ago. Neither do the mountainous walls. Nowhere to run. No escape.

A sudden shiver wracks her body.

She picks up her jumper from where it hangs from the anchor trapdoor.

There is a flash, lightning dancing across the Milky Way. A crash like thunder that resonates in her face.

She looks at the deck, brown wood in her eyeline. She struggles to understand. The teak comes closer until she is resting her forehead on it. A streak of red sullies the previously clean planks.

Her forehead throbs. The skin is split.

Feet push at her, heavy boots that shouldn't be allowed on the deck. Pirates have climbed aboard. It is a hazy thought, and it is not correct, because they don't exist here, in the Greek islands.

Do they?

She looks up to the sky, all those stars. Flashing and sparkling. She feels something solid at her back. She is in the small boat now. It rocks gently beneath her.

Something smacks lightly against her chest. She peers at the object through smarting eyes. It is green, small and partially burned.

It is the charred remains of Annie's provisional driving licence.

Another slap as something else lands on her. Blue this time, burned and cut but still identifiable as what it once was.

Robyn licks her lips, suddenly dry.

In a terrible moment of realisation, she understands everything.

She hadn't thought there were many others like herself, who enacted their own punishment. Can't quite believe that this group of professional, proper people intend to go as far as this.

Then she remembers the times that *she's* turned feral, wild, bloodthirsty.

She wonders if later – after – they'll be able to live with themselves.

Would love to stick around and find out.

Knows that won't happen.

At the first touch of cold metal on the flesh of her neck, Robyn holds her breath.

She promises herself that she won't scream, but at the sudden sound of machinery, that promise is a lie. The sound is cut off instantly by a hand across her mouth. She snaps and clicks her teeth, but her persecutor either doesn't feel her bite, or doesn't care.

The sound of rolling steel. She is held aloft now, in the hot Greek air, going up, up, up.

Against her wishes, she begins to thrash the lower part of her body. It is no match for the motorised anchor.

The fibre-reinforced plastic slides into steel at her back. The edges of the anchor pocket.

So, this is what it feels like.

PART SIX

1

ELLA

PRESENT DAY

When Ella left the rooming house after the interview, for the first time, her mind was clear and focused.

Danny was on the boardwalk when she marched determinedly towards *Ananke*.

'All right?' he called.

'I found her,' Ella said without preamble.

She hadn't found her. She'd just been doing her job, attempting to let all the trauma go. But fate intervened.

Fate and circumstance.

She produced the provisional driving licence that she'd plucked out of the fireplace, blackened around the edges, the name Robyn Seever still intact, and a bank card, Annie's name just visible, and the passport, burned and charred, the smudged photo of the girl they knew as Ashley.

'She's got herself a fake ID. She calls herself Roberta.' Ella pauses for just one moment. 'She starts work on board tonight.'

There was never any question that the girl would survive the night. Not in Ella's mind, anyway. And, as it turned out, not in the rest of the crew's.

Ella sat with them in the guest cabin. Captain wasn't there; neither was Sid. Just Ella and Danny, Luca, Brandy and Cat.

Ella told them everything that she had gleaned from all her sources. Nikki, Pippa and Roxy, and Shaneece. She watched as these souls she'd worked alongside for a long time – lovely, gentle, kind people for the most part – turned feral before her eyes.

There was no great plan laid out. There were not hours of discussion. For a crew that was only successful due to process, practice and procedure, it was surprisingly easy to agree that only the end game mattered.

Luca made them all a dinner, a feast that only charter guests normally got. Fresh, local lobster and potato cakes, prefaced with a crab bisque. They all enjoyed it, only Captain and Sid got a portion of Halcion crushed up in theirs.

Yawning widely, they went off to their respective cabins before the new girl neither of them even knew about arrived. Ella will make a call to Joan in a couple of days, complaining that the girl they hired from her never showed up.

The evening passed quickly and in somewhat of a series of flashes. The girl's arrival. The crew's silence. The girl dispatched to her bunk. The crew collective on deck, quiet, still.

Waiting.

Ella felt nothing as they surrounded her, coming together as one. *Ananke*'s teamwork at its very finest that night.

Once she was immobilised, they all held the long remote that pulled the anchor home. Then, Ella had thought of them like a firing squad, just one bullet that nobody would ever be sure of whose trigger finger was responsible for a life ended. Later, thinking about it, she dismisses this theory. They wanted to share the responsibility, not shy away from it.

And here they are, on the final approach now, as the anchor tries to fold itself home.

There is a snap, a gush of blood. It stains the port side with its spray.

The girl will have felt it for a long few seconds.

Now, she is gone.

They work in silence as they take the anchor chain from around her neck. She pools like a puddle into the tender. Ella takes the old, rusted, heavy chain that was lying in the bosun's locker and secures it around her feet. From there, collectively they move her weighted form over the side. Here, the Aegean Sea is over two thousand meters deep. This girl will remain down there for as long as it takes for the sea life to desecrate her flesh and turn her into nothing but a pile of chains and clothes.

They clean in silence. There is no direction. They see what needs to be done and get on with it. Luca and Brandy in the tender, Danny with his long broom, scrubbing the side until it is back to gleaming white. Cat moving along the teak, going against the grain. The passport has gone overboard; Ella watched as it drifted away on the tide. The bank card is still here, and she picks up the little plastic rectangle that once belonged to a stranger named Annie.

It is a reminder that sometimes, when justice is an impossibility, fate and karma will visit.

It is a reminder of what they – *she* – did. They did it. But she sparked it. Because she couldn't let it go.

She puts the charred piece of plastic in her pocket, liking the feel of the sharp edges digging into her thigh. She will look at it sometimes. And when she does, she will think of Ashley, and Annie, and her brother Hades.

Because this was a little bit for him, too.

The thought has been swirling hazily in her mind for a while. To find them, those that wronged her brother, those that made him think there was no other way.

It could be even easier to locate them. Finding Robyn was fate and that is *Ananke*'s namesake.

Ella's own surname, Themis, means 'divine law, justice, and moral order'.

Her crew drift away from the spotless deck as the sun is beginning to rise on the horizon. Ella walks behind them, noting the fingers clasped, hands trailing on shoulders, looks exchanged. They hold this secret in their eyes, this shared few, and Ella knows they will never mention it again.

Danny falls into step beside her, and, like the others, he entwines his fingers in hers.

They break apart at their cabins. Ella slips inside and packs quietly, but he is still waiting in the corridor when she emerges, rucksack on her back.

'You're leaving?' His voice is low. He isn't surprised, she sees.

'Yes. I'm going home.' She feels a thrill as she says the words. She realises she can't wait to get back to that house that has fallen foul to a misery that hangs low like death over the roof.

She can't wait to see her broken parents. She wants them to see that though life will never be perfect as it once was, with one of theirs gone, it can get lighter. She wants to locate her remaining brothers and bring them home. She wants to live near to the base where Hades took a bullet along with his last breath.

She wants to continue with her divine law and moral order.

She doesn't tell Danny this, but she thinks he knows anyway.

He walks her out. 'Say goodbye to the others for me,' she tells him.

He nods. Embraces her. She feels his lips on her cheek before he turns and is swallowed up by the interior of *Ananke*.

On the marina, by the sides of the swaying palms, she sits and surveys the landscape. Home for a lot of summers, as familiar to her as the back of her hand. It feels alien now, like she's overstayed her welcome and needs to move on.

Or move back.

It is time to go. Like the area, she also knows the times of the airport transfers, but something keeps her sitting there for a while longer.

Two minutes… five more.

The sunrise commences. A slice of orange cutting through the night, heralding the beginning of a new day.

A new start.

A figure emerges in the distance, backlit by *Ananke*'s night-lights.

She stands upon his approach, reaching out a hand to grip Danny's fingers. He has his own bag on his back. He is with her, now.

Hands entwined, they walk away from *Ananke*, from Athens, from the bodies that will stay here.

Walking towards the future, whatever it might be.

For the first time, Ella is relaxed, no longer dependent on rigidity, rules, regulations. For now, she is confident to leave what may be to fate, and circumstance.

ACKNOWLEDGEMENTS

As always, I'm so grateful to have so much support. Firstly, I send so much love and all my gratitude for my family. Top of the list are my parents, Janet and Keith Hewitt.

And to Marley, my friend and constant writing companion.

Big thanks to my agent, Laetitia Rutherford of Watson, Little. My editor, Siân Heap, thank you for your support and enthusiasm. Copyeditor Becca and Proofreader Rachel, who both did a wonderful job, picking up those things that needed detail or attention, big and small.

The writing community – thank you to those extraordinary groups of wonderful crime (and other genre!) writers who I am so thankful to call my friends. A special mention to Sheila Bugler, Rachel Lynch, Marion Todd, and Sarah Ward; four women who provide a fantastic listening ear, brilliant advice and also make me scream with laughter.

To the bloggers, publishers, and book clubs; everything you do is appreciated.

My friends, of which I am blessed with many, who shout out about my work on social media. Darren and Cat, who champion my writing and point out (and sometimes meddle with) displays of my novels at bookstores.

Finally, a huge thanks to you, the reader. As always, as long as you keep on enjoying my books, I'll keep on writing them.